CW00815845

SPIRIT MIRROR

SPIRIT MIRROR

Stephen Marley

COLLINS
8 Grafton Street London W1
1988

William Collins Sons & Co. Ltd
London · Glasgow · Sydney · Auckland
Toronto · Johannesburg

For my mother and father

And with thanks to Brigitte Delorme, last met in Lyon; and Wong En Yin, last heard of in Kuala Lumpur.

Not forgetting Janet and Sarah, dwellers in the mysterious and mythic town of Long Eaton; Professor David Jary, who gave me the chance to study dynastic China in some depth; Fatima Deen, who was around at the right time; Keiko, for being so charmingly Japanese; Jane Judd, for her faith and tolerance; and last but not least, Laura Longrigg and Rachel Hore at Collins for being such pleasant and helpful editors.

First published by Collins

Copyright © Stephen Marley 1988

ISBN: 0–00–223368–1

Made and printed in Great Britain
by Robert Hartnoll (1985) Ltd., Bodmin, Cornwall

1

DRAGON SHADOW

It was in the quiet time of the forest that they came, when the shadow of their enemy was long upon the mountain.

They came, sliding from thickening shadow to thinning sunlight, grey mantles rustling and silver masks glinting in the early dusk. They were stealthy, the two silver-masked figures in flowing grey cloaks, stealthy as they neared the dancers at the foot of Black Dragon Mountain, and neither the dancers nor the watchers of the dancers heard or saw the two Silver Brethren.

The quiet of the forest was in their footfalls. Where the bare feet of the Brethren trod the grass slowly withered until it was as dry and dead as the long grey hair that trailed from the crowns of the silver mask-helmets.

It was the Eve of the Feast of the Dead.

The Silver Brethren came and halted within a few steps of the entranced audience that spread in a crescent around the animated dancers. Unmarked, unheeded, two Silver Masks observed the performance.

Upon a platform slung between two low boughs of a mighty oak the dancing troupe spun and pranced in flamboyant costumes ablaze with the colours of a hundred symbolic flowers of Spring Coming, and each dancer's face wore a sun mask of burnished bronze. Below the dancers issued the music of celebration: the squatting drummer beat the rhythm of the earth thunder on the stretched deerskin hide of the chieh-ku as the hsiao flute's notes swirled and hovered like miniature birds and a moon-lute plucked dreams from the air to the brash accompaniment of a clashing gong.

And behind the bright world of swarming colours and leaping dancers and jubilant music, beyond the paper lanterns of red and yellow and blue – was quiet forest; was the unfathomable, dark green silence of the forest.

It was the Hour of the Hound, the hour that begins in day and ends in night.

The arc of spellbound villagers that grinned and swayed in sympathy with the joyous dance between the oak boughs were dressed in old rags wrapped in newer rags. They were the remnants of ten villages in Celestial Tiger Forest, villages that had been torched and butchered in the outbreaks of mass slaughter following the Yellow Headband uprising of five years past. Of the ten villages, just one hundred and thirty souls survived from a total population of more than four thousand. With crops burnt by imperial soldiers and forest game hunted to the edge of extinction by rebel bands, the survivors that sat watching the dancers had been carved thin and angular by sharp hunger. All they had to offer the Lo-an performers were the wooden masks and simple theatrical props which the few skilled woodworkers left alive had fashioned for the travelling troupe. The gifts of oak and elm and pine were heaped in front of the suspended stage.

The twenty or so scrawny children had forgotten their hollow stomachs for a magic hour or two in the enchantment of music and wild motion and vivid colours. And the gaunt men and women were reliving a lost childhood wonder in the hopeful Dance of Spring Coming. One woman, who might have been young but who wore the ageless face of poverty, moved her thin lips in a prayer: 'Green Dragon, Lord of Spring, rise from your palace beneath the eastern sea and descend upon the land with your green breath of life. Let the trees and the bushes and the plants give birth to the food of the forest.'

6

A wizened old man at the woman's side nodded as he listened to the fervent prayer. 'And may the Green Dragon of the East defend us from the shadow of the Black Dragon Sorceress,' he added, conscious, as were they all, of the towering mass of Black Dragon Mountain at their backs.

But the inbred fear of Black Dragon Sorceress had receded far into the background for the villagers in this brief span of time in which glowing myth and legend ruled. Most hands clapped in time with the drum. Most gap-toothed mouths smiled. The watchers were beginning to move into the ritual patterns of the dance of growth and new life. They became one with the dance of life. Winter was over. It was the new birth.

And the Silver Brethren who stood behind them knew they were ready for the words.

One of the Silver Masks turned from the vibrant spectacle in front of the armies of pine and oak and tilted his metal visage to the high cliffs and steeps of Black Dragon Mountain. A bloated sun rested on the crest of a rugged crag far above the roof of the forest. There – on that crag – was the enemy. He could not see her but he sensed her shadow reaching down to him from her lofty stronghold. There she was in the high places – the Green-Eyes, the enemy, the Death-bringer.

It was time to bring death to the Death-bringer.

The Silver Brethren faced one another and exchanged nods as they shaped words in their minds.

The Death-bringer looks down from the mountain, they thought as one.

The dancers will dance the measure of the Mirror, was the second thought.

And the watchers will watch until the dying time.

The silent communication concluded, they fixed their attention on the exuberant performers. The Brethren's voices, conjoined in a single utterance, were hardly audible. They had learned long ago that the true word of command is spoken in a whisper.

And below the music and the beat of the heart, down where the darkness hears, the musicians and the dancers caught the tone of absolute command in the soft whisper.

Dance the dance of the Mirror. And the words echoed endlessly inside their heads.

And the swift Spring Dance became the slow Mirror Dance.

Watchers, watch until the dying time.

Again, the killing words were the quiet words.

And the watchers became lost in the dancers. And the dancers were lost in the dance. And the dance was lost in a music of whispers.

And there was a quietness in the forest that did not come from the forest.

The black silhouette, long and lean, stalked across the grey slopes. The dark shape, thin and stretched in the afternoon sun, undulated over the dips and rises of Black Dragon Mountain. The long shadow meandered over the mounds and hollows, pace for pace with the wandering steps of Chia's bare feet.

Chia's deep green eyes tracked her sunset-lengthened shadow to where it fell on the lower cliffs and jumbled boulders. Soon, she thought, soon it will be time for me to die again. And that will be another kind of shadow.

Ah yes, thought Chia the sorceress, death, once more, was near. Death always followed the madness. And the madness was returning.

And there is an evil growing where the forest meets the foot of my mountain. But I will turn my face from it. I will not heed its call.

She halted her slow walk at the jagged edge of a jutting crag and stood gazing into the darkening east as the dying sun split into the rich red of an open wound that bathed her lonely black figure in blood-glow.

An evil has killed the Dance of Spring far below. But I close my eyes to the vision of evil. I renounce the summons of the suffering. I remain within myself.

As her shadow stretched further into the east it lost its definition, its outline becoming blurred. At last, when it threatened to become a dusky giant lying across the lands of China, it started to fade. It blended into the gathering gloom, and quickly vanished.

It was the Eve of the Feast of the Dead in the reign of Ling Ti, child-emperor of the Eastern Han Dynasty, and China was riven with civil war. A mere ten li from Black Dragon Mountain, beneath the leafy canopy of Celestial Tiger Forest, there were corpses on the ground with their blood soaking into the loamy soil. Imperial China was disintegrating into a cauldron of warring states, and centuries might pass before a new unity was forged by a fresh dynasty. But the impending collapse of the House of Han did not overly dismay Chia. Although no lover of internecine strife, still less was she a lover of the effete customs and outmoded traditions enshrined in the decaying House of Han. Han Dynasty China was becoming a vast prison walled by mandarin protocols and prejudices. It was time for the dragon paths to shake the earth and bring down those imperial walls in a crash of thunder.

It was time for uncertainty. Without uncertainty, there could be no growth of the spirit. And where there was no growth there could only be decay. It was time for new thoughts. It was time for the Way of the Buddha to join with the Way of the T'ao. When the Chinese Empire rose again it would contain a hundred philosophies. Diversity would thrive.

Far to the west, she mused, was a truly diverse empire. Thousands upon thousands of li across the Moving Sands, beyond Fergana and Parthia, sprawled the empire of the Romans ruled by two centuries of Caesars since the Emperor Augustus. The Empire of the Eagles. Even the once-mighty Egypt was now a province of Rome . . .

9

'Egypt,' the sorceress murmured, fingering a silver ankh that dangled on her breast from a silver chain. 'Nefertiti, Queen of Egypt.'

Nefertiti, Daughter of the Nile – I'll always love you.

Chia's slender hand dropped from the ankh as a tear fell from a pensive green eye. With a brusque gesture she brushed it from her cold cheek with the back of her hand. To hell with memories. Memories kill.

I am young. I am old. And I, also, am that which kills.

The sorceress, wrapped in the long black folds of her hooded cloak, was still as a statue as she stared into the east. There – where her erstwhile shadow had pointed – was the deep cleft between conical peaks at the far side of the forest. And beyond, hidden by the peaks, the steep valleys of the River Fen. And further, hundreds upon hundreds of li, the mountainous expanse of the T'aihang range, before the mountains dwindled to foothills and sank into the vast plains of the Yellow River, distance upon distance, until swerving up into the rearing summits of the eastern range. And behind the eastern mountains, the immense Forest of the Ancestors. And beyond the Forest of the Ancestors . . .

Spirit Hill.

A tremor of dread ran through Chia's lithe young body. Spirit Hill. Spirit Hill – almost three thousand li to the east. Why did that name make her shake all of a sudden? Why this trembling in the breath of the wind? Why this fear?

Mirror.

'No!' she snapped at the voice in her head as she averted her face from the east. No. I turn my face from evil and the victims of evil. I renounce all action. I remain within myself.

Spirit Hill . . . Mirror . . . Nyak.

'Nyak,' she hissed between clenched teeth. She shut her deeply slanted eyes and tightened her right hand into a fist. 'Have you come to haunt me again, you walking nightmare?'

10

She started to breathe in the rhythm of pranayama in order to compose her spirit and drive out the voices in her skull. She tried to flow into the harmony of the T'ao. But the whispers in her mind would not abate.

Spirit Hill . . . Mirror . . . Nyak . . . Silver Brethren . . . Spirit Hill . . . grey shrouds, black shrouds, white shrouds . . . knives . . . Mirror . . . Nyak . . .

'Silence!' she screamed as she opened her eyes and covered her ears in a vain attempt to still the voices within. Realising the absurdity of the attempt, she let her hands drop and hang loosely at her sides. 'Silence,' she sighed to the feeble breeze.

Chia's gaze wandered over forest and mountains and sky. Her young, exquisite face was the face of one born in the morning of the world and her green eyes had the look of eyes that have looked at everything. Her wisdom was deeper than first love. But the madness had touched her again. And she knew that the madness would grow like a tumour in the head. And the madness was the Death-bringer.

She trembled in the chill breeze. 'Somebody help me,' she whispered.

The Mirror Dance was a quiet dance, a dance where the sounds were like shapes of silence. Its music was the chorus of a thousand whispers. The Mirror Dance was a slow dance, a dance for sleeping dancers.

Only two dancers remained on the platform perched between the boughs – the others had merged with the mute musicians under the stage. The musicians swayed as the crescent of villagers swayed, heads lolling, eyes hooded, like dreamers. All moved with a slow, languorous harmony.

All, that is, but the two female dancers on the suspended stage, who stood as stiff and upright as the Silver Brethren outside the circle of lantern-light. Both women had cast off the bronze sun masks, revealing rounded, pleasant features so alike that it was clear the two dancers were sisters, if not twins.

One of the Silver Brethren reached underneath the loose folds of his grey cloak and drew out a silver mask, which was unadorned except for ornamental green eyes painted around the eyelets. With a sweep of his hand the Silver Brother sent the green-eyed metal mask spinning through the air in a long arc, to thump at the feet of one of the women on the stage. She picked it up with a fluent motion and placed it over her head with the same fluent ease. For a moment she stood there, with blind green eyes in a silver face.

Then, gradually, her arms slid around her narrow waist as her head bent forwards and her legs folded until she knelt at the feet of her partner. Her body contracted further until it was a squashed bundle resembling a small shadow at the foot of her lantern-framed sister.

The Silver Brethren departed as quietly as they had arrived, the grass under their bare feet withering with each soft footfall as they merged into the darkness of the forest. All around them they could feel the presence of the long shadow of the Death-bringer, invisible to normal vision now that it had become one with the night but no less present merely because it had joined with the shadow of the world. And the long shadow of the enemy on the mountain would soon feel another darkness rising to meet her. Now that the Mirror Dance had begun in earnest.

On the tree stage the dance began under the flickering glow of a crowd of coloured lanterns hung on dangling branches. Whether they were dancers, musicians or villagers, whether they watched or sealed their eyes, they were all one with the dance. And they were all one with the music of a hundred whispers, and each whisper was so soft that it was quieter than the deep silence of the forest.

A dark shape congealed from the painted feet of the

unmasked woman on the stage. The humped form enlarged as it emerged from the erect figure, gradually
unfolding as it crept around the unmoving woman. As
the shape circled the unmasked woman it grew taller
with each step. By the time it had reached the end of its
outward spiral dance it had assumed the form of a full-
grown woman in a silver mask with painted green eyes.

The masked woman spread her arms in a gesture of
invitation to the sister from whom she had arisen. And
the other dancer responded, weaving slowly in an inward spiral centred on the blank green eyes of the metal
mask. And with each curve of the inward spiral, she
stooped lower. Her chin pressed tight on her breastbone,
her shoulders hunched, her knees bent. Her whole body
started to close in on itself. Soon she was crawling as she
contracted to a ball of flesh and bone. To the music of a
hundred whispers she wriggled with small, rhythmic undulations to the feet of the silver-masked dancer. She lay
like a dark lump at the feet of the masked figure.

The silver mask raised its moulded features and
ornamental green eyes to the sky, then lowered its
changeless expression to the shadowy bundle. Then the
masked woman lifted the metal from her face and placed
it on the face of the thing at her feet. She raised her
unmasked face to the faint stars of dusk and smiled a
crooked smile. Spreading her arms in a sign of triumph,
she began to stretch every muscle and tendon in her
supple body.

And as the unmasked stretched, the masked shape was
crushed into itself. The ribcage cracked and caved in
under the relentless tightening of the enfolding arms.
The jawbone was torn from its sockets. Teeth ground
each other into fragments. Finally the neck snapped in
one of its fragile joints.

Chia yelled in pain at the crushing embrace that drove
her to her knees, gasping as her ribs bent under the

pressure. For a fleeting moment she swayed over the jutting lip of the high crag as the breath was squeezed from her compressed lungs. A flailing hand sent a scatter of stones tumbling over the edge of the drop.

The shade that diminishes has ascended the mountain but I will not bow under its weight. I deny its oppression. Illusion is power according to the strength of belief. I will not believe. The power of illusion is the power of doubt. I renounce all doubt. The diminishing is not in me, it is not of me, it is not around me. Where I am, it is not.

The spasms of her contracting body subsided as her mind resumed control of her rebellious muscles. Still swaying, Chia regained her feet and focused her green gaze on the firefly lights of the Lo-an dancers in the dark at the base of Black Dragon Mountain. The fireflies were coming adrift, separating in the darkness. The shadow in her knew that they had trodden the measure of the Mirror Dance, but that now the dance was done and each went their own way with their lantern against the impending night. One sacrifice, it seemed, was enough.

'So again, Silver Brethren, you issue a challenge from your master,' the sorceress observed with a wry twist of her mouth. 'But you'll not lure me down from the mountain. Not with my madness returning. Not with my death so near.'

Spirit Hill . . . Mirror . . . Nyak . . .

Chia groaned aloud at the renewed clamour of voices in her head. Was the madness making short shrift of her this time? Or was it the echo of the Mirror Dance? Or —

'Or nothing,' she sighed deeply. 'Nothing.'

She suddenly stiffened as she caught sight of a flicker of blue on red at the foot of the gnarled crag. A figure in blue and red. Chia frowned. Few dared to climb her mountain, even those rare few who believed themselves to be her friends. Who could this be?

The figure in blue and red ascended the twisted and treacherous trail which skirted the looming crag. As the figure drew nearer Chia perceived that the fearless visitor had the shape of a young woman, a young woman clad in a scarlet gown which was partially covered by a blue cloak. Nearer still and Chia was able to discern the face of the climber.

'Fu,' she breathed, deep memories in the forest green of her eyes, 'Fu the Unlucky.'

As the tall, slender girl approached the even taller sorceress, a wave of loving memory swept over Chia.

Fu. Fu the Unlucky. It had been almost two years ago and three thousand li to the east. Fu was just sixteen then when they met in the elm woods north of Spirit Hill. There had been very little talk, as Chia remembered. Love had come easy and flowed as naturally as the stream by which they had lain. There had been no wild passion – just an affectionate, sharing love for an hour or two with gentle stroking and whispered confidences. Fu had told her that she was called the Unlucky out of sheer irony because she had known such an abundance of good luck from birth. Chia had laughed and given the girl a talisman to add to her wealth of good luck – a black dragon pendant of pure jade.

Think of me now and again when you wear it, lucky Fu the Unlucky. A kind thought can travel further than a Fergana steed, and maybe your thought will touch me wherever I am.

Chia had known from the beginning that their brief love-making would be the one and only time together. At the heart of her, Fu needed to get back to her familiar life in San Lung Town with its family faces and sense of home – she could never have withstood the terrors that crowded Chia's life.

I love you, Green-Eyes. But who are you? There's a mystery in your eyes. Have I made love with a goddess?

'Are you still fool enough to think I'm a goddess?' inquired Chia in a good-humoured tone as the girl in red and blue crested the rim of the towering crag. She noted, with a smile, that Fu was wearing the black dragon

15

pendant. Chia spread her arms in welcome and her smile broadened. But as Fu drew closer the smile faltered.

There was a blank look in the girl's delicate features. An air of unreality hung around her slim shape. And – and now that Chia came to think of it – how could anyone have climbed the treacherous trail as quickly as this girl had seemed to do?

The madness has come.

It was with little surprise that the sorceress witnessed the abrupt disappearance of the image of Fu. She vanished like mist in the wind. She was no more than a vapour of memory. A dream.

Chia lowered her arms and inclined her head, face hidden in the drooping hood of the long black cloak. A dream. A waking dream was always the harbinger of the madness. And the dreams and voices would drive her to the silence of death. She would welcome that death.

At length, she threw back the hood, undid the silver clasp of the cloak and slid the black woollen folds off her shoulders to fall in a heap around her bare feet. The supple muscles of her lithe physique were plainly evident beneath the black silk gown that hugged her body from high-collared neck to ankle-length hem. With a slightly nervous gesture she ran a long-fingered hand through the wild and lengthy locks of her night-black hair before letting the fingers slip from her unkempt tresses to the hilt of a silver dagger which was tucked into a crimson sash girdling her narrow waist.

Before she returned to the safety of Black Dragon Valley in the upper lap of the mountain, she had to restore at least a measure of harmony to her spirit. Chia's lover was waiting for her in the caverns of Black Dragon Valley, and she might be in danger from Chia if the sorceress returned with the madness mounting in her soul. Wei was a gentle and loving woman and Chia would sooner be torn to pieces than harm her full-lipped, full-breasted lover. No – she must never hurt impish little Wei.

Chia knew she must hurl out some of her inner darkness in the ritual of the Outward Spiral. The Outward Spiral would cleanse her mind of silent voices and black memories and remove any threat she might pose to Wei —at least for tonight. Tomorrow Wei must leave Black Dragon Caverns until the dying time was done. As for now . . .

'The Outward Spiral,' whispered Chia, drawing the long silver dagger from the crimson silk sash.

With deft motions she loosed the sash and threw it aside with her dagger hand as her left hand opened her collar and laid the upper chest bare. Stooping, she undid the tiny silver hooks that secured the side-slit which slashed the right side of her gown from ankle to upper thigh. Gown fully loosened, she pulled the black silk up her body and over her head.

Naked but for the silver ankh suspended on its chain between her small, firm breasts, Chia closed her green eyes and allowed her body-spirit to merge with the ch'i force and flow with the wind- and water-forms of feng-shui. After a lengthy seeking of the feng-shui powers, her skin began to tingle as flesh and spirit started to resonate with the hidden energies of living Nature. Her eyes opened and the grip on the dagger tightened as the dark force of Yin and the bright force of Yang coalesced into the exultant vitality of T'ao.

Sensing the raw power throbbing in her racing bloodstream, Chia sank into a crouch in a slow, sinuous motion, weaving the dagger to and fro. A savage smile curved her wide lips. She was energy, tigerish energy.

With a fluent lilt of heels and hips, Chia began to turn in her low stance. Slowly at first, with a stealthy feline grace, her slim form circled in the dry grass; but with each widening circle her body rotated with increasing speed until she spun like a crazed dancer within the spiral path that she followed. Brimming with violent exuberance, Chia whirled through the air like an elemental, her dagger a silver lightning-flash.

And as the sorceress whirled, the winds whirled also. Raw

winds. Wild winds. Winds as raw and wild as the naked dancer. And the winds converged into a single raging entity. It was primal power. It was the fierce Spirit Breath of untamed Nature. And Chia laughed and screamed as the Outward Spiral carried her into its boundless exaltation.

I am the wrath of the dragon. I am the fury of the tiger. I am naked love. I am the killing love. I am the madness. I am the Death-bringer.

Chia yelled out her inner darkness as the Outward Spiral neared its culmination. Her seismic body, buffeted by a bawling whirlwind, swept to the jutting rim of the crag.

The Outward Spiral climaxed in an instant as Chia brought her orgiastic dance to an abrupt halt with her toes dangling over the edge of the crag. With a howl she stabbed the air in front of her and the silver dagger seemed to burn with the passion that poured from her quivering muscles.

Directing the momentum of the Outward Spiral, Chia propelled the inner dark into the outer world. The fury – the madness – the death – streamed through her dagger arm and the burning dagger, and were swept away in the winds of the Spirit Breath.

The ferocity in her heart quickly subsided but the winds that lashed her skin did not abate in accordance with her vanishing savagery. She became like a gentle child as the wind continued to rage like a vengeful god.

As Chia's wits cleared she realised that she was still holding the dagger at arm's length. It pointed to the east. She had projected a small element of her inner shadow into the east.

The dagger no longer glinted pure silver. There was a smudge of red at its sharp tip. The smudge spread into a dribbling red stain. Crimson drops started to spill from the silver blade. Chia trembled at the sight.

Blood . . . the silver dagger weeps tears of blood.

And as Chia's gaze travelled into the east where the blood-weeping dagger pointed, a blurred vision of a strange sky formed in her mind. It seemed to her that the bloodied dagger pointed at a sky thronged with clouds that billowed like shrouds in a storm. It was a sky of grey shrouds, black shrouds, white shrouds savaged with flashing knives of silver lightning.

And a shadow was rising into the torn sky. It loomed above the T'aihang mountains. And it wore the shape of Chia.

Chia stared at the apparition as it rose high into the phantom sky and her arm slowly lowered the blood-weeping dagger. Then, as abruptly as the torn sky and giant shadow had appeared, they vanished. The eastern sky was quiet once more, and dark, with a faint haunting of stars.

The sorceress took a few deep breaths, and glanced at the dagger. The blood had disappeared from the silver blade. But nothing could stop the shivering of her limbs or the tightening of her skin into goose-flesh, because a cold wind had sprung from the east at the instant the mad visions ended.

And the wind from the east blew stronger with each swelling of her lungs. And with each breath she inhaled a subtle mist of the spirit darkness she had so recently exorcised by the Outward Spiral. Intangible shadow substance seeped into the tight pores of her contracting flesh. Expelled voices and memories returned with the beat of each cold gust. And the warmth of her spirit shrank in the face of the icy east wind. The dark she had rejected now filled her once again.

I cast my shadow into the east. And the east throws my shadow back.

There were whispers in the keening tone of the rising wind. Familiar whispers.

Spirit Hill . . . Mirror . . . Nyak . . . Silver Brethren . . Fu the Unlucky . . . Death Whisperers . . . Death-bringer . . . Mirror.

19

After a time, the voices and the memories were lodged in her head. And the wind was just a cold wind, nothing more.

The Hour of the Hound gave way to the Hour of the Boar as Chia stood on the rocky ledge and gazed into the east and the depths of memory. She spoke only once.

'Death-bringer.'

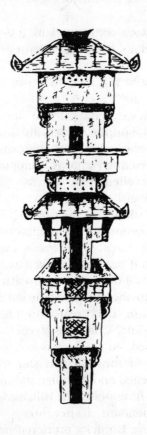

2

HOUR OF THE RAT

The night sky was a sky of turmoil. It was a sky of ripped and tattered clouds like ragged banners in the dragon-wind.

Into the torn sky hunched round-shouldered Spirit Hill.

Two silhouettes scaled its ribbed slopes.

A bluff wind bounded over the middle slopes and buffeted the two climbers, plucking grey cloaks, fluttering a creaking lantern, flapping conical hats, whipping dishevelled hair across the man's harsh features and the girl's wary eyes.

'Bitch,' Chao snarled at his captive.

Fu the Unlucky looked up at Chao with a mixture of fear and disgust. A rusty iron chain fastened to a rustier iron collar around her neck clinked as her captor jerked impatiently at its loose end. Her breath was laboured as she struggled up the steep incline and she had no intention of wasting her breath on Chao the Braggart. What was the point? Chao was a cruel, ignorant bastard.

As they climbed, Fu's stare was averted from the burial mound on top of the hill. But she spared a nostalgic glance for the veiled and unveiled moon in the turbulent skies above the hump of Spirit Hill, and she clutched the black dragon pendant at her breast. *I remember you, Green-Eyes.* Fu the Unlucky proffered no silent prayer to T'aoist immortals or Buddhist divinities – she had despaired of them. Although barely eighteen she had clung

21

to many beliefs, but here and now the black jade dragon pendant hanging from her neck was her sole comfort – her hand clasped it tightly as if the warmth of her skin might kindle life in the amulet. *Aid me, Little Dragon, aid me.*

And she thought of the green-eyed goddess who had laughed at being called a goddess and then given her the little black dragon. That had been a golden time then, in that elm wood two years ago. A night of love and mystery.

But now a single thought throbbed in her skull . . . *I'm going to my death.*

She gasped as Chao gave a sadistic tug at the chain. 'Move your feet, whore. It's a long path to Spirit Hill Tomb.' Then she thought she heard him muttering something about the Hour of the Rat.

Perhaps she was dreaming. *Little Dragon, let me be dreaming.* But when other dreams turned into nightmares she awoke. Why not now? This nightmare had begun with the Silver Masks at the foot of Autumn Willow Tower, masked men who brought her to Chao in Shen Lung Gorge. Why did the tower and the Silver Masks and Chao and the iron shackle seem to be undeniable destiny? Why had her slender neck bent so meekly to the metal collar?

Oh, Black Dragon Sorceress, my one-night lover, hear me! Help me!

Chao scowled into the gusty night air and forced his gaze up to the summit of Spirit Hill with its ancient death mound. It wasn't a tomb he would have freely chosen to enter – even tomb robbers had their superstitions – but he had the sworn assurances of Ming. Ming, preening himself before the bronze mirror in his mansion, had passed on the orders of the Master: 'You realise, Chao, that you can't hoodwink the Master. Obedience is the only course. Spirit Hill's a fearful place, but the Silver Brethren will allay your fears.'

It was true, Chao reflected; the Silver Brethren had smothered his doubts. It was as though they had made up his mind for him.

Yet the robber was uneasy as he trudged up the winding

path. The timing of this enterprise was inauspicious: the Eve of Ching Ming, known to the Buddha Followers as the Eve of the Feast of the Dead. And Spirit Hill, aside from its reputation, was in a hazardous region – a mere twelve li east of the Forest of the Ancestors with its hushed trees and (some said) vampire tombs. Shaking his head clear of misgivings he gave another jerk on the chain and swore as the girl stumbled.

The wind gave a last growl, a final bluster, then prowled into the black ink of the east. Fu darted a glance at the looming bulge of the tomb on the hill. The tomb was ancient, for it had no spirit road – no path flanked by stone sentinels to its doors. Spirit Hill Tomb, an uneven dome against the fleeing flags of the clouds, was the most shunned burial mound east of the Forest of the Ancestors. She felt, for a childish moment, that the rearing tomb was waiting to slide soundlessly down the slope with its doors flung back and its mouth gaping wide. She stifled a sob. Chao tugged again on the chafing iron collar.

Her shoulders still shook when they ascended near enough to discern the heavy doors of the verdigris-smeared bronze.

Nearer still it was possible to distinguish the embossed figurations on the bronze doors. The mound hung massive above the erratic nimbus of Chao's lantern which played on the lower branches of spreading elms standing one to each side of the doors. Chao halted at the portal and pursed his bloated lips at the archaic designs on the gold and green bronze. Puzzlement creased his brow at the abstruse pictograms and ideograms snaking in sinuous whorls across the dull metal. Patina muffled the golden symbols like moss burying an antique tablet of sorcery. Some of the signs bore superficial resemblance to Chinese character writing but were nonetheless indecipherable. Was this an ancestral form of Chinese? If so, what kind of men had their ancestors been? The convoluted designs were ominous, inviting the eye along emblematic mazes.

For an instant he wavered, then pride renewed his determination. He was Chao the Intrepid, wasn't he? Chao with the bones of iron, with the sinews of stout rope, with the skin of tanned leather. With a mighty shove he opened the doors and they swung inwards with the long protest of a low groan. Dank airs gusted out of the blackness and chilled his seamed face.

Earth and mould and damp and decay.

Fu's heart was drumming. She licked lips as dry as silk on hot rock. She was looking at the doors of her death.

Her voice trembled between quivering lips. 'Chao – what's happening? No robber has ever returned from Spirit Hill Mound. You know that. Why have you brought me here?' *But why did I come so meekly? The masked ones* . . .

Her words struck chords in his memory and he frowned. But he recalled the whispered promises of the Silver Brethren and brushed off the doubt she had instilled. He stepped into the blank interior of the mound, his burly figure a sooty profile in the dithering aura of the lantern. Lifting the light he peered at the ruddy reflections from bare walls. Fu the Unlucky directed a farewell look at the barren hill slopes, the rippling moor below, Shen Lung Gorge and the swelling terrain that dipped to the south. Chao's tone had a hollow timbre as it bounced back to the girl.

'Skeletons.'

Swinging back with a start to the gaping doors she viewed the parched remains illuminated by the light of the lantern. Two dry skeletons clad in corroded armour sprawled on the floor of the sinking tunnel, gripping sword stumps that pointed like signs to the doors.

Chao tilted his head and shrugged. 'Bones in a rusty iron skin,' he dismissed them. He shook the chain. 'Come on.'

'I told you that no one returns from the mound,' she whispered.

A hundred heartbeats of shuffling down the tunnel and

past a scatter of brittle skeletons huddled by the walls brought them to a pair of bronze doors identical to the first. Fu shuddered at the sinister pictograms and spirals revealed in flashes by the lantern. The doors were slightly ajar and opened with a gentle push.

With humming heart she followed Chao into the darkness, their shapes encircled by a pallid aureole of lantern-light. The ivory outlines of the bones of past men were strewn on the dank flagstones. Chao stumbled on a sodden plank and cursed. Kicking aside another plank he approached the ramshackle remnants of a wooden enclosure around a triple coffin. His thief's eye noted with regret that all the funerary articles were absent, even the mu yong and tao yong – the wooden and pottery figurines that represented relatives, friends and servants of the dead occupant. The corpse and its cerements were also missing.

'Shang Ti's blood!' he snapped. 'Not so much as a dead fingernail to take as a trophy . . . just stagnant water, intruders' bones and rotting wood.' His voice boomed in the voluminous chamber. Fu, remembering the stories whispered in Sang Lung Town, was unable to drag her vision from the ruinous coffin. A silver drop of water rang like a fragile bell in a pool at the end of the chamber.

'The roof must have a thousand tiny cracks to let this much water in,' surmised Chao. His brow contracted. 'There must be an inner chamber . . .' The lure of funeral treasure was not included in Ming's original promise, but still – most tombs had a hidden chamber.

'If you twitch a finger I'll split your skull,' he threatened, releasing her shackle. 'And if you as much as breathe too loudly I'll throttle you,' he added. She nodded, too frightened of the man to express her fears of the burial chamber.

Sparing the occasional glance for his downcast captive Chao skirted the clammy walls in the hope of discovering a niche which would secrete the honey of gold, the moon-water of silver, the hard, cold magic of jade. But

25

there was nothing but flat stone, dull stone, drab stone under his sliding hand. Then his theft-sensitive fingers detected a hairline crack on the far wall of the chamber, beneath which the pool of water had gathered. Fingertips traced down, up, across, down. Smiling, he stepped back – a door, a secret door into another chamber: perhaps a treasure-house of gold, silver and jade. Grinning, he strode to where Fu the Unlucky stood above the feeble lantern.

'This venture is turning out well for me, little brat,' he mocked. 'Not that it will benefit you . . .'

Sudden as a striking snake she grasped the heavy chain and whirled it at Chao, but the weighty links and her combative inexperience sent her aim astray and the chain thumped on the side of his bull neck. Although misdirected, the blow sent him reeling and she grabbed the opportunity to make for the door. Gathering the chain in her arms she raced up the tunnel like a panicked doe. She could hear the groggy steps of Chao lumbering in her wake.

Run, run, run, her mind urged. Run to the open air. Lock the tomb doors on your pursuer. Run. Down the slopes. *Run*.

The salvation of the open portal was a mere stride away. A backward glance. The bobbing firefly of Chao's lantern was far behind.

Ravenous for freedom, she leaped at the open square of the door.

She was spun back by an invisible force, her thoughts spiralling in on themselves. In a few breaths she regained her balance and cleared her head of that perplexing inward spiral of images.

Chao was less than twenty strides from her.

Quaking with fear, Fu once more flung herself at the open doorway. Again she was spiralled back, thoughts spinning, vision whirling.

When she recollected her wits Chao was two strides away.

The tomb robber's brutish features split into a grin. 'Feeling dizzy, little bitch?' He placed the lantern on the sloping floor, his bright slits of eyes avid with rage and lust.

'You'll pay for striking me, little girl,' he growled. 'I've got a ram that will split a spoilt little virgin like you.' His savage grin broadened. 'You don't want to die a virgin, do you, bitch?'

In the moment that followed, memories of light and love rushed in a torrent through the trembling girl . . . her gentle mother, cuddling her as a child after awaking from a nightmare. *Safe now, safe. Not to worry. Not to worry* . . . the colourful exuberance of the Birthday of a Hundred Flowers . . . Fen-lai, grown from a boisterous boy into a shy, handsome youth, pressing a gold tiger brooch into her palm. *A sign of my heart, Golden Flower* . . . Grass-Stomper, her pony, prancing in the sunlight . . . Green-Eyes in the elm wood . . .

All lost now. All kindness gone. She faced the stark reality of darkness and rape and death.

Her spirit suddenly rebelled. 'No!' she howled, swinging a fierce kick into Chao's groin. The robber doubled over with a moan. Seizing her advantage, Fu whirled the iron chain at Chao's bent head. The cumbersome links thudded on the ruffian's skull and he yelled in shock before swaying, folding, then crumpling to the floor.

She turned back to the inviting portal. A few hours' journey beyond that open frame was San Lung Town, her wing-roofed home, her kindly parents, her future husband, her friends. Whatever force had repelled her from the tunnel doors was a powerful illusion, and could be overcome by force of will. She was thankful that a Wu magus had taught her the basic techniques of surmounting illusion.

Fu shut her eyes and breathed slowly, seeking union with the T'ao – the way of harmony. Gradually the spirit of the T'ao flowed into her meditation.

'There is no barrier,' she whispered to herself. 'There is only the illusion of a barrier. That illusion has dissolved.' She opened her eyes to the moonlit landscape outside the tunnel. Escape. Freedom. Home.

She stepped towards the opening, avid for home.

She was hurled backwards by the rusty chain and crashed to the floor of the corridor, nearly choked by the bite of the iron collar. Above her loomed Chao the Braggart, blood trickling down his face, chain secure in his sturdy grip. His decayed teeth were displayed in a feral grin.

'Bitch,' he hissed. 'Damned dung-bitch.'

With a roar he heaved the chain and dragged her on her back down the dark slope. The metal collar dug into her throat as she slid backwards down the tunnel. Halfway down the corridor he wound the chain around one brawny arm and grabbed her long, scented hair in a savage fist. Fu bit back a scream at the agony in her scalp as Chao hauled her by the hair down into the burial chamber. She felt as if the roots were tearing loose as her tormentor pulled her threshing body across the ruin of the triple coffin and the sodden surface of the tomb floor.

He finally halted by the pool that fronted the hidden door to the inner chamber. The chain was cast to one side. For an instant he glared down at his prisoner. Then he delivered a sharp kick to her head. Her teeth bit her tongue with the impact of the blow.

'Get up, whore-daughter,' he ordered.

Fu's ravaged mind ran like a child to her mother, her father, her friends, kind faces. She shut her eyes to the fearsome countenance above.

'I said get up,' Chao bellowed, seizing her hair again. With a vicious yell he hauled her up by her long tresses and thrust her against the wall.

The terrified girl fingered the black jade pendant resting on her chest. 'Little Dragon, help me,' she implored.

'Bitch,' he snapped, then kicked her hard in the stomach. The air whooshed out of her lungs and she slumped to the margin of the shallow pool, fighting for breath. 'Now you're going to feel my thick ram rip your scrawny body, little girl,' he chuckled. Relishing her screams, he caught her by the ears and hoisted her up by the tender lobes.

Then with a bellow he launched his massive weight on her and bore her to the floor. He pushed his swart face into her delicate features. Her face was a white paper mask of terror. 'I'm going to tear your crotch in half, little bitch,' he whispered with a smile.

Chao's throat muscles suddenly tightened. Fu's eyelids trembled. Her eyes dimmed. Her head slowly tilted to one side. The eyelids closed. 'Little Dragon . . .' she sighed. The head flopped at an angle.

A frail trail of blood threaded from her hairline to the blue cloak and the red silk gown. She had struck her head badly in the fall. Alarmed, Chao gnawed at his lip. Ming, the Silver Brethren, and the Master – whoever he was – would be angry. He had injured the wretched girl and would have raped her. There could be trouble ahead for him. His orders had been explicit and he had disobeyed them. Ming had been adamant about the treatment of the girl, had shaken a warning finger: 'Take the girl into Spirit Hill Mound before the Hour of the Rat and then wait, do nothing but wait. And while you're waiting, don't shed a drop of her blood either in rape or wounding.'

But, Chao reasoned, the cut was superficial and the girl was not dead, merely stunned. Stunned, that's all. She would soon revive. Yes, everything would be well. He had to believe that. In the meantime there was the door to the secret chamber to consider . . . Unlocking the iron collar, Chao flung the chain aside and left the insensible girl by the pool.

After an extensive investigation he found that the door obdurately refused to budge. His clumsy knife was in any case inadequate for the task. Admitting defeat, he slid to the ground and rested his back on the stubborn stone.

A bead of water plipped into the pool, spreading ripple rings.

The red silk expanse of the girl's breast rose and fell in a slow rhythm. The cold, the silence and the darkness of the chamber made the waiting seem long. They played on his nerves until he started at the splutter of the lantern or at insignificant, perhaps imaginary noises outside the rim of sight. How much longer would the light last?

He huddled over the saffron shudder of the lantern, his broad hands and craggy lineaments bathed in a lustre that seeped into the enfolding dark. He nervously scratched the Black Serpent tattoo on the back of his right hand. He glanced at the pool: it was an inky well that threw back the shimmer of the lantern. He thought of the hidden chamber behind the secret door at his back, and of the drenched wooden remnants of the ancient triple coffin. What had happened to the body it once housed? Had it been stolen? Had it been drummed into dust by the beating of centuries and sunk into the slime on the floor? He became sensitive to the oppressive nearness of the slate wall of darkness. The yellow ring of his world was contracting. The lantern flared and whiffled, conjuring a dance of shadows.

In a short space it would be the Festival of Ching Ming, or what many called the Feast of the Dead.

The Feast of the Dead.

A memory sprang like a weed in his skull. Six years old. Or was it seven? No matter – a long time ago. A distinct picture of scrubbed pinewood floorboards (he remembered the sweet smell of pine). He was playing toss-and-catch with five cowrie shells. A grey twilight outside the open door and geese honking in the distance and a sense of rain coming. His mother leaned down. 'It's the Feast of the Dead,' she said. 'It's time for the sweeping of the tombs. You can hold the candles for the ancestors.'

The lantern spluttered and threw a shadow on the memory. The candles for the ancestors. The relic of the threefold coffin was shrouded in black velvet air but its image settled behind his raw eyes. Childhood fears were resurrected, rising and moving on stealthy feet.

30

Waiting. Bringing the girl and waiting. It had seemed a simple business in the radiant candlelight of Ming's San Lung Mansion. But it wasn't a simple matter. Perhaps if the girl were conscious it would be more bearable – he would have someone to goad, to divert his attention from the implacable darkness. He observed her features, their contours inconstant in the wavering light beams.

'Bitch of a girl,' he cursed, unconsciously attempting to exorcise a misshapen dread that slouched in his head. He worried at a grimy fingernail with eroded teeth.

Beyond the walls of Death Mound it was deep night. It was the Hour of the Rat on the Feast of the Dead. He knew this with a sure instinct and the knowledge made his heart patter like a rat in a trap. In the lore of tomb robbers it was an ill-omened time; a time of conjurations and curses, of ice voices and stone hands. Here, in the dark, it was easy to believe in such things. Grimacing, he locked his eyes and struggled to summon recollections of sunlit hillsides, the teeming streets of San Lung Town, robust shouts of gambling in gaudy pavilions, wine and musky female sweat . . .

But he was unable to banish the thought of the Hour of the Rat, the Feast of the Dead.

'*Whispered to death.*'

He gulped and peered into the dark. Whose was the voice that sighed in his ear? Whispered to death . . . Had the girl spoken?

'*Whispered to death.*'

No, not the girl. She was drowned in a well of sleep, her lips didn't tremble with the sough of the voice. Chao bared his teeth and fished beneath his threadbare cloak for the bronze hilt of his knife. Had an intruder come, or the one for whom he was bidden to wait?

Had the darkness spoken? *It's time for the sweeping of the tombs. You can hold the candles for the ancestors.*

He grasped the knife in a moist palm as he thought he heard a whisper, a shuffle, a murmur.

31

The pool tingled with the slap of a water drop.

Chao pressed his shoulder-blades to the secret door, strained to catch the slightest sound, strove to steady his knife hand. And waited.

On the northern slope of Spirit Hill the monk Vinaya, of the brethren of the Celestial Buddha Temple, had contrived a rudimentary shrine. The cave that housed the Mahayana clay figurines was even more cramped than his tiny cell in the monastery and while the cell was dry the cave dripped with moisture. But the lean, ascetic Indian loved solitude, and in the whole of San Lung prefecture there was no corner more solitary than the cave on Spirit Hill. Except, of course, for the Death Mound that crowned Spirit Hill.

Vinaya welcomed the notoriety of the hill. Folk seldom visited the rises by day. And by night – he smiled – utter solitude.

The beasts, too, avoided Spirit Hill.

The desolate wind which had keened through the Eve of the Feast of the Dead had dropped at the approach of the Hour of the Rat. The flames of the tallow candles burned steadily in the rocky chamber, warming the simple idols, softening Vinaya's lupine features, brightening the mirror into which he stared. The mirror was a black bowl brimming with water and set firmly on the ground. It would lead him on the path to deep meditation. The reflected visage in the dark liquid was dim and unfamiliar – a drowned stranger. It diminished the silent gazer, dissolved the self.

Vinaya forgot the ardent glow of the candles, the measured *tap tap* of water and the serene smiles of the clay pantheon. Presently he was only conscious of the image in the water. Finally he was conscious of nothing.

The Hour of the Rat slid over the rapt form of Vinaya. In the saffron radiance of the pungent candles the monk, seated cross-legged in the lotus asana, looked like a member of the Mahayana divinities – an embodied silence. His vision, a blind seeing, rested inperturbably on the black water mirror.

For an instant there was a subtle breath of awakening – a sensation of almost touching – a sense of a huge secret about to become manifest – it was there, and here, this side of breath . . .

The blissful trance was ravaged by a sudden black lightning and ground thunder of the spirit. Vinaya's gaunt frame arched in shock and pain and a lashing foot caught the black bowl of the water mirror, spilling the liquid on the smooth rock. Vinaya threshed in violent spasms on the cold stone.

The empty mirror bowl rolled and rolled.

Chia sprang out of sleep like a hare from a trap, flung off the pelts from the straw pallet and blinked at the sandstone walls of Black Dragon Caverns. The familiar ochre of her cavern, etched throughout with huge spirals, glimmered in mild reassurance with the lazy glow of the fire. Propping her weight on an elbow she stared out of the cavern mouth into the night rain. Anxiety receded with each slowing breath.

'Spirit Hill. Hour of the Rat.'

Chia's companion stretched beneath the disturbed pelts. Drowsy eyelids opened. 'What is it?' she yawned. 'Did you say something?'

Chia gave a thin smile. 'Words to the rain.'

Wei rolled her eyes at the woman by her side. 'A typical Chia reply. Evasive as ever.' She snuggled close to the sorceress, naked skin to naked skin. 'Can't sleep?'

'Not any more. But it was a dream – not desire – that woke me.'

Wei carefully studied her pensive lover. 'Those green eyes of yours have a strange distance in them.'

The sorceress did not respond.

'I love you, Chia.'

33

'There's nothing in me to love.' The reply was low and hollow.

'Then see yourself in my face, Green-Eyes. You'll see a Chia to love there.'

The sorceress shook her head.

'There's a small death in you tonight,' observed Wei.

'No death. A dream.'

'Can it talk?'

The sorceress sprawled out on the pallet, hands folded behind her head. 'Two people were climbing a hill,' she commenced, her voice little more than a murmur. 'One of the climbers was Fu the Unlucky.'

'Oh – was she the one you . . .?'

'Yes. And in my dream I saw her climbing Spirit Hill.'

Wei compressed her pert lips. 'There are many spirit hills.'

'This one is in San Lung prefecture, three thousand li to the east. It has a death mound on the summit. I saw Fu being dragged on a chain into Spirit Hill Mound.'

'You're not going to the Spirit Hill of San Lung,' Wei asserted firmly.

Chia raised an eyebrow. 'Did I say that I was?'

'You don't need to. I know you. But you can't go – you know you can't. The madness has touched you already, hasn't it?'

Chia nodded. 'I felt the first touch at sunset. Or it may have been the echoes of a dance in the forest.'

'Dance in a forest!' Wei snorted dismissively. 'It was the beginnings of the madness. The Death-bringer.'

Chia sighed. 'I know.'

'Will the dying time be soon?' the other asked hesitantly.

'Yes, soon.' The flat tone betrayed no emotion.

Wei's elfin eyes brightened a shade. 'I could go and ask Liu Chun to visit Spirit Hill, if you like.'

'What?'

'Liu Chun. He'll be glad of a chance to leave Luminous

34

Cloud Mountain for a while. He wears the life of a hermit like an unbecoming coat and he'll pounce on any chance to throw it off. Also he relishes adventure. You can't go, but Liu Chun can go in your place. Not with your death so near, Chia – you mustn't think of going.'

The sorceress turned a disturbing green gaze on her lover. 'I never know where I'm going. I don't even know who I am.'

Wei shrugged off the unsettling look and snuggled back into the warm, musky pelts. She mumbled herself back to sleep. 'Fine, Green-Eyes. Liu Chun goes. It's decided. Good night.'

Chia remained awake, brooding on an inconstant past. The hours dragged by.

Fu in Spirit Hill Mound, beaten senseless by a brute called Chao the Braggart. Chao waiting in the tomb with knife in hand – there the dream had ended.

But was it more than just a dream, gentle Fu?

Spirit Hill . . . Mirror . . . Nyak . . . Silver Brethren . . . whispered to death . . . Mirror . . . Outward Spiral, Inward Spiral . . . shadow . . . the dagger that points east is the dagger that bleeds . . . Spirit Hill . . .Nyak . . .

Dawn dripped wearily into the valley outside her spiral-decorated caverns. She stared into the persistent rain. Its dull beating depressed her spirit but did not quench it.

'More than a dream,' she whispered to the rain. 'It has happened. It has begun. And each day it will grow. There will be a burying of the living and a dancing of the dead.'

DROWNED STRANGERS

It came, not from the unknown, but from the known. Its face, if face it could be called, was drawn from the familiar, not from the alien.

It was more than a dream, this thing that knew your name.

At first it was quiet and discreet like a rumour whispered in a confidential ear. And as fast as a rumour, the whisper spread.

It was odd. It was subtle. It killed without hate.

And the madness it brought you was a sign of its love.

Sung was a vagabond and young and footsore and his unwashed bony frame was almost as shrunken as his starved stomach. He had sat begging for hours on the North Road from San Lung Town but it seemed that nobody had any food to spare these days. If you didn't own land (and if Imperial or rebel soldiers didn't burn your crops or steal your animals) then you starved, unless you could get into the army or find employment in serving one of the merchant-smugglers. All over the Dragon Empire the granaries were running low. On his journeys he had passed many grain mills with their rice huskers broken and neglected, their winnowing machines tumbled, with twisted crank handles and their corn grinders askew. So many dead, deserted farms. As for livestock – they had a higher value than people. But then, perhaps they always had.

Sung glanced up and down the road. Not a soul. Well, an unusually well-disposed Imperial courier had informed him that there was a plentiful supply of fish to be had from Shen River where it looped a few li south of Spirit Hill. With a sigh the vagabond left the dusty road and headed for Shen Lung Gorge.

Sung slithered down the moist bank to the creamy bustle of the river that rushed through the cramped, beetling gorge of Shen Lung, the Spirit Dragon. His mouth tasted imaginary fish and his eyes beheld imaginary fish and his nimble fingers twitched in anticipation of grasping the cold, vibrant thresh of energy that was fish. Ah – there – the lean youth grinned at the bronze and silver scurry of sleek fish in the foam and mutter of Shen River.

He skipped over a boulder, splashed through a shallow pool, waded into the shallow margin of the river, bright teeth bared, hands hooked into claws. The river gurgled by. He dived like hawk-drop. And in his clutch was struggling food. Ravenous, he ate it as he stood, and cast the skeleton into the hurrying waters. He gulped the icy liquid with grunts and gasps.

With a satisfied sigh he returned to the bank. Soon he would build a fire and his next fish would be cooked. Luxury. Then he would sleep like a cat in the sun. He angled his head and studied the sky – it was bland blue and the sun was young. His lids blinked and he yawned. He would rest for a time on a rocky lip overhanging the river. Later there would be time for fishing and fire-building.

Squatting on the rippled rock he peered into the rela-tively calm inlet below, sand-bedded and sky-mirroring. Minnows darted like minor agitations beneath the surface. The scrawny youth observed his wavering re-flection in the trembling water. His indistinct face stared up at him from under the water like the visage of a drowned stranger.

Suddenly he became deaf. Completely deaf. And there

was a shape leaning over his reflection in the water. He jerked round to confront the newcomer and his mouth gaped in amazement. There was no one. And his deafness had departed the moment he turned around. The pounding of his heart quickly subsided.

Again he regarded his watery reflection and deafness smothered his ears once more. And there was a shape leaning over Sung's shoulder. It was the shape of a man, slim and effeminate, with a vivid white face and rose eyes. A slender, milky hand was stretching to touch the nape of the youth's neck. For an instant Sung gaped at the image, then sprang back and rolled away. As before, there was nobody behind him. And the deafness vanished in an instant. He discovered that he was shuddering uncontrollably.

A fit of nausea came and passed. Sung gingerly regained his feet and climbed the southern slope by which he had descended. Not once did he look back.

The perfect madness does not rage. The complete madness does not shout, or howl, or bawl its despair. The perfect madness is restrained.

The perfect madness is devoid of malice. It takes no pleasure in pain. It does not seek revenge. The perfect madness means you no harm.

The perfect madness understands you. It knows everything about you. Above all, it knows what you keep hidden.

It slips in everywhere, through locked doors, shuttered windows, closed eyes. It has slipped in here – where the drying sheets flap in the narrow courtyard and the thick aroma of boiling vegetables wafts from the glazed earthenware bulge of the cooking pot. The housekeeper with her brawny arms is arranging the hanging sheets and singing a song of young love in the forest as her ageing feet tap to the rhythm of an ancient dance.

The perfect madness is not rash or importunate. It is

patient. It works slowly. The housekeeper will sing her sentimental songs and stomp her clumsy feet for some time yet.

But in a little while she will learn to listen to the perfect deafness and her feet will dance to the perfect silence.

There – she has looked up. She has begun to listen.

Nua peered beyond the swaying beaded curtains at the translucent tumble of rain on the muddy lane, then went back to her favourite mat and resumed polishing the bronze mirror her husband had recently forged. Married three months, she was proud of the skills of her youthful, ambitious husband. One day he would work in the smithies of the Emperor Ling and she would parade in sumptuous silks and satins and brocades. She rubbed the bronze mirror briskly in an effort to allay anxiety.

It was the fifth day after the Feast of the Dead and twenty li south of Spirit Hill.

The modest house of Nua and her husband Fang-ch'i was behind the northern walls of San Lung, on the Lane of Axes near the Gate of the Black Serpent. The lofty wooden gates were drab ghosts through the opalescent gauze of the rain. The lane was deserted. Soon it would be time for the closing of the gates, heralded by the striking of gongs and the rolling of drums.

Why was her husband so late?

The rain drubbed the blue-tiled roof and effervesced on the muddy lane but the sheltered porch was dry in the lee of the wind so Nua could comfortably leave the door ajar and gaze through the rustling curtain beads at the cascading rain, thinking of her missing husband.

Where was he? The polishing of the bronze mirror became an unmindful action as Nua reflected on the brief months of marriage and the plans they shared for the future. She knew that Fang-ch'i was proud of her deportment and her full, pretty face with its strikingly even features; he had often affirmed that she made an excellent

39

wife. But what if he became a renowned artisan with sufficient means to buy another wife, as young in that future time as she was young now? What then? She flicked a speck of dust from her simple blue silk gown with a pettish gesture.

The downpour swiftly diminished and died as she brooded on the future, her hand imperceptibly slowing in its circular polishing motion until it rested with its soft cloth at the centre of the gleaming circle of bronze.

She was hauled from her sunken thoughts by the brazen beating of gongs and the thundering of drums from the four gates of the walled town. The gates would be closing soon! Dashing off a small prayer to the eponymous god of the town she hurried out the door, still clutching the mirror. The lane was empty, although a babble of voices drifted from the surrounding houses that wound from the Black Serpent Gate to the southern Square of Execution. Wincing at the strain of her unnecessary burden she placed the bronze disc carefully against the door-jamb and scanned the lane for signs of Fang-ch'i's homecoming. But the rutted track was dull and vacant in the drab light. The puddles were muddy wells pitting the desolate lane.

Then she caught a glimpse of something odd – a glimmer of gold from the northern bend of the lane, quickly fading. Then another golden glimmer, slightly nearer. Astonished at the mysterious sight, Nua stared at the gold-dust glitter as it wove towards her. Her superstitious fingers gripped the orange jade t'ao-t'ieh talisman that hung from her neck, but the amulet was cold to her warm touch.

As the golden radiance drew closer she realised that it moved by shifting from one rainpool to the next. She became uneasily aware that the clangour of the gongs and drums and the distant clamour of the townsfolk were being steadily muffled. Sound receded as the golden light approached from pool to pool. Nua shrank into herself

40

and her glance slid to the bronze mirror leaning near the door . . . it was blazing with a fierce golden glare. Her gaze returned to the advancing light as it diminished in a nearby pool and was reborn in the ring of water at her slippered feet.

As Nua stared into the golden water the last sounds of the world died.

Then there was perpetual silence.

Ming was a vain man as well as a cruel one. Shortly before the Hour of the Rat on the Feast of the Dead he had preened himself for over an hour in front of his huge bronze mirror, striding up and down, puffing out his chest, regarding his reflection with smug approval. Then he had dined lavishly in the Spring Cloud Room of his San Lung mansion with five wealthy merchants (bemused at the late hour of the feast) and a score of alluring bondsmaids.

That had been seven days ago, but he still recalled the amusement he had gained from speculating on the fate of Chao and Fu in the ancient tomb of Spirit Hill. It had added an extra savour to the meal.

Ming smirked as he oiled his eyebrows in the golden reflection of the mirror. How easily the Silver Brethren had persuaded the normally shrewd Chao to enter Spirit Hill Mound! Fu the Unlucky had also played her unwitting part. And Ming had orchestrated the plan to perfection. The Master would be pleased.

Just seven days, and the ripples he had set in motion were already gliding through San Lung Town. Four hundred steps from the gates of his mansion the house of Nua and Fang-ch'i stood tenantless.

Ming sat on a heap of velvet cushions and admired his bulky profile, draped in a lavish yellow silk robe, reflected in the gleaming bronze of his circular mirror. His bound hair and dangling band of a beard were sleekly oiled. Gold rings shimmered on his bulbous fingers. An opulent pendant rested on his chest, constantly fingered by the ringed hands. Absorbed in his reflection, he ignored the incised patterns on the bronze mirror, being more concerned with his looks than with mystic intaglio.

The mirror was of a reputed antiquity and was unusual in that its designs were grooved on the front side – the viewing surface. At the centre of the mirror was a plain square panel representing the ts'ung – the earth symbol at the centre of all things – surrounded by the Twelve Earthly Branches and the four sacred animals of the serpent to the north, the phoenix to the south, the tiger to the west and the dragon to the east. It was a cosmology in miniature. A board game that resembled it had once been popular but was now of little interest to all but T'aoist magi; the game known as Liu Po involved forcing the opponent's men into the angles in the outer margins and consolidating one's own men in the central square to achieve a symbolic cosmic dominance. In the early decades of the Western Han Dynasty the game and the mirror patterns were treated with reverence as symbols of mimetic magic, but in these later years of the Eastern Han the cosmic import of the game and its designs was overlaid and lost in extravagant and inane formalisations.

Thus Ming did not speculate on sorcery and cosmology as he studied the great mirror suspended from its mighty oak frame, but rather considered his own image, smiling.

Tall orchid-scented candles brightened the green and gold room with windows unshuttered to a mild evening. The late sounds of San Lung Town floated through the open windows together with the odours and scuffles of the kitchen below. Ming stirred, and scratched his ample belly, thinking of food, his nose responding to the smell of cooking. He became attentive to the hubbub and clatter of cooks and cookery. They would be ready soon. His brow creased into a frown. They had better be ready soon.

He almost toppled from his heap of piled cushions as the door swung open. His mouth opened to roar at whichever servant had dared to intrude upon his privacy. The full mouth froze into a gaping oval. Reflected in the bronze mirror, the silver masks were dull surfaces. But the Silver Brethren were unmistakable.

Ming swung round to greet his two visitors, forcing an expression of welcome into his features. His heart hammered. 'You grace my humble house with your esteemed presence, noble Brethren,' he stammered. 'I hadn't expected –'

He was cut off by the guttural sounds that issued from a Silver Brother's strained vocal chords. 'We have brought the Body and the Hearing. You will hide them here and keep them safe until the enemy comes.'

The fat merchant was terrified, but he knew better than to gainsay the Silver Brethren. The barbaric mask helmets with their long, swirling manes of dead grey hair and the sickening stench that flowed from their grey-mantled bodies were daunting enough, but Ming knew what was hidden by the masks and the mantles and his contracting throat could hardly draw breath, let alone defy the Brethren.

'Whatever you say,' he managed to croak.

Peng-t'ai had been a deaf-mute from birth but she had learned to read lips and judge faces and gestures and she was skilled in interpreting the silent communication of hand and eye. It was difficult for a deaf-mute to survive in the world of the hearing, but Peng-t'ai, in the twenty years since her sixth birthday, had struggled hard to achieve her humble niche in the hierarchy of San Lung society. Even in these war-torn, poverty-crushed times she managed to make a subsistence living from her stall near Red Phoenix Gate. There were always a few customers who were keen to buy her wooden sculptures of gods and goddesses and mythical beasts. People, in general, had treated her with respect. Sang Lung, all things considered, had been a pleasant enough town.

It was no longer a pleasant town. There had been two other deaf-mutes in San Lung. Both had died of two different plagues in the last five days, and the plagues had taken less than a day to run their course from start to finish. At the end, San-ch'i's body had resembled a bloated black bag while Lai-ko's six-year-old shape had swollen into a crimson mass of supurating boils. And there had been six blind people in San Lung. All had been stricken by the black and red plagues over the last five days, and all had died in a matter of hours. What kind of plagues were they that only chose the deaf and the blind?

Peng-t'ai nervously put the finishing touches to her display of wooden figurines and took up her usual position behind her rickety stall. Despite her jitteriness, she did her best to adopt a friendly smile for the milling crowds at Red Phoenix Gate.

The faces in the bustling crowd were familiar from a thousand mornings but today (how could she express it?) they were strange in their familiarity. She was aware that they had been infected by a madness that was worse than the swift black and red plagues. She had seen them talking of the dead as if they were still living. And sometimes they spoke of the living as if they were dead.

A movement at her side made her turn and widen the welcoming smile she wore for customers.

A blood-red hand with nails like metallic talons stroked her cheek. It was like a lover's caress, that red hand of death. The hand drew away and the visitor departed.

Peng-t'ai returned with a low sigh to the statues on her small stall. Her cheek had already started to itch.

She knew that she would be dead of the red plague in a matter of hours but she continued to stand in her customary place, ready to sell her sculptures. She could have fled screaming, or fallen on her knees and welcomed the plague as the justice of the gods. But that wasn't in Peng-t'ai's nature.

In a world where everyone has gone mad it is all the

44

more important to retain your own humanity, she told herself. Even when you're dying. Especially when you're dying.

The itching had become a burning.

There is something in this place that hates the deaf and the blind. Is it because you can't bring deafness to the deaf or blindness to the blind?

Peng-t'ai maintained her friendly dignity as she stood her ground behind her collection of skilfully carved statues on the makeshift stall. And she managed to retain her cheerful smile.

The brazier by the gate flared as if responding to the mounting heat in her body. The guard by the brazier glanced at the flames, then glared at her with open hostility. He glanced once more at the fire. His mouth bent into a vicious smile.

Within minutes, her stall and statues were burning.

Ming's mansion, emptied of slaves and servants, was a dark, quiet maze of rooms.

In the quiet darkness the Body lay in its perfect madness.

And from the hearing, the Mimic slowly grew.

And the Mimic's first thought was voiced in a whisper . . .

'Chhhiiiaaa . . .'

The chimes of the sacred chung bells resounded in the Temple of the Celestial Buddha as Dharmapala walked under the shadow of Cloud Tower in the northern courtyard. From time to time he glanced hesitantly at the closed door of the abbot's cell.

Dharmapala stopped pacing. He took a deep, decisive breath, then strode briskly to the abbot's door.

Abbot Nagarjuna made a sign of welcome as the young monk entered his room. The earnest, agitated brother

45

bowed before sitting cross-legged on one of the rush mats strewn about the lantern-hung, incense-smoking room with its blackened rafters and earthen floor. Dharmapala cleared his throat but didn't speak. The aged abbot regarded his pupil with keen eyes before his mouth widened into a friendly grin.

'Well?' prompted Nagarjuna.

'Well,' mumbled the young man.

'Yes?'

'I've just got back from San Lung.'

'I know.'

'And I'm troubled, Master. I've heard such things in San Lung Town . . .'

The old man's brow was crossed with a frown. Dharmapala was customarily the most carefree of the brethren; the change in his manner was disturbing. He patiently waited for the young brother to continue.

'Master, I might have discounted the stories I heard but I witnessed a portent on the return journey.'

'Perhaps you had better begin with some of the tales,' suggested Nagarjuna.

'Yes, well – the first story came from the mouth of a vagabond called Sung. He was sleeping outside the town walls when I visited San Lung Town two days ago. After I had given him a little food he told me what happened almost two weeks ago in Shen Lung Gorge. Apparently he had looked into the river and seen an unearthly figure standing behind him, reflected in the water, but when he turned round there was nobody there.'

The abbot was unable to smother a roguish grin. 'I've heard similar stories many times, Dharmapala. These Chinese almost outdo us Indians in the weaving of fanciful yarns – it's that patchwork T'aoist religion of theirs.'

The monk shook his head. 'I'm convinced the boy was telling the truth. I was told scores of other tales by many people that day. There have been disappearances. There was a man named Fang-ch'i who returned to the town

46

barely in time for the closing of the gates to discover his wife missing and a bronze mirror he had newly fashioned tilting in the doorway. The neighbours came rushing when they heard him cry out. It seemed he babbled something about seeing Nua – his wife – in the mirror. The next day he took his own life.'

The news had expunged the smile from the abbot's face.

'And there have been odd tales about Ming the robber-merchant – tales of that huge bronze mirror of his. It seems that Ming ejected all of his slaves and servants a few days ago. Since then he has locked himself inside his mansion and no one has seen him. One ex-servant believed that the ancient bronze mirror had swallowed him. And there have been plagues of deadly swiftness that seem to have struck only the deaf and the blind. And everywhere I heard reports of visions, dreams . . .'

Dharmapala ceased speaking and lowered his head.

Nagarjuna ostensibly studied the blue branches of veins on the backs of his root-knuckled hands. 'We all live within the Veil of Maya,' he declared. 'Illusion is the substance of the unenlightened life. We live in a world of dreams and nightmares. But sometimes a dream can seem very real.' He paused and looked up. 'However, you mentioned a portent you witnessed on your return journey . . .'

The young monk lifted his shaven head and sighed. 'I did see something, or rather there was something that I did not see . . .'

'Spoken like a true Buddhist!' interjected the abbot with an attempt at a smile.

'A wayfarer told me that he had come from the Pavilion of the Red Phoenix – you know it? – just south of the town. He had found the building deserted and a sign of warning posted over the portal, a sign which, predictably, fired his curiosity. He explored the pavilion, uncovering nothing until he threw an idle glance into the water mirror near the door. Then he ran like a madman to the town. It took me more than an hour to calm him. Then I set out for the pavilion myself. I looked into the water mirror.'

'A water mirror!' snorted the abbot. 'You sound like Vinaya in his Spirit Hill shrine, testing the strength of your spirit like that. A little presumptuous?'

'I believed it to be necessary.'

'What did you see?'

'Nothing.'

Nagarjuna raised his eyebrows quizzically.

'Nothing,' the monk repeated. 'There was no reflection. A night robbed of stars. I lit a candle and held it over the water but the flame cast no shimmer on the surface. The mirror reflected nothing.'

'You were fortunate to take no harm.'

'The All-Compassionate One protected me.'

A long silence ensued. The great chung chimes in the Cloud Tower were calm. The saffron-robed men were still as statues.

'We'll speak of this again in the morning.' The old man's voice had a tired, hollow ring.

Dharmapala moved to the door, half-opened it, looked over his shoulder. 'Master, what is happening?'

Nagarjuna shook his head and signed the monk to leave. The door closed quietly.

The abbot stared at the closed door. 'Dreams,' he muttered under his breath. 'Dreams that kill.'

Early in the morning the abbot called Dharmapala to his cell. The old man rose and they exchanged bows. A lifted hand and a cough preluded his request.

'Last summer you undertook a mission to Sung An in the T'aihang mountains. Are you prepared to embark on the same journey?'

The monk nodded, darting an uncertain glance at his mentor. 'I'm always ready to follow your instructions.'

'Good. Then you'll bear a message to someone who

48

lives near the summit of Luminous Cloud Mountain thirty li north of Sung An.'

Dharmapala's jaw went slack with surprise. 'Luminous Cloud Mountain! Then the message must be for Liu Chun! I had thought . . .'

'What had you thought?'

'Chia – the Black Dragon Sorceress – it's common knowledge that she helped to found the monastery. She has powers . . .' the young man stammered, wishing he had swallowed his earlier exclamations. 'I assumed that if you sought aid it would be from Chia, but perhaps legend has magnified her skill as it has exaggerated her lifespan.'

Nagarjuna's worn lips curved in a weary smile. 'Legend, of course, tells its lies, but not concerning her skill or lifespan. The lies about Chia touch on other matters. She's dangerous, my eager young friend, to herself and to others. Are you acquainted with one of her titles – the Death-bringer?'

'I have heard it.'

'It has some justification. Although I deem it an honour to be counted as one of her friends I would have to admit that death is also numbered among that company. Death is her unwelcome companion. She mustn't come to San Lung region. Liu Chun must stand in her place.'

The young monk nodded assent. 'As you say, Reverend Abbot. I will pray that the light of Amitabha brightens my path to the western ranges and Liu Chun of Luminous Cloud Mountain.'

Nagarjuna chuckled. 'You were always prone to pomposity when abashed, Little Dragon. Your desire to see the sorceress is understandable – you've doubtless been talking to that heretic Vinaya – I hear he has become obsessed with her recently. I too would like to see her beautiful face again, but it cannot be. Chia must never come to San Lung.'

'Never?' queried Dharmapala.

'*Never.*'

4

THUNDER UNDER
THE EARTH

'Fifteen days since he departed,' remarked the abbot as he leaned on the parapet of the temple's west wall.

'Fifteen days,' confirmed Vinaya.

Below the two men Celestial Buddha Hill dipped to its encircling river. A dense white mist surged up the gentle slopes and caressed the sandstone walls of the temple. Nagarjuna shivered and pulled the saffron woollen folds of the Buddha-garment tightly around his beaten dwarf of a body. The tall young monk at his side appeared impervious to the clammy fog; his lupine lineaments were tense and his bright eyes fixed on distance.

The feeble yellow sun sank into the mist and the mist made golden cloudscapes of the hilled and hollowed lands. Weakening sunlight made the billowing vapour an impenetrable curtain – rock and soil contours were dissolved and the subtle horizon was finally obscured. It was with a weary air that the abbot turned his back on the west.

'I wonder if Dharmapala is riding with Liu Chun on the homeward journey,' he pondered. 'Fifteen days. It *is* barely possible to complete a return journey in fifteen days.'

'A Mahayana monk riding a Fergana horse like an Imperial courier,' laughed Vinaya. 'That will arch a few pious eyebrows of those versed in Buddha doctrine.'

The old man shrugged. 'We should use our own legs, I

know, but the mission required the fleetness of a stallion's hooves. You cannot found the first Indian monastery in Ch'i Province without learning flexibility. After all, Wolf Mask, you should be the first to recognise the value of my compromises – you've taken the fullest advantage of them.'

Vinaya made a wry line of his mouth. 'Ah – you mean Spirit Hill.'

'Spirit Hill – and other ventures – but Spirit Hill most of all. That was foolhardy. But I'll confess to several reckless forays when I was young in India. However, you must tell Liu Chun of your experience on the Feast of the Dead – it's of a pattern with the strange happenings that followed.'

'I'll tell him . . . if he comes.'

Nagarjuna renewed his western gaze. 'He will come.'

Outside the monastery, fog was the world. The mist was shading to grey and the unseasonal cold deepening with the darkening of the evening. The abbot entertained the fanciful notion that the fog was boundless, a mask that made a secret of a hundred countries. The temple seemed a mellow lantern floating on a diaphanous ocean of fog. A private smile – how plausible were Nature's tricks! Here was he, thinking of an ocean of fog while the temple was rooted in the firm earth. It was humbling to realise he was still subject to the illusion of isolation; the monastery, the Buddha Sangha, was simply a segment of a strand in the web of the world. Distant tremors in the mist would rumble under the ground and the wall he leaned on would vibrate below hearing, below touch. A clash of sword on sword at the far rim of China and a mote of dust was unsettled in the temple. Thunder under the earth. All is One.

Nagarjuna broke into a low chuckle.

'What's so amusing, Reverend Abbot?'

'The idle ramblings of senility, my raw young pupil. Perhaps my mind was impelled on its wanderings by a misbegotten spring.'

51

Vinaya rubbed his assertive jut of a chin. 'The weather is indeed capricious. Hardly the inimitable Chinese spring – thunder under the earth.'

The teacher eyed his pupil with surprise. 'If I didn't know you for an addle-pated heretic I would suspect you of seeing into my head.'

'A simple trick, Master.'

Suddenly the young man stiffened and his stare twisted south.

'What is it, Wolf Mask? A hare coughing in the fog?'

'Someone's coming to Red Phoenix Gate. This Wolf Mask has ears to match.'

The monk's saffron drapes, hanging loosely from his gaunt frame, swirled in the breeze of his rush to the stairs. Nagarjuna, perturbed by the young man's agitation, shuffled flap-sandalled in pursuit.

As their feet padded across the clay ground that skirted the wing-roofed Buddha Hall an intimidating knock thudded from the Red Phoenix Gate. The abbot's old heart thumped at the sound; some people had a distinctive way of rapping for admittance, and this was one he recognised. Rounding the ornate dome of the stupa in the southern courtyard the two men approached the arched gate where an elderly brother struggled to lift a heavy crossbar. Vinaya strode briskly to assist while Nagarjuna hung back a short distance from the stone arch.

The crossbar was raised and the gate opened to a square of mist with a central figure of condensed vapour – a tall shadow whipped from fog into tenuous substance. The shadow slunk into the torchlight and its outlines hardened. The full-length woollen cloak was black and the eyes green. She strolled with a nonchalant grace into the courtyard.

'Chia,' the abbot greeted, forcing his mouth into a smile.

'Nagarjuna,' she responded drily.

The old Indian had forgotten the full force of her personality, the awe-invoking cast of her slanted green eyes, the stern refinement of her features. But the abbot's chief sensation was shock, the shock of seeing the living past. Thirty years had passed since he last encountered the Sorceress of Black Dragon Mountain; she looked now as she had looked at that last meeting: a tall girl of less than twenty summers. An obsidian pillar could not be more impervious to time. Nagarjuna could almost believe that Chia was her own daughter, self-procreated with trans-migratory soul. Judging by his expression even Vinaya was impressed. Aware that he was gaping in a manner unbefitting a venerable old man, he hunted for speech.

'Ah – are Liu Chun and Dharmapala following after? Did the sage perhaps suggest that you come in his stead?'

She shook her head and smiled her unique, unsettling smile. 'I don't know who Dharmapala is and I haven't seen Liu Chun for two years. I came on my own initiative. As for Liu Chun, I can only express a fervent wish that he stays well clear of this place.'

Vinaya's spindly back shook in mirth.

Chia folded her arms and studied the abbot's expres-sion. 'Could it be, Reverend Buddha Master, that there's no longer a welcome for the Green-Eyed Sorceress in the Buddha Temple?' Nagarjuna registered the undertone of menace.

'You'll always be a friend to this monastery,' he replied. 'It's just that your arrival has taken me by suprise. Allow me to make amends – I'm sure you're ready for a meal and a sound sleep after your journey.'

'I'm ready for a meal, yes. Sleep must wait.'

Following the abbot and the young monk across the courtyard she halted at the sandstone dome of the stupa with its exuberant Indian reliefs. 'The oldest edifice in the temple,' she remarked. 'Your nostalgic link with the Land of the Ganges.' The others refrained from comment. She resumed her walk only to stop again at the symbolic gate to the stupa, placed thirty steps from the northern door of the dome; it was a torana, marking the beginning of the sacred path to the stupa. Chia's gaze rested on the volutes at each end of the three architraves surmounting the two chiselled columns. 'The volute,' she noted. 'The spiral – these spirals draw the eye outwards from their whirling centres.'

Vinaya laughed. 'While you're musing on higher realms I'll take the opportunity to ready a meal to sustain your earthly frame.'

Chia looked askance at the departing monk as she joined the waiting abbot. 'A master of sarcasm, your young pupil,' she commented.

Nagarjuna was quick to the young man's defence. 'There are worse faults. And you won't find any Buddha-follower, myself included, who's as well versed in Chinese lore. Sometimes I think he's more T'aoist than the T'ao Seekers. It may interest you to learn that he has a considerable knowledge of the legends surrounding you, Black Dragon Sorceress.'

'It doesn't interest me. And stop calling me Black Dragon Sorceress – it makes me feel like some damned inscription.'

They were nearing the door of the abbot's room before Nagarjuna posed the question prompted by Chia's observations on the torana. 'The spiral is your emblem, is it not, Black Dra- er, Chia?'

'It is. All along the walls of my caverns are carved the Outward Spirals. They're taken from an ancient symbol of truth – truth inevitably leads men outwards from the blind inner core of the self.'

He frowned. 'And if the spiral should be drawn inwards, leading the eye to the centre?'

'Then, Man of the Mantras, it is time to start praying.'

The abbot continued to frown as he opened the door for his guest.

Chia handed the chopsticks and the emptied bowls to

Vinaya and assumed a more comfortable position on one of the many rush mats strewn about the abbot's cell.

'An acceptable meal, Vinaya,' she complimented. 'At least it was recognisably Chinese – my mouth isn't on fire with exotic spices.'

'It would be a pity to burn your low melody of a voice to cinders,' the young man declared with a bow. 'And there's a great deal of instruction I wish to glean from that dark voice.'

'Are you usually so formal?' she yawned. 'What do you want to know?'

Nagarjuna fidgeted in his cross-legged posture. 'Vinaya – it's hardly your right to –'

'It's all right,' assured Chia. 'Curiosity becomes the young. Ask as you wish, but don't always expect an answer.'

The monk's olive eyes shone fervently. 'Tell me of that silver amulet you wear. It's said that it comes from a kingdom many thousands of li to the west, far beyond the Moving Sands.'

'Egypt,' she replied quickly. 'It comes from Egypt. It's called an ankh.'

As she spoke her slender finger touched the silver metal. Nagarjuna recalled the gesture as a sign of anxiety. Whenever Chia was troubled she fingered the ankh as if it fed solace to her spirit. His brief study of the ankh made the abbot pay closer attention to her attire: she had doffed the hooded black cloak and sat in a long black gown girdled with a red sash in which was secured a silver dagger. So dusty and worn with travel were her clothes that it looked as though she had dressed in the same garb for years. He wondered if Chia stayed faithful to the same style of apparel for the same reason that she clung to her ankh.

Nagarjuna's gaze moved up to her hair. It looked as if it hadn't been combed in months.

'And how long have you possessed the silver ankh?' Vinaya was asking.

'Since before the Buddha sat under the Tree of Enlightenment.'

'What's its purpose?'

Chia's green eyes clouded. 'Mind your own business.'

Nagarjuna took the opportunity to weigh in with his own question. 'Chia, what made you come here?'

She seemed all of darkness when she spoke. 'Night visitors,' was her enigmatic answer. 'Dreams. Shadows.'

'Dreams and shadows brought you?'

'They called me. That's all I'll say.'

'At least tell me what you know of what's happening here,' the abbot pleaded.

She shrugged. 'Why should what's happening here be any worse than what's happening anywhere else?'

'There's a dark power growing in San Lung,' stated Vinaya. 'A dark power from the hidden world.'

Chia's laugh was hollow. 'Dark power, Vinaya? The dark power of this world sits on silk cushions and orders armies to massacre the innocent in their thousands. The dark power wears the yellow robes of a Chinese lord and has children dropped into boiling cauldrons in order to enjoy the music of their screams, and he forces slave girls to open their legs to beasts and their mouths to his vomit. The thought of millions starving only adds relish to the sumptuous feasts he indulges in. The blind and the crippled are a source of amusement to him. That's the dark power, Vinaya. It's everywhere. And there's nothing hidden about it.'

Vinaya was undaunted. 'We're all acquainted with human suffering, sorceress. You're not the proud discoverer of its existence. The Buddha had much to say on the subject, as you may or may not be aware.'

'That's enough, Vinaya!' admonished the abbot.

The sorceress waved the incident aside. 'He's right, Nagarjuna. I spoke out of turn. I know that what's happening in San Lung is not to be taken lightly. Dreams and shadows and whispers can destroy as surely as the

56

largest army. The world is evil enough without adding the evil of . . .' Her low voice sank into silence.

'Of ghosts?' suggested Vinaya.

Chia's brooding eyes became fixed on the night that pressed in from the small window. 'Yes,' she said at length. 'Call them ghosts, if you wish.'

'And what ghosts should we be afraid of, Chia?' the abbot softly inquired.

For a long time she sat hugging her knees in silence. When it came, her reply was barely above a gentle breath: 'Ourselves.'

Nagarjuna and Vinaya traded glances. Was the sorceress being deliberately obscure, adding mystery to mystery? Or, the abbot speculated, was it the malady? Were her wits crumbling into madness?

'You're about to die again, aren't you?' the old man hazarded.

Chia's response was a slow and rueful smile. 'Yes. I'm about to die. I should have died weeks ago.' Her gaze became withdrawn. 'Wei begged me not to leave the safety of my home. I haven't slept since I left Black Dragon Caverns. I daren't sleep.'

'Just one moment,' Vinaya butted in. 'I may be showing my ignorance, but I received the distinct impression that this lady asserted that she made a habit of dying now and again. My hearing must be going.'

'Sarcastic bastard,' muttered Chia.

The abbot raised a conciliatory palm. 'With your permission, sorceress, I'll inform my inquisitive pupil of the rudiments of your malady.'

His request was met with a shrug of indifference. 'It's your monastery, monk. Do what you like.'

'From time to time a malady strikes our noble guest,' Nagarjuna began. 'It is a malady of the mind. Her memory crumbles . . .'

'My memory isn't too wonderful at the best of times,' commented Chia.

'. . . and her wits become confused. At such times she becomes – unpredictable. And – ah – some might say, dangerous. To put it plainly, our good friend here falls into madness. The madness ends with her death. But when she dies her body doesn't decay. After a month or so life re-enters her body and she rises renewed in flesh and spirit.'

Vinaya stroked his sharp chin. 'Hmm . . . interesting.' He settled his gaze on the tall woman in her gown of black silk. 'Do me one favour, sorceress. An intriguing woman such as yourself must have many exploits to her credit. Would you recount one for me? Just one? Please?'

Firmly and slowly, she shook her head. 'I'm bored with men telling me how intriguing I am and asking about my past. Ask Nagarjuna if you want to hear one of those Black Dragon Sorceress adventures – he knows about some of the disasters I've been involved in.'

As the abbot reluctantly introduced Vinaya to one of Chia's more foolhardy forays into the Forest of the Ancestors, Chia closed her eyes and let her thoughts drift away from the aged voice in the monastic cell. Scraps of memory floated through her mind.

My shadow on the mountain and my shadow in the sky. And below, at the edge of the forest, the dance of the shadow. Outward Spiral. The east draws blood from the point of a dagger. Spirit Hill. The death whispers of the Silver Brethren. The tall shape of Nyak the necromancer. Spirit Hill Mound. Mirror.

When she left a tearful Wei at the narrow entrance to Black Dragon Valley, Chia had sensed the Chinese spring vibrating through the soles of her feet. It was the stirring of the dragon paths under the ground, a pulsing of the earth's veins that made the rocks tremble.

Thunder under the earth. And the ground thunder was the pain of awakening and new life. It was the sound and motion of the real. It dispersed the dream that diminishes and the whisper that lies. The thunder under the earth sustained and quickened her spirit as she traversed the bleak T'aihang peaks. It enlivened her as she crossed the

Great Plain and climbed up into the mountains of the eastern range. And it kept her from sinking into the death sleep as she skirted around the southern borders of the silent Forest of the Ancestors. But as she reached the southern boundary of the San Lung region, the power of the Dragon Spring deserted her. The echoes of the thunder under the earth were hardly discernible in San Lung. The sound of the real was absent from its land- and water-forms. And in the space of a few li the weather became erratic and ambivalent, a troubled marriage of fog and winds.

'Spring Feast of the Dead,' mumbled Chia. 'Thunder under the earth.'

Nagarjuna, catching the garbled words, recalled the cloaking fog outside the monastery, the fog that hid the links between the temple and the world, the cloud that hid patterns. The abbot hastily concluded his brief story of Chia in the Forest of the Ancestors and turned his attention to the sorceress.

'Chia?'

She opened her eyes. 'What?'

'We were discussing the moody weather moments before you arrived,' Nagarjuna said. 'What's the cause, do you think?'

'The land seems deserted. Where are its inhabitants?' Chia asked the abbot, bluntly ignoring his question, but thinking. *Mist and wind – the Spirit Breath, but not the breath of the Spirit Dragon, soul of the budding earth . . .*

Nagarjuna gave a resigned sigh. 'Most have fled the region in the past two weeks . . .'

. . . not the breath of the Spirit Dragon but the breath of the Spirit Shadow . . .

'Only a few hundred are left in San Lung Town and a handful in a scatter of villages south of the town. And in the north there's no one – all fled. Those that remain wait for the word to flock to the monastery in the faith that the Celestial Buddha will protect them here.'

59

'Why hasn't the word been given?'

'The people were awaiting the word from me, and I was awaiting the word from Liu Chun. I was delaying the decision until the arrival of the sage.'

'Forget about Liu Chun. I give the word,' Chia stated in a manner brooking no contradiction. 'Let them come.'

The abbot displayed a submissive pair of palms. 'They will come.'

Vinaya, who had watched the exchange with amusement, chose this juncture to catch Chia's attention. 'I was on Spirit Hill on the Feast of the Dead.'

She fixed him with a green stab of a glance. Her stern features paled. After a stretched moment she regained command of herself, stroking the silver amulet with a meditatory motion. 'So – you were on Spirit Hill. What of that?'

He proceeded to relate his experience in the rustic shrine on the northern slope of Spirit Hill, and neither he nor Nagarjuna failed to mark the woman's deepening absorption in the tale. At its conclusion she heaved a deep breath.

'Well,' Vinaya exclaimed at the growing silence. 'What do you make of my story?'

'It was the Hour of the Rat,' she reflected. 'You were peering into a water mirror. You were seized by a paroxysm. Then you fled in fear.'

'However,' he grinned, 'the fear abated with the running of my feet.'

'Have you ever tried to enter Spirit Hill Mound?' she asked sharply.

'Never.'

With startling suddenness she reached out and thrust her palm onto the young man's chest. The abbot was baffled but the monk seemed unconcerned. In a few moments a faint smile touched her wide lips and she withdrew her hand.

'I believe you, Vinaya. Now go and assemble the

brethren in the Buddha Hall. The abbot's going to give them a message. My message.'

Neglecting to seek the abbot's confirmation of the order the monk bowed and left. Nagarjuna was the first to break the silence that ensued.

'Sorceress, you must go. Whatever has to be done will be done without you. San Lung is a threat to you and you're a threat to San Lung. I don't know why I'm so certain, but certain I am. Call it a hint from the Buddha if you like, but somehow I know that your presence will bring us harm.'

She stared into an abstract distance. 'I'm going nowhere, old man. Not until the task is done.'

He raised his arms in defeat. He was familiar with Chia's temperament; there was no gainsaying her. 'Very well, but at least tell me what task you expect me to perform.'

'You will instruct the brethren to avoid all mirrors. You will ensure that their eyes are averted from all reflections of themselves.'

The abbot shrugged. 'This is what I've been doing for many days. Did you think I wasn't aware of the danger of mirrors in the light of what is happening here? Did you think I was unversed in the tales about Spirit Hill and its death mound? The message you wish me to pass on is a message I have already imparted.'

Chia gave an airy wave of the hand. 'Excellent. Then pass on more of the same message.'

Nagarjuna, suppressing a twinge of exasperation, leaned forwards. 'For the last time, sorceress, I want to know why you've come here.'

She ran slim fingers through her unruly mane of dusty hair. 'I don't suppose you heard of my last visit, but I was in this area two years ago on my way back from T'ai Shan,' she said, seeming to ignore his question. 'I came across a girl called Fu the Unlucky. You wouldn't know how she is, would you?'

He shook his head. 'I'm afraid not. There were reports

61

that she was seen heading for Spirit Hill on the Eve of the Feast of the Dead. She hasn't been seen since. Nor have her family. They vanished a few days after the Feast of the Dead.'

Chia nodded slowly, her expression indecipherable. 'After you've spoken to the monks,' she said quietly, 'I'll have a few words of my own with them.'

'So be it. And what is this knowledge you intend to impart to the brethren?'

Her smile when it came was not pleasant. 'The knowledge of fear, Buddha Master. But before I frighten your holy monks I need an outline of the events in San Lung since the Feast of the Dead.'

Reluctantly, he complied.

Ming, at first, had wandered from room to room of the darkened interior of his mansion, fearful of the Body and the Hearing hidden behind the locked door of one of the loft chambers. But as the days slid by in the empty house he wandered less and less and spent more of his time squatting outside the door beyond which lay the Body and the Hearing. Now he just sat outside the locked door from night to day to night again. And from night to day to night again he heard the whispering of the voice in his skull. It was the voice of the Hearing, and day and night it called upon the name of Chia.

Ming was starving, but the food was downstairs, and that was too far. Physical effort of any kind was too wearisome. He hardly had the energy to lift the hand that held the long knife.

There were so many voices in his head. So many whispers. All from the same mouth. All from the mouth of the Hearing. The whispers in his head were making him ill but all would be well when his master trod quietly up the stairs, his hands of healing reaching out to drive the illness away.

The flabby folds of his shrinking belly shook as he

started to sob. I'm not in China anymore, he thought. My flesh is the border of the world and I and all the phantoms move within it. The dark hall and stairs are part of my flesh.

'Chhiiaa . . .' whispered the Hearing in his head. 'Hungry for you . . .'

'No,' spluttered Ming. My belly is the world, he thought. And the world is hungry. Hungry for pork. Juicy pork.

Perhaps his master would come soon, bringing him luscious chunks of pork. Yes, Nyak would come soon. Nyak the Master wouldn't forget his dedicated servant.

Is Nyak a part of my flesh, too?

There was a crash and a crack behind Ming's back as the lock on the door burst asunder. The door swung open without a sound.

The whisper roared in Ming's head. 'Chhiia . . . I come for you. You should welcome me, Chia. Because I know who you are.'

Ming grinned at the Hearing as it emerged from the door and walked down the hall. Then he lost interest in the departing shape and stared at the knife in his oily hand.

'Pork,' whimpered Ming.

5

BUDDHA HALL

The brethren were gathered in the raftered and incense-wisped Golden Hall of the Buddha, mute and attentive, a saffron congregation squatting in rows. Inside each shaven head there buzzed the same question: why was a woman allowed to enter the Buddha Hall? It was unseemly.

And such a strange woman.

1w4,6,10   Green eyes. They had never seen a Chinese woman with green eyes. And so tall. And with such a shamelessly revealing side-slit in her black gown. And her hair so wild. And her face contoured in candlelight had such a look . . .

They were uncomfortable. They had sought refuge from temptation and temptation had invaded their refuge. It was wrong to admit a woman into the Golden Hall. And it was hard to drag their eyes from the firm expanse of thigh that curved so seductively from the open slit in the black silk.

Chia stood with wide-sleeved arms folded under the tableau-enlivened far wall, beside the bronze Buddha seated in the lotus asana, its bronze hand uplifted in the mudra of blessing. She knew what the monks were thinking and cared nothing for any of it, paying scant attention to the abbot's words as he addressed the assembly of the Sangha, the monastic community of Buddha brethren.

'Greetings, fellow-followers of the Noble Eightfold

Path,' Nagarjuna commenced. 'You will have heard of the ancient tomb on Spirit Hill thirty li north as the raven flies. Many tales are told of the mound on Spirit Hill and most of the stories are of mirrors and ghosts. You have probably heard the tale of the mirrors as recited to every child under a Chinese roof. Children are told that in the time of the Yellow Emperor there was a world beyond the sacred bronze mirrors, which a mortal could enter so long as one of the Mirror People took his place. The tale goes that in those innocent days the Mirror Realm hadn't yet been reduced to a mere imitation of the human world and the domain beyond the mirrors rejoiced in its own colours and landscapes and beings. It was a time of magic and harmony between the two worlds, and life was enriched. But one day the Mirror People invaded our world. After a lengthy battle they were exorcised and forced back into the mirrors. And they were punished. They were reduced to the lowly status of reflections of ourselves. It was ordained that they smile as we smile, frown as we frown, dance as we dance, wearing our colours and shapes. They were condemned to be our mimics and their world a mimicry of our own. Thus the Mirror Realm became the — ah — Mime Realm. This cradle story ends with the warning that the Mirror Folk are biding their time until the chance comes to escape from their prison.

'This is just a colourful yarn, I know. But often such stories can throw light on spiritual truths. The Enlightened One himself frequently used such stories to illustrate a moral principle. The Mahavastu tales, for example —'

'I haven't got all night, abbot,' called out Chia as she leaned against the wall and crossed her legs. There was a low murmur of laughter from the monks.

Unruffled, Nagarjuna bowed in her direction before resuming his speech. 'The Mahavastu tales, for example, are treasure chests of symbolic truth. The symbolic truth in the mirror tale, as I see it, is that there is a false self in the image that men behold in mirrors. The longer a man worships his own image in a mirror the stronger that false self grows until the false self and the man become one. Symbolically, the mirror self becomes the man and the man becomes the mirror self. There is a moral here for all of us . . .'

The abbot's keen ears just succeeded in catching Chia's exasperated groan, but he disregarded it. 'The moral is that we must not dwell on the false image or we may become prey to dreams and illusions. Those who would follow the path of rightness must discard all images of the self . . .'

Chia smiled a faint, wry smile. Nagarjuna was doing his best with what little knowledge he had of Spirit Hill Mound but he was trying to knit a full-length cloak from a small ball of wool. The old man hardly had a clue of what was happening in San Lung. And how long was he prepared to trot out his moralistic speech?

Ah, Fu the Unlucky, my love of a night, are you suffering at this very moment as I idly stand and listen to an abbot's speech? Are you still in Spirit Hill Mound? What has happened to you, my gentle Fu? I've travelled three thousand li to find you and now I waste my time in this damned Buddha Hall. Beloved Fu. Are you still alive? Are you a corpse in Spirit Hill Mound? No I can't bear to think of you dead. I refuse to think of you dead. Ah, Fu, are you in some small hell awaiting salvation by the hand of the mad goddess? I'm no goddess. But I'm as near to full madness as I can be without falling into the dying time.

Am I too late? It's been a month since the Feast of the Dead. So long a time. Be alive, beloved. Be alive . . .

The voices rushed into Chia's head without warning.

Mirror . . . Nyak . . . Glak-i-kakthz . . . Thzan-tzai . . . shadow . . . Spirit Hill . . . Outward Spiral . . . Inward Spiral . . . grey shrouds, black shrouds, white shrouds savaged with knives . . . Celestial Ones . . . Death-bringer . . .

Mirror . . . the dying time . . . Nyak . . . Silver Brethren . . .
Death Whisperers . . . Mirror.

'Spirit Mirror!' gasped Chia.

My death breathes down my throat. The Death-bringer madness is hurling me into the dying time. The dying time – what the few who know of it call the Sleep of Rebirth in the need to make of my death a gentle, mystical thing of legend. But the dying time is flight from the madness and the madness is flight from the shadow within. And everywhere I look there are nightmares that walk in the day and I run and I run and there's nowhere to run and there are mad voices in my mad mind and Nyak laughs at my weakness and I can't remember can't find my . . .

Aten.

find my refuge . . .

Aten.

My refuge.

'Aten,' she whispered softly. 'Sun Disc.'

The Aten. The Sun Disc of Akhenaten and Nefertiti. The Aten – her symbol of refuge. The solar symbol of the Unknown One worshipped centuries past in the Land of the Nile. The blazing Sun Disc drew her shattered mind together until the Death-bringer voices gradually receded. She released a long sigh of relief.

It was only then that she realised her eyes were closed. She opened them to the sight of Nagarjuna addressing the brethren in the Buddha Hall. Chia hoped that her inner turmoil hadn't been expressed in her appearance apart from a closing of the eyes and a low murmuring of the lips. A swift glance around the hall showed that no one seemed to have noticed her interlude of madness. She steadied herself with another deep breath as she withdrew her restored wits from the healing symbol of the Aten.

Somehow, Fu, I'll save you from Spirit Hill Mound. I'll save you from the breath of the Spirit Mirror for I have the power of the spiral. And if Nyak comes near me I will kill him.

'Yes, Nyak,' she whispered under her breath. 'You're

close – I sense it – but not close enough to kill. Come closer, Nyak. Come to me. The battle has gone on long enough. It's time to end it in your blood or mine.'

The abbot's words to the assembly finally filtered into Chia's awareness.

'Fifteen days past,' the abbot was saying, 'I bade you shield your eyes when drinking from bowls of water. Do so still. It wasn't difficult to adhere to this rule within the confines of the Sangha but now some of you must venture outside as Ananda and Vinaya have been doing these last weeks. Amaravita has the names of the eight who must go. Two will leave for San Lung Town and inform the townsfolk that the temple is open to all who desire its sanctuary. The remaining six will travel through the region and invite the remnants of the villagers to the refuge of Celestial Buddha Temple. Bid those with metal mirrors to bury them. Tell those with water mirrors to pour the water into the earth. Urge those who live by streams and rivers to leave for places where water doesn't flow. Persuade them to close their eyes when they drink water from the well. Warn them to avoid glancing into pools. Teach them to shun all reflected images. That's all I have to say, but stay where you are – our guest wishes to speak to you. May the Lord Buddha be with you.'

A frail arm lifted a seamed brown hand in a mudra of blessing before Nagarjuna sat down on the floor with benedictory hand still raised.

Chia strode past the seated abbot and stood in front of the assembly, unfolding her wide-sleeved arms and resting her hands on narrow hips. She paused momentarily, her long, slanted eyes scanning the light and shadows of the hall where the monks were as immobile as the Mahayana figures lining the smoke-smeared oak walls. She glanced at the square of the hall door beyond which wisps of mist scudded over the ground, impelled by a breeze from the north. Mist and wind. Spirit Breath. A thick cloud that dampened the thunder under the earth.

She had two tasks to perform in her words to the Sangha. To scare them, and then to squeeze information from them. When she spoke, it was with a strong undertone of menace.

'This whole region and everyone in it are being lifted clean out of history. The hidden power in San Lung is a draining power, and it will make a nothing of you all. You can't see it or hear it. It is stealthy. Like a shadow, it doesn't truly exist. But it will draw you into oblivion. For each of you it will wear a different shape. It is a power of thought, this subtle power that crowns our lies and clowns our truths. Thoughts, noble brethren, thoughts become eagles that soar to the celestial palaces or plunge to the nethermost hells. Ideas assume form. And the shadow form that can't be seen or heard will consume your thoughts. It will whisper death into your ears and you will not hear it. And there is a Death Whisperer for each one of you. It is your dark self. Your dark self is searching for you. It is coming. It knows your name and it wears your face and it thinks the dark side of your thoughts. And your Death Whisperers are trickling down from the north, from Spirit Hill. If you wish to imagine them simply as your mirror selves, as the abbot suggests, then imagine them shifting from reflection to reflection as they seek you out. Wherever there are mirrors or pools they can move at will. They slide from mirror to mirror. They slip from rainpool to rainpool. And always, they search for you. And when they find you, they will suck out your soul with a look.'

She noted with satisfaction that the majority of the monks looked thoroughly unnerved. It was time to move on to her main purpose.

'But you have one hope,' she said. 'A haunting of this nature and magnitude cannot have arisen of its own accord. Nothing comes from nothing, as you must surely know. What is happening in San Lung must have been orchestrated by someone, and the only one I know who is capable of such a feat is a self-styled necromancer. His name is Nyak. His servants are the Silver Brethren who know him as the Master. It's my belief that Nyak is behind this haunting of Death Whisperers, mirrors, shadows and bad dreams. And if I can find him and destroy him then I'll be able to bring the haunting to an end. So – tell me – have you heard the name of Nyak mentioned in the last few weeks? Any mention at all?'

Blank faces. Rows of blank faces. All eager to help, but blank nevertheless.

'Very well, you haven't heard the name. But you may have seen or heard rumour of the Silver Brethren who serve him. They are very conspicuous – they all wear silver masks. What have you heard of the Silver Brethren?'

The faces were as blank as before. They knew nothing of Nyak and the Silver Brethren.

Chia was about to turn away in defeat when Vinaya signalled with his hand.

'What is it, Vinaya?'

I heard someone say that the Thzan-tzai were behind the evil in San Lung,' he announced. 'Thzan-tzai, whatever they are. That's what he said. I don't suppose that's any help but –'

'Any help?' laughed Chia. 'More help than I hoped for. Nyak's father was Glak-i-kakthz, the last of the Thzan-tzai. Nyak's power is the inherited power of the Thzan-tzai. It is the power of an elder race that was destroyed by the Celestial Ones ten thousand years ago. Nyak is half human and half Thzan-tzai. He is the final legacy of the Thzan-tzai on earth. If the Thzan-tzai are behind the evil in San Lung then it can only mean that Nyak is behind it. And that means I can track him down and send him to join his father in the lowest of the Ten Hells.'

'Were these Thzan-tzai disposed towards evil, then?' asked Vinaya.

'Disposed towards evil?' echoed Chia in a loud tone. 'They were living nightmares, whirlwinds of spirit power. The name Thzan-tzai means Unshaped Masters, and Glak-i-kakthz was the last and worst of . . .'

She dammed the wild flow of her speech. She was here to glean information from the brethren, not impart it to them.

'Who told you the Thzan-tzai were behind the San Lung hauntings?' she inquired of Vinaya.

'Ming. He's a merchant of sorts. He lives in a mansion in San Lung Town.'

Chia nodded. 'I know him.'

She turned to Nagarjuna. 'That's all.'

The abbot signed the monks to depart. They shuffled to the door in respectful silence, leaving the hall to Nagarjuna and Chia.

He was the Hearing and through hearing he saw.

He was the Clown with hands that wore blood.

He was the Whisperer of Deceits, the Shouter of Dreams.

The Mimic.

He sang a ballad and San Lung danced.

He played a dirge and the people died.

He, the Mimic, was master.

His ripe lips bowed into a grin. She had come. She was near. The sorceress. The Green-Eyes. The enemy.

Welcome, Chia, laughed the Mimic.

Welcome in the Blood Spiral.

Greet your shadow.

6

BLOOD IN WATER

Vinaya, the last to leave the Buddha Hall, cast a backward glance at the abbot, his bony countenance evincing an inquiry of some kind.

'Ah yes, Vinaya,' called out the abbot. 'I remember. Wait in my cell. I'll join you presently.' He shook his head affectionately. 'Gautama Vinaya, he's incorrigible.'

'*Gautama* Vinaya?' Chia echoed. 'Called after Gautama Sakyamuni – the Buddha himself? I'm out of touch with recent practice, but isn't that what the Confucians would call "irregular"?'

'It's unusual but not unprecedented. Why do you ask?'

Chia pursed her lips, then relaxed into a fluttering laugh. 'It's just ironic that he's named after Gautama Buddha. That fellow is tall and lean and intense whereas Gautama was short and plump and fairly uncomplicated. Almost opposites.'

The abbot's mouth was wide with awe. 'Chia – you didn't actually – you didn't *meet* the Lord Buddha, did you?'

'Why yes – haven't I told you before? I only met him a few times. We argued about religion and such matters. He tended to be evasive.'

A conflicting meld of wonder and disapproval fretted Nagarjuna's age-grained lineaments. 'All those centuries ago . . .' he marvelled. 'Were you not – *overawed* by his presence. Did his divine words not enlighten your mind?'

'Not especially.'

The abbot was excited and insistent. 'But what was he like? What – what did you think of him?'

She shrugged. 'He was very acute in the diagnosis and remedy of human suffering, but he refused to discuss deep philosophy – I found that irritating. He wouldn't have approved of Mahayana, you know, with its fleshing out of his doctrines. Theravada was more his way – the bare bones of religion. Sometimes I suspect that in his zeal to reform the religion of the Brahmins he cured the boil by severing the arm. Still, most Hindu gods have arms to spare . . . However, I've strayed from the issue at hand – I must leave for Spirit Hill before the malady tracks me down.'

'I wonder how the Buddha would have diagnosed your malady and what remedy he would have prescribed,' the abbot said with a trace of a grin.

'He knew nothing of it. Some say it springs from the inordinate length of my life. Reality falls from me and my identity dissolves like a snow figure in the flame – such is the nature of the attacks. But even in my periods of relative sanity my memory of the past is episodic and jumbled. Too many centuries, Nagarjuna. Too many centuries. My past is an indistinct giant.'

'If you wrote down the chief happenings of your life the malady wouldn't be so devastating,' he remarked. 'The giant would be supplied with the rudiments of a face.'

'I have done so, many times.' Her tone was remote. 'But the result was invariably the same. An instance – some twenty years past I inscribed the experiences of the previous four or five years on a set of stone tablets. I hid them near a waterfall in Silver Water Valley, which is my second home. I had hoped they would be safe there, but it wasn't to be. I can't remember whether the day was hot or cold, dry or rainy in Silver Water Valley. The river was brown and silver like the slick back of a trout – that I recall. The malady swamped me without warning, bringing oblivion. I woke to moonlight bouncing its silver coins in the branches overhead. I lay in the grass for a long time, stiff as wood. The valley brimmed with cold as the night aged and I saw from the shape of the moon that weeks had glided by while I was sprawled beneath the tree. When dawn crept over the ground it illustrated the relics of my madness – a heap of chipped and flaked stone. The stone was slate. It was on slate stone that my memories had been carved. My fears were soon confirmed – I searched in the hiding place by the waterfall but the tablets were gone. Remorse was keen as I returned to the shattered slate beneath the silver birch . . .'

Nagarjuna looked askance at the withdrawn gaze of the sorceress, puzzled by the idiosyncratic inflection and resonant timbre of her speech. Also he was troubled by a lucid image of the events she was describing: he was *seeing* Silver Water Valley – the cliffs, the waterfall, the pines, the silver birches, the pile of pulverised slate. He had heard of her power of depictive speech, but never experienced it. It was unnerving, even for a Buddhist abbot. How far he must be from Nirvana . . .

Chia's breath-pause was followed by a cataract of self-recrimination. 'It was I, Nagarjuna, I who destroyed the inscriptions. I with my shifting under-currents of the spirit, I with my sudden inchoate storms of madness. How much I must have secretly resented – hated – those tablets and the knowledge they contained. What demented strength I must have possessed to dash them into a jumbled mass of fragments, as jumbled as the memory of my past. For weeks I struggled to recall the inscribed messages, but my mind had rejected them.'

'The work of an intruder, perhaps?' His tone was as feeble as the explanation.

'No. The power of Silver Water protects the valley like the stone dragon and tiger sentinels that guard palace gates. It was I who was to blame.'

He thought deeply for a space. 'Chia,' he began gently.

74

'I followed your speech closely, but – are you *sure* that the Celestial Ones and the Thzan-tzai truly existed? After all, you've beheld neither. The Thzan-tzai legend in particular is an elephant which this thin throat baulks at swallowing.'

'Don't concern yourself, abbot. I'm aware that my cosmology is unorthodox. Stick to your beliefs, my friend. I've no desire to shake them. Perhaps the Buddha was right – all that matters is the operation of Karma resulting in continual rebirth or the eternal liberation of Nirvana . . .'

'And the Pure Land of Buddha Amitabha's Western Paradise,' the old man added.

A hollow laugh fell from Chia's lips. 'A recent acquisition to mould flesh on the bare bones of the Buddha. The Western Paradise is a Buddhist version of a Chinese myth as old as the Shang tombs. The Middle Kingdom is transmuting your religion, Nagarjuna.'

'As base metals are reputedly transmuted into gold by T'aoist alchemists, you mean?' There was a residue of pique in his voice.

'Or gold into base metals,' she rejoined with a whimsical smile.

Her smile evoked a grin from her host. 'Just like the heated discussions of long ago, Chia. I'll never convert you to the Noble Eightfold Path.'

'Don't let it worry you. The Buddha couldn't convert me, either. What a battle of words we had in the fields near Benares! When Gautama realised he was getting the worst of the argument he announced to his disciples that I was Mara the Tempter, but I didn't oblige him by vanishing when he wove Hindu sigils with those plump hands of his. That's one incident you won't find in the Tripitaka Canon or the Mahavastu tales, or any other sacred book. But I'm carping – the Buddha was an inspired reformer, and he was genuinely compassionate. There were few other teachers willing to befriend whores and outcasts, but he did so.'

The abbot assumed a meditative expression. 'Sorceress,

75

you say that your memory comprises shattered relics, so how can you be certain that your meeting with the Buddha transpired exactly as you assert? After all, following the malady you described you were left with indecipherable slate fragments. How do you judge false from true in your fragmentary vision of the past?'

The sudden tense set of her supple frame showed that he had struck at the core of her being. Yet why should the question be like the swing of an axe to her? Surely she must have considered the problem a hundred times . . .

He looked away from the green flare of madness in her slanted eyes and winced at the stab of her voice.

'We've chattered trivia long enough, old man. I peer into a warped mirror at my past, but that past far outstrips your miserable lifespan. How dare you challenge me, you insignificant stumbler on the Buddha Path? What do you know of truth and falsehood, with your interminable sutras, tedious mantras and naïve mandalas? Remember to whom you speak and keep in mind the stories of those that opposed me.'

'I do not fear death,' he stated quietly.

Her tight mouth curved in a lethal smile. 'Because you'll be reincarnated or pass into Nirvana? Do you seriously believe that? What if there's nothing but terror on the far side of the grave? Eternal terror?'

'I know that cannot be true.'

'You can't know!' She was almost strident.

'I know.'

Her hand bunched into a fist and slammed into the abbot's chest, sending him spinning to the foot of the tall bronze statue of the Buddha. Her fist remained clenched and she stood rigid as iron while the old man gasped for breath and struggled to his feet. Leaning against the base of the bronze image he gazed at Chia more in pity than in accusation.

'I'm sorry if I offended you, Sorceress of the Black

Robe,' he managed to wheeze from bruised lungs. 'As you say, I'm an insignificant stumbler on the Buddha Path. Who am I to question you?'

His apology apparently failed to mollify the strange girl. She seemed enclosed in an alien realm. She wore the visage of a terrible goddess in the rich yellow candlelight and the green eyes glared supernatural madness. He thought of Kali, Hindu goddess of death, and shuddered. Eternal terror, she had said.

She started to whisper a deep incantation. 'I am Chia, Celestial Daughter . . . Hated by the Maw . . . Feared by the Thzan-tzai slaves . . . Adversary of the necromancer . . . Beloved of Nefertiti . . . Sorceress of Black Dragon and Silver Water . . . Wanderer of worlds . . .' The litany ceased. The madness faded. And Chia was Chia once more. She blinked and squinted at the trembling abbot. Her laugh broke free and normal.

'What are you, Nagarjuna? A mouse quivering before the cat?' Her brow clouded. 'What happened? We were talking of the Buddha Gautama, were we not? Why are you propped against a statue, gaping at me as if I were a demon?'

'I – I think you suffered a fit of some kind. You lost yourself. At the end you chanted a litany that released you from the trance. Do you recall it? You intoned it in a whisper.'

She shook her head with a disturbed expression.

'You referred to yourself as Celestial Daughter.'

'Did I? Well – it's true. There are many legends from the Hsia Dynasty of the mating of a Celestial and a mortal woman and the birth of a green-eyed girl who partly inherited the immense lifespan of the father. That was over three thousand years ago. Some of the legends hold that I grew as normal until my twelfth year but from then on aged but three years in every thousand. There's little doubt that I'm a Celestial Daughter. A demi-mortal.'

As she spoke she fidgeted with the silver ankh and her

glance was wayward, and the abbot received the distinct impression that she was trying to convince herself, not him, of the veracity of the legends. But he dared not risk incurring her wrath again with a direct personal question.

'In your speech to the assembly you portrayed the Celestial Ones as the defenders of humanity against the demonic Thzan-tzai, but supplied few hints as to the nature of these protectors.' Or of the Thzan-tzai, he thought.

Again the nervous eyes, the fumbling with the ankh. 'The Celestial Ones were spiritual beings from the Otherworld – the domain of bliss. They were emissaries of the Divine Light.'

'Then they weren't beings from any part of the cosmos, but spiritual – er, visitors from what you call the Otherworld? Pure spirits?'

She nodded affirmation.

He did not pursue the subject. If she shrank from facing the implied difficulties, that was her affair. Colourful legends apart (including the legend of the Buddha's virgin birth), could a pure spirit mate with a corporeal being, let alone cause a child to be conceived? Anything was possible, but he doubted this, and so, he suspected, did Chia. Her origins remained as great a mystery as ever. He rubbed his throbbing chest with a weak exhalation.

'Nagarjuna!' Her voice tingled with shock. 'You're ill. Is your heart faltering?'

'No. In your distraction you struck me. It's nothing.'

'Struck you! What devil was in me? Here – lean on my shoulder. I'll take you to your cell – you must lie down. Curse my madness!'

He politely refused her arm. 'It was but a soft blow, by your standards. Even with a clouded mind you wouldn't hit a friend with a hard blow. It's not in your nature.'

'Even with an unclouded mind I've done so, many

78

times,' she muttered quietly. Recovering her composure, she strode to the door of the hall. 'Come, Nagarjuna, these bronze Buddhas and Bodhisattvas and holy candles and sacred sandalwood odours make me feel like an unclean trespasser.'

Following, the abbot attempted to reconcile the nonchalant Chia he had met in middle manhood with the deadly apparition that had hurled him to the floor. It was as if there were two Chias: one casual and affable, the other lethal.

The sorceress halted at the portal's square of evening, allowing the frail Indian time to hobble to her side. She indicated an eight-spoked wooden wheel mounted on one side of the door. 'That caught my eye as I came in. What does it represent, apart from the Eightfold Path?'

'It signifies the Wheel of Samsara, the cycle of rebirth spun by the hand of Karma.'

'Karma and Samsara,' she smiled. 'Two Indian gifts to China. But it should be a spiral, my friend, not a wheel.' Abruptly, the fine muscles in her cheek began to work in tiny spasms as she stared into the evening wind.

'Nagarjuna,' she murmured. 'Have you ever had the feeling that something is waiting for you? Something you fear to confront yet cannot avoid?'

The abbot nodded.

'The thought of Spirit Hill troubles me,' she confessed. 'Once, long ago, in a village near the eastern span of the Great Wall, I rested a few days from my pursuit of the sorcerer Pan Chou, an acolyte of Nyak. I was unsure of myself and afflicted with turbulent memories and random surges of panic – no state in which to challenge Pan Chou. I had to find a measure of harmony, so I meditated on my reflection in a water mirror provided by the villagers. After some hours my conscious self was submerged and I battled through a nightmare world, slaying scores of misshapen figures in silver masks. When I regained my wits I discovered that I was washing blood from my hands in a stream. The broken-backed body of a child lay in the water an arm's length from me. I grew numb. I turned and saw a squashed red fruit in the wet mud of the bank, then realised it was a heart – near it lay a female corpse with a raw gap where her breast should have been. Flies swarmed on the heart and into the ragged wound. I lifted my bloodied hands and studied them as if they were alien claws grafted onto my arms. It was hot, and very quiet. Swarms of flies everywhere. Then the buzzing flew into my head and I screamed. As I stumbled through the village I was still screaming. Torn bodies everywhere. The lanes were blood. I would have slain myself then if I hadn't sworn to slay Nyak one day. What had I invoked from the water mirror reflection? What evil had the mirror summoned from my spirit? What had I seen in the water mirror? The shadow of my soul?'

Nagarjuna was aghast at the account. His senses shook and he shouted a resounding 'No!'

Yes, contradicted the sorceress in her thoughts, silent as snowfall.

'Couldn't it be your memory that's at fault?' he suggested anxiously.

A slight lift of the shoulders. 'I admit sometimes the recollection is different . . . I emerge from the trance washing my hands in the water mirror, and the broken child and the woman with the torn breast are in my hut. There is blood in the water mirror and the villagers are gathered outside the door, paralysed with hate and fear. The memory is inconstant. But something hideous happened there – in that region near the Great Wall, and in other regions also, I'm known as Chia the Death-bringer. And whenever I see my reflection I remember water and blood. Blood and water.'

The Indian looked up at the long, bedevilled eyes of the Chinese. 'I've been considering how to present this request since you arrived. But now I know of your burden of guilt I feel it's a request you'll be willing to grant. A mirror may once have made you act as a monster – would you now save someone from the monsters beyond a haunted mirror? I mean the girl Nua I spoke of earlier – the one who disappeared in the Lane of Axes, leaving a bronze mirror leaning in the doorway.'

'What of her?' *He's going to ask the impossible of me.*

'Well, Dharmapala brought the mirror here – the mirror cast by Fang-ch'i, her husband, who later committed suicide at the loss of his wife. The mirror was covered and locked in a chest, of course. No risks were taken . . .'

'There are always risks.' *It's impossible, but . . .*

'Dharmapala was conscious of the dangers. I had hoped that you might . . .'

'Might bring the girl out the mirror and restore her to the world?' Chia said. 'Abbot, don't take this matter of mirror selves too literally. There are phantoms similar to the Death Whisperers I mentioned and a Death Whisperer might be inside that mirror, but Nua herself isn't trapped in some mirror world. It doesn't happen that way. The most that could happen is that I might release a Death Whisperer into the world, and we would be its victims. Whatever befell Nua, she's lost. She can't be saved. Even if there were a mirror world in the same sense that there's a human world I still couldn't save her.'

Nagarjuna's eyes pleaded. 'I understand your reticence, but I knew this girl. She was good-hearted. I can't bear to contemplate her imprisonment. She's an innocent victim, Chia. I believe that the Mime Realm exists, and I also believe that the All-Compassionate One cannot wish her to remain trapped in it. I'll pray to the Celestial Buddha for the success of our venture. Vinaya is waiting in my cell to assist us in the ordeal . . . Chia?'

She hesitated. 'As far as I'm concerned the Mime Realm has no more existence than the Celestial Buddha of All Worlds in whom you believe so fervently. But I'll help you for old times' sake. I'll pretend to believe in mirror worlds and mirror selves for a little while, for the time it takes to perform a summoning. I'll do it as reparation for striking you.'

She hadn't expressed the real reason for her assent and her tone was unconvincing. The abbot was right – she did bear a burden of guilt from the slaughter she had dispensed in that village by the Great Wall. Slight as the chance of success was, she felt obliged at least to go through the actions of releasing Nua. It was an inadequate act of reparation for losses of blood in a village. For Chia, mirrors and guilt were almost synonymous.

She didn't speak as she left the hall, for inside her skull swirled blood in a water mirror.

UTTERED INTO LIFE

損

Haloes of candle flame highlighted patches of the abbot's cell – the outline of a simple straw pallet – a low table with a clay bowl – a camphor wood figurine of the Buddha Amitabha meditating in a sculpted alcove. Cool stars peered in through the nine squares of the window grille. Chia leaned on the wall by the Buddha shrine, studying the craftsmanship of the carving in order to keep her mind from dwelling on the task ahead. Nagarjuna and Vinaya stood patiently beside an oak chest at the foot of the pallet, arms folded. The abbot blinked as Chia turned abruptly.

'We require another mirror.' The edge to her voice made it more of a command than a comment.

'The temple possessed just one such mirror, and it was buried weeks ago.'

'Then have it resurrected.'

The abbot inclined his head and departed.

'Go and help him,' she ordered the monk. With a mock bow Vinaya took his leave.

The girl, left alone with the room, grasped the silver ankh at her breast and prayed aloud. 'Aten, Unknown One beyond the Solar Disc, Lord of Worlds, aid me. Protect my spirit from the shadow. And – and protect Fu until I come for her.' *Why is it that I feel this presence, this invisible presence behind me?*

Releasing the ankh she opened the oak chest and gingerly drew out a velvet-swaddled disc and laid it on the earthen floor. Her lip twitched into a snarl as she regarded the object. 'It was a black moon when you forged this mirror, husband of Nua.' *Is there someone in the room with me?*

In preparation for the summoning she sat beside the mirror and adopted the cross-legged posture of the lotus asana, drooped her eyelids, breathed slowly in the gentle rhythms of prana, and composed the elements of her being in the harmony of T'ao. Gradually she settled into deep meditation.

She was roused by the abbot's return and hastily swam up to the light and shadows of the austere cell. The old man carried a small disc swathed in muddied hempcloth. With a peremptory gesture she signalled Nagarjuna to stand over the larger mirror on the floor. Vinaya, she waved to one side.

'You had best start praying, Men of the Saffron Robe.' The aside was aimed especially at the young monk. 'Pray to whichever Buddha-aspect you prefer – any will do – but pray, reach outside yourself.' Wheeling back to Nagarjuna: 'Hold the haunted mirror so that it rests upright on the floor and then close your eyes. On no account open them – that also applies to you, Vinaya – even though I scream like all the demons in the netherworld. No – don't uncover the mirror yet. When I give the word, pull off the velvet so that the whole mirror is exposed – keep your eyes tight shut – and leave the rest to me.'

As he lifted the mirror Chia ranged round the cell blowing out the candles, leaving nothing but the pale illumination of star- and moonlight in the room. Finally she knelt facing her companion at a distance of two arm's lengths, heaving an audible sigh before raising the smaller disc to confront the mirror fashioned by Fang-ch'i. Again she breathed in the flow of prana, harmonising her spirit and concentrating her will.

'Uncover the mirror,' she whispered. 'And try to still

the shaking of your hands. Both of you – think hard on Nua. Picture her. Hear her voice.'

Nagarjuna fumbled with the wraps, tilting the mirror to and fro. Chia cursed in a soft breath. 'Keep the mirror in place,' she admonished. 'The discs must face each other directly.'

As the velvet fell from the haunted mirror Chia tore off the cloth from her own and a flash of gold lit up the drab cell. Mirror reflected to mirror and a silence sank into the room. She gritted her teeth and forced her gaze to remain on Nagarjuna's mirror. She sighed with relief on finding that the circle threw back no reflection, not even a hint of the bronze of which it was composed. It was utterly without light: a black hole in the world. Her intent mind had conjured that emptiness which shielded her vision from the aberrations of the Mime Realm although, curiously, the black mirror enlightened the surroundings with a golden glow – an ink-black well with a golden nimbus.

The silence was so thick that it nearly muffled the beating of her heart and the drumming of blood in her ears. An almost soundless cough shook the abbot's scrawny frame and streaks of gold lashed across the ebony surface of the mirror as his hold on it wavered.

A sound akin to a shape of silence bulged out from the flame-flashed circle and crammed her ears with sound-less words . . . *whispered to death . . . whispered to death . . . whispered to death . . .*

'The Whisperers,' hissed Chia. *There's a fourth person amongst us.*

The tremoring of the abbot's hands increased and the sounds and silence mounted.

'Keep still!' she yelled through the thronged air. 'Be still or they'll flood into the room.'

The trembling halted but the gold bursts and the whispers persisted. Weird images sparked behind the girl's green eyes. In her struggle with the malign influences she bit her lower lip and blood welled into a tremulous drop from the punctured skin.

The momentary glimpses of the Mime Realm resonating from the unstill mirror rattled into her maze of brain with a myriad echoes: glimpses – visions – intimations – phantasms. She stifled a scream and fought to retain her concentration on the entrapped Nua, battling to wrest the haunted bronze to her own purpose, striving to impose her own image onto the whispering circle. After a scatter of anxious moments the mirror resumed its blackness. The blood drop trembled on her lower lip but she paid it no heed.

Her shoulders relapsed from tension as she conjured the image of a tunnel within the mirror: it was a tunnel perceived in blackness, a tunnel unseen, a tunnel sensed. The whispers swelled and wove like serpents but she ignored them and continued staring down the endless invisible tunnel.

She was almost beginning to believe in this mummery performed for the sake of Nagarjuna (or as a sop to her grimy conscience?)

'Nua,' summoned Chia. 'Nua. Uttered into life. Nua. Uttered into life. Nua. Uttered into life . . .'

A human hint quavered in the dark tunnel and human breath clouded from the black mirror. Astonished, the sorceress extracted the Night-Shining Jewel from the cowl of her cloak. The so-called jewel was a luminescent stone which magnified the thoughts of its user tenfold. Holding the Night-Shining Jewel like a weapon against the black disc in Nagarjuna's hands, she sought a vibration of the imprisoned girl.

And it came. To her mounting astonishment, it actually came. A suspicion of Nua blew down from hidden realms. Chia caught the suspicion and held it, exerting her influence through the potency of the blue stone which waxed brighter with each second. Nua's breath rose like a gust of steam from the tainted metal. Still no visible image appeared in the mirror.

'Nua. Uttered into life. Nua. Uttered into life. Come forth . . . Walk by day . . .'

The sorceress stiffened, sensing a presence on the inner threshold of the dark mirror, the near end of the forever tunnel. The mirror misted with a swirling silver vapour threaded with hues of the rainbow. A shape was revealed in a burst of light within the bronze. Then the form stepped out of the agitated circle and into the room. Nua had returned. Her rescuer gaped, seeing the girl standing apparently unharmed outside the reflecting field of the two mirrors. Suddenly, a huge rush of energy swept from Chia and she fought for breath.

She felt as if something had died inside her.

Chia, panting with the shock she had suffered, prepared to cover her mirror, telling the abbot to do likewise so that both surfaces would be masked simultaneously. But as she bent forwards to drape the hempcloth over the disc, the drop of blood shivering on her lip fell onto the bright bronze in a thin crimson smear, causing her to cry out in alarm. For an instant the presence of the Death Whisperers surged into the grim monastic cell. The floor quaked and the ceiling trembled. Candles were hurled across the moonlit room as if an invisible hand had swept through it. But Nagarjuna had sufficient wits to cover his mirror and Chia was just able to do the same.

The tumult subsided and the breath of the Whisperers flowed back into the Mime Realm. Now there were two haunted mirrors; the smaller disc had been infected by the reflections of the other. But the immediate threat was averted. Chia released a long, thankful exhaltation and replaced the Night-Shining Jewel in her cowl.

'By the Ssu Ling, that was close. That was very close, Nagarjuna.'

The abbot nodded, smiled, and promptly fainted. The sorceress gave a low laugh and let the old man lie undisturbed. The laugh sank without trace when she turned her deep green eyes on the girl who leaned in Vinaya's arms.

Chia could not accept the reality of what had occurred.

A thought scurried like a squirrel in her head. She regarded Nua with a faint suspicion. Why was she so quiet? Why didn't she open her eyes and scream? To outward scrutiny the girl was human, but what if she was a skilful mimicry of Nua? It was unlikely that the Mirror Kindred could so accurately imitate a human, but it was possible. Vinaya and Nagarjuna would be more reliable judges than she – they could compare her with the girl they had known. And, unlike her, they had truly believed that the summoning might work. She explained her dilemma to the thoughtful monk, omitting her original lack of faith in the ritual.

'I'll judge as best I can,' he promised.

'It won't be any use asking her questions about her past,' she pointed out. 'She has been in the Mime Realm – it will have warped her identity. Just note her appearance, her voice – if she speaks, mannerisms of face and body. These rarely change.' And there's an infallible method of ascertaining the truth, she thought. But the method eluded her. How could she have forgotten? She felt so ill – the summoning had drained her low reserves of vitality.

It took Vinaya less than a minute to judge who it was that shared the room with them, and by that time Chia had roused the abbot.

'It's Nua,' the monk declared firmly. 'Much changed in spirit. But Nua. I'm sure of it.'

The sorceress nodded. 'As you say. But I'd like Nagarjuna to confirm that.'

After a short interval the abbot confirmed that the girl was Nua. But Chia couldn't dispose of a disquieting emotion. The girl was so serene – like a sleeping child. And the two men were unaware that Chia had not envisaged the success of the summoning. It had been performed as a step towards the expiation of guilt. Blood swirling in a water mirror . . .

And Chia hadn't yet recovered from her surprise at being confronted with powerful evidence that the Mirror World and mirror beings actually existed. Still unwilling to pin her faith on the monk's opinions, Chia moved up to the girl and stared into her dreaming face. Chia sharpened her attention to the point where it was like a dagger probing into the hidden nature behind the dreamy features.

And in the face of Nua, Chia saw her own face.

Taking a deep breath she stepped back. Could it be? A mirror being from a mirror world?

She faced Nagarjuna. 'She could be just what you say — Nua, wife of Fang-ch'i. But she may be something of another kind. I can't leave her in the temple. For your sake, I can't take that risk. She must come with me, much as I regret it. Refugees will soon be pouring into the monastery, and it must be kept secure. She goes with me.'

'But you can't watch her continuously,' protested Nagarjuna.

'True,' she conceded. 'That's why I need a companion to keep watch on her. This also I regret. In danger, I prefer my own company. If I'd foreseen the success of the summoning I would also have foreseen its consequences. However . . .'

Again the blood-and-water image of guilt.

'I would go with you,' the abbot said. 'But I'm needed here.'

Vinaya turned a meaningful stare on his mentor. Nagarjuna cleared his thin throat. 'Ah — Vinaya would seem to be the obvious choice. He has been privy to our discussions and deeds so far.'

'So be it. Vinaya will accompany me. Now remember, Nagarjuna, when the refugees come, that everyone must be searched at the temple gates, even the monks. And, of course, bury these two mirrors immediately.'

'There's no time more immediate than the present,'

89

Vinaya replied, picking up the mirrors with extreme care.

'Come back as soon as you've finished,' she called out as he passed through the door.

'I will bring both myself and a light for the candles,' he said. 'Your green eyes may be able to see in the dark but those old orbs of our esteemed abbot don't serve him so handsomely.'

With the departure of the monk, Chia confronted the dim, blue-gowned figure of the placid girl before her. 'What are you, Nua?' she asked rhetorically. 'Are you body or shadow? Form or reflection?'

Soon the young man returned and candlelight filled the room.

The candles had melted barely the width of a finger when they had concluded a swift meal and a brief debate. Nua had vaguely refused the meal and slunk into a murky corner where she sat hugging her knees. Her eyes, which had been closed, were now hooded, reminding Chia of the eyes of women dosed with dream potions.

'It's time to go,' the sorceress announced at last, donning her black cloak. 'It's time for Ming's mirror and the Game of the Immortals.'

Vinaya fixed her with a keen stare. 'And where precisely are we going?'

'First to San Lung Town, then to Spirit Hill.'

The monk smiled. 'Excellent. An adventure. I'm honoured to be your companion.'

The abbot frowned disapprovingly.

Chia moved to the door. 'Come, young adventurer,' she invited, 'bring Nua by the arm. I want to reach Spirit Hill well before dawn.'

'But won't you require a pack of provisions?' inquired the abbot.

The dismissive wave of her hand was all but a gesture

of contempt. 'We won't need provisions. And I never carry a pack – the jewel in my cowl and the dagger in my sash are all I require.'

It was the dark Hour of the Rat when Nagarjuna stood at the north Black Serpent Gate of the temple and watched the departure of the three figures – black, saffron and blue – on the winding brown road. On the nearest bend Chia glanced back and waved, then turned her face to the twisting road. The moon had sailed high in the sky by the time the three were finally lost to sight.

'Chia,' sighed Nagarjuna. 'You should have stayed in your valley on Black Dragon Mountain. You should have stayed.'

8

DREAM WALKER

The perfect madness, unfolding in its perfection, had begun to perceive an unfamiliarity at the heart of its loving being.

The perfect madness came, not from the unfamiliar, but from the familiar. It distrusted the unfamiliar. It feared it, a little.

What was this sundering, this ripping at the centre that split the one into one and one? What was this division of the indivisible?

It was like a separation of Body and Spirit, Body and Spirit being cleft asunder.

But the division would soon be healed. The Body and the Spirit of the perfect madness could not remain in schism for long.

Even in schism, the madness of the Shadow Spirit had touched a hundred human souls, had drawn them along the path that led into itself. They would all become one with the supreme love which is the love that kills.

I know everyone in the world, whispered the perfect shadow. I know everyone in the future as I know everyone in the past.

And I love all of you.

And I will never let my love be denied.

I will always be waiting for you.

'Master,' sobbed Ming. 'Where are you, Master?'

But there was no answer from the dark stairs or the

shadowy hall. Nyak the Master had not yet come to feed his servant. And Ming felt the pangs of hunger all the more keenly with the departure of the Body and the Hearing. But Nyak would come because Ming had served him faithfully. The Master would not desert his faithful servant.

The empty house seemed noisy to Ming's abnormally enhanced hearing. It was loud with a hundred creaks and cracks of settling wood. *But that is just the bone joints stirring in my flesh which is the flesh of the house.* There was nothing he couldn't hear: the patter of a mouse was a rumble that echoed through the old house. *But that is only the beating of my heart in the world's flesh.*

'Master . . . when will you come to reward your servant?'

But the old house of dark flesh didn't answer. Doubts started to trickle through Ming's brain. He slowly twisted the knife in his gold-ringed hand. Hadn't there been a time, long ago, when there was a world called China? Hadn't he lived in China, once upon a time? He thought he remembered sumptuous feasts lit by scores of candles, each candle a different colour, a different scent. Had he not owned a vast wardrobe of lavish costumes and chests bulging with jewels, long ago? Surely there had been a hundred girls, naked and obedient under the touch of his sharp knife? Hadn't he once lived as Ming the merchant in a land called China?

'Just a dream,' his heavy mouth mumbled. *I am the world. And I once had a dream in which I lived inside myself. But now the world has awoken and the China dream has vanished.*

Ming's eyelids blinked as he studied the knife in his hot palm. He exhaled a slow, wheezy breath. His slick brow creased in puzzlement.

But if I'm the world, he pondered, then who is the Master?

For a moment Ming's fuddled wits almost cleared and

93

he came near to recalling who and where he was. But the echoes of the Hearing that resounded in his head and the lingering silence of the Body that sighed into his spirit soon scattered his thoughts like small clouds in a wind.

'Pork,' he moaned witlessly. 'Master, the flesh is hungry.'

Ming was filled with a sudden upsurge of faith in Nyak the Master. He had never seen the Master but he had served Nyak all his life as his father had done before him. Ming's father had never set eyes on Nyak either, nor his father's father, but knowledge of the Master was passed down from generation to generation. For Nyak, Ming had learned as a small child, life was not a matter of morals and philosophy or good or evil. Life was a game which was played for its own sake and the supreme value in life was cleverness. The game was to the clever. The path was to develop and demonstrate the cleverness of the mind. And the mind proved its cleverness in creating complex games, then playing and winning them. Everything was the game, and all that mattered was winning. There was no hatred in Nyak, no will to evil – just love of the game.

'Does that mean that my flesh is the game, too?' muttered the bulging lips.

Where are you, Master? The Silver Brethren promised that you would come. They promised that you would give me the reward, the reward of being changed into a Silver Brother. That was the promise, the reward of walking with the Silver Brethren, fearsome, ageless, and wielding the power of the killing word. Century to century, walking with the Silver Brethren.

Ming's swimming vision ran up and down the murky hallway. Was Nyak perhaps hiding behind one of the hall doors, ready to spring out and surprise him with a reward of juicy pork in his hand?

He shifted the knife in his loose grip. The bright knife

94

could cut the pork into dainty morsels. The belly of the world was hungry.

'Pork,' he murmured again.

There was a noise downstairs. The sound of a door opening. It sounded like a crash of thunder to Ming's sensitive ears. His febrile muscles tightened in the excitement of anticipation. The knife was clenched harder in his slippery grasp.

The thud-thud of feet ascending the lower staircase. Ming's heart pounded with the tread of the feet. The thudding halted as the feet reached the lower landing.

The Master . . . he'll climb the upper stairs now . . he'll come to me, up through the house of my flesh . . . he'll emerge from the darkness at the head of the stairs, a reward in his hand . . .

A voice floated up the stairs. 'Ming . . .'

Yes, Master, I'm here . .

'Ming . . .' repeated the voice.

Ming grinned. The Game Master was here. Ming would have his reward . . .

The abbot was small and frail in the wide mouth of Black Serpent Gate as Chia gave him a final wave, but the walls of the temple were tall and staunch: a foursquare fortress against marauding bands and a refuge for the lost and the haunted. With a leaden heart she turned her back on the monastery as she descended the gentle hill it surmounted.

Her attention switched to Vinaya who kept a strong grip on the drowsy Nua. The monk cast Chia a quizzical look. 'May I ask your purpose in visiting San Lung Town?'

'There's an ancient bronze mirror there. I think I may need it.'

'And where is this mirror?'

'In Ming's mansion.'

'And what's special about it?' the monk asked.

'It's one I stole from a vampire. It has a certain power. I may need that power.'

A gasp of admiration escaped the monk. 'You stole a sacred bronze mirror from a vampire tomb? That was a brave act! Where was this tomb?'

'In the Forest of the Ancestors,' she replied absently.

'But if you stole this mirror why don't you still possess it?'

An old hatred trembled a muscle at the corner of her fresh mouth. 'The Silver Brethren stole it from me. Some time later they entrusted it to Ming's father. I had no important reason for taking it back until now.'

Vinaya pursed his narrow lips. 'I find this curious. If the Silver Brethren serve Nyak why didn't they give it to him instead of Ming's father?'

'Nyak wouldn't go near the mirror. It has a trace of the Thzan-tzai spirit in its metal. It would give him pain.'

'Oh, why?'

She glowered at her companion. 'I'm not an abbot, monk. I don't give lectures.'

He gave a light shrug. 'Talk makes a journey pass quicker.'

'And the feet move slower.'

'Touchy,' murmured Vinaya.

She ignored the remark, slanting her gaze instead to Nua. The dreamy girl trailed from Vinaya's arm with a lazy air as she veered from side to side like a drunkard. The simple blue gown swished softly as she swayed.

There was an absence in Chia since the exertion of Nua's summoning (she could still hardly accept the reality of Nua's magical emergence). The summoning had battered her memory almost to powder. She was not the same woman as she was before. The ordeal had brought the dying time a few steps closer.

The cool wind from the north ruffled Chia's long hair and fluttered her black cloak. Evanescent snakes of mist writhed and vanished in the gusts, only to reappear in the teeth of the wind. This mist wind from the north was ominous – the wind would blow from wherever the Spirit Mirror was hidden.

'The mouth of Spirit Hill,' she whispered, thinking of Fu and trying not to think of Fu.

What is this thing that I have forgotten?

Wind and mist. In San Lung the weather was a series of skirmishes between wind and mist. Her slanted green eyes scanned the surrounding terrain. Low hills. Shallow hollows. Tiny boulders bleached by moonlight, resembling skulls. Near, nestling in the lap of an oak-groved hill, the conical yellow hat of a thatched cottage. Distant, a three-tiered house crowned with a tiled roof hued dull red at the head of an arrowed valley and the remote din of honking geese. The clamour of geese – an alarm? Intruders to the peace of the tall dwelling? A wry expression stole into her face. Peace? There would be little enough of that in San Lung this night.

Fu . . . I think of you but I must not think of you . . . the dying time is near and the madness is strong . . . I must think only of the task if I am to save you . . . I must turn my face from the memory of your face . . . I must think only of the game . . . I must think of the game and I must not sleep . . . If I sleep, I die . . .

She threw a sharp look at the dream walker called Nua. Who was the sleepy girl who weaved gracefully at Vinaya's side?

When I looked her full in the face, I saw a brief vision of my own mouth and eyes.

Withdrawing her eyes from the dream walker in blue, Chia began to ponder the mystery of mirrors as she strode along the dusty road. Mirrors – not just sacred bronze mirrors, but all mirrors, all reflections. Gaze into the polished bronze or silver and what do you see? Peer into the water mirror and what is revealed? The room is reversed, the face is reversed, the hands are reversed. What is the right hand here is the left hand there.

97

Mirrors. Reflections. Approach a mirror and the reflection approaches, retreat and it withdraws, step for step. As you advanced to the mirror was something on the far side advancing to meet you? Your own opposite? Your own denial?

To meet yourself is to die.

A distant commotion alerted her hearing and cleared her head of speculations – a muffled rumble behind a bend in the road at the foot of a rock-boned hill. Chia peered ahead, clenching and unclenching her right hand with an ingrained habit inspired by millenial experience of menace, violence, sudden ambush. But the remote rumble was soon identifiable as the prosaic rolling of wagons, and Chia's hand relaxed. A party of about twenty peasants appeared round the corner, some sitting on the three heavily laden wagons, most walking alongside the sturdy oxen that pulled the precarious vehicles with plodding hooves and lowered heads. As the foremost wagon rattled near a shout went up from one of its passengers, a man of middle years in a dishevelled green smock stained with ox dung.

'Tell him nothing,' Chia ordered the monk.

'Brother Vinaya!' the passenger greeted. 'It's Ho-li! We're on our way to the holy temple. Two of your brothers passed through our village a small hour ago. They told us to seek sanctuary in the temple from demons that jump out of mirrors and streams. Will the abbot take us in?'

'Of course,' assured Vinaya. 'The monks were acting under the abbot's orders. You'll be welcome.'

The villager laboriously descended from his shaky perch and walked up to the monk. His stench was almost as strong as the smell of steaming oxen and he noted the presence of the sorceress with a wary glance.

'Your brothers in Buddha wouldn't escort us to the temple,' announced Ho-li. 'Will you come with us?'

'I'm afraid not.'

'Hmm . . .' grunted the other. 'Then permit the two women to join us for their protection.'

Chia rolled her eyes and her mouth formed an angry line.

'This tall, somewhat peevish woman is in no great need of protection, Ho-li,' explained Vinaya. 'She is Chia, Sorceress of Black Dragon Mountain.'

'You fool!' spat Chia, spinning vehemently on her companion. 'Can't you keep your mouth closed? Were you lost in Nirvana when I spoke to you a minute ago? Shall I scrawl my name in lightning-strokes across the sky?'

'Don't speak to the holy man in that fashion, wench,' blustered Ho-li.

'Go and jump into the netherworld,' Chia reposted, stalking past the wagons and the inquiring, underfed faces. 'Come, Vinaya,' she ordered, 'and make certain Nua doesn't slip away.' With a suppressed grin the monk followed, gripping Nua by the crook of the arm.

'What madness boils in your head, green-eyed vixen?' shouted Ho-li after the departing figure in black. 'The holy brother was only making a jest. Everyone knows that the Black Dragon Sorceress is a children's tale. Oh, but you're stupid enough to believe it, are you?'

She looked over her shoulder, halted, and made an obscene gesture with her fingers at the outraged Ho-li. With a contemptuous twist of the head she resumed her journey.

'There are monsters in the stream ahead, whoredaughter! I pray they drag you down through the Ten Hells!' the man yelled derisively between cupped hands. 'They've taken four of us already. I hope the water demons make you the fifth!'

Chia frowned. Monsters in the stream . . . water demons . . . Ho-li's wild fancies might indicate the presence of Death Whisperers in the stream ahead. But four disappearances in one small village? Was that possible?

Hopefully there would be a bridge – fording a haunted stream by stepping stones wasn't a prospect she relished. After they were well out of earshot of the villagers and their irate leader she beckoned to Vinaya. 'How far is the stream that oaf was bellowing about?'

'Less than a li – five minutes at an easy pace.'

'Is there a bridge?'

'There is.'

'Just as well,' she breathed quietly.

'How so?'

She waved at the somnolent, blue gowned figure of Nua. 'Because of her, monk. If Nua has a mirror spirit in her and if the stream is haunted by mirror spirits then she might draw an evil to us. Unlikely, but possible.'

But why so many disappearances? The abbot calculated that there had been at least two hundred disappearances in San Lung Town alone. If the power in Spirit Hill Mound was fully released, all would be swallowed into another world – the world of perfect madness. And if it was only partially released it could take only a tiny handful of souls from the whole of San Lung region in the space of mere weeks. Why so many vanishings? I knew the answer before the summoning – I'm sure I knew it then. What took it from my mind?

They had skirted the foot of the hill and started on a straight stretch of road dipping to a moonlit stream bordered by a small huddle of huts and spanned by a humped wooden bridge. The sorceress flicked a sidelong glance at Nua who ambled with a lilting, chignon-crowned head set with doe-soft eyes under hooded lids. Had the dream walker, Chia wondered, affected her mind in some fashion? Was that why she felt so tired and her memory was blank?

The three travellers were a hundred steps from the warped and weathered boards of the humped bridge. Loose red balustrades carved in the likeness of fabulous beasts ran along the bumpy brinks of yellow planks. The throng of huts on the far bank had a desolate air. Apart from the silver gurgle of the stream, there was silence. As they neared the bridge the silence mounted.

Sound poured into the ears of the Mimic and he saw the sound in his jovial head.

Sight flowed into the ears of the Mimic and he listened to it, grinning.

Madness streamed into the ears and out of the eyes of the Mimic and he sniffed and tasted it, chuckling.

She was coming, the Green-Eyes. The enemy was near.

Dance in the dance of the Blood Spiral, Chia.

Dance into your death, Chia.

Lovely Chhhiiiaaa . . .

Dance with your shadow dancing partner, Green-Eyes.

Dance into the Mirror, all unknowing.

Meet your face in the Mirror, smiling.

Fall into yourself.

Plunge into the spiral.

Become your shadow, sighing sadly, Green-Eyes.

Become a regret, Dream Walker.

As they came within thirty steps of the humped bridge, Chia tapped Vinaya on the shoulder.

'Grip Nua's arm firmly,' she whispered. 'I'll hold the other arm. We must keep her between us as we cross. Close your eyes when I give the word. And meditate on the compassion of the Buddha – the wonder of the Western Paradise – whatever symbols inspire reverence.'

His hold on Nua tightened as Chia grasped the girl's left arm; her free hand she cupped over the girl's hooded eyes.

Ten steps from the foot of the bridge.

The sorceress conjured an image of the Solar Disc of Aten in her imagination, then visualised Nature gently breathing in damp sunrise. She inhaled deeply.

101

'Close your eyes,' she commanded. The moment she gave the order she shut her own eyelids.

The boards protested in drawn-out creaks as Chia's bare feet, Nua's slippered feet and Vinaya's sandalled feet padded over them. The incline rose, rounded, dipped.

'Keep your eyes shut for ten more steps,' Chia advised. Ten steps more, then Chia released Nua's eyes and opened her own to the brown path as it climbed in mild undulations to a swollen rise. She exchanged glances with the monk. 'Don't look back until we've put more distance between ourselves and the water,' she insisted. 'It may be that the Whisperers weren't aware of us until we crossed the stream. They can still reach into our minds.'

But their progress was unhindered as they ascended the swells and surges of the grassy rise.

'We're safe now,' declared Chia as they wound through a rustling grove of daimyo oaks near the breeze-rippled crest of the slope. Then she laughed in reaction to tension.

'Safe is what we are,' confirmed Vinaya. 'Something of an anticlimax.'

'What a strange Buddhist you are,' she commented, her nervous laughter subsiding. 'Anyway, we've walked unharmed with the dream walker over haunted currents. And nothing happened.'

He raised an eyebrow. 'Perhaps we're being gulled into complacency.'

She disdained a reply, but cast a withering look in his direction. A supercilious smile broadened his lips.

'There's something you should tell me, sorceress,' he declared. 'As I'm your invaluable companion on this journey there's something you should tell me all about.'

'Is that so? And what might that something be, Bald Man of the Saffron Robe?'

'Nyak.'

'And why should I tell you about Nyak?' scowled Chia.

102

'Because I'm your companion and if he's a danger to you then he's a danger to me as well.'

The sorceress reflected for a moment, then conceded the point. 'All right, Vinaya. I suppose you have a point. Nyak, son of Glak-i-kakthz, last of the Thzan-tzai, has lived for some ten thousand years.'

'But who were the Thzan-tzai?' His olive eyes were intent on her refined face.

'An elder race, as I said in the Buddha Hall. The name Thzan-tzai means Unshaped Masters in the ancient tongue. In their origins they were similar to humans, but over millenia they altered through their power of shape-changing. In the end the Celestial Ones destroyed them. Glak-i-kakthz was the last to be exterminated, but not before he squirted his seed into a woman's belly. That seed grew into the being known as Nyak – the name means Game Master. Nyak is a nightmare, and my lifelong enemy.'

'What if he's watching us now?' asked Vinaya, a troubled expression invading his ascetic face.

She shook her head. 'He may be near, but not that near. There is a power flowing south through San Lung region. It flows from Spirit Hill. And that flowing power is a living memory of the Thzan-tzai. There's a Spirit Mirror to the north that distils a Thzan-tzai dream. All of San Lung is slipping into a Thzan-tzai dream. It is sliding out of history . . .'

'But why should that keep Nyak at a distance?' asked Vinaya.

'Anything that bears the scent of Thzan-tzai, however faded, is pain to his flesh,' she replied. 'He couldn't even touch a Thzan-tzai relic like Ming's mirror. It would dissolve his fingers. All of San Lung is haunted by a dream of the Thzan-tzai. If Nyak entered San Lung it would mean death to his flesh. Only his servants – the Silver Brethren – can enter. Nyak must keep his distance.'

'Interesting,' the monk remarked. 'Tell me more of this mighty being.'

But Chia lapsed into a moody silence and stared straight ahead as they mounted the brow of the slope and pursued the road where it twisted and fell into the rich plains of San Lung. Nua, drowsy with calm, meandered along the road, oblivious to everything but her dream walk. Three li distant, an earth-brown square in the moon-silver plain, squatted San Lung Town. In between the travellers and the town wound a stream, and where the road to the southern gate met the stream there was a pavilion. At the base of the slope that sank into the plain two figures in saffron headed a long column of people with palanquins, wagons, carts and wheelbarrows.

'The townsfolk were ready to depart for the temple weeks ago,' Vinaya remarked. 'Poised, you might say.'

'I'm glad the town will be deserted,' she said. 'I don't want too many eyes on me when I take Ming's mirror. Come.'

They descended the incline and stepped to one side of the path as they encountered the head of the procession. The monks halted and traded ceremonial bows.

'Oh, come *on*,' groaned Chia as she witnessed the formalities.

As they walked by the rag-taggle exodus Chia began to experience a disconcerting sensation that the entire population of the town were dream walkers. It was very subtle, very obscure, but there was something wrong about the townspeople. They were a long row of inquisitive stares that made Chia feel alien. At the tail of the column she idly noted a haggard old couple hobbling along with the use of crutches, a burly man in a tattered grey mantle bearing a slim man on his wide back, a huddle of bemused children in a rickety wagon.

The stragglers trailed past and the three were alone once more. The stone bridge over the coiling stream was less than a hundred steps away.

Chia tapped the monk on the arm. 'We'll proceed as at the last crossing. There's no need to become lax.'

Vinaya lifted his hand in compliance.

Her pulse quickened as they came closer to the grey stone bridge. There was need of caution, but why did anxiety growl like a beast in the breast? The townspeople had poured over the stream unharmed, and she had almost discounted the notion that she and the girl were a draw to the Whisperers. Yet still she was disturbed. Vinaya, she recognised, was suspicious of their companion. More than fifty steps from the gnawed rim of the banks a palpable silence began to smother their footfalls.

'Sorceress . . .' the monk's voice was a distant susurration. 'The silence is like a thick mist from the stream. The townsfolk couldn't have experienced this — they would have stampeded.'

Her own thoughts exactly. Her green eyes flashed a vivid hostility at the girl. Vinaya caught Chia's gaze in a meaningful stare. 'I don't think it's you that inspires this unholy silence,' came the remote echo of his voice. 'It's her.'

An alien thought intruded into Chia's head: I am coming for you. I am searching for you, sister. I wear your face with the subtle alteration of nightmare.

'Act as we did at the first bridge,' she shouted through the thickening air, ignoring the inner voice. With the girl pinioned between them they advanced to the worn mouth of the bridge. Fifteen footsteps more . . . ten . . . five . . . Chia closed her eyes. The silence squeezed into her ears and a disquieting sensation of deafness shivered her mental image of the divine Solar Disc like wind on water.

Smooth cold stone beneath her unshod feet. Under the stone, running water below the brink of muffled hearing. Crisscrossing currents in Chia's mind ruffled the solar image of Aten. Yellow desert trembled. The Nile deluged archaic temples . . .

The visions fled and alarm rang in her body as Nua lunged and knocked her to the parapet where she nearly toppled into the stream. Struggling against the compulsion to open her eyes, the sorceress seized the girl's arm in both hands and forced her to the middle of the bridge. In view of her slight physique, Nua's resistance was amazing: Chia had encountered less trouble with doughty warriors.

Ten strenuous paces with the threshing girl and the soles of Chia's feet felt the rutted earth of the path again. The silence receded and Nua relapsed into lassitude. Chia hurled a fiery glance at her small companion, then swung her gaze to meet Vinaya's. His features mirrored her thoughts.

'She tried to pull me to the left,' he accused.

'And she tried to push me in the same direction.'

Out of the corner of her eye she observed the Pavilion of the Red Phoenix to the left of the road; an angular, wing-roofed edifice of painted wood. A red paper sign inked with black characters overhung the chained and boarded door: 'The Black Serpent has swallowed the Red Phoenix, and it will swallow you if you enter this mouth!'

'Dharmapala came to no harm when he gazed into the water mirror of the Red Phoenix Pavilion,' Vinaya remarked thoughtfully. 'Wouldn't it be worth a brief look? If my brother in Buddha could survive the ordeal, surely a mighty sorceress could undergo it with impunity? Why not chance a look, Green-Eyed One? We might learn something.'

She declined with a wave of the hand and a shake of the head. 'You are Mara the Tempter, Saffron Robe. I hope I'm not so arrogant that I'd put my skill and luck needlessly to trial. The girl is risk enough. Either she's a Death Whisperer or she's vulnerable to their breath. We might have been hurled into the haunted stream.'

The monk nodded. 'She almost succeeded in dragging us over the parapet. She is one of the Whisperers, Chia.'

The lift of her eyebrows was expressive of perplexity. 'No. We can't be sure of that. Not yet.'

Chia noticed that the mists had totally disappeared, and

106

that the wind which had blown unceasingly from the north now suddenly veered to the west. Curious. She frowned. Swiftly, the wind wheeled round until it blew from the south. The south? She finally shrugged. There were enough mysteries.

Her vision shifted to the swaying profile of Nua and then rose to the impassive walls of San Lung Town. Brown, bell-towered ramparts crowned a rumpled eminence. There was no sound.

'Hurry,' she urged. 'We *must* be inside Spirit Hill Mound before dawn.'

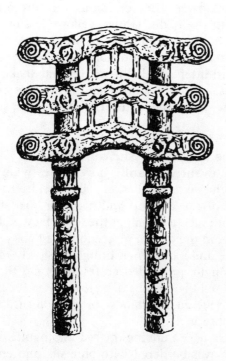

9

MIRROR BREATH

No voice greeted them as they stole under the massive lintel of the town's Red Phoenix Gate. No arm was raised in salutation or challenge from open belvedere or fortified watchtower. The ponderous wind from the south, laden with the night, fanned yellow dust down hollow streets, plucked trampled straw from neglected corners and scattered it in profusion along orderly avenues. Haphazard litter scuttled in circles and snake-curves. A wicker basket rolled and rolled northwards in the wind that blew from the gate. The oak gates swung and creaked.

'No one,' Vinaya remarked.

'No one we can see,' she corrected.

They advanced warily down the wide, deserted avenue, the discarded basket rolling before them. At the junction of the avenue and a minor road the wicker basket thumped to a halt at the foot of a wooden portico where, from the carven projection of a t'ao-tieh visage, a rigid rope and a limp man hung and slowly rotated. The purple tongue protruded grotesquely and the eyes resembled the bulging orbs of a frog.

'They severed his hands for good measure,' Vinaya quietly observed.

Chia nodded, studying the red silk mantle draping the corpse. It was bordered with blue silk and embroidered with stylised trees, mountains, dragons and thunder-spirals. It was the Kang-i garment, the apparel of a T'aoist magus. What futile task of mirror exorcism had he essayed to be so savagely punished? Magicians were customarily revered by the people, but in times of calamity blame often fell upon them. They were straw dogs that were worshipped for a space, then torn and trampled underfoot. Chia herself had frequently been treated like a straw dog.

'The sight sickens me,' she snarled. 'Let's move on.'

A whale-cloud gulped the moon as they entered the Square of Execution and the dismal courtyard filled with blackness, obscuring the central scaffold and executioner's block.

'Necks sawn through – necks severed with an axe – human justice.' Chia did not reply to the monk's laconic comment.

The moon was still in the glimmering cloud as they came to the courtyard gate of Ming's mansion. Passing through the bronze gate they walked among the luxuriant gardens to the porticoed entrance of the opulent mansion. The ornate, lacquered doors were unlocked; they opened with a belligerent shove from the sorceress. Darkness stood within.

'Where is the mirror kept?' she inquired in a soft breath.

'In the room at the top of the first flight of stairs. I'll come with you.'

'No!' she exclaimed. 'Stay here with Nua. That's your mission – to keep her under guard.'

'You may need help.'

'Not from you.'

He shrugged unwilling consent and Chia crept into the unlighted hall without another word. Using the faint illumination of the Night-Shining Jewel she scaled the creaking stairs, her free hand sliding along the top of the red balustrade. Hesitating on the landing, she studied the outline of the door indicated by Vinaya, then, with a deep breath, pushed it ajar.

Light flooded through the gap – the light of lanterns, the

light of candles. Startled, she slipped distrustfully into the richly furnished room. The bronze mirror was draped in a voluminous sheet of red silk. And a man with long, dishevelled hair and a red Kang-i garment sat before it on a pile of luxurious cushions, brandishing a peachwood wand and challenging her with hostile gaze. 'Begone, Fox Spirit!' he commanded.

A dash of humour mixed with her surprise. 'Fox Spirit? Not so, witless one. I'm a Black Dragon. And it's *you* who must go. The Mirror of Ming is beyond your mimetic magic. It's fortunate for you that I arrived.' She glanced at the swathed disc. 'However, you're not entirely bereft of wisdom, it seems. Was it you who cloaked the mirror?'

Sulky and suspicious, he shook his head. 'No. Dharmapala did it some time ago. He's a bald-headed barbarian from the Buddha Temple. Masking mirrors is all he's capable of – it takes a Wu magus to perform a successful exorcism.'

Chia examined the antique Liu Po board set beside the pile of cushions. Six elmwood rods were tied in a bundle at its side. Liu Po – the game of gaining the centre and establishing dominion.

Evidently this Wu practitioner *was* something of a magus.

She nodded at the wooden board. 'Yours? Or Ming's?'

'Ming's,' came the disgruntled reply. 'I have my own, of course,' he added hastily. 'I found this one in that chest over there. It's much older than my board so I knew it would be imbued with strong magical properties. The casting sticks were with it. I was about to play the game to win the mirror back from the demon when you burst in.' His eyes narrowed to sceptical slits. 'For all I can tell you might be a demon yourself. You look fairly human but your eyes are green. I've never seen a Chinese with green eyes . . .' Then his wisp-bearded jaw dropped slack. 'But I've heard tales of one. A tall,

green-eyed woman in black. Black Dragon Sorceress . . .'
He began to move his wand in signs of protection from
evil.

'That's me, Wand-waver,' she confirmed. 'And you
can cease your wand waving. I won't hurt you. But I
can't speak for Ming. I can't imagine he invited you in.'

'I called his name out a couple of times, but he didn't
answer. At least, not at first.' The magician's nervy eyes
swerved up to the ceiling. 'I heard a voice from up there a
few minutes ago. Ming's voice. I couldn't make out the
words – they sounded like gibberish. His mind's gone,
sorceress. And the whole house is going with him. Did
you catch that whiff of wood mould downstairs? And
you can't escape the stink of rotting food in the kitchens.'

'I didn't miss them. Nor do I care about them. All I
want is for you to go. Now.'

Ming had heard a voice downstairs and now he heard
two voices, but he didn't mind.

The voices were just noises from his stomach. He wondered if one of the stomach noises was going to rise up
into his throat.

He had thought the first voice was Nyak the Master,
but it seemed it was not. Ming didn't mind. He had faith
in the Master. Nyak would come and Nyak would bring
the gift of Silver Brother flesh.

Ming dribbled thick liquid down the oily black of his
beard. He grunted contentedly, and tried to scratch his
belly.

He was happy, for the moment. And he wasn't hungry
any more.

'You've got to go, magus,' Chia insisted.

'But I can't!' he shouted. 'The people killed one of my
order for failing to drive a demon from a mere water
mirror in the Street of the White Crane. They cut off his

111

hands – then they hanged him. And they'll do the same to me unless I bring them proof of my power – the infamous Mirror of Ming the Swine, freed from its curse. I must restore my honour among the San Lung folk!'

'Those who treat men like straw dogs aren't worthy to be served,' she remarked coldly. 'Leave this mansion. Leave San Lung. The Dragon Empire is wide – it contains many provinces where you can resume your trade.'

The rising wind beyond the gold and green walls of the chamber rattled the shutters. The wind moaned with a mournful cadence. The magician angled his head to the mounting bluster.

'I was intending to use the Celestial Breath of the Four Winds when I cast the elmwood sticks in the game of Liu Po,' he confided. 'I believed it would defeat my demon opponent and throw him back into the netherworld . . .'

Chia was about to order the wizard to leave for the last time when a squeaking sound at her back made her spin round. The oak door had been pushed further ajar. Vinaya and Nua stood in the rectangular frame. For an instant Chia's tongue froze. Then she yelled in fury:

'Why did you bring her here, you dolt?'

A low moan from the magician made her glance over her shoulder, and she saw with dismay that the man was staring blankly at the figures in the doorway. She recognised that stare – it was the look of a man whose will was in thrall to another. The wizard's hand lifted to the red silk drape on the mirror.

'Get out!' she roared at the intruders. 'Out!' Lurching forwards she pushed the two out and slammed the door shut. Whirling round she faced the dazed magus. He was raising the silk sheet from the mirror.

'Stop!' Her desperate entreaty met deaf ears. In the blink of an eyelid he threw aside the red drape so that it slithered to the floor behind the mirror.

The massive bronze disc was revealed: cold, impassive, lethal. The Mirror of Ku Pang, Vampire King. Now called the Mirror of Ming. A drop of time lingered like water hesitating at the tip of an icicle.

Then a wind blew from the mirror. The cold breath tingled her skin and stirred her hair. The magus, his wits regained, staggered back from the icy gust. He threw an imploring look at Chia. 'What's happening, sorceress? Whence comes this wind?'

For a fleeting instant the wind ceased. Then it returned – but not from the same quarter. This time it blew *towards* the mirror. It beat against Chia's back and forced the wizard one step to the mirror.

'Hold your ground!' she warned. 'Don't let it drag you in!'

He planted his slippered feet staunchly on the floor and bent into the chill wind. It was as if the mirror was a yawning mouth inhaling all before it. For the second time the wind halted momentarily, then poured once more with redoubled force from the bronze disc. The savage gale threw Chia against the wall, punching the air from her lungs. The magus was flung clear across the room and pressed to the wall just outside the reach of the sorceress.

'The thing's *breathing*!' he screeched above the shrieking gale. Her eyes widened to his words. Breathing . . . They had been thinking of the wind that juddered the shutters. He had mentioned the Celestial Breath of the Four Winds. The Mime Realm always worked through human minds – the endless undercurrents of random thoughts and associations, the unrecognised flow of self-imagery. The magus must have *pictured* himself enrolling the aid of the Celestial Breath. That was how the mirror wind was unleashed – it was conceived from themselves. The wind had no effect on the objects in the chamber: she and the magus were the sole victims of the gale – even their clothes were unruffled.

If she was to save them both she had to steep her mind in the long moment – a technique that would speed the ch'i force within her to such a pitch that the surrounding world would seem to move at a snail's pace.

113

Abruptly the violent exhalation stopped, but before Chia could collect her scrambled thoughts and submerge her mind in the long moment, the mirror began to inhale. She slid into the long moment too late to save the magus: the suction of the huge disc dragged him screaming across the chamber. As she fell deeper into her trance his threshing form appeared to slow in its flight.

Finally, to her ch'i-speeded vision, he seemed to float into the waiting mirror, his slow gestures of panic eerily graceful as his blurred reflection glided to meet him. Man and reflection merged into one another as the shape dissolved into the haunted bronze surface.

Sorrow at the magician's fate was tempered by fear for herself. Leaning at a near horizontal angle into the gale, the edges of her feet digging into the velvet matting, she was being pulled, step by step, to the golden disc.

Chia released her mind from the long moment, for it hadn't altered her experience of the gale. Under the long moment, an ordinary wind would seem to have abated, the air moving more slowly. But this mirror breath fed on her sensations: the wind was for her alone, and it did not abate. By lengthening her experience of time, she was only lengthening her ordeal.

Just two steps from the glowing disc, when the straining sinews were ceasing to respond to her will, the mirrorward roaring wind stopped. In that squeezed second of silence her intellect sprang awake and she cursed herself for emerging into normal awareness; by returning to normal experience of time she had let a precious chance slip by.

In the wake of this revelation came the wind.

It thundered from the haunted metal like an invisible demon and threw her with stunning force to the far wall where she was pinned more than a foot from the floor. The violence of the collision with the stout timbers drove all the breath from her body and all but broke her spine. A crushing vice compressed her rib-cage making it impossible to inhale – she could feel the sharp bones thrusting into her lungs. The blow she received on the back of the head almost knocked her senseless and the eyes in her skull were pushed deep into the sockets. The flesh on her face stretched and quivered as if it were being torn loose.

Spreadeagled on the wall, she struggled to remain conscious. If she could survive this onslaught she could still escape, but precise timing was vital. Soon, she thought, soon it will inhale. A few seconds . . .

She sank into the long moment. Deep into the long moment. After excruciating seconds the gale ceased. Utter silence.

She staggered across the room to the back of the mirror where the silk drape lay in a mass of folds. Her guess had proved correct: it was only during the rush of winds that the long moment was ineffective – the instant of stillness was free from the mirror's influence and could be extended to some ten seconds under the slow time trance. Seizing the red silk sheet she flung it over the face of the mirror and hastily secured it at the back with deftly tied knots. She dropped to her knees, her bones aching, her muscles trembling. The pounding of her heart echoed in her head and her vision swam. But the evil spell was broken.

A long, wavering procession of heart-beats thumped by before she regained her feet and walked unsteadily to the door. Her hands shook as she opened it.

'Vinaya –' she called out, then gasped at the pain in her chest. Leaning on the wall she closed her eyes. In seconds they blinked open to the monk and the girl as they shuffled into the room. Vinaya was shame-faced.

'I'm grieved that I disregarded your orders, Chia. Something urged me to climb the stairs. A compulsion . . .'

She silenced him with a contemptuous gesture. 'I need transportation for the mirror . . .' She paused, refilled her throbbing lungs. 'There must be a few vehicles left in the town.'

He pondered for a moment, then brightened. 'Why yes! I have the ideal solution.'

'Then go and bring your ideal solution to the mansion door.' She inhaled painfully. 'And take Nua with you.'

He looked around. 'Where – where is the magus?'

'Don't ask.'

He bowed and left. Chia scooped up the six casting rods and deposited them in her cowl. She approached the muffled mirror with dragging steps. The great bronze disc had to be removed from its oak stand. Normally, the iron pivots that secured bronze to oak would have snapped in her hands like twigs under the Yogic control that summoned the ch'i force in her body, but in her bludgeoned state she was doubtful of maintaining Yogic mastery of her being. Fortunately the pounding of her heart had subsided or she would not have dreamed of allowing the ch'i breath to surge through her veins because the circulating ch'i energies caused a massive acceleration of the heart-beat. If such an acceleration was imposed on an already palpitating heart the risk of death was very real. She placed her fingers on one of the iron pivots and her stare grew remote and intense.

The blood, urged by the ch'i breath that dwelt dormant in the body-spirit unless awoken by the inner vision, started to rush like a torrent through the labyrinth of veins. An invigorating flood gushed through her body. Invigoration expanded into exhilaration. Heart banged against ribs.

With an effortless twist of the wrist Chia snapped the pivot, moved swiftly to its companion and broke it with a slight effort. The mirror fell backwards and crashed like thunder on the floor. Before the ch'i force dissipated she heaved the mirror up and rolled it like a wheel to the door, pointed it in the direction of the stairs, and gave a mighty shove. The mirror spun and bounced down the steps, smashing several boards in its Jagannath progress before rolling and swaying across the hall to collapse with bone-shaking impact near the door.

As the ch'i force drained away her gaze slid to the

blackness at the head of the upper flight of stairs. The doomed wizard had said that Ming was in the upper storey of the house. Dazed as she was, and anxious to discover the fate of Fu, she couldn't resist the lure of those dark stairs. There was something in the dark of those upper rooms. And it wasn't just Ming.

Her bare feet induced only the faintest of creaks from the pine treads as she scaled the flight to the top floor. Right hand hovering over the hilt of her silver dagger, she stepped onto the landing and moved like a shadow down the hall.

A squat shape in a yellow silk robe was slumped against the jamb of an open door. The dangling ribbon of its beard was sleek with a wetness that dripped onto the bared chest and belly. The greasy mouth slobbered as it chewed. The gold rings on the knife hand glinted as the blade did its work. The sweaty hulk stank like fly-blown meat.

'Pork,' mumbled Ming as he carved another slippery chunk from his belly and popped it into his mouth. The ragged wound in Ming's belly was the size of a fist – the exposed entrails swam in viscous blood and juices.

Chia stared down at Ming with a dispassionate air as the mess of viscera bulged out of the raw hole. She felt no pity. A man like Ming deserved no pity.

Whatever had pushed the merchant down into madness had left the after-scent of fear in the open room. She recognised that ineffable scent. It was the Thzan-tzai odour. It was the aroma of perfect madness, as delicate as the smell of Ming's carcass was rank.

Some power Chia didn't fully understand had been the source of that lingering aroma. It was Thzan-tzai power, but that power had a thousand after-scents haunting the world. This scent perplexed her – it reminded her of Nyak, but was not quite the same as the necromancer's distinctive odour.

Swaying with the giddiness which was the price of

117

evoking the ch'i force, Chia drew away from the open door. With a last glance at the mindless bulk which dined on its own meat, the sorceress wove unsteadily down the hall and the narrow stairs.

Chia peered with swimming vision at the mirror-cracked boards of the flight leading to the ground floor and edged groggily down the ruined stairs as dizziness eddied her thoughts. With faltering paces she advanced to the wide portal. She crumpled into a dead faint as she reached its threshold

Roused from blissful oblivion by a rattling, jangling jumble of sounds Chia rose wearily and leaned on the doorpost. A tired smile gradually widened her mouth. If Vinaya had acted foolishly before, he had made amends. A sturdy, imposing chariot drawn by two stately Fergana horses clattered to a halt in front of the portico as Vinaya pulled on the reins. He leapt from the chariot and approached her with a light step, leading Nua by the hand. The stout, iron-banded wheels rolled back and forth as the horses stomped and steamed. The monk gave an imitation of a bow.

'A princely chariot drawn by the noble blood-sweating horses of Fergana,' he announced. 'I remembered that the T'aoist magic-monger who – er – disappeared upstairs shared a comrade in sorcery. You know, that hanged wizard we saw. Those two had the incredible luck to be given the chariot as a gift from some local lord for a pretentious display of miracle-working. Their most prized possession. They had to have left the chariot and team somewhere safe and near. I found them in the North Gate stables. The Buddha beams good fortune from his holy visage, no?'

'Not for the two magicians,' she murmured, finding his levity distasteful. 'Come, help me hoist this damned mirror onto the chariot deck.'

'Hm . . . you're going to need help – it's as tall as a

man,' he observed. 'But how did you get it off the stand and down the stairs?'

Still repelled by his callousness, she declined to answer.

After the huge mirror had been tilted and fastened inside the chariot with a network of ropes scavenged from Ming's outhouses, Chia squeezed her supple shape into the only available corner, beside Nua. Vinaya hunched over the front rail with a firm grip on the reins, ready for Chia's signal.

'Tell me, Saffron Robe,' she asked intently. 'Why did you bring the girl up to Ming's chamber?'

He frowned. 'It's difficult to say – it was a sudden impulse – I thought you might require assistance. It was just an idea I had . . .' He paused as if struck by a thought. 'But perhaps the idea didn't come from me – perhaps *she* put it into my mind. It was at her the magician was staring when he went into a trance.' The monk was glaring at Nua. Chia conceded the point by a gesture of the hand.

'Where are we heading, sorceress?' asked Vinaya.

'Is the Black Serpent Gate open?'

'All the gates are open – I think the townsfolk believe that the evil spirits will fly out the gates.'

'Then we head for Black Serpent Gate – the north road. We're going to Spirit Hill.'

The unlikely Buddhist laughed as if in anticipation of adventure and shook the reins. The horses responded eagerly, galloping across the courtyard with the bumping chariot swerving in their wake.

As they thundered through Black Serpent Gate and onto the north road, Chia attempted to relax and breathe in the flow of prana. She tried to withdraw her mind from the discomfort of her position in the jouncing, lurching chariot. The last voice she heard before sinking into restorative meditation was Vinaya's.

'To the Death Mound!' he roared to the whistling wind. 'To the destruction of evil!'

'Half-wit,' she muttered to herself.

10

ROLLING WHEELS,
SPINNING DREAMS

Beneath the Forest of the Ancestors, far underground, the dark held its silence in the cavernous vault.

From the roof of the vault a girl named Yi hung from hooks in her eyes and ears.

The girl had committed a crime:

She had once been a friend of Chia.

Yi's body, naked to the dark and clothed by the dark, dangled from the hooks and the rusty chains.

On the dank walls of the vault, the wavering flames of torches shuddered with a ruddy glow.

Crimson drops fell from the suspended girl and settled on a long, narrow, naked figure inside an open stone sarcophagus.

Apart from the intermittent splutter of a torch, nothing disturbed the deep silence in the vault.

There was no word spoken. There was hardly a breath.

A frail phantom, subtle and invisible, ascended from the lean figure in the stone sarcophagus. It was a tenuous exhalation of the spirit.

The rising exhalation was the heart of the silence and the dark.

And the heart of the vault was the Deep Self.

It was the essence of stillness.

As the chariot thundered north from San Lung Town Chia glared moodily at the receding Black Serpent Gate.

She knew that she had escaped the dying time by the breadth of an eyelid when she fell into a faint at the door of Ming's mansion. It must have been some deep inner resolve that saved her from plunging from sleep into death while she lay unconscious for those few minutes. If she were not to go mad or drop into the death sleep she had to wander for a while in waking sleep.

Gradually, she drifted into the meditation that led to the waking dreams.

A wild jolt of the chariot shook her from meditation and she nearly fell from the deck. With a mild oath she heaved herself back to her former position.

'No need to worry,' the monk called down, his robe a yellow agitation in the wind. 'The man we ran over was already dead.'

'How do you know?' yawned Chia.

'No head.'

She studied the shaven-pated charioteer for a space, then shrugged and let herself slide into the waking sleep.

As intermittent moon-flashes between scudding black clouds, such were her dreams. Then the clouds cleared and the lucent light of a dream gleamed steadily . . .

A red and black sign on the lintel of an open door: 'House of the Twilight Owl' . . .

Then she stood in a dark hall and the door was closed behind her . . .

A massive eight-spoked wheel rumbled down an endless corridor . . .

A door in her dream swung on hushed hinges, and she stood in a room ablaze with candles. She looked into the black jade bowl of a water mirror – blood swirled outwards in the dark water. The water mirror tipped over and the blooded water streamed on the table and trickled over the floor to the far wall. On the wall hung a large disc swathed in black velvet. Blood started to dribble from beneath the hidden mirror. A flicker of motion on a nearby table attracted her attention: a weird T'aoist figurine was rising into the air – a winged sylph with taloned hands and a broad, misshapen head. The wooden figurine twitched and flexed as it flew to the mirror. It was going to tear the protecting fabric loose . . .

But her swift hand locked round the sylph and it struggled frantically in her fist. Then the figure began to merge with her clutching hand; wood grew into skin and bone, skin and bone grew into wood, and the wooden hand groped of its own volition at the lush drape. Chia fought to gain control of the claw at the end of her arm, but to no avail.

'It's only my hand – only my hand.' The voice was her own, but it seemed to heave from her stomach (for a flying moment her eyes flickered to the narrow vision of the pitching chariot and she was aware that she was dreaming, then wakefulness fled). She stared at the jerking wooden claw and realised it to be an illusion. .Where the claw twitched and tore at the velvet she started to imagine, to the last detail of knuckle and vein, her long-fingered hand. The texture of skin replaced the grained wood, the firm shape of her hand succeeded the twisted form. And with the image of her hand came the freedom of its command.

A wheel thundering down a long corridor flanked by bronze Buddhas and Bodhisattvas . . .

A silver mask peering through a window . . .

The neglected upper room of the house, dusky and fearful. Something in the room. A macabre vision of bloated owl-eyes peeped at her from a far corner. A ghost owl, enormous and insubstantial. It whisper-winged about the room and wove a nest of black spells. The door slammed shut. Entrapment and burial. A brush of broad feathers stifled her scream. She felt the probing scrutiny of the evil owl spirit; hostile, interrogative. Questions thrummed from the bird presence.

'Who? Who?' The owl eyes were baleful yellow

123

lanterns. 'Who? Who? Who?' The yellow-moon owl eyes enlarged to fill the room and the dream. 'Who?' the owl hooted.

Chia recoiled from the onrush of the lambent eyes and toppled back into the waking world of the shuddering chariot where a sudden jolt threw her against Nua. The road behind raced out of view round the corner of a jagged crag. She caught a fleeting glimpse of a dark mass crouched crookedly across a deep wheel rut, then the sight was obliterated by a fang of rock. Chia gave a light tug at the hem of Vinaya's robe.

'What did you run over?' she asked.

'A wolf,' bellowed Vinaya.

'It looked rather large for a wolf.'

'It was a large wolf.'

She dismissed the incident and began to ponder the dream, for it had relieved some of the darkness from her maladied memory. A long-forgotten discussion with Lao Tzu was resurrected: 'The man who reflects upon himself will lose himself. The man who forsakes reflection will find the T'ao.'

Chia compressed her lips. If she were free of self-reflection the spell of the Death Whisperers would be ineffectual. But who could honestly lay claim to such freedom? Lao Tzu, for all his later reputation, had not achieved it. Still – to have travelled but one li on the road to freedom was to be one li further from bondage.

What was it that Chuang Tzu had written? 'The heart of the sage is quiet, it is a mirror of Heaven and Earth, a mirror of all things.' Yes – freedom from self-worship signified freedom from the mirror self. Ah – the corners of her mouth assumed a wry set – that revived the old dilemma: how could she, by an act of will, cease from reflecting upon herself?

She had presented the problem to Wei three months past: 'Wei, try *not* to think of – let's say, a lotus. See if you can avoid thinking of a lotus for as long as ten breaths. Just try.' Wei had passed a dubious look, but agreed to what she obviously regarded as an absurd experiment. After a number of attempts she was forced to admit failure. It was impossible to fight consciously against thinking of the suggested object, for the very effort ensured the retention of the object in the mind.

It was from this axiom that the Ching Masters derived much of their method: whether they were itinerant showmen or court sorcerers the technique was identical – authoritative command. In folklore, such men were supposed to possess 'ching' – a power that resided in hands, eyes and mouth. Often a Ching Master would breathe upon his subject before inducing the characteristic trance, giving rise to the superstition that it was the ching breath which drove out one of the hun souls from anyone who became the target of the Ching Master's 'sorcery'. But the truth was that everything depended on belief in the magus. Where the shallowest residue of belief in the Ching Master existed, it could be used against the believer to force him into a trance. The technique itself was simple – command a man who has full belief in you to perform a certain act and he will perform it, even if he has no surface recollection of the command.

In many cases the belief in the magus was slight (few totally disbelieved) and it was in such cases that the mettle of the Ching Master was tested: less than one in a hundred practitioners was able to overcome determined resistance to the supposed hun soul expulsion; those who could accomplish this feat adopted the title of T'ai Ching, and were feared or revered according to the disposition of the Master. Where a man offered stubborn resistance to the command of a T'ai Ching, his strength was turned back on himself for he was willing *not* to will as the magus bade him. To oppose the dictate of a T'ai Ching Master was to play a game according to his rules, rules which ensured his victory: try not to think of a lotus.

So, how do you cease reflecting upon yourself?

Chia interrupted her trail of thought to study the girl at her side, crouched in drowsy silence. At another time she might have experienced a twinge of desire for the soft bodily curves and the rounded prettiness of the face crowned by an intricate chignon, but her present feelings were far from sensual. The face was an enigma that reminded her of whispers, reflections, presences in streams. She glanced warily at the silk-draped disc of Ming's mirror.

The Mime Realm. Plucking the notion of the wind from their minds it had turned it on herself and the wizard. Although she should have realised at the time that the mirror wind was an illusion it was unlikely that the knowledge would have been of much assistance – if she had rejected its reality the *idea* of it would have remained in the manner of the suggested notion in the minds of obstinate T'ai Ching victims. Either way it won.

But there was a third way.

The Mimic hearkened to the booming of a thousand heart-beats.

The heart-beats of men, women, children, animals and birds in the night.

He was the Hearing.

The shapes of the ten million sounds of the world formed clear images in his otherwise blurred vision. The ears fed the eyes.

And the lips formed the vision of the humans around him. Their world was moulded by his words. They saw in him a hundred people. They saw through him a thousand sights.

He was the Trickster, the Clown.

The Mimic.

He danced in his skull and drank in the sounds and the sights.

He sang from his mouth and the fools saw new shapes,

heard new sounds. And soon the Green-Eyes, too, would see the shapes and hear the sounds.

But who are you, Green-Eyes? Who?

Then the Mimic forgot Chia and gathered the sound.

He laughed with the fullness of sound.

The Mimic capered and dispensed his visions.

He strangled a child and nobody saw.

Chia slowly rubbed her chin. Yes – there was a third way. Instead of agreement or opposition to the suggested image there was the alternative of a different image. She could will against, or with, or *otherwise*.

A T'ai Ching adept, she had accustomed her mind to concentrate on the Egyptian images of the Sun Disc of Aten – the shimmering yellow desert – the Nile; and often she would grasp the silver ankh and imagine its glistening shape suspended among crystal stars. It had saved her life more than once when she had been attacked by T'ai Ching Masters who had bound themselves to the cult of the Thzan-tzai.

But there was one in the Han Empire whom she could not challenge: Nyak. The necromancer was the greatest of the T'ai Ching Masters. He could cast his thoughts into the heads of his prey without the intermediary of eyes or mouth. He could manipulate or kill over vast distances. Against Nyak, mystical adepts could only resort to desperate defence and flight from the Dragon Empire. Yet, for a reason she had never fully comprehended, Nyak was unable to strike her by the casting of thoughts. There must be . . .

A lurch of the chariot tipped her against the rim of the slanting mirror, and her fingers brushed the wrinkled silk. The mirrors. And the dream. She berated herself for allowing her attention to wander from the dream House of the Twilight Owl – her mind strayed like a vagrant caravan on the Moving Sands.

'Attend to the dream, rambler,' she muttered.

Dream symbols: House of the Twilight Owl . . . what did it signify? The name had an irritatingly familiar ring. Had she visited such a place at some forgotten date? The draped mirror in the dream room – Ming's mirror? But it had oozed blood – symbol of her guilt? The water mirror also had carried blood, spiralling outwards. Blood curling in a water mirror had preceded blood dripping from the metal mirror . . . The inconstant memory of innocent blood in the stream or the water mirror in the village near the Great Wall . . . Chia the Death-bringer . . .

She squared her shoulders and contemplated other aspects of the dream; to drink too deep a draught of guilt was poison.

The figurine that merged with her hand to become a wooden claw . . . in her musings on T'aoist philosophy and the art of the T'ai Ching Masters she had already uncovered the meaning of that. Imagination preceded action. As soon as she beheld the true hand, freedom of action was regained. While she saw an alien claw her hand behaved as an alien claw . . .

'River ahead,' announced Vinaya.

'Is there a bridge?' she asked, struggling to her feet in the pitching vehicle.

'Yes – humped and wooden. And a steep road beyond up to the Tower of the Autumn Willow.'

Chia surveyed the squat bridge and the argent skin of the river. Beyond, a rising ridge of rock spined the contours of round-shouldered slopes ascending to a swollen summit. Foliage was sparse, the trees were stunted spokes. Were the rattle of the wheels and the thud of the hooves growing quieter? It was as if silence lay in thick folds about the bridge. She summoned the Sun Disc, the Nile, the desert.

'Drive like a wind spirit, Indian brother,' she ordered grimly. 'Clear the water in the space of a breath.'

Sun . . . Nile . . . desert . . .

The monk shook the reins and roared the horses on-ward. A wild lurch threw them back as they thundered onto the steeply rising boards, almost dislodging the mirror from Chia's grasp. Then they were hurled for-wards as the bouncing wheels rushed down the declivity to the far bank. The sorceress allowed a few moments to pass before she withdrew from her Egyptian meditations.

'Congratulations, charioteer,' she complimented sarcastically. 'We flew so fast the mirror nearly fell in the river.'

'Holding the mirror in its harness was your business, racing over the hunchback bridge was mine,' he retorted. 'In the space of a breath, you said. And in the space of a breath I did it.' He sounded piqued.

'I'm breathless with admiration.' Her sarcasm drew a scowl from the monk.

The sorceress remained standing at Vinaya's side as the chariot mounted the slopes of the hill. The pace became slower and the path more winding as the angle of ascent increased. The weary moon was sinking behind the Forest of the Ancestors. Chia's green eyes were baleful and feline as they filled with the deep past.

'I remember this hill.' Her tone was like snakeskin. 'The Hill of the Silver Sorcerer. Many things happened here, long ago . . . and in the Tower of the Hound of Heaven — what you call the Tower of the Autumn Willow.'

The monk spared an apparently uninterested glance. 'Oh? Do you know more?'

Absently, she shook her head.

'And how do you come to know what little you know?'

'You talk too much. You are a wearisome distraction to me, Vinaya.'

He pulled a face and chuckled. The austere slopes fell gradually behind them as he guided the Fergana team up the uneven trail.

'The tower,' Vinaya indicated with a jerk of the head. She looked up. The tower. Angular and ruinous, a Chou Dynasty relic; its power dormant, yet still overlording its tiny kingdom – the Hill of the Silver Sorcerer. Past the tower the land dipped sharply to Shen Lung Gorge just three li south of Spirit Hill. There was little time left to prepare.

Hastily she considered the remainder of the dream. The owl. It was a bird of ill omen in the folklore of the Dragon Empire, a forewarning of death. 'When an owl enters the house, the master is about to leave' . . . thus ran the oracle. But the dream owl meant more, she felt sure. What was the significance? Twilight Owl – the house itself had been named after it. Twilight . . . Owl . . .

She exhaled in exasperation. Twilight Owl meant nothing to her, except – had it been a name? The name of a village? Her own name, in a past age?

Chia frowned. The explication of dreams was a notoriously fallible undertaking – a dream could be made to mean anything one wished. The owl had asked 'Who? Who?' . . . and she was unable to shake off the idea that the question had been addressed to *her*. 'Who are *you*?' Who? Huge yellow owl eyes, deepening to green.

She gave a low moan. She was so tired – tired from the onset of the malady, from the summoning of Nua, from the bludgeoning of the mirror wind in Ming's chamber.

To hell with dreams.

The taste of pork on the palate and the feel of pork in the stomach was good, very good. It made Ming glow with satisfaction.

He was feeling very happy with the world, the world of flesh. He hadn't minded when that cat-woman with shining green eyes had crept up on him like a shadow and peered at him in the dark.

He didn't mind at all, about anything.

The Master would come and touch his flesh and his flesh would become ageless and deathless.

Will I be red, black, green or white? wondered Ming.

There was a noise in the body of the house. The booming sound of steps that echoed in Ming's acute hearing. They scaled the lower stairs and reverberated on the landing.

Ming grinned happily and looked down at the pink expanse of the world's belly. Who would have thought that a little knife could have excavated such a deep crater in the belly of the world? And the crater seemed to be erupting . . .

The footfalls resounded on the boards of the upper flight of stairs. Was it the Master? Had Nyak come at last with the reward of immortality?

A tall figure loomed at the end of the hall. It approached with the soft swish of a long grey mantle. Its silver mask was a vague blur in the murkiness.

Silver Brother . . . It's a Silver Brother . . . But is he red, black, green or white?

The Silver Brother stretched out his silver-gauntleted hand. A whisper flowed from the tiny mouth-hole of the mask. A whisper so quiet it was deafening.

'Awake.'

The world of flesh contracted with bewildering speed at the sound of that whisper. Ming's abnormal hearing diminished. Dreams dissipated. There was a sudden pounding in his head and a tearing in his guts.

For the first time in weeks, Ming remembered who he was and where he was. He was the most cunning merchant and smuggler in San Lung prefecture and he was sitting in the upper storey of the most imposing mansion in San Lung Town. And – his body . . .

His stomach . . .

His horrified gaze slid down to the ragged hole where his belly had once been and the sloppy mass of entrails that hung in abundance from the bulging gap. The agony

131

that seared through his quivering frame brought forth a vomit of half-chewed skin and tissue.

'*No pain.*' The whisper bounded and rebounded in his skull and there was . . . No pain . . .

There was horror, but there was no pain.

Ming spat out the remainder of sour meat from his mouth and nodded his thanks to the Silver Brother.

The word that heals . . . Thank you, Silver Brother . . .

'Where's the Master? he managed to choke out. 'And the reward?'

'The Master has come to you but you never knew it,' grated the harsh, guttural tone of the Silver Brother.

'And immortality?' gasped Ming, feeling the heat of life slithering out of his stomach. 'My flesh made Silver Brethren flesh . . . the promise . . .'

'The Master always keeps his promises,' replied the Silver Brother as he pulled the gauntlet of silver mail from his right hand.

The Brother reached down a hand that was black as the blackest spider. The long, sharp nails were curved like claws. The hand wriggled into the gaping wound of Ming's stomach, squeezing and fondling the viscera.

Ah, thought Ming, the Brother is making my flesh one with his. I will walk with the Silver Brethren from generation to generation and my gauntleted hands will hold the death of the black plague and I will whisper the words of command and death will herald my coming and death will lie in my wake . . .

'Immortal,' he sighed as he felt the black fullness spreading through his stomach and chest.

The Silver Brother's hoarse voice dispelled Ming's euphoria. 'The Master promised immortality. Only the dead are immortal.'

'Wh-what . . .?' croaked the merchant as he witnessed the darkening of his belly and guts.

'And the flesh of a Silver Brother spreads through your flesh, as was the promise,' ground on the remorseless voice.

'What's happening?' yelped Ming from his swelling throat.

'Immortality. Death. The black plague.'

The black hand slipped from the blackening stomach and the Silver Brother glided silently down the hall. 'Pain,' he whispered in the word of command.

Ming tried to shout after the tall Brother but black fluids flooded his throat and spurted from his mouth. And pain ravaged his ripped, infected shape.

The wound tore wider as his torso swelled like a black wineskin pumped too full with wine. As his stomach split, it was black wine that gushed out.

Drowning in its own liquids, Ming's bloated body threshed violently as it filled up like the lungs of a man under the waves. Ming's bulk bulged to twice its normal size.

Black liquid spurted from his nostrils and ears, and his protruding eyes wept black tears.

It ended when his brain bathed in a black pool.

11

TOWER OF THE WOLF

The buckled path veered around a sandstone face to the barren dome of the hill. Tangled clumps of tall grass. A brisk whoop of a wind rushing from the south. Shushing of wind in ragged grass.

A four-storeyed derelict with gabled eaves, faint smears of faded paint on warped willow timbers, a broken shutter that clapped in the wind, fragments like autumn leaves around the trunk of a tree.

'Tower of the Autumn Willow,' the monk murmured thoughtfully.

'Tower of the Hound of Heaven,' Chia stated, scanning the creaking edifice. 'Tower of the Wolf.'

Vinaya gave a dismissive snort to show that names were of no consequence. Normally she would have agreed with him. In a past dynasty, Nyak had made this tower his home for a time and given one of his titles to the hill – Silver Sorcerer. Surveying the northern terrain she spotted an ominous bulge on Spirit Hill some five li distant. The Death Mound.

Then a motion nearby, at the mouth of the tower, caught her gaze.

Shapes were emerging. Four shapes. Shapes of men. Men swathed in long grey cloaks. Men wearing silver masks. The foremost raised a mailed hand, as if in salutation.

'Shang Ti's blood!' she shouted in horror. She took the reins from Vinaya with a frantic grab, shook them frenziedly, yelled, 'North! North! Go!'

The horses responded like beasts racing from a forest fire, hooves flashing, manes streaming, nostrils flaring, heads dipping and rising. Headlong down the bumpy slope the chariot bounded and pitched, throwing its passengers from side to side and shifting the precarious mirror in its intricate network of ropes.

'Shen Lung Gorge! Watch out for the gorge! You'll have us in the river!' The monk's voice was a cachinnation in the din of the chariot and the bellow of the wind; his leaning stance and alert face were animated.

Darting a glance at her companion she gradually eased the pace until the Fergana team cantered down the lower reaches of the gorge with heaving flanks in a cloud of steam. She restored the reins to the monk as the chariot wheeled onto the undulating riverside path and steadied herself on the handrail, her body rigid.

'Trying to solve your problems the quick way?' Vinaya inquired. His eyebrows were aloof and there was a curious twist to his mouth.

'What?'

He waved a gaunt hand. 'Let it go.'

The mind of the sorceress was rabid, thought chasing thought, frantic hounds. The slaves of the necromancer had been waiting for her – the mailed hand had been raised in grim greeting. Nyak knew of the mirror hauntings. Perhaps he had planned them. Most certainly he was directing events from somewhere outside the margins of San Lung. Most likely he was instated to the north, for the haunting had spread south with the flow of the rivers and only a thin region to the north of Spirit Hill would be infected by the breath of the Whisperers. If only the Celestial Ones had destroyed Nyak instead of merely barring him from places and relics tainted by the Thzan-tzai. If only . . .

Acknowledging ruefully that she was indulging in vain wishing she mocked her regrets and bared her teeth in a feral smile. What was she? A child? Be grateful to the

Celestial Ones that the necromancer was forbidden to tread the slopes of Spirit Hill, otherwise she could never hope to reach her goal. But she had to contend with his many slaves wielding their single weapon – disease.

Chia bit her lip and her gaze slid up to the looming crest of the burial mound on Spirit Hill. Her memory sprang at the words to the abbot in the Buddha Hall: 'Nagarjuna . . . have you ever had the feeling that something is waiting for you? Something you fear to confront yet cannot avoid?'

Dragging her eyes from the bulging summit of Spirit Hill she studied the northwesterly bend of Shen Lung Gorge with its grey stone bridge to the northern bank. The bridge was less than a li ahead.

So gripped with foreboding was she that Vinaya's sharp tone made her jump like a startled hare. 'Listen!' Listen, Green-Eyed Enchantress!'

'Listen? To what?' she snapped.

'Ordinary nocturnal noises.'

Her glare would have quelled the Yellow Emperor. 'Don't play children's games with me, Saffron Robe . . .' Then her eyes widened in comprehension . . .

There was no silence, no smothering silence. They were the width of three chariots from the reed-ranked border of the river, but there was no silence. On impulse, she glanced at Nua who sat hugging her knees, staring into vacancy.

'No silence,' she pondered. 'Yet it should be seeping like mist from the river. Are the currents no longer haunted? Spirit Hill is so near – the area ought to be steeped in illusion . . .'

'Plagues move on,' her companion observed. 'It has evidently travelled south – Shen Lung Gorge is now free of its infection. When you come to think of it, it's not really so strange.'

'On the contrary, it's exceedingly strange,' she contended. 'While the Spirit Mirror is active its environs

136

should remain poisoned by its breath. I expected the air to be thick with the aura of the Death Whisperers, but this region is apparently untainted. Under the shadow of the Death Mound, yet unaffected by the Thzan-tzai legacy. It's a perplexing riddle.'

He gave a casual lift of the shoulders. 'The obvious inference is that the fabled mirror is now inactive, temporarily or permanently. Perhaps it's having a respite from vomiting contagion.'

Chia ignored the other's insouciance. 'If it has become inert, it will stay inert. The wonder is that it was ever animated – it was buried in a complex prison of masonry, shackled in spells, enmeshed in its own infinite reflections. How could it breathe its spirit from the mouth of the mound? Some other power was at work.'

'What about the necromancer? Couldn't he have set this Spirit Mirror free?'

She frowned pensively. 'I'm the only one who can do that, as far as I know.' She caught Vinaya's dubious expression. 'Naturally, you assume the culprit to be Nyak but . . .'

'It seems disrespectful to apply the word 'culprit' to a mighty sorcerer,' he butted in.

'. . . it couldn't have been Nyak himself,' she went on, brushing aside the interruption. 'The Spirit Mirror is Thzan-tzai. The slopes of Spirit Hill are tainted by the lingering scent of the Thzan-tzai. Nyak couldn't get within two li of Spirit Hill Mound without his flesh rotting from his bones.'

'But why?'

'I told you before,' she sighed. 'Thzan-tzai relics or the scent of their memory are death to his flesh. Without that limitation he would be invincible. He can only deal indirectly with Thzan-tzai relics, scents, hauntings.'

The monk was mystified. 'Why is it that Thzan-tzai relics and scents are death-poison to a being who is part Thzan-tzai himself from his father – what was his name – Glak-i-kakthz?'

137

She shrugged. 'No one knows. I wish I could tell you.'

'So do I,' he said with feeling.

'It hardly seems credible that the Mirror has spread its dream through San Lung. But it has, it seems.' Chia's muttering voice was barely above her breath. 'How? The Yin-Yang rods have been cast, but I can't discern the pattern.'

Vinaya shrugged. 'I'm sure there's a simple explanation. There must be.'

Chia smiled grimly. Oh no, not simple, my clever young monk. Not with Nyak involved somehow, somewhere. It's complex. Nyak is the player of complex games. The Game Master. And winning isn't enough – he must make his opponent appear foolish. He's often made Chia the Death-bringer into Chia the Fool.'

'By the way, sorceress, I appreciate you allowing me to string along. It's an honour to be permitted a rôle in this great adventure.' The monk beamed in gratitude.

'You should curse me for including you,' Chia said under her breath. 'It's no honour.'

Yi hung from the ceiling of the underground vault by iron hooks in her eye-sockets and iron hooks thrust into her ear-cavities. From time to time, the chains from the hooks to the ceiling stirred and creaked their ancient links.

She should have been dead, but she lived.

An unwholesome power shook the dark air and fluttered the fire-ribbons of the torches set in the walls of the vault. A shadow power preserved life in the mutilated girl and enticed small tears of blood down her waxen cheeks. Now and again, a teardrop of blood would drip onto the supine figure below the dangling girl.

The long figure lying in the open stone sarcophagus never moved, barely breathed. A few of the descending blood drops smeared the silver mask that covered the face and stained the lengthy grey hair that sprouted from the crown of the mask and draped half the body.

From the lean shape in the open stone sarcophagus a faint exhalation rose to the sacrifice above, giving a wispy breath of unnatural life to the hook-hung girl.

From the suspended victim descended a flow of vitality to the masked figure in its drape of dead hair. It absorbed the vitality without the flex of an arm or the twitch of a finger — it was the dwindled spirit of the figure that drank the spirit of the sacrifice, the spirit of the blood.

In the vault, the air itself shivered at the violation.

All flesh is pain.

The Sight was flesh.

The Sight was pain.

In the pain of the flesh the strength of the Sight was tested, its sharp resolve honed.

The Sight was absolute clarity. It was the clarity of exquisite pain in the movement of bone-joints, the flexing of muscles, the stretching of tendons, the pumping of blood.

The Sight was thought made flesh.

It was subtle reasoning, it was delicate judgement, it was precise assessment.

The Sight dwelt mostly in the folds of the brain where it reasoned, judged, assessed, but the pain of the Body was one with the brain and the words of command from above were answered by calls of pain from below.

But the Sight was firm purpose. It never faltered.

The way was prepared. The pattern was set.

Chia would be led into the centre of the maze — and left there forever.

It was not that the Sight hated Chia. The Sight hated no one.

The Sight simply followed what logic dictated.

The Sight was always rational, in its pain.

It was always logical when it killed or tortured. It felt no pleasure in such activities. Nor did it feel regret.

And the Sight feared nothing.

It did not even fear the perfect madness and a mirror that is a spirit and a spirit that is a mirror. It fostered and fed the perfect madness of the Spirit Mirror with its own orchestration of mimicry.

The Sight always knew the path through the maze.

The Sight had constructed the maze.

The Sight feared nothing.

Except, perhaps, for the Hearing. It feared the Hearing, a little.

Chia eyed the gorge distrustfully as the chariot neared the stone bridge. Vinaya startled her by suddenly shouting and pointing to a clump of trees and bushes on the far side of the bridge. She peered at the trees – had there been a glint, a motion, in the dense shadow of the foliage?

A weak ray of moonlight stroked the rim of the valley and glanced off the leafy canopy. Three sparks of silver flashed from the dark grove.

'Silver Brethren!' she cried in dismay. 'Nyak's slaves are waiting in ambush on the north bank!'

Her mind raced as Vinaya brought the Fergana team to a halt: the river was not haunted beyond this point . . . the foot of Spirit Hill lay two li from the northern bank . . . Nyak could walk anywhere not tainted by the Thzan-tzai legacy. She clenched her right hand as the left fingered the silver ankh. Now that Shen Lung Gorge was free of the Death Whisperers it was possible for the necromancer to exist in it. He was free to stand with his slaves on the far side of the river. Nyak might be waiting in the thick covert, waiting to thwart her mission at the last spot at which he was able – once over the northern crest of the gorge she would arrive at the base of Spirit Hill outside his reach. Of course, he might not be with his masked band under the trees, but should she take the risk? She was unprepared . . .

'Well, sorceress?' Vinaya was evidently mystified by her alarm, doubtless wondering why a fabled Champion of Light was daunted by the prospect of a few diseased slaves.

'Turn back,' she ordered. 'Head southeast down the valley.'

'Turn back?' he echoed disbelievingly. 'But we're so close −'

'Turn back,' she repeated.

With a brief shrug and a long sigh he pulled the horses round in a wide curve.

'Hurry,' she urged. 'There are foes on the southern bank as well as the northern.'

'And at our feet, too,' the monk added.

She looked at the silent Nua in response to the remark. The girl seemed to be asleep. Yes, she thought, perhaps her real foe was within the stretch of a hand.

At Vinaya's signal the horses surged forwards and Chia bundled the problem of the girl to the back of her mind as she apprehensively surveyed the rugged rises tilting up to the blurred smudge of a column in the sky. The Tower of the Hound of Heaven. In an age long past Nyak had installed himself as close as he dared to Spirit Hill. Tower of the Wolf. Dreadful rites had once been enacted within its creaking walls. Chia craned her neck as they passed under the edifice − no evidence of cloaked shapes where stone crest met starlit sky.

Her gaze descended the slopes. Figures. Moving figures.

Vinaya saw them in the same instant. His low note of warning mingled with her cold hiss of recognition. She discerned eight silver-masked shapes swooping down the lower slopes just ahead of the path of the chariot.

'Don't be concerned, Green-Eyes,' the monk said. 'The dust of our wheels will have settled long before their feet touch the path.'

She managed a smile. 'That's a pity. Otherwise we might have been able to run over a couple of them. After all, you went over two innocent bodies on the way here.'

A strange look skimmed her companion's face, but he said nothing. The foremost slave was high above the path as the chariot rushed beneath the descending figures and

141

raced round the southwestern bend of the gorge. Soon the hunters were lost to sight. Gradually the valley opened out as it began to veer eastward, and as the valley broadened the river became wider and quieter. Chia gave the horses a swift look of appraisal. The team was tiring. She glanced ahead at a lofty spur that swelled from the valley wall and almost met the river bank. Her keen vision spotted furrows and angles near its upper surface, betraying the existence of a cave. But before seeking cover she had to put her pursuers off the scent, and the river at this point was ideal for the purpose.

The river — suddenly she was aware of silence, deep silence.

Vinaya stiffened. 'The silent cloud,' he growled. 'It hangs over the waters.'

She nodded. 'This must be the northern limit of the haunted region, its power will be weak here. Don't worry — that which works against us on our right hand may work for us on the left. Give me the reins.'

With discernible reluctance the monk handed over the reins. Reluctance changed to dismay when he saw Chia swing the Fergana team into the shallows, dashing up sheets of spray. He shook Chia's arm in protestation. 'Are you trying to deliver us into the Mime Realm?' he yelled, his words all but swallowed in the engulfing silence.

A soundless breath blew into their ears.

The foaming turmoil about the horses' legs was a boiling cosmos in the silent, limitless deeps. The terror-stricken whinnying of the Fergana horses was like a remote echo from an underwater cavern.

Chia felt as though she were suspended in a universe of grey, silent water.

A vast spiral of blood streamed through the watery cosmos.

She grappled to regain her vision of the valley. Momentarily, her sight cleared and she saw that they were nearing the great spur of rock and that the chariot still followed the southern shallows. Leaning to the right she urged the team out of the water and onto the comparative safety of a shelf of stone. Using all her strength and skill to restrain the frightened horses she coaxed them up a natural trail to a serrated ledge jutting below the jagged crest.

Her earlier guess had proved accurate – the tangled mass of damp vines draping the near face of the ledge masked a cave mouth. A trickle of water coiled from the cave and spattered over the rocky lip.

Vinaya eyed the runnel with distaste, obviously still suffering from his ordeal in the river.

'Be at peace, Saffron Robe,' Chia reassured. 'There's no danger of this water being tainted. It comes from the earth – it hasn't mixed with the flow from Spirit Hill.'

Dismounting the chariot, she led the stomping horses by their jingling harness into the dark cave. 'I'm sorry about the dash through the river,' she called over her shoulder. 'It was necessary to shake off pursuit.'

The monk grunted in disagreement. 'You won't fool our masked hunters with that old ruse, Black Dragon. They'll soon discover our trail.'

'Unlikely. They'll assume we crossed the river to reach Spirit Hill and became caught in the Mime Realm. I doubt that they will realise how weak it is at this limit of its influence. If they suspect we reached the further bank they'll waste time scouring in shingle and stone paths. Besides, this cave is well hidden and the route to it mostly over rock – it will be difficult to trace us. In addition, the Silver Brethren are weaker during the daylight hours – the sun has an enervating effect on them. As the Death Whisperers wax with the growing light, so the Silver Brethren wane.'

The murky interior of the cave was damp, but sufficiently spacious to allow the chariot and its team to move unhampered. Chia unhitched the horses and they drank gratefully from the thin rivulet, misting the chamber with steam from their throbbing flanks. Chia joined them, splashing her face and sipping handfuls of water while Vinaya fastidiously sauntered upstream to quench his thirst.

Nua, looking like a soft doll clad in blue silk, remained seated in the chariot as if asleep.

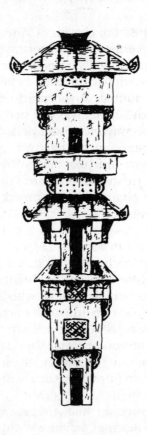

12

SHEN LUNG CAVE

The sorceress parted the curtain of vines and stared out into the night. Overtopping the northwestern crown of the valley was the bruised summit of Spirit Hill, roughly six li distant as the white crane flies. Below – the curve of Shen River, unhaunted to the north, haunted to the south. Surprisingly, there was no sign of the masked followers of the necromancer. Vinaya strolled to the cave mouth and attempted to ply her with questions of the Spirit Mirror, Nyak and the Silver Brethren, but she waved him aside. He showed chagrin at the curt dismissal. Her gaze became pivoted on the crown of Spirit Hill. It would be daylight soon – the friend of mirrors and re-flections.

A droplet of rain in a dish-sized pool. Another on a miniature natural obelisk, trickling. Time became moist and unhurried. More drops, near, distant. Rain tapped on stone, pattered on wrinkled wood, whispered on waving grass. Soon the stars were drowned. Blank dawn stooped below the humped horizon. The Hour of the Tiger dis-solved into the Hour of the Hare. 'Too late.'

'What was that?' asked the monk, starting from his cross-legged posture just inside the clammy vines.

'Too late,' she sighed. 'We cannot reach the Death Mound before sunrise, and the daylight hours are hazardous in any dealings with the Whisperers. This cave must be our home until sunset . . .'

The sorceress sucked in a snatch of breath as a group of

distant figures came into view round the northern bend of the valley: the Silver Brethren were tracking the grooves of the chariot wheels in the patches of pliant turf fringing the river. Chia slid through the wet foliage and crept cautiously to the rim of the ledge. Far below, eight tiny shapes skirted the banks. Arriving at the spot where she had driven the Fergana team into the Shen River, the trackers stopped. Chia's lips bent into a cold smile. The hunters scoured the vicinity for some time, always keeping three or four steps' distance from the haunted currents. The sorceress frowned. She had hoped that they would conclude that their prey had been foolhardy enough to brave a crossing of the river and unfortunate enough to choose a point where the waters were haunted. She wanted the Silver Brethren to believe that she had been swallowed by the Mime Realm. Whether Nyak would believe it was a different matter.

The east was fresh blood before the Silver Brethren retraced their steps up the northern twist of the valley. Unhappily, they left two of their number at the foot of the scarp. Her enemies had not been fully duped.

'May the demon arrows transfix you,' she cursed.

Lithely and lightly she stole back to the cave, finding Vinaya sprawled in sleep within the hanging curtain of foliage. Even in sleep he shivered with the cold. The girl in the blue gown, slumped in the chariot, had opened her eyes and was staring vacantly at nothing, or something beyond the range of normal vision. Nua evinced all the signs of being a threat to their mission, and yet – the sorceress did not feel her to be a threat. It was simple instinct that countermanded the dictates of reason; but then, her instincts had often led her astray. The evidence was against the girl – had not Nua tried to push her into the stream before San Lung town? Had she not displayed an uncanny imperviousness to the breath of the Whisperers? But then . . .

Chia shrugged off the dilemma and sat near a rent in the

masking greenery. If the girl was a mirror self, or possessed by a mirror self, she was not likely to attack until they had entered the Tomb of the Spirit Mirror. Best wait until then. Why fret over an hypothetical danger when hedged about by immediate danger?

The Silver Brethren. They had known she was coming. But what was their plan? Or rather, what was the plan of their master, Nyak? To capture her? Simply to prevent her reaching Spirit Hill? Had she done exactly what he wanted when she fled and secreted herself on the wrong side of the river? Through relentless centuries of conflict with the necromancer she had learned that it was difficult to fathom his cunning; the very move you took to avoid him was the move he intended you to make. However, the situation would be more unpredictable for Nyak if she pursued the Third Way of T'ai Ching – think otherwise. And spontaneity – there was another breeze which would upset his web.

Her furrowed brow smoothed as she studied the drab downpour. She must not attempt to guess what Nyak had planned, and then scheme against it; nor, of course, conspire with him. She must not think of his plans at all. Her actions must flow from her own being, and if her being was dissonant her actions would be dissonant. 'Begin with yourself,' she whispered. A full breath expanded her lungs. 'Whoever you are, Chia.'

Assuming the lotus asana she visualised the blazing Solar Disc of Aten as her breath undulated in the rhythm of prana. She felt the tension in her larynx as she repeatedly uttered the name of Aten. Gradually she relaxed the tension and ceased to speak the name out loud. Now the name was in her mind only: *Aten . . . Aten . . Aten . . .* Still aware that the muscles in her throat were continuing to respond each time she thought of the word, Chia sank deeper into quietude. When the throat muscles were completely relaxed she allowed the name of Aten to recede into the brimming abyss of her spirit. The Solar Disc remained, a fitful image. At last the image flickered out, leaving her in that simplest and most difficult of states – bare attention.

Waking light pervaded the upper levels of meditation, bringing illumination. Visions blossomed: a hoofprint filled with water; a snowstorm in a jungle; a gem-encrusted crocodile scaling a pyramid; a fierce bronze mirror hung in Egyptian skies . . .

Sinking lower, the light and the flitting visions faded. A silence too intense to be called soundless enveloped her being. Identity spiralled away like vapour as the small self and the Ten Thousand Creatures dropped into the abyss of uncreated self. Self was one with Other.

Tat tvam asi: Thou art That. Blissful void.

Shantih.

T'ao.

But the depths return their sunken bodies, in a day or the four billion years of kalpa. Even pebbles dropped onto the bed of the ocean are one day washed onto the beach. Likewise Chia. She felt the tug of the upper world and resurfaced. The cave and the valley had the look of fresh creation, the paint still wet on the silk hangings. It had been many seasons since she had experienced such peace. Many years . . .

There was a poignant moment between peace and the ending of peace when the enigma of Chia's life was sharply highlighted – the inexplicable twist in her mind, the paradox at the hidden core.

She feared peace. She evaded revelation. Calm and certitude disturbed and confused her.

Like an old, accustomed illness that the sufferer will not exchange for health, the prospect of joy was a menace. She was a fish that drowned in the sea, a bird that choked on the air. Who was she? Was there a creature, she brooded, that endlessly rose and dipped through sea and air, compensating one for the other? There were flying fish, but they did not breathe the air. There were birds that

148

plunged into the sea, but they did not breathe the water. Was there some strange beast that belonged to neither world – that breathed water then gagged for want of air, that breathed air then gasped for want of water? If so, such was she.

The Mimic had grown in the Hearing.

The Hearing was now bright sight.

His own vision he imposed upon the fools of the world and all in the world were fools.

I'm the ear that sees, chuckled the Mimic.

All around him milled the fools, seeing nothing or seeing the wrong thing. Many of the dead were still living, and some of the living were dead. And all were fools.

All were fools except the Fool, the Clown, the Mimic.

He took an old woman by the white hair and wrenched the head from the stalk of her neck. Whistling, he swung it by the hair as he walked. Everyone smiled at the dream in their eyes and the voice in their ears. And the old woman's husband kept chatting to his wife all along the road.

And the Green-Eyes will wallow in hell, laughed the Mimic in his skull.

He snapped a young man's spine and the young man's bride continued her love-whispering into empty space, her looped arm cradling a shoulder that wasn't there.

The Mimic shook with mirth.

He kicked the old head into a fresh shrub and strode on his way with a jaunty air.

In the dark cave, Chia puzzled over the brief peace she had gained from meditation. As far back as she could recall, all her trances of deep contemplation had been marred by the haunting of an intangible presence – an ineffable threat just outside the rim of knowing. Yet this time the yoga meditation had not resurrected that obscure ghost: there was no sense of danger – no hint of the shark – in the deeps. Surely danger must always be present in the deep

places? Or was it that she persistently wished peril –
inflicted suffering – on herself?

She cursed softly.

If only her malady had not robbed her of so much of her
past.

She knew the secrets of the stars and the paths of the
planets, but how she came to learn of them she had no
notion. She recollected meetings with the sententious
Kung Fu Tzu, the eccentric Emperor Wu, the brutal
Emperor Shih Huang, the lackadaisical Chuang Tzu, the
placid Gautama Buddha, but she could not remember her
own mother. Nor could she remember her father – but
then, was he not a Celestial One, an eternal spirit? From
what other source could she have derived her lengthy
lifespan? But that was not a subject on which she cared to
dwell.

An aching head and soreness in the chest reminded her
of the sudden wind from the Mirror of Ming. Although the
wind was an illusion her body had reacted as if it were a
reality. The mind believed the body was to be crushed, so
the mind ordered the body to crush itself. She had
witnessed similar feats of muscular control exhibited by
individuals subject to T'ai Ching Masters. In spite of the
unreal character of the Mime Realm its effects were
nevertheless quite real. Against this threat, she reminded
herself of Chuang Tzu's words: 'The heart of the sage is
quiet, it is a mirror of Heaven and Earth, a mirror of all
things.'

Nua gave a drawn, subdued sigh. The sorceress wheeled
round to observe the weird girl, but seemingly she had
relapsed into slumber: curved lashes shaded her upper
cheekbones. Her full mouth was moist and slightly parted.
She huddled in the chariot like a puppet with broken rods.
Chia swivelled her gaze to Vinaya. The monk was alert
and nervous in sleep, like a fretting hound on a leash.

Down the valley the diluted red disc of the sun reared
above a weathered ridge as the rain beat down with

increasing vigour. A tentative breeze ruffled the tangle of vines. Chia shivered a little with the cold. The Night Shining Jewel she had placed near the back of the cave as a source of illumination slowly faded as the external light stealthily invaded the chamber.

Almost in reaction to the inclement weather a vivid memory of Egyptian sands sparked behind her thoughtful green eyes. Yellow distance, hot and hushed. Blue infinity overhead. Seen from below, linking sand and sky, the inscrutable visage of the Sphinx confronting the East, the rising sun, her distant homeland.

The golden body of Nefertiti swimming in the deep, vibrant Nile . . . the golden limbs of Nefertiti flashing through the earth-brown ripples of the Nile shallows as they swam, stroke for stroke, by the green ranks of palms on the western shore . . love-making as fierce as the desert and as subtle as the Nile under the green canopy of lofty palms . . . Nefertiti, Queen of Egypt, Daughter of the Nile . . .

Chia smiled, a little sadly, at her vision beyond the rain. 'Left-handed', that was what the scheming priests of Amen-Ra had called Nefertiti, a popular term for women who lay with women – it was also used in the Dragon Empire.

The Land of the Pyramids. The world had seemed good then. Some things she did not forget. Bright times. Chia ran slender fingers through her hair, remembering.

Bright days. But the brightness was ultimately eclipsed. A magus with ebony skin came from the remote southern jungle, a sandstorm his herald, a python his companion. Around the seamed, baked brow wound a circlet fashioned in the likeness of a viper. About his shoulders hung a green cloak of snakeskin. Arcane talismans flashed and jangled on his carven, painted staff.

Kabo the Wise. Kabo the Sky Watcher. In ecstatic trances he had glimpsed worlds both seen and unseen,

151

apprehended the stupendous inner thunder of the stars, perceived times past, times future, other realms.

And he knew of Chia's origin, and of her destiny.

Nefertiti pleaded with her not to exhume what her memory had buried, but Chia could not resist the offer of knowledge from the black shaman.

'Speak, jungle sorcerer,' she had demanded, a tremble in her voice. In a high, nasal tone Kabo began to chant. Then came a darkness and the light of her thoughts was quenched. When she recovered the shaman was gone and Nefertiti refused to repeat his words.

'Kabo the Wise spoke truths you couldn't endure, Green-Eyes,' Nefertiti murmured. 'A madness came on you with his speech. I thought you were going to kill him. It was as though Set himself had sprung from the desert wind and taken possession of you.'

Then came the day when Nefertiti and her husband the Pharaoh Akhenaten were killed, overthrown by Horemheb's military, and a new reign under the child Pharaoh Tutankhamun made Egypt old. With the death of Nefertiti the magic of Egypt died for the sorceress. Chia, her heart a cracked stone, departed the Land of the Nile for the long trek home to the Shang Kingdom of the Yellow River, forerunner of the Chinese Empire. The capital of Anyang had changed little during her long absence, and the Shang rulers treated her Egyptian lore as fanciful and subversive. Disheartened, she withdrew to her ancient refuge on Black Dragon Mountain. Often she would mourn for Nerfertiti through the bleak hours of night, gripping the silver ankh and staring into lonely space.

But a handful of sorcerers had not disregarded her exotic lore, the more astute among them dressing the Egyptian images in Chinese garb in order to satisfy the masters of the Yellow River Kingdom. The new knowledge led some to good, some to evil, as was the way in all lands. Most influential of all, perhaps, was the doctrine of the Ten Essences, as it came to be called by the Shang sorcerers. Chia had reported originally that the Nile Kingdom held to the belief in the existence of seven essences or elements that combined to compose a human being . . .

She inhaled sharply as her thoughts jumped from past to present. The Ten Essence doctrine. In the original Egyptian hierology there were three upper 'souls', and four lower, known as Sekhem, but in the Dragon Empire this had been altered to the doctrine of three upper hun souls and seven lower pho souls. The sorceress carefully reviewed the characteristics of the seven essences described by Egyptian priests – the three upper elements, the Ka, Ba, and Khu, and the four lower elements of the Sekhem, the Khaibit, Ren, Khat and Ab.

Three above, four below. The Seven.

But in the Dragon Empire there were ten – three above and seven below. The Ten essences. Nyak had never left China and was unfamiliar with other doctrines of selves within selves. He was restricted to Chinese soul theories. She was not. And the struggle against the Spirit Mirror was of identities – of selves within selves. That was the way. The Third Way. Attack the familiar with the weapon of the unfamiliar.

'Yes – the Ka and the Khaibit,' she whispered.

The Sight would have smiled if a smile had been required.

It knew what Chia was thinking. And it knew where her shadow was placed.

It always knew what Chia was thinking. And it knew what her shadow would do.

The Sight despised Chia's confused wits although it had helped to confuse them.

Chia was deep in the maze.

She would soon be in the centre of the maze.

There was no return from the centre.

*

Chia's green eyes brimmed with sadness. For most of the journey she had succeeded in putting Fu's fate to the back of her mind through an immense effort of will. For a few moments, the wall was breached and Chia was racked by grief and anxiety. Fu's loving arms. Her quiet, serious eyes. Gentle girl. Gentle, affectionate girl. What has happened to you? Are you in the Death Mound?

With a massive inner struggle Chia finally forced the tormenting thoughts to the background. She had to concentrate on Nyak and the struggle of selves.

And she would focus on just two 'souls' – the Ka and the Khaibit. The Double and the Shadow. The Other Self and the Dark Self.

The torches shivered in the dark vault far beneath the trees.

From Yi's hooked eyes and hooked ears the blood gently trickled, drop by drop.

And drop by drop, the masked shape in the stone sarcophagus sucked in the spirit of suffering. Thus it was sustained. And a febrile breath of that sustenance was returned to the impaled girl hovering above.

The victim, locked in her skull, shared it with madness. Behind her mute, maimed visage, nightmares jostled.

Inside the silver-masked head of the prone figure, there was no madness. There was deafness and blindness, but no madness. In the masked head, there burned diamond-bright thoughts: the Two that are One . . . the Spirit and the Body . . . Chia the sorceress sinking in the mire . . . the rites of desecration . . .

The torches trembled once more, then were still.

Chia gazed bleakly out of the cave. The rain was unrelenting. The sun was a smudge of thin blood in the drab, monotonous cascade. This dawn had a dead heart. The rustling tangle of vines grew sodden with the downpour. The dome of Spirit Hill was barely visible, a phantasmal blur at the edge of the world. She hugged her firm contours with the black woollen cloak to preserve the warmth within; there was little enough of that.

The saffron shape of the monk was still folded in sleep. The enigmatic girl in the blue gown stared vaguely from the sturdy chariot.

Shivering, Chia lifted the cowl over her head for warmth, but as she did so six elmwood rods tumbled out and dropped into the shallow rivulet. Fishing them out and shaking them free of glistening waterdrops she was reminded of the purpose for which she had taken them from Ming's mansion: Ming's mirror and the six Yin-Yang rods – with their aid she would struggle with the Whisperers in the Death Mound. However, that would not be until after sunset – for the present she could cast the rods according to the lore of the I Ching to gain some insight into her spiritual condition.

The traditional method of I Ching casting was one she eschewed, as the technique of dividing and subdividing a bundle of fifty yarrow stalks resulted in too much conscious manipulation. A successful casting required a major element of apparent chance which allowed the caster's deeper self to achieve expression. The most effective means to this end was the ancient and virtually disused method of the Six Rods. The elm rods gripped in her hand were adequate for both the I Ching and a variant of Liu Po.

'In the dawn, the oracle – in the night, the contest,' she breathed softly.

She shut her eyes and slowly emptied her mind, grasping the Yin-Yang rods at the end of an outstretched arm. As the dark-light vacancy expanded behind her hooded vision, sun-flash tableaux heat-shivered the emptiness. The visions abruptly coalesced into an illimitable field of lopped yarrow stalks. Winds started to blow on the field – the Red Wind of the South, the White Wind of the West, the Green Wind of the East, the Black Wind of the North. The contrary winds, battling for supremacy, scooped up the stalks and hurled them high into the air where they clashed and stormed, agitated armies. Unconsciously, the sorceress was gently shifting the elm rods in her hand in accord with the currents of her spirit. As swiftly as they had pounced the winds withdrew and the myriad stalks settled to the ground. At the same moment, Chia instinctively roused from the trance to behold the sleeping but unsettled form of Vinaya sprawled nearby. Satisfaction creased the corners of her mouth – the casting had been successfully per-formed.

But satisfaction changed to dismay when she regarded the hexagram formed by the fallen rods. The Yang sign on each rod showed uppermost. It was impossible – out of character with everything she knew of herself.

Yang. First hexagram of the sixty-four patterns. Yang. The product of two trigrams – Heaven Above and Heaven Below. Symbol of light, force, the male principle. Others would have regarded the oracle as favourable: 'Heaven in motion; the strength of the dragon'. But the oracle did not augur well for her and she suspected a more covert meaning in the hexagram. Skilled exponents of the I Ching did not cast in-appropriate hexagrams out of sheer randomness, so she could not delude herself that the Yang pattern was the result of capricious forces. If she had posed any other question than that of her inner balance she would not have been taken aback – any answer was permissible for external events. But in all the centuries of using the I Ching to clarify her spiritual state she had been an-swered by just four hexagrams – all disposed towards the Yin force. Now she was presented with the with the hexagram of pure Yang. It disconcerted her in much the same way that the menace-free depths of her meditation had afterwards perplexed her. The hexagram and the yoga meditation were too benign for one such as she. The sun does not share the night with the moon.

And there was the rod slightly askew at the base of the hexagram; it signified that the Yang force was in some measure still dormant: 'The dragon lies hidden in the deep'. It counselled abstention from action and decision until she was certain of the right course.

Chia tightened her lips. It was possible that the elm rods were weighted in some peculiar fashion. In the middle of each rod was notched a black Yin mark on one side and a red Yang mark on the other. Was the wood loaded so that the Yang sign always showed uppermost? To test the idea she swept up the rods and dropped them haphazardly, asking the oracle – in mock-serious vein – what the coming night had in store.

The result disproved the notion that the rods were weighted: the hexagram showed two Yin signs and four Yang signs. She experienced regret, a regret reinforced by the hexagram revealed. It was Teh-kuo, the twenty-eighth hexagram, with two inauspicious moving lines. Teh-kuo was the hexagram of impending disaster, symbolised by the trigrams of the Wind Below and the Marsh Above. It was an evil augury, and the moving lines compounded the evil. The third rod was askew, signifying 'The beam is weak'. An ominous augury, warning that she was heedless and stubborn and that she resisted the advice of the I Ching. The sixth rod was also angled, an even worse omen: 'The man walks straight into the stream'. The sixth moving line spelt catastrophe.

Was that what the night held – catastrophe?

The rustle of silk on silk slithered into her musings. The blue gown of Nua. A wooden creak. The deck of the chariot. Again the sussuration of silk, approaching. Chia did not turn; she waited, tight and alert. The silken whisper ceased behind her. A cold hand stroked her hair, pushing back the cowl.

'Chia . . .' The voice was attuned to the sough of the rain.

The icy fingers moved to caress her cheek.

'*Chiiiiiaaaaaa . . .*'

The sorceress kept her stare fixed to the ground.

The caressing stopped. Again the *shush* of silk. Chia continued to look at the damp rock in front of her knees. A shadow slid across the moist surface. Chia's gaze travelled to the end of the shadow and up the blue-gowned figure of Nua, framed in the dull arch of rainy daylight. The girl had undone her chignon and the freed hair tumbled loosely over slim shoulders and full breasts. Her ripe lips were parted in a voluptuous smile, a striking contrast with her previous demeanour. Most of all, the eyes which had been vacant were now full, full of wildness and feral lust. The primitive nudity of the girl's gaze ensnared Chia like a fish in a net, and like a fish she struggled against the drawn mesh.

'This net comes from the sea, Chia,' came the rain-whisper of the girl. 'It is cast on land by the creatures of the deep. Come and join your Unborn Sister, Chia. Enter the sea.'

Anger crackled inside the sorceress. No one commanded Chia, Black Dragon, Celestial Daughter. She advanced on her enticer, not in desire or obedience, but in fury. 'When you invite me, little girl,' she menaced, 'you invite the Dragon Storm.'

Nua sank to the wet ground and lay spreadeagled with hooked hands twitching spasmodically. She started to writhe as if to grind herself into the very rock, become one with the earth. Chia was repelled by attraction – attracted by repulsion.

'Hate me, Chia Left-Handed,' the girl sighed. 'Hate me as I hate you, Sky Sister.'

And Chia did hate her with a hatred so intense that it

158

sought unity with its object. A cold, cruel sensuality tingled her skin and her heart beat lust. She straddled the prostrate girl and seized two strands of her hair. She pulled hard, and the girl screwed up her features in a pain indistinguishable from pleasure.

As Chia pulled the hair and delighted in the other's pain, an opposing emotion impelled her to stoop and press her lips on Nua's parted mouth. With the touching of lips, Chia's right hand released the black tress and slipped under the girl's gown to cup the warm breast. Her nails dug deep into the breast, the squeezing as brutal as the kiss was tender. Chia's desire kindled stronger cruelty in the pincer-fingers and in turn the cruelty inflamed the passion.

A low laugh escaped Nua's pliant mouth as she averted her profile from Chia's open lips.

'Sister Below governs Sister Above,' chuckled Nua. Then, with an indolent, insinuative sneer: 'What happened in Egypt, Chia? What happened in Egypt?'

Chia stared for what seemed a moon-phase at the alien, yet tauntingly familiar face, breath mingling with breath. Her right hand she quietly withdrew from the gown. Her left hand let go of the girl's hair. She saw in her enticer's eyes a kindred spirit, and that intimidated her more than any threat from Nyak or the Death Whisperers. She rose numbly as if she had just discovered a lover, dead.

'Ah! So the mummery is over,' the sardonic edge of the monk cut in. 'A pity. The spectacle was entertaining, as far as it went. It would have been pleasant to watch the fabled Black Dragon Sorceress debasing herself bare-fleshed with a mere mortal.'

Chia shot a stark glance at the lounging curve of the awakened monk propped nonchalantly on an elbow. Nua twisted in vehemence and spat at the lean, derisive countenance.

'Filth!' shrieked Nua. 'Those who can, do. Those who

can't, watch. Eunuch! Half-man! Corpse! You think you're better than her? You're worse!' She grabbed Chia by the hand. 'Beware of the womanless man, Black Dragon,' she warned. 'He tells you I'm your enemy, but he's lying. I've always been with you. *He* is your enemy.'

'Don't listen, sorceress,' begged Vinaya, springing to his feet. 'I repent of my affrontery. Don't misjudge my caustic tongue. She's using my words to divert suspicion from herself.'

Nua jerked up, quivering with outrage. 'Liar! *You're* the enemy. You think you're so sly, but you can't go on fooling Chia forever.'

'It's you who lie, Mirror Creature,' Vinaya replied calmly.

Chia, bewildered, varied her gaze from one accuser to the other, weighing evidence. The scales were tilted against the girl, but how could a Whisperer so expertly mimic a human being? Mystified, she surrendered the problem with a sigh and walked with bowed head into the rain.

Shunning the rim of the ledge she surveyed the valley from northwest to southeast. Barren and deserted, muffled in a pall of rain. The weighty sky was the hue of stone. Her head sank further as she stood, insensitive to the downpour.

'Sorceress...' The monk's hand touched her shoulder. She did not react. 'You must believe that Nua is our enemy,' he insisted. 'She hates us both and wants to destroy us.'

She nodded vaguely. 'I know.'

Satisfied, he retraced his steps, brushed aside the dripping vines and sauntered into the cave. With an arrogant stance he stood over the girl who returned his keen stare with a look of sheer hatred.

On the rain- and wind-swept ledge, Chia continued to ponder the ominous hexagrams and the strange character of the deep meditation and the cryptic question from Nua: 'What happened in Egypt, Chia? What happened in Egypt?'

All reflections were chased by the sight of ten or more tiny shapes emerging from the northern bend of the valley. Instinctively she ducked behind a bush. The distant figures were the Silver Brethren, silhouettes robbed of substantiality by the rain.

The downpour gradually abated as the Silver Brethren approached. By the time they rejoined their comrades at the foot of the spur, the rain had diminished to a weak drizzle. Filtering sunlight sharpened the contours of the dips and rises furrowing the valley. The opposite ridge became firm and distinct. Her eye tracked the battered line of the crest on its jagged journey north until it alighted upon the hazy summit of Spirit Hill. Though the rain was light, at this distance the domed mound was grey gauze, a flimsy apparition. For an instant she forgot the Silver Brethren's gathering as she stared at her goal.

She was so weary and confused. And there was an elusive piece to the pattern, a piece her memory had mislaid. Blood swirling in water? No. But something . . .

THE WHEEL OF SAMSARA

Nagarjuna shuffled from his cell into the milling crowd in the courtyard. The deluge had left numerous puddles that reflected the grey of the heavens. A swarm of feet splashed in the water as the refugees jostled and haggled for the more sheltered corners of the temple. Oaths and insults were bandied freely although the scramble for places did not reach the stage of violence.

The old man estimated the number of arrivals to be in the region of four hundred, with fifty or so more still to pass the scrutiny of the four inspecting monks at the gate. The townsfolk were understandably irate at being drenched while lingering outside the monastery, stamping their feet in impatience at the meticulous searches of property and person and railing at the standard of the makeshift stables one li east of the garan – the high-walled monastic enclosure. A few grumbled over the impounding of weapons, unfamiliar with the Buddhist pacific principle of ahimsa. The abbot regretted the necessity of the searches but he had to ensure that nobody brought a reflective surface into the temple. When the last impoverished stragglers were within the enclosure he would try to make amends to the drenched and disgruntled company.

From first light Nagarjuna had been on the lookout for the young vagabond, Sung. The youth had been the first to experience the Whisperers when he saw a pale reflection behind his shoulder in the River Shen a few li south of Spirit Hill just two days after the Feast of the Dead. The abbot was especially concerned to question Sung.

Nagarjuna looked up and sniffed the air – the rain had moved northwards and the sun promised a bright day as it peeped through widening cracks in the slate sky. Was Chia, he wondered, emerging from the Death Mound and looking at the sun at this moment, triumphant from her quest? Hard to believe, somehow.

If only Dharmapala had found Liu Chun. There was a man who might challenge the Spirit Mirror. But Luminous Cloud Mountain was a thousand li to the west, and the young brother had been gone scarcely sixteen days. It was asking too much of Dharmapala to locate and bring back the sage in so short a time. Why had Chia not waited for Liu Chun? She was too rash, too arrogant.

Thoughts of Chia vanished as he caught sight of a Wu magus dressed in the characteristic Kang-i garment. The magus was striding at a fast pace to the far side of the Buddha Hall. The magician's manner seemed furtive. But then, perhaps he was the butt of the people's anger, a man to lay blame upon for the mirror hauntings, a straw dog.

'Reverend Master!' bellowed a stout voice in an irreverent tone. The abbot looked away from the wizard to the half-open gates where a burly figure stood. He was slow to recognise the new arrival – the man had changed a little since their last encounter. And who was the limp passenger he bore on his muscular back? The bobbing throng parted in fearful respect as the massive newcomer approached the abbot in long, sure strides. He halted with a slight swagger and stared down contemptuously at Nagarjuna.

'What's wrong, Indian?' he boomed.

'Nothing.'

'Good. Now, I want one of your miserable cells for my friend and me.'

Nagarjuna glanced at the blanched face lolling on the man's shoulder and the slender hands clasped about the brawny neck.

'He's sick,' confirmed the overbearing guest. 'We'll need a cell to ourselves and woe fall on anyone who dares to intrude.' He grinned a mockery of amiability. 'I trust I make myself plain?'

The abbot nodded calmly. 'Perfectly.' He signed to a nearby monk. 'Take these two – ah – gentlemen to your cell and see that they are undisturbed. You will share with Amaravita and five of the townsfolk.'

The monk nodded in compliance and nervously ushered the sauntering giant and his torpid passenger to the monastic quarters on the southern side of the garan. The abbot regarded them thoughtfully.

He was startled from his reverie by the earnest tone of Amaravita. 'Master, you wished to speak with Sung the vagabond.'

'What? Oh yes – yes, of course.' He squinted at the youth standing beside Amaravita.

The youth was angular and stick-like from starvation. His head was like a skull, a skull swaying on a stalk of a neck. Empty eyes stared out of etched sockets. He was a hungriness.

'You'll be the first to be fed,' promised the abbot, moved by the boy's plight.

'Fed,' echoed the flat voice of Sung. The blank eyes stared past the abbot.

'Ah – if you could just tell me a little about the face you saw twice in the river near Spirit Hill.' The abbot felt that he should not be questioning the lad at all – he needed care, not questioning.

'Spirit Hill,' repeated the hollow voice. The eyes continued to stare past the abbot.

When it became clear that the youth would say no more unless prompted, Nagarjuna phrased the simplest question he could think of: 'What was the vision?'

A short silence.

'Vision,' vibrated the echo.

Compassion overwhelmed the abbot; he felt guilty at

164

putting inquisitiveness before concern. He beckoned Amaravita.

'Starvation has scrambled the poor lad's wits. Take good care of him. The best possible care.'

Amaravita bowed and led the youth to the southern cells. As they departed, Nagarjuna saw the wisp-bearded Wu magus, resplendent in the embroidered red silk of the Kang-i, standing a short distance away. He looked even more furtive than before, his narrow eyes meeting, then not meeting the abbot's, his fingers fiddling with a peachwood wand. He seemed about to speak, then thought better of it, if Nagarjuna was any judge. Then the wizard hurried away as if afraid of the abbot.

Is my imagination getting the better of me? wondered Nagarjuna. He was not normally given to suspicion. Probably it was a simple matter of age and exhaustion. He was tired. It had been a sleepless night and a hectic dawn.

He yawned involuntarily. Yes, he was worn out from lack of sleep. And with the formidable task of settling all the refugees he would be lucky if he could catch any sleep before noon.

He yawned again.

The Mimic stalked past the Buddha Hall and smirked at the dozing San Lung refugees. *I have made you blind, dreamers.*

The Mimic capered under the torana and sneered at the sandstone dome of the stupa. *Pious lies and childish rites.*

The Mimic paced about the southern courtyard and laughed in the faces of a small group of villagers. *I have made you deaf, babblers.*

And I have made you mad.

You see me. You don't see me. You see me and greet me.

You say 'Greetings, Brother Amaravita!' or 'Lo-kai, my

friend!' or 'Our regards, esteemed abbot,' or 'Are you lost, little girl?' or 'Old man, you look familiar' . . . And often – often I'm not there at all . . .

'I have made you all mad!' chuckled the Mimic to an unheeding monastery.

Blind and deaf and mad.

Sunset was nine orange squares between the crossed bars of the cell window. Nagarjuna blinked at the window as he woke from a long, refreshing sleep. A loud snoring rumbled from an unidentifiable member of one of the two small families sharing his room.

One of his guests was awake – an undergrown youth scratched and muttered to himself, shifting restlessly on the makeshift pallet that he shared with his younger brother. There was barely room for a cat to squeeze between the sprawled bodies but the abbot managed to edge through, inadvertently rousing a few grumbling sleepers as he missed his footing.

The door groaned and he winced as he slipped through the daylight gap, anxious not to disturb his tired guests further.

Nagarjuna walked at a steady pace over the wet clay to the southern perimeter of the monastery, wondering as to the works and whereabouts of Chia. He acknowledged the occasional salutations from refugees with a polite nod but did not loiter to exchange pleasantries. He sought solitude.

Solitude was difficult to find. Hunched shapes lined the flamboyant walls of the Buddha Hall to the left and the severe rows of cells to the right. Fatigued eyes met him as he passed, some in trust, some in suspicion. Rounding the southern corner of the wing-roofed hall he was confronted by the oldest building in the temple – the stupa.

Time in the past. Nagarjuna saw into boyhood India as he mused on the ornate, voluminous dome of the stupa

166

thrusting up like the scalp of a mud giant from the stained clay of the southern courtyard. The sandstone dome, blood-rusted by the diffuse slant of the low orange sun, was a monument to India, a homage to the hallowed stupas of Sanchi, a Shatavahana relic in a foreign land. Over forty years ago he had left his native Mathura and his adopted sacred order on the vast Ganges plain on a mission to the Land of the Yellow Emperors. Eleven of his brethren had died on that journey. After a year of arduous travel and a series of hostile receptions they finally settled in San Lung at a safe distance from the teeming city of Loyang – the insecure capital of a precarious empire.

The first stones laid by the brethren were the foundations of the stupa, and in less than two years the work was finished. And in under ten years the last brick of the monastery had been slotted into place. Other monks came, braving the perils of steppes and cities, and the numbers swelled. Buddha, so the abbot liked to think, had left a million footprints in Chinese soil through the missionary zeal of his later disciples. They had come to convert. And indeed they had made many converts, although by Imperial decree no Chinese was allowed to join a Buddhist Sangha; instead, the converts became what were popularly known as 'Mendicants of the Middle Road', often mingling with the T'ao Seekers. The indigenous religion of the T'ao had been increasingly influenced by the precepts of the Buddha Followers, much to the distaste of the Confucian mandarins and the more traditional T'ao priests who suspected the Mahayana Way of the Buddha to be a potential threat to their power. Perhaps it was.

And yet – could any religion truly transform the Han Empire? They had come to convert, but was it not true that the Indian visitors had undergone a Chinese conversion? The stupa itself, the earliest edifice of his missionary order, testified to the delicate infiltration of the Chinese alchemy.

By the time they had come to sculpt the exterior of the dome their lungs had breathed Chinese air for a thousand days, air particled by the dust of multitudinous Chinese ancestors, air resonant with the cadence of a million Chinese stories, poems, songs, flute and stringed melodies; their bodies were nourished by Chinese food; their vision was greeted by Chinese towns, faces, landscapes and skies. Chinese alchemy. As their brown hands sculpted elephants, the Tree of Enlightenment, the Manushi Buddhas, the yakshas and yakshis and a veritable jungle of sensuous apsaras and ferocious rakshasas; the bamboo-yellow hands of the dynastic ancestors nudged an angle here – guided a curve there – and a foreign element permeated the Indian reliefs, a crosscurrent shifted the Ganges sediment. And the alien mythology intruded: Hsi Wang Mu rose to share the Western Paradise Throne with the Buddha Amitabha; rakshasas cavorted with turbulent kwai spirits. The Faith of the Buddha co-mingled with the Way of the T'ao.

The stupa sank into a dull copper as the sun dipped below the west wall. The dome was India drowning in China. The abbot experienced a pang of loss, then straightened his back in a sharp reaction. Drowning? What had he been thinking of? There was no death here – here was symbolised the marriage of three religions, here was creation. Luxuriant divinities of the Hindu pantheon weaved in concert with rapt Buddhas and Bodhisattvas who in turn consorted with the Sage Immortals of the T'ao. Following the serpentine forms and tracery it was difficult to discern where one religion ended and the others began. It was like an eternal cosmic wheel . . .

He pulled himself short. A wheel? The Wheel of Samsara? Was his religious eclecticism a form of Maya – an elaborate illusion which condemned him to the endless repetition of the Wheel of Rebirths, spun by the hand of Karma? He relaxed his tautened shoulders. If so, let it be so. He had done what he thought best. He had brought the Buddha Light to the Empire of the Dragon

Throne, and if the sacred flame acquired a yellow hue from the Chinese earth, what of it? Each country had its own colour for the cosmos. Purity did not lie in dogmatism. He preferred to believe that the enrichment gained from the mingling of religions would itself lead to release from the deceptive Veil of Maya. Long ago, in templed Mathura, his master in Buddha had taught him that no religion was sufficient to achieve Nirvana, not even Mahayana.

So – it seemed that his life's work was to some purpose. Ten years past, another Sangha had been established in the city of Chang'an. The religions had already met; soon they would undergo a mutual transformation. New religions would arise from the meeting of China and India, invigorated by the confluence. Yes, that was surely the way. The abbot's life had often seemed to him to be an uphill climb to an unseen summit, but at times like this he was convinced of the value of his work. He would gladly offer his old life in furtherance of the conversion of China.

Learning to bend with the wind like the bamboo, he had constructed the Buddha Hall and the tower in the northern quarter of the garan on Chinese principles, gleaned from a shrewd appraisal of the architecture of Loyang. The tower had recently been renamed 'Yun-t'ai' – Cloud Tower – after the imposing edifice destroyed in the Loyang Fire. Clouds were the perennial emblem of the T'ao Seekers, and the Imperial Cloud Tower of Loyang was sorely missed by the aesthetes within the shih class: much latent hostility had been erased and a degree of favour obtained by the diplomatic dubbing of the tower. With a child-emperor plumped on a cracking throne and a bevy of eunuchs embroiled in political machinations at the court of the Son of Heaven, survival depended on diplomacy. The Temple Master's expression was wistful as he stepped closer to the decorative dome of the stupa: he disliked unnecessary compromise, but – in his own words of thirty years past – 'Wear the skin of the wolf in the forest of the wolf'.

He halted under the isolated torana which fronted the stupa at a distance of thirty steps. The three architraves surmounting the two upright pillars of the torana were sculpted at all six ends with a spiral design. The spirals had always drawn the abbot's eye outwards rather than inwards to the ever-receding centre. In reverential Mathura on the far side of the Himalayas, the spirals on the torana architraves were representations of venerated scrolls, but here in the Dragon Empire the schematic scrolls were transmuted into a new symbol – the volute became a vortex, a universal whirlwind, a cosmic whirlpool eternally spinning a million somethings from the heart of its no-thing.

From the abbot's position within the ochre rectangle the dome of the stupa was precisely framed. On the western pillar of the torana, deep in shadow, was the maternal figure of Hsi Wang Mu enthroned on the summit of Mount K'un-lun and attended by a cluster of minor immortals; on the eastern pillar glowed the stately form of Tung Wang Kung – a dull ember in the shrinking radiance of the sun. Tung Wang Kung, Eastern Lord of Mount P'eng-lai; Hsi Wang Mu of Mount K'un-lun, Mother of the West: Chinese deities on an Indian gateway. Somewhere the creeds of his boyhood had been mislaid, but the loss was gain, and the creeds had contrived the loss. He had heard of certain insects which die as they give birth – of such fibre were creeds.

And what summed up the ceaseless activity of dying into birth as perfectly as the stupa? The creed of the Brahmins submitting to the Path of the Buddha, the Path of the Buddha uniting with the Way of the T'ao, each fulfilling – not supplanting – the other.

And before all these sacred phases of the dome, before the mystic signs and the holy relics and the esoteric sigils and the eidolons and the benedictions, the primitive stupa was a simple burial mound. A crude dome of death. He rubbed his white-stubbled chin and narrowed contemplative eyes: even the tomb had died into birth. In the ochre dome the cycle of rebirths was pre-figured. The Wheel of Samsara.

Nagarjuna bowed his gaze to the ground between the symbolic gateway pillars. A vision formed on the clay between the columns. A trail of blood winding inwards to form a red spiral. He blinked and the vision disappeared.

As the sunset leaned into night and the monastery became astir with the drone of voices and the kindling of lanterns like hovering fireflies, the abbot remained in his bowed stance beneath the tall, florid torana as if petrified in communion with the spirit-sculpted stone.

A straggling ribbon of primrose was swallowed in the darkness of the western sky. Insubstantial stars began their eastern haunting. The huge chimes installed in the top storey of the Cloud Tower bounced brazen reverberations about the temple.

It was only when the chimes died that a dull knocking could be distinguished at the Southern Gate.

An apprehensive silence greeted the steady beating, lantern-lit faces turned quizzically to the gate. Nagarjuna shook off his speculations and assumed command of the situation, bustling with a springy step that belied his age to deal with the unknown caller. At his nod two monks raised the crossbar. The gates screaked open and lanterns were thrust into the dusky arch to reveal the strangers. Leading steaming horses by the bridle, the travellers emerged from darkness to lantern-light, one clad in the traditional saffron robe of the Buddha Followers and the other swaddled in a gown of warm grey wool overlaid with a thick blue woollen cloak.

The abbot beamed. 'Dharmapala! You have found the redoubtable Liu Chun! Praise be to the Celestial Buddha!'

'Praise be to the Will of Heaven and the Spirit of Mo Ti!' retorted the Chinese sage in a humorous tone.

14

CLOUD TOWER

The Hour of the Hound was falling to the Hour of the Boar as Liu Chun devoured the remaining scraps of a six-course meal, rubbed his full lips with the back of his hand, scratched his bearded jowl with coarse, stumpy fingers and heaved a sigh of satisfaction as he deposited the chopsticks in a wooden bowl scoured of the last particle of food.

'That's better!' he boomed in a voice as large as his bulky build. 'After a week of grubbing plants with that reptile-stomached pupil of yours I needed a good meal.'

The two families in the abbot's cell eyed the sage with veiled curiosity: the legend of the Master of Luminous Cloud Mountain was widespread, and considerably magnified in the telling and retelling. His awesome presence was ramified by fable.

Nagarjuna, on the other hand, was not awestruck by the guest. He sat facing Liu Chun over the crowded food mats with a benign serenity that would have done credit to the Buddha himself. Between the two men there was the easy familiarity of old friends. Their friendship, the abbot ruminated, was as firm as it was unlikely. Liu Chun had, for twenty years, been a renowned warrior and an exponent of the robust philosophy of Mo Ti, a sage of the Warring States era some six centuries past. Liu Chun was generally regarded as a worthy disciple of his long-dead hero. At the ascension to the throne of the child-emperor Ling, the weathered veteran had

172

terminated his chivalrous career in protest at court intrigues and settled in seclusion on his beloved mountain amid the solemn T'aihang peaks. In marked contrast, Nagarjuna had practised a monastic mode of existence since childhood and observed the basic Buddhist precept of non-violence – ahimsa. The ethics of Mo Ti and the Way of the Buddha were as divergent as the climates of China and India. Yet, somehow, a tacit companionship endured.

Liu Chun took a deep swig from the wineskin that no one had ever seen him without, licked his lips, and jumped to his feet with wineskin in hand. 'How about sniffing out a quiet corner somewhere? Some place where I can play Wei-ch'i and we can both talk our heads into a spin . . .'

'There will be few quiet corners,' the abbot apologised, rising. 'But we'll find privacy if we talk above people's heads.'

'I see what you mean,' Liu Chun muttered ruefully as he dropped his hands from his ringing ears and the echoes of the chimes wandered into the distance. 'Who would be so addle-pated as to pick a spot like your Cloud Tower for sleep or talk?' The sage could still feel the clangour of the chimes juddering through his skull although the raucous din had departed. The stout brother who had struck the sets of chung bells – metallic bells that were oval in shape and decorated with t'ao-t'ieh masks – released the weighty wooden beam suspended from the sturdy roof of the Cloud Tower and descended the angled staircase.

Nagarjuna and his companion sat on the low parapet of the blue-roofed, bell-hung crown of the tower, gazing into the northern darkness. Below their perch the temple was bubbling with life and flaring with lanterns and torches. Beyond the walls the land was still and night.

'Why the constant thundering of the chimes?' complained Liu Chun.

The abbot smiled. 'Surely you can guess? The people believe that the bells keep evil spirits away. It's a belief common to all the race of Han.'

The other grunted. 'Hm . . . Chimes as loud as those would scare *anything* away. However . . .'

'Yes – however.'

'I'm sorry I missed Chia,' the sage began. 'We should have gone to Spirit Hill together – safer for her, safer for all of us. I'm to blame for not heeding my premonition – I should have hurried here straight away.'

'Premonition?'

'Yes. On the Feast of the Dead. In the Valley of the Five Ways. A troupe of mummers danced an imitation of the Mirror Dance for about an hour. Afterwards they couldn't explain why they had done it, except that they had been possessed by the vision of a deadly dance far away, beneath Black Dragon Mountain.' He scowled. 'Why did I tarry after that omen in the valley? Stupid sage!'

'Don't accuse yourself,' the abbot remonstrated. 'I ignored clearer portents. It was Dharmapala who opened my eyes to the full extent of the danger.'

'Yes, he's a good lad. He told me that he trekked all the way from Mathura at the age of sixteen to become a missionary, *and* against monastic orders. If all your monks had his spirit the entire Dragon Empire would be Buddhist within twenty years!' He laughed and lifted his eyes to the Cloud Tower roof.

Nagarjuna remained silent as his companion surveyed the Yun-t'ai roof with its four massive supporting pillars. The sage assumed a meditative stare. Was it conceivable, the abbot wondered, that Liu Chun was seeking a clue to the mirror riddle in – architecture?

'What's that wheel-shaped thing on the other side of the chimes?' The sage jabbed a thick finger at the southern parapet.

'Just that – a wheel,' shrugged Nagarjuna. 'It's spun by

hand. You can see it has eight spokes to represent the Noble Eightfold Path of the Buddha. It has no utility. It's simply an aid to contemplation. The hand that spins the wheel is a symbol of Karma. The spinning of the wheel signifies Samsara, the cycle of rebirths resulting from the operation of Karma. I constructed the wheel almost a year ago along with another that was instated in the Golden Hall. Ah – now I come to think of it, the sorceress remarked on the Wheel of Samsara . . .'

'And I'll wager my wineskin that she said it should be a spiral,' Liu Chun butted in.

'Why – yes. How did you know?'

'I know Chia,' winked the burly sage. 'She sees the spiral at work anywhere and everywhere. It's her emblem. The Inward Spiral is evil because it signifies diminishing essence, while the Outward Spiral is good because it represents a broadening – an embracing – of truth. Thus the spiral is a symbol of good or evil, depending on whether the eye travels from the centre to the rim, or from the rim to the centre.'

He took a hearty gulp of wine. 'Outwards good, inwards bad,' he summed up with a tinge of facetiousness. With a hoarse exhalation he opened a box of black and white Wei-ch'i stones. A spell of silence ensued as Liu Chun set up the latticed Wei-ch'i board with its three hundred and sixty-one intersections for the placement of the stones.

Nagarjuna recalled the volutes on the torana architraves and the blood spiral between the torana pillars. He pondered Chia's ideogram of existence. 'Will she use the spiral as a form of talisman against the Spirit Mirror, do you think?' he asked.

The other laughed and placed the first of his black stones near a corner of the board. 'You just try and stop her! Whatever she intends to do in Spirit Hill Mound, it will involve spirals. Of that you can be sure.'

The sage placed a white stone near the solitary black.

175

'Now I take the part of my enemy,' he announced. 'I am the black, but now I think as the white . . .'

The Mimic slipped through the chattering crowds like a ghost shadow.

The Mimic slid into the streaming light of a torch and no one saw.

'I am your dreams,' the Mimic chuckled, and no one heard.

Your eyes see what I want them to see, thought the Mimic. My words weave your sight.

And the Sight itself fears me, for it fears what I know.

'Master of mimicry, how well I perform for my audience! How well I vanish when I must vanish, hidden in air!'

How well I cloak the Brethren, thought the Mimic. How well the Brethren whispered illusion into your ears.

'I am the Black Serpent,' declared the Mimic, left hand lifted in a parody of greeting to the blind, the deaf, the mad.

I am all of you.

The hooded woman stared at the Mimic and his attendants from the sheltering shadows of the stupa.

I see you, she whispered in her mind. I see you and I hear you in the moving of your lips. But my deafness defeats your deafness of the spirit, you strolling nightmare.

You boast. You parade and you boast. But I can see you and you can't see me. The sacred stupa hides me and protects me. The power of the Buddha has joined with the way of the T'ao in the stone of the stupa and the sacred presence is strong in the candlelit dome. You can't enter, boaster.

But the ones that walk with you, they can enter.

Buddha Spirit, be with me. Immortals of the T'ao, stand by my side.

I see no one in the temple who can see, or hear. There is a madness in them. But the madness is calmed and constrained by the spirit of the temple. While the flame of the spirit burns in the temple you cannot subdue and enslave them for long, strutting braggart.

The woman in the stupa, in a gesture of habit, pulled the hood firmly over the right side of her face.

She kissed the burnt stump that she clutched in her work-worn hand.

That burnt stump had been her salvation.

But what would save the townsfolk and the villagers?

What would rid the temple of the strolling nightmare?

'Do you think you could leave your Wei-ch'i game aside?' implored the abbot as politely as he was able. 'Surely it's your duty to rush to Chia's aid?'

Liu Chun looked up from the Wei-ch'i board and shook with irrepressible mirth. 'Rush to *Chia's* aid? The mouse scurrying to defend the dragon! You have quite a sense of humour, Nagarjuna. The sorceress has no need of me.' Liu Chun's deep sigh betrayed more than affection for the absent Chia.

The older man fumbled for words. 'But she didn't appear to be well in her mind. Not in complete control of herself. There ... there were signs of violence in her ...'

Liu Chun tossed his muscular shoulders in a dismissive shrug. 'So what? She's quick to violence when roused. I called her a bitch once, and she gave me one hell of a kick in the groin. I walked funny for days afterwards.'

'But her memory —' persisted the abbot.

'Oh, she's always had that memory malady. She's used to handling it. And she'll handle the Mirror, too.'

The abbot sank into a tired sigh. 'This whole business of the Mirror hauntings is spinning my wits.'

'My head is whirling too,' came the gruff response. 'I'm versed in the folk-tales of the Spirit Mirror, but they all contradict each other.'

'Indeed,' concurred the abbot. 'But perhaps you could enlighten me further as to the Thzan-tzai. I confess to wondering whether these demons are merely a figment of Chia's rich but muddled imagination.'

He waited patiently while Liu Chun added three more stones to the existing twelve and downed another swig of wine. 'The Thzan-tzai are real,' he stated firmly after wiping his lips with the back of a rough sleeve. 'It's generally held that they were overthrown some ten thousand years ago. Their rule was ended by the Celestial Ones, from whom Chia claims descent. Unfortunately, the Thzan-tzai legacy remained.'

'And do you belive that her father was a Celestial One?' asked a sceptical abbot.

'Frankly, no. But Chia does, and it seems to make her happy.'

'And what are the Thzan-tzai? What is this legacy you speak of?'

'The Thzan-tzai!' snorted Liu Chun. 'Where there are no written records there's no history. You know that. Do you think demons sit down and write their biographies for the benefit of posterity?'

'There are oral traditions.'

'From ten thousand years ago? Even if stories were passed down from such a misty time do you think they wouldn't be altered beyond all recognition by now? Have you ever tried that game called Indian Whispers?'

'We call it Chinese Whispers.'

'Whatever. A story passed from mouth to mouth over ten thousand years would be changed a thousand times in the telling. There are no Thzan-tzai written records. There are no Thzan-tzai oral traditions. There is only Nyak, and the Thzan-tzai cult he formed and nurtured. That's where the knowledge comes from –

Nyak. And that is the knowledge which Chia has garnered.'

The abbot nodded. 'Yes. I see.'

'Good,' smiled the other. 'Then I'll tell you the tiny fraction of the story which Chia saw fit to tell me.' He recrossed his legs and propped an elbow on the parapet. 'It seems, he began, 'that there was a race of beings from the dawn of the world. They were closely related to humans. Indeed, they were human in all but one aspect – the power of thought over flesh. As they extended and deepened their powers of thought over flesh, they began to change. And the change accelerated with the birth of each new generation.' He paused. 'Imagine it like this, Nagarjuna. You have a power of thought which enables you to open and close your hand. What if the power of your thought were a hundred – a thousand, times stronger? Thought of that force and intensity could stretch or shrink the skin. It could stretch or shrink the bones of the hand. It could make the hand ice cold or molten hot. It could make the hand a claw, or paw, or just a lump of living matter. That was the power of thought over flesh which the Thzan-tzai possessed, and that was only the beginning. Succeeding generations nourished the power from century to century until the ultimate goal was reached. Thought achieved total dominion over the flesh. They could mould and alter the substance of their flesh with a single thought. They could change shape in an instant. They could become anything. They could do anything. Thought was the absolute master of flesh. They could transform themselves into a tiger or a worm, an eagle, a flower, a spider, or a drop of dew on a leaf. There was nothing they couldn't become. And thus they became immortal.'

'And evil?' suggested the abbot.

Liu Chun waved the suggestion aside. 'They weren't demons, although I'll admit I've called them that for brevity's sake. Talk of demons is just temple-fodder. These weren't monsters from some Buddhist hell. They were human-like beings who gradually mastered the art of shape-changing. They achieved a natural immortality. They became what Chia calls the Masters of the Infinite Flesh.'

The Indian rubbed his chin with a meditative motion. 'You call it natural, my friend,' he observed. 'But they used nature against nature. They violated the Way of Being and Becoming.'

Liu Chun scratched his tangled beard. 'Quite true,' he acknowledged. 'And they paid the price. Our shape is constant, our flesh fixed. We have a definite nature. We have an identity.'

'This isn't in full accordance with the Buddha's teachings on —'

'Never mind about the Buddha,' the sage groaned. 'As I was saying, we have a fixed shape and a definite identity. But the Thzan-tzai became nothing but a conglomeration of ever-changing shapes. The power of thought over flesh turned back on itself and the unceasing contortions of the Infinite Flesh wrought havoc with the very power of thought which was once its master. They lost their identities. They lost the power of thought. They became the Infinite Flesh.' Liu Chun, his wide brow furrowed, moved another white counter on the Wei-ch'i board. His serious gaze skimmed over the crowded temple to the north. 'They became Thzan-tzai — the Unshaped Masters,' he muttered. 'And mindlessly, without hate or malice, they tore into the very fabric of the earth. They would have transformed the earth and all its creatures into the thoughtless writhing of the Infinite Flesh — but something intervened. Spirits from the Otherworld fell upon the Thzan-tzai and carried them off into the netherworld. Glak-i-kakthz was the last Thzan-tzai to be forced out of the world, and before his expulsion he left his seed in a human womb. So Nyak

180

was born of a woman from the seed of the Last of the Changers. And he formed a cult in memory of the Un-shaped Masters. And for ten thousand years he has sought to resurrect the power of the Thzan-tzai in his flesh. 'And that's all Green-Eyes told me.'

He was about to raise the long neck of the wineskin to his lips when Nagarjuna caught him by the arm. 'And the Thzan-tzai legacy . . . What of that?'

The sage firmly disengaged his arm from the abbot's grip, then slowly waved it over the temple and the surrounding night lands. 'The legacy?' he smiled grimly. 'The legacy, dear abbot, is all around you.'

The Mimic stood under the Cloud Tower and smiled his malice at the abbot and the sage.

The Mimic blinked once and the sage was made blind to the Mimic. Another blink and the sage was made blind and deaf to the four Brethren.

'Join my blind, deaf, mad audience,' invited the Mimic.

'No one claps my performance, but I don't mind,' said the Mimic. 'I am the most retiring of entertainers.'

I will make my audience one with me.

You will become me, Liu Chun.

'You will all become me,' whispered the Mimic.

The sauntering nightmare had moved out of sight of the hooded woman in the stupa. And the four tall grey shapes in silver masks had followed him out of her vision.

A fine black powder smeared the light green fabric of her gown where her left hand clasped the burnt stump to her breast. The charred wood was a charm, a magic fashioned by her own supple hands. A talisman against the touch of death.

There was a breath of death in the temple.

She had discerned the killing words formed by the heavy mouth. They killed the spirit, not the flesh. And the killing words were dispensed in generous profusion. They settled into numerous faces and brought empty dreams to numerous eyes.

But the hooded woman also sensed the living spirit in the dark sanctity of the stupa. It was the radiant spirit of the Buddha – a newborn Buddha in Chinese flesh, one with the Yellow Earth.

It was a profound consolation, that glowing spirit.

But outside the stupa, outside the spiritual centre of the temple, what could the glowing spirit do against the killing words and the hands of death?

In her deafness, she was safe from the deafening whisper of death. No madness would dance into her hooded head. And she was wise to the colours of the killing hands.

All over San Lung, the thunder under the earth had sunk below the level of touch and hearing. The season was receding into a dream of years plucked at whim from time going and time coming. In San Lung, China was becoming a dream. But here, here in the temple, China throbbed in the bob and sway of dragon- and tiger-lanterns and the thump of chieh-ku drums and the swirl of dancers whirling dragon-beard streamers from bamboo sticks. The killing words and the killing hands had muffled the throb of the Yellow Earth, but in the temple, muffled as it was, China's heart still beat.

But how long could it beat in the teeth of the death breath? How long?

Would the Buddha send a saviour, a redeemer, a Bodhisattva? Would a Bodhisattva descend from the gate of Heaven, forsaking Heaven for love of China?

Could it be, she wondered, that the green-eyed one they had passed on the road from the town was a saviour, a Bodhisattva? She had the look of a goddess. And she remembered seeing this goddess before. Two

182

years ago. She had been dressed in the same strange black clothes then, with the same crimson sash and long silver dagger and exotic silver pendant.

Chia . . . Are you a Bodhisattva? Will you save us?

Chia. Black Dragon Sorceress. The sorceress had been kind and friendly to her, forcing a silver ring into her palm in payment for a simple wooden statue. That silver ring – worth a hundred of the statues she carved – had paid for her green cape and a month's supply of food. She remembered that the gate guards had tried to arrest Chia with drawn swords. And she remembered that Chia had killed them.

Do redeemers kill, Chia? Even when threatened with swords, do redeemers kill?

The woman in the stupa tensed as the nightmare strolled back into view around the corner of the Buddha Hall. He was flanked by four of the silver-masked figures. Her hand flew instinctively to her right cheek under the cover of the dark green hood.

You have a name, nightmare. And I will remember it. And when I remember it I will shout it out.

The woman's strong fingers stroked the livid, puckered surface of the burn that had seared deep into the flesh of her right cheek and scoured its whole area with an angry mark she would wear to her grave. She was glad of that savage burn. It was the symbol of the fire that healed.

The charred stump of the wooden statue grasped in her left hand was also a token of the healing flame.

The deaf-mute in the hooded cape was still and silent in the shadowy dome as she probed her memory for the name of the nightmare.

Just once, in her long search for the name, did another thought intrude for a moment.

Chia, where are you? Where are you?

Nagarjuna pondered Liu Chun's words for a space. At

length he shifted a little in his cross-legged position on the hard floor.

'The Thzan-tzai legacy – all around us, you say?' the abbot reflected. 'But what is this legacy that is all around us?'

Liu Chun's vision drooped to his booted feet. 'A scent, so Chia says.'

The abbot's grey eyebrows lifted. 'A scent?' he echoed.

'A scent,' repeated the sage. 'Like the scent in a room where everyone has left and closed the door behind them. Like the odour of a sandalwood necklace that clings to the skin and clothes after it has been unclasped and locked away for the night. Like the pungent aroma of quenched candles that lingers in a shrine long after the vanishing of the flame. A scent, an odour, an aroma. The Infinite Flesh of the Thzan-tzai has gone, but the scent remains. Each year it fades, but so slowly, so very slowly. In some places it has faded so much that even the sensitive nostrils of a dog or deer can't sniff it out. But in some locked corners of the world the scent is so rank that dogs will bristle and bark and slink away from the source.'

Nagarjuna nodded pensively. 'I took serious note of the desertion of San Lung by all animals, apart from a few domestic birds and suchlike. It has happened since the Feast of the Dead.'

'Oh yes,' declared the sage. 'The scent drove them out or drove them mad. People are less sensitive to such things – they go mad, but gradually, without any sudden turns or signposts. The scent permeates living bodies subtly and insidiously, and changes the body from within. The sights of the world recede, its sounds fade.'

The abbot rested his chin on the interlaced fingers of his cupped hands and stared somewhere outside or inside of himself. 'Chia said that San Lung was being lifted out of history. I feel now she was right. Our moorings are coming loose and we are starting to drift out of China.

Soon its mountains and plains and cities will be lost in the mist. It will become a memory, then the memory will be forgotten.'

Liu Chun heaved a deep breath of the night air. 'Yes, old friend, the legacy of the Thzan-tzai is all around us. A scent. And thirty li north as the raven flies you'll find its source. The summit of Spirit Hill was always a hidden wound in the world, a dark corner locked away from air and life. Long ago, long before history, a mound was built over that dark wound, that strong scent. The mound has imprisoned it for thousands of years. But now it seems that a trace has escaped. The scent has become a memory, a dream, a ghost. And it's haunting San Lung.'

The abbot glanced up. His voice was unsteady. 'I've heard all the tales of the mirror or mirrors on Spirit Hill, but what's the truth about the Spirit Mirror? Do you know?'

The sage gave a slight shrug. 'I know as much as Chia, which is not a great deal. The Spirit Mirror is a Thzan-tzai relic, but it isn't an object. It is a concentration of the scent so thick and pungent that it has a shadow substance in our world, and a shape formed by drinking directly from the hidden springs – or should I say cesspits? – of the human spirit. It mirrors the darkness within us, and it sips from it. No one forged it in the smithies of some mythical past. It was never designed or planned. No one intended its creation, Thzan-tzai or human. It just grew from the scent, taking its essence from the shadow self, the darkness within. It is the mimic of everything in us that we wish to deny. It's the mirror of the devil in us.'

The abbot buried his face in his hands. 'Liu Chun – what are we going to do? Despair is all around us. What can we do?'

Astonished, Liu Chun leapt to his feet. 'Despair? What are you babbling about? It's true that the Spirit Mirror and Nyak are terrifying prospects, but have you forgotten about Chia, the Green-Eyes, the Black Dragon Sorceress? Has that slinky, thigh-revealing, wild beauty of a warrior woman totally escaped your memory? For the sake of your Buddha, look on the bright side, will you? And – by the way – to cheer you yet further – there's an ultimate safeguard on the Death Mound. It's a sort of prophecy. It goes 'From the brother, the Body. From the sister, the Spirit. Two spirals for the Two that are One.' Now I don't fully understand it, but Chia assured me that all it signified was the use of the spiral in the containment of the Spirit Mirror. And the spiral is her sign of power. Do you see? All she has to do is to wield her spiral and the Mirror will be imprisoned.'

The abbot nodded his pleasure.

Liu Chun's weathered features softened as a lovelorn, faraway look stole into his face. 'Ah, Chia,' he sighed. 'Strange, gentle, wild, mystic. Brimming with paradox. Older than the dynasties of India or China and younger than the morning. Time, for her, flows like a torrent. She meets a lover from a past decade and the lover has withered like the flame of a single day.'

Nagarjuna's brow, brown as the skin of an over-ripe, bruised apple, wrinkled its grooves into a scrawl of thoughtful patterns. 'For all but Chia, the Wheel of Samsara fulfils itself by rebirth in another womb. True death, true birth. An old man dying into a girl-child in the womb, a dog dying into a foetal man. But Chia is tied to her life as Chia – that is her Karma. And her death and rebirth in her own life is the form of Samsara which results.'

Ignoring the abbot's comments Liu Chun shifted his broad frame onto his elbow and leaned over the parapet. Bright lanterns danced amid the crowds, making shining masks of eager faces. Grizzled ancients debated in shadowy corners. Ebullient men diced and quarrelled. Women chattered over improvised stoves. Children played as children always played.

'You'll have a chain of converts before another day has passed,' observed Liu Chun. 'See how unmindful they are of watching ghosts and whispering streams. The temple walls are their refuge. The Buddha will beam at the swelling of his Chinese flock!'

'And if the walls are breached?'

'Then they'll drive you out with curses and blows. You can't have it both ways.'

'True,' acknowledged Nagarjuna. He paused. 'There is *one* detail about Chia's plans that puzzles me.'

'Yes?' asked Liu Chun.

'What does she want with Ming's mirror? Just before she left she said it was time for Ming's mirror and the Game of the Immortals.'

Nagarjuna was taken aback by the look of shock in his friend's face.

'Liu Chun – what's wrong?'

'Ming's mirror . . . the Game of the Immortals . . . Liu Po . . . primitive mirror exorcism . . .' mumbled the sage.

'Tell me what's wrong!' the abbot cried in mounting alarm.

Liu Chun turned dead eyes on his companion. 'She's using primitive mirror exorcism. That means she's forgotten. She's forgotten the spiral. And the spiral is the only means of imprisoning the Spirit Mirror. Without it, she'll be destroyed. We'll all be destroyed.'

Nagarjuna felt his heart die within him.

The Mimic frowned.

Sung was staring at the Mimic.

The youth who ate raw fish and had twice glimpsed the Body reflected in Shen River, was glaring at the Mimic. Sung the scrawny vagabond could see the strong, stinking body the Mimic inhabited. And the Mimic had, for the moment, donned invisibility.

The Mimic tensed. If the youth could see the brawny

body in which he resided, could he not also discern the four Brethren? Had the repeated sight of the Body in the river cleansed Sung's vision of illusion?

Had he seen the Silver Brethren in the weeks since the Feast of the Dead?

Could he see the four Silver Brethren who were now emerging from the cell and mixing, unseen, with the throngs inside Celestial Buddha Temple?

The Mimic strolled casually to where Sung squatted by the eastern wall of the garan. The vagabond's haggard eyes followed his movements.

Ah – he knows me, thought the Mimic. Not just the bulky skeleton and flesh I inhabit, but *me*.

'I can see what you are, Black Serpent,' the youth growled.

The Mimic knelt in front of the hostile vagabond. He grinned merrily at the youth. 'I'm sure you can, my lad. But I think you've seen enough.'

The Mimic grasped Sung's narrow head in his huge hands and pressed his thumbs into the youth's eyes. With his grimy thumbs he pushed the eyes back in their sockets until the jelly of the orbs splattered into the brain and down the cheeks in a flood of blood and watery fluid.

Sung screamed and kicked but no one noticed. Blind and deaf and mad.

The threshing body went limp.

The thumbs dug further into the two red rents until they were buried inside the dead head. Then the thumbs withdrew.

All around them, people chattered happily about the relief of being safe within the temple walls. When they glanced at Sung they saw a quietly sleeping youth. Blind and deaf and mad.

Except one.

A tiny girl nearby, standing between her parents, gaped at the bloody eye-sockets of the dead vagabond. She turned an accusing glare at the Mimic.

He took a single stride to the girl and clasped her neck in one massive hand. In one swift motion he lifted the infant and squeezed her neck. The neck bones cracked and the little head lolled at a grotesque angle. He dropped her to the ground like a broken doll.

'Your daughter is tired and sleepy,' whispered the Mimic.

The mother immediately looked down and sighed. 'Look – poor little Red Blossom is tired and sleepy.'

She swept up the small body with its dangling head and swollen tongue.

'There, sleep now,' the mother soothed, cuddling the body in her arms. The father stroked the dead hair and murmured gentle words to his daughter.

The Mimic left the mother rocking the dead child to sleep.

Blind and deaf and mad, laughed the Mimic, striding back to his cell.

The women in the hooded green cape stole warily to the door of the stupa.

She was on the verge of identifying the name of the walking nightmare. His face was altered, but she was on the edge of recognising him.

And when she found the name, then what? Seek out the abbot? Shout the name from her awkward mouth? Would the abbot be able to understand the half-sound issuing from her mouth and the gestures of her arms?

She still feared the red hand of death that had stroked her right cheek as she stood at her stall by Red Phoenix Gate. That caress had spilt the red plague on her skin. For the first few moments she had reacted stoically, then her eyes had alighted on the glowing embers in the brazier by the gate. That was when Peng-t'ai had seen her salvation. Salvation from the fire. Picking up one of her wooden statues from the rickety stall she had dipped it into the bowl of oil laid by for feeding the fire, then

189

plunged the statue into the brazier. The statue, a pine carving of the Buddha, had ignited almost immediately.

Peng-t'ai then scoured the red plague from her cheek with the burning Buddha statue. She played it over the flesh until the skin scorched and sizzled, then, in the aftershock of pain, dropped the burning Buddha at the foot of her stall.

Within minutes, the stall and its statues were burning.

Peng-t'ai stroked her right hand over the memory made flesh in her cheek.

The red hand of death.

The walking nightmare in the temple.

And the name of the nightmare was . . .

The burnt stump of the Buddha statue nearly dropped from her hand as the name came.

Oblivious, in her excitement, to the nightmare and the four Silver Masks stalking the temple, Peng-t'ai dashed from the cover of the stupa to find the abbot and warn him.

Liu Chun had made a marginal recovery from the stunned spectacle he had been a short while since.

Nagarjuna had also managed to compose himself sufficiently enough to be able to present a mask of calm befitting the abbot of a Buddha temple.

'What,' he asked, 'is the Game of the Immortals?'

Liu Chun downed a deep draught of wine before resuming his seat. His tone was low and subdued. 'In folk legend,' he murmured, 'Tung Wang Kung and Hsi Wang Mu play their immortal game between east and west on a bronze mirror symbolising the cosmos, each player winning and losing in turn, Yang succeeding to Yin succeeding to Yang, and so on. A legend, no more. The original Game of the Immortals was the Mirror Game. Exorcists discovered that haunted mirrors could be turned back on ghosts of reflection. From this grew the Mirror Game, a battle of wills later stylised into the game of Liu Po. The link between Liu Po and the Mirror Game is still recognised by a number of Wu magi.'

'There were two such magi in San Lung,' informed Nagarjuna. 'One of them is here. I saw him at dawn. I have no idea what became of the other.'

'Little good, I fear,' growled Liu Chun.

A sudden commotion in the courtyard made the abbot rise to his feet and peer over the parapet. A woman in a dark green cape stood under the Cloud Tower, surrounded by a trio of remonstrating monks.

After a few moments he recognised her. It was Peng-t'ai, the deaf-mute who sold her wooden statues from her stall in the town. She was mouthing a word as she stared frantically up at the abbot and her fists beat against her chest in some sort of sign. What did the sign mean? The old man concentrated, his brow contracting. Ah — it was the gesture of a boaster. A braggart.

And the mouthed word? Ah yes. It must be T'ao.

He nodded his understanding and the woman smiled in gratitude and fled into the southern precincts of the temple.

The sound of Liu Chun's voice startled him.'Chia is walking into a trap.'

The Indian nodded, unsmiling. His narrow shoulders drooped. 'At least she is not alone.'

'Not alone? What do you mean?'

'One of my monks and a San Lung girl are with her.'

Liu Chun scratched his tousled head with a frantic hand. 'But why?'

A nervous tic plucked at the abbot's cheek. 'The blame falls on me, I'm afraid. I asked her to release a girl called Nua from the Mime Realm. There was some doubt as to whether the girl was genuine or – a replica. The sorceress thought it unsafe to leave her in the monastery so she took the girl with her. Vinaya — one of the younger brethren — accompanied them to keep watch on Nua.'

'Vinaya?' The sage leaned forwards, striking the abbot

191

with a penetrative stare. 'Dharmapala mentioned that fellow. It's possible . . .' He checked himself. 'But Nua is the more obvious danger. The solution to her identity is straightforward. Were her clothes and facial features reversed?'

Nagarjuna pulled at the lobe of his ear. 'In all honesty I can't be sure. She wore an unadorned gown and her features were strikingly even. It's . . .'

Suddenly, the mention of the reversed image shook awake a memory of the morning. The abbot sprang to his feet in consternation.

'Chao!' he exclaimed. 'Peng-t'ai mouthed the name of Chao. Chao-Braggart.'

'Chao?' the other echoed.

Nagarjuna was already moving to the stairs. 'Chao,' he repeated. 'Chao the Braggart. A notorious tomb robber in these parts. A giant of a man. He was one of the last to enter this morning and I gave him a private cell because of a sick man he bore on his back. I thought him oddly changed. In fact, I didn't recognise him at first.'

The tall Chinese strode briskly after the hurrying figure of the frail Indian. The abbot's haste had his sandalled feet padding out of the tower before Liu Chun reached his side.

'Where are we going?' demanded the sage.

'To Chao's cell. Chao has a Black Serpent tattoo on the back of his right hand. I wasn't looking for it when he arrived but I *do* remember that his features were strange and that the tunic under his rag of a cloak was fastened right over left.'

'Unusual.' Liu Chun grated the word between tight teeth. 'Few people wrap their tunics in that fashion. And you say his face was strange . . .?'

The crowd they plunged through was a throb of threshing light and shadow, and the two men were jostled in their progress. The people of San Lung were celebrating their deliverance from the scourge of the mirror demons, effervescing with faith in the strong magic of the Buddha brothers.

'See how they rejoice,' the abbot shouted in his companion's ear. 'They trust us. The temple is their sanctuary. Let's hope the Black Serpent hasn't invaded it.'

Wary of the truculent Chao, the townsfolk had steered clear of his cell. An empty crescent fronted the small pine door. The heavy chimes of the Cloud Tower thundered about the lantern-glowing walls, signalling the end of the first quarter of the Hour of the Boar. Next would come the Hour of the Rat.

Disdaining caution, Liu Chung flung open the door and burst into the dim room with fists clenched. Nagarjuna followed apprehensively. An imperious silence greeted their abrupt entrance.

In a dark corner, the white-faced, red-silked stranger was bundled up on the rush mats like a lavish, unwholesome bale. The tall, brawny figure of Chao stood grinning in the centre of the room, arms akimbo, feet spread wide and firmly planted. His visage wore an unfamiliar expression like a mask.

Chao's mouth opened and an incongruously sleek voice slipped between the stained rows of eroded teeth as the chapped lips formed a tilted smile.

'Why this intrusion, my feverish friends? My privacy must be total.'

'That's not Chao's voice,' the Indian croaked hoarsely. With a deep breath he summoned his courage. 'Show us your right hand – your Black Serpent hand.'

A peculiar, modulated laugh trickled from the crooked smile of a mouth. 'My tattooed right hand? So you've finally crawled your way to a little truth, little man. Here, Buddha Groveller . . .'

Slowly and deliberately the leering Chao raised his right hand. Knotted red and blue veins branched the back of his grimy hand, but no tattoo. The skin was untouched by the needle. He lifted his left hand, and the abbot sucked in a cold snatch of air as he gaped at the Black Serpent motif writhing on the rough flesh.

The tattoo was on the back of the wrong hand. And the Black Serpent emblem was itself reversed.

Damp fears settled on Liu Chun's skin. This mirror image of Chao evoked the sage's childhood dread of ghosts.

'You are Chao's dark brother, his mirror self,' accused Liu Chun.

'Chao?' chuckled the huge man. His laughter faded as he lowered his hands. A stern, glittering quality seeped into his deeply slanted eyes.

'I am not Chao. I'm the Hearing, the Imitator, the Parody, the Shadow. The Mimic.'

He held his prey in an iron stare. They felt the breath squeezed from their lungs.

'I am Nyak,' said Chao's mouth.

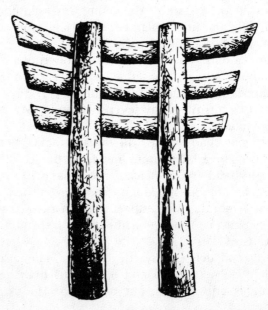

194

15

SPIRIT HILL

Somewhere, the last drop of rain fell. The rainclouds sailed north over Shen Lung Gorge and sunlight filtered into the morning valley. The Silver Brethren sat in a circle on the banks of the Shen River, their vitality sinking with the rising of the sun.

'To hell with you,' Chia sneered, averting her gaze from her enemies far below.

With careful steps she stole back into the cave, praying silently that the Brethren would remain inactive until nightfall. Vinaya and Nua were asleep. The horses were quiet and docile. Only Chia was wakeful and over-wrought, brooding on the coming night.

She was lost and bewildered.

The Yang hexagram: inexplicable. The Teh-kuo hexagram: menacing. The mysterious placidity of her yogic trance. The malaise she had suffered since summoning Nua from the mirror. Her sadism as she lay upon the girl. And the words, always the words: 'What happened in Egypt, Chia? What happened in Egypt?'

For hours the sorceress fretted over the innumerable problem that beset her as her companions slept in peace. Time after time she beat her palm in exasperation. There was a central flaw in her schemes — what was it? What, in all the chambers of hell, was she forgetting? Just once, in all her convoluted speculations, the thought occurred to her that there might be a simple answer that would cancel the necessity of the complex Liu Po exorcism. Her arch symbol – the spiral – would that be sufficient? For an instant she almost recalled . . . the illumination wavered, died.

There seemed no alternative to the hazardous game of Liu Po.

Noon waxed and waned, bringing little warmth to the shrouded cave. The horses grew restless, stamped their hooves and whinnied. 'Hush, gentle beasts, hush,' she soothed.

Afternoon slithered through the rocky chamber. Tension mounted in the heaving flanks of the stallions. The monk and the girl were still buried in dreams.

Afternoon deepened to early dusk. The eyelids of the sorceress drooped with fatigue. She bit her lip in worry and glared at her slumbering companions, debating the reason for their extended sleep. None too gently, she roused them and crept stealthily to the lip of the ledge. The Silver Brethren were sprawled in an untidy circle, but with sunset near they would soon be stirring. And in a short time the power of the Mirror Kindred would decline. Now was the time.

She coiled round as Vinaya stepped out of the cave mouth.

'Keep out of sight!' she hissed. 'Hitch up the horses as quietly as you can, and check the mirror harness. We must leave soon.'

Vinaya responded with a sardonic bow.

Orange dusk glowed in bars through the rank green curtain of vines as Chia wheeled the horses towards the cave mouth. She wound the reins around her wrists as the stallions strained against their breast-straps, eager to depart the damp confines.

'We'll have to descend quietly and carefully, sorceress,' advised the monk as he gripped the hand-rail.

'We'll have to descend quickly,' she replied, raising

196

an eyebrow. A deep breath. 'Now!' she yelled, shaking the reins.

The horses stormed out of the cave with such ferocity that the chariot was nearly carried over the rim of the ledge. Chia pulled violently to the left and steered the team onto the headlong path to the foot of the spur. Vinaya clutched the rail and swayed like a drunkard in the toss and tumble of the descending chariot. Nua, squatting beneath the draped mirror, laughed intoxicatedly above the pounding of the hooves and the thunder of the whirling wheels. Chia's hair flew like a black flag in the wind, but her cold green eyes were hard and fixed.

The chariot was bumping over the lower rises before the Silver Brethren reared to their feet and raised their silver-masked visages to the oncoming vehicle. The shallowest part of the river lay directly in front of Chia's path, and it was this potential ford that Nyak's servants were presumably guarding. Crying out in their guttural voices they lurched forwards to block the way. The sorceress caught one with the right wheel and sent him spinning. Another was crushed under the flashing feet of the sprinting stallions – Chia relished the brittle sound of snapping bones. An eruption of spray brawled around the speeding chariot as it thrust into the Shen River.

Chia laughed in exultation. 'So much for those diseased bastards, Vinaya! And the waters are free of the Mirror, the river haunting has moved further south!'

The ascetic monk seemed unimpressed. 'Take care you don't drown us in your enthusiasm, Black Dragon. The current is strong, and there are treacherous deeps hiding in the shoals.'

'Killing Silver Brethren always fills me with enthusiasm,' Chia said in a low voice, but was not too proud to heed the advice and exercise care in guiding the Fergana horses to a broad stretch of grey shallows.

A mighty lunge up the steep mudbank of the northern

shore brought them to firm ground. Chia glanced back in derision at the Silver Brethren floundering across the turbulent river. The disconcerting thought crossed her mind that it had been far too easy, but she rejected the misgiving and headed the team north along the rolling turf of the shore. As they rounded the wide bend of the gorge the scatter of oaks and elms thickened to clusters until the clusters swelled into gladed woods. The Tower of the Hound of Heaven, roseate in the shimmer of the sunset, loomed into sight on the southern crest of the gorge. Her mood darkened when she darted a look at the dull red tower. The edifice was of no concern to her present venture, but it reminded her of Nyak. It reminded her of his incalculable intelligence and inexhaustible malice.

'What of Nyak?' The monk's inquiry gave her a start. Could he see into minds?

She tossed her head with a carefree air, hiding her feelings. 'What of him? I'm turning up the slope long before we come to the bridge – I spotted a trail earlier. He won't have anticipated my chosen route, and when he realises it will be too late. Once over the lip of the gorge it's slightly downhill over the last li or so to our goal. Even Nyak can't outrun a chariot on a straight course.' *And the scent will face him like a wall.*

'So – it must be the Hour of the Hound by now. It's appropriate that we run like hounds.'

'Not quite, it's the hounds that chase us. We run like hares in the Hour of the Hound.'

With fluent motions she edged the horses away from the rippled bank and urged them up a narrow, pebbled gully that led like an ascending aisle between bowing ranks of trees to the rounded rim of the gorge. Hampered intermittently by boulders lumping across the gap and skidding wheels on shale, the ascent was not as rapid as Chia had hoped. Rattling over a low bank of stone where the wheels' iron bands clanged and emitted crimson

198

sparks in the lowering gloom, Chia cursed the din of the chariot. Even at this distance, Nyak and his servants could not fail to distinguish the source of the noise.

She swung the team onto the crest of Shen Lung Gorge with a profound sigh of relief. The Silver Brethren and their dire master were nowhere in evidence. The vista was empty, a mild stretch of dips and slopes gradually falling to the foot of Spirit Hill over a li distant.

Spirit Hill.

A lofty, irregular pyramid of swollen rock, shifting soil, starved grass and stunted trees. And for its crown, the overgrown bruise of the burial mound.

The sight was familiar, yet she was unable to recall the nature of her previous visit, or visits. There had, of course, been the dream of Chao and Fu the Unlucky scaling Spirit Hill and entering the Death Mound on the Feast of the Dead. It was a dream she scarcely re-membered, but one powerful enough to impel her on her long journey east. She suspected the dream had portrayed a real event. But it wasn't the dream that made Spirit Hill and its surrounding terrain look familiar – it was the unremembered prior visit or visits that enabled her to recognise the hill in the dream.

'The sky is the orange of a funereal mural,' Vinaya observed superciliously.

'Reserve your flippancy for when our troubles begin in earnest – you'll have need of it then,' Chia countered, rattling the reins and flexing her arms as the Fergana team hurtled down the rolling moor.

Periodically, her green gaze scanned the landscape: it was deserted. Nyak had failed to halt her journey to Spirit Hill, and on its bleak slopes he was forbidden to tread. The Brethren, sharing a small portion of the fate of their master, suffered considerable pain if they came near the hill, and agony if they approached Spirit Hill Mound. She was almost out of reach of the necromancer.

She looked over her shoulder. No signs of pursuit. Her

gaze lingered on the southern horizon for a moment, dwelling with affection on Abbot Nagarjuna and Celestial Buddha Temple. At least the temple would be safe. Her eyes skimmed to the west and the orange effulgence of the setting sun. Were her friends in the monastery also staring at the sunset, anxious on her behalf?

Suddenly, a vague vision shimmered in her mind . . . Nagarjuna staring at an inward spiral of blood on the ground between the two pillars of the torana . . .

'Sorceress! Between the trees on the first rise! Look!' The monk's pitch was shrill.

The obscure vision vanished abruptly.

Chia peered at the arch of the trees wrapping the hill's lowest fold. A figure, black in the dimness of dusk, stood gauntly beneath the arch. The figure stood directly on the path that wound up to the summit, its arms out-stretched, its face a silver mask. Chia's features tight-ened, then relaxed. She drove the team straight at the tall shape.

'Look at the height of the man!' exclaimed Vinaya as the chariot rumbled close to the leafy arch. 'Is it Nyak?'

In answer, she drove right into the figure. It crumpled under the horses and in a breath was behind the chariot, scattered over the friable soil. The monk laughed.

'It was a stick man!' he spluttered. 'A couple of crossed poles draped with a robe and crowned with a mask! No wonder you weren't alarmed.'

'It had to be an artefact,' she said. 'Nyak couldn't exist on this hill. And it would be curious indeed to find a Silver Brother confronting us in solitary defiance. They're not given to heroics.'

There was no further discussion as they pursued the meandering trail through swaying coverts and sighing grass. Above the rock-boned steeps the pale moon began to make known its presence. Nua rose and stood by her companions as the sturdy horses plodded up the wandering incline.

Chia broke the long silence. 'Where is your cave shrine?'

Vinaya waved a vague hand. 'On the north side of the hill, about two hundred feet below the summit. Do you wish to go there?'

'No. I just wondered. Quite a coincidence, isn't it?'

He frowned. 'Coincidence? In what way?'

'It's a coincidence that you were here at the precise moment that something went amiss in the Death Mound. At the same moment that I woke from a vivid dream in Black Dragon Caverns. The Hour of the Rat.'

His eyes narrowed. 'Of what are you accusing me, Black Dragon?'

She smiled distantly. 'I make no accusations. I mention mere coincidence.'

Nua swung a provocative glare on Vinaya. 'She knows, Skull Face. She's pierced your deceptions. She knows you're false.'

'One of you is, that's for sure,' Chia muttered under her breath.

The exhilaration inspired by crossing the river had dissipated, and her perennial anxiety reasserted itself. Soon she would have to play the unpredictable Mirror Game. And there was something vital she was forgetting . . . If only she had embarked alone on her quest, without distraction . . .

The whinnying of the horses caught her attention. They were nervous. Rounding a sharp outcrop the sources of the stallions' perturbation came into sight. They flicked their ears and frisked their tails as the huge dome of Spirit Hill Mound loomed above. She had to coax them as they slowed to a reluctant trot and halted in disquiet in front of the two elms that flanked the bronze doors. The doors were open.

They dismounted and studied the open bronze doors. The darkness within was absolute. The air was damp and cold.

'I wish I remembered more of my dream,' she mumbled, thinking back to the Feast of the Dead.

'What dream?' snapped Vinaya.

'Thinking aloud,' she replied. 'Now let me see – the Hour of the Rat, the hour that spans midnight. It's the time when the Mime Realm is at its weakest and all other evil forces at their strongest. Supposing that the incident – whatever it was – occurred during the Hour of the Rat; that suggests that the cause of the haunting doesn't lie in the Spirit Mirror itself. It must have come from outside. And there arises the maddening paradox again – only Nyak could have freed the Mirror and Nyak is the one person who couldn't have been here.' Her right hand clenched to a bone-white ball. 'How? How was it done? Damn my memory!'

Nua sauntered unconcernedly to the ancient doors. 'Shall we go in?'

'Not yet, my impetuous one. Stay clear of the entrance. You too, Vinaya.'

The girl shrugged casually and stepped back. The monk, with a show of reluctance, also retreated. Chia moved to the musty green bronze and scanned the primordial ideograms half-buried and eaten by the corrosion of millenia. Patina choked the sinuous symbols, but they were still decipherable. And recollections came of other times she had stood in front of these doors. Fragmented, elusive memories. Someone had been with her on those earlier visits – who was it that had stood at her side?

Dropping on one knee she studied the inswarming patterns on the bronze, tracing their paths with a light fingertip. Her brow furrowed in concentration. *Ah, Fu – are you beyond this door? No. Mustn't think of you yet. Grief-craze.*

Silence and solitude, bleak rocks and crooked trees encircled the black, saffron and blue figures. A ragged primrose cloud sank into the western sky. The sun swam in its blood on the horizon. As the Hour of the Hound died into night the sorceress suddenly drew a sharp breath. Wheeling round to the others, she raised a forefinger.

'There was a warning,' she said. 'A warning about this place. I think it began: "From the brother, the Body. From the – from the" – What comes next? In the name of all the hells . . .' She glanced at Vinaya. 'Have you ever heard such a warning?'

He shook his head.

'"From the brother, the Body,"' she intoned. 'Ah – let it go – the tomb doors haven't nudged my memory. And it'll soon be the Hour of the Boar. It's time to enter the mound. Untie Ming's mirror, Vinaya – we're taking it with us.'

As the monk set about his task Chia pushed the bronze doors fully open. The darkness shrank back as she held aloft the Night-Shining Jewel. The outlines of two brittle skeletons in rusted iron armour were revealed, ginger-rust swords broken in twig-bone hands. They sprawled with skulls and snapped swords pointing to the entrance.

'They look as if they died trying to escape,' said Nua.

'I fail to see what difficulty these rotted doors presented,' Vinaya remarked. 'Something else must have imprisoned them.'

Chia abruptly thumped her brow. 'Of course! How stupid I've been! They *were* imprisoned by another force – a force that makes the Mirror Game superfluous. All this time I've been worrying needlessly! The answer is simple!'

She stooped low and surveyed the stone threshold. She snarled in triumph and pointed to a faint pattern of lines, green threads in basalt.

'There! I was right! The ancient symbol. The spiral. Emblem of Good and Evil. This is the power which chained the Mirror for ten thousand years, a spiral composed of an ancient metal from a vanished age, and I forgot it was here! And there's another spiral – under the secret door to the Golden Chamber where the Spirit Mirror is housed. Yes, I remember – two spirals for the Two that are One.'

The lean monk folded his arms. 'Is that all that held the Mirror in check – two spirals?' His tone and expression evinced disbelief.

'These spirals were drawn by a mighty opponent of the Thzan-tzai, a hero whose name is lost in history. They can imprison anything.'

Vinaya was still sceptical. 'Then why the enormous construction of the burial mound, with no one to bury? Why the chambers and secret door?'

'Aren't you familiar with the paraphernalia of carnival magicians?' she asked. 'When magicians are encased in stout boxes it isn't the elaborate locks and sturdy chains that imprison them – they're only distractions to divert the onlookers from the single element that releases the magician from his prison. Shackles are distractions in carnival displays. The doors and chambers of Spirit Hill Mound are distractions from the spirals. My memory has been so much at fault that I was blinded by those diversions myself. As were these poor wretches who failed to uncover the means of escape.'

'You mean that the spirals confined everything within the tomb, men included?'

'Yes. Once an intruder entered, he couldn't escape. The Spiral of Power would present an impassable barrier to his will. And even if he identified the Spiral as the source of the obstacle he would be unequipped to deal with it. Only I know the full secret of the symbol.'

'And Nyak?' queried Vinaya with a lift of the shoulders.

'Nyak knows half the secret, and his feet can't touch the soil of this hill,' came the acid reply.

'As you say.'

'I've had my fill of brooding on the necromancer,' she

muttered. 'Silver Brethren . . . T'ai Ching trances . . . Liu Po mirror games . . . Hexagrams . . . My brain has been whirling like a leaf in the dragon wind. Undisciplined speculation defeats the purpose of speculation. All that mattered was the spiral. Just that.' *Fu – at the back of my skull, grief-mad, your cries resound.*

Her slanted, numinous eyes carefully assessed the delicate green spiral. The blue phosphorescence of the Night-Shining Jewel bathed her features with the calm glow of the mystic. Nua crossed her arms and watched in silence. Vinaya shuffled impatiently. At length, the sorceress lifted and dropped her shoulders.

'The spiral doesn't move,' she said vacantly.

'Could you elaborate?' the monk requested after a lengthy pause.

She didn't answer at first, then spoke in a hushed tone as if to herself. 'The Outward Spirals of Light. The Inward Spirals of Darkness. All the Spirals of Power should move. The spiral is frozen. Some influence has suspended its motion. The eye is drawn neither outwards nor inwards. This could be what released the Death Whisperers . . .'

Vinaya pursed his thin lips. 'But would this frozen spiral – whatever *that* means – be sufficient to animate the Mirror? The Mirror Kindred require light and reflections. There is no light in the tomb.'

'The torch of an intruder would be sufficient if there are pools in the chamber.'

'What of the other spiral – the one beneath the secret door? Is that not enough to restrain the Mime Realm?'

She shook her head. 'The two symbols act as one. As one moves, so moves the other. As one is stilled, so the other is stilled.' She jerked up her chin. 'Wait – I remember another part of the warning . . . Something about a sister . . .'

'Apart from all this abstruse pondering, do you think that the Mirror is still within the mound?'

'It has to be,' she replied with less than certainty, 'or the direction of the spiral would be reversed, not simply frozen. The freezing of the vortex would permit the Mirror to spread its scent, but I can't imagine that it would be able to escape the tomb.'

He lifted his palms, feigning exasperation. 'Then what needs to be done, Black Dragon?'

'The spiral must be restored to its previous flow and direction. And if you'll close your mouth that's exactly what I'll do.'

Chia did not voice a huge doubt. She did not admit aloud that she was unsure of the correct direction. Was it outwards or inwards? She was convinced that she had once been familiar with the proper flow, but her treacherous memory had betrayed her as so often before and the essential knowledge was withheld. The outward flow attracted her most, but by favouring it was she falling into one of the necromancer's intricate traps? However – there was the Third Way, the technique she had used against T'ai Ching Masters. The Third Way. Empty the mind. Act on impulse from the deep self. That was sure to thwart Nyak's plans – the spontaneous is that which cannot be predicted. She gently closed her eyes and drifted into meditation . . . Down through the days and domains . . . The descent into Primal Self was blissfully effortless . . .

The yellow-robed monk and the blue-gowned girl stared intently at the rapt, kneeling sorceress. Moonlight sifted through foliage-clouded elms and fell softly as a spirit on the rough, stubbled ground. The Night-Shining Jewel at Chia's side distilled blue radiance.

Vinaya drew a quick breath as Chia's hand moved as though of its own accord to the spiral. Her fingertip touched the centre of the spiral. Her whole being was concentrated in that touch.

And slowly, very slowly, she traced the faint green path outwards in ever-widening circles.

As her finger moved from the outermost limb of the spiral her eyelids opened to the black tunnel. Awareness flooded back and she sprang from the door. She stood between her two companions with bated breath, glancing at the spiral animated by the outward flow. The dark tunnel looked as before – implacable.

Time crawled. Nothing burst out of the dark corridor. There was silence. Chia began to feel a tentative hope . . .

At first it was very feeble, the breath that came from the door.

As feeble as the breath of a rat, and with the scent of a rat.

But Chia sensed it, and her muscles went rigid. The breath grew to a sigh. The sigh strengthened to a foetid breeze. Darkness bulged from the open doors. The breeze rose to a wind. The wind mounted to a black gale, pouring from the gaping mouth of the mound.

'It's coming,' moaned Chia. 'Aten protect us! It's coming . . .'

The blast blew them aside like straw dolls and tumbled them over the bumpy turf. Its vast roaring tormented Chia's ears and its brutal buffets knocked the breath from Chia's lungs.

But the gale passed quickly. Its violence ceased. Its bellow faded. Chia staggered to her feet and watched numbly as the trees on the slopes just below the ledge threshed and groaned in the unnatural, misty gale before lapsing into stillness as the trees on yet lower slopes were hit with the same ferocity. The savage breath from Spirit Hill Mound was beating a slow path down the hill.

Vinaya ran to a despairing Chia. 'Sorceress! What's happening?'

She turned dead eyes on him. 'The Mirror Breath is moving down the slopes. It's moving south. I made the wrong decision with the Spiral Flow. Chia the Death-bringer they call me. The Spirit Mirror wasn't fully free before I interfered but by my blundering I've set it free. I went to help a sick man and made him a corpse. The Mirror Breath moves south, and the monastery is in its path.'

The spiral, she reflected bitterly, the spiral. If, by some miracle, Nyak had stood in front of the tomb he would be restricted to moving the spiral in the inward path. Nyak's spirit was limited to the inward path. Chia was the sole one who could move the spiral in both directions. The Inward Spiral imprisons, the Outward Spiral frees. Chia had freed the Spirit of the Mirror.

'Chia the Fool,' she whispered. 'Chia the Fool . . .'

Vinaya flinched slightly as a feral rage blazed in her forest-green eyes. She spread her wide-sleeved arms to the south like the splayed black wings of a bat. She screamed her fury.

'May you be damned to all the Hundred Hells, Nyak! Damned for eternity!'

The Sight, if it loved anything, loved the perfect madness.

The perfect madness came not from the unknown but from the known. Its face, if face it could be called, was drawn from the familiar, not from the alien.

At first it had been quiet and discreet like a rumour whispered in a confidential ear. But now it roared with glee as it bounded from the summit of Spirit Hill.

The Spirit of the perfect madness had, for a time, been divided from the Body.

In its prison, the perfect madness had been whole, whole for ten thousand years. Then there came the split in its wholeness with the freezing of the spirals. The Two that are One became one and one.

But the split in the perfect madness of the Spirit Mirror would be healed in the approaching Hour of the Rat. Just a little while.

The Sight, too, was divided, divided from the Hearing

and the Deep Self that lay under the Sight and the Hearing. But the time of waiting would be short. As the perfect madness made itself whole, so would the Sight be made whole with the Hearing. The Sight and Hearing would also be the Two that are One.

The Spirit scent moved south, streaming to unite with its old flesh.

Then the Spirit Mirror would don more flesh – Buddha flesh.

The Sight noted, dispassionately, that the end of the game was in view.

Chia had almost arrived at the centre of the maze.

Soon she would walk into it. And her inner refuge was the trap at the centre.

And the centre would suck her down in the Inward Spiral.

Forever.

The Sight was about to win the Game of the Immortals.

16

BLACK
SERPENT BREATH

Chao again lifted his left hand with its reversed Black Serpent tattoo and reiterated the chilling declaration: 'I am Nyak.'

Liu Chun fought to regain his stolen voice. 'Liar,' he managed to croak. 'You are Chao's mirror self. A demon.'

Chao's bronzed face split into a cold smile. 'A demon? Not a bad title, although I prefer the Mimic. But Nyak is who I am, Master of Desecration, and by the Hour of the Rat this temple will be a relic of desecration. Now leave before I make you tread the measure of the Mirror Dance.'

Nagarjuna shot a glance at the supine stranger in the red silk gown. 'Who are you?' he demanded. 'Can you hear me?'

'He cannot hear you for the moment, but you'll soon discover who he is,' rippled Chao's mouth. 'Now leave, crabbed Indian.'

Liu Chun pulled himself up to his full stature. 'He takes no orders from you, Mirror Creature. By the spirit of Mo Ti, I'll wring payment from you for making threats!' Lurching forwards truculently he bunched his fists.

Unperturbed, Chao remained in his insouciant stance. Opening the moist cavern of his mouth he expelled a soft breath. A dark mist swirled from his stretched lips and expanded to meet the sage's onslaught. Liu Chun recoiled from the unnerving spectacle. The black breath tendrilled out to the two shaken men like a cloud of ink swelling in water. The abbot choked, fighting for breath. Liu Chun's capacious lungs battled for air as his vision swam and his head reeled. The noxious vapour embraced them in branched tentacles. Gripping his spluttering friend by the arm, Liu Chun staggered to the door and out into the blessedly clean air of night. The door banged shut. Amazed townsfolk gathered at a discreet distance as the two coughed from burning chests.

Finally recovering from the harsher effects of the vapour, Liu Chun wheezed out sporadic sentences. 'By my ancestors, it seared like ice and fire!'

The abbot nodded in mute agreement. 'It rolled my breath . . . cold fire . . . black gale . . .' He swayed to his feet and weakly signalled the sage to follow as he tottered to the northern end of the monastery.

Nagarjuna drank air like precious liquid and observed the disorganised departure of the San Lung families while his craggy companion struggled with the strategies of Wei-ch'i. Harassed monks bustled hither and thither in an effort to bring an element of order to the chaos.

The two men had resumed their perch on the topmost tier of the Cloud Tower where they could survey the evacuation to best advantage and discuss their plight in private. Liu Chun glowered at the turmoil below. The brethren had been instructed to persuade the townsfolk to leave through the Red Phoenix Gate for the southern road, but many insisted on returning by the Black Serpent Gate to their homes in San Lung and at least a hundred obdurately refused to flee the illusory sanctuary of the temple. Those who were leaving had lost faith in the protection of the Celestial Buddha; those who remained would soon find the apparent refuge a terrible prison. Either way the Indian mission had foundered.

'The Indian candle of the Buddha flickers in the Chinese wind, Temple Master.'

The other bowed, head in hands. 'Yes, and the light may not be rekindled for generations if it's quenched now. There is no greater anger than the anger of faith betrayed. Those who refuse to believe there is a threat from the Mirror Being have the strongest faith – their faith will turn to wrath when they're faced with the truth.'

'And what is this Mirror Being?' growled Liu Chun. 'He appears to be Chao's mirror self, but he claims otherwise. Could he be Nyak in disguise? It seems possible. And what can his purpose be, whoever he is? Also there's the mystery of the ailing stranger in red.'

The abbot's leathery features were drawn with despair. 'Events have outrun my comprehension. And I'm weary and sick at heart. Decades of work wasted. Chia confronting the power in Spirit Hill Mound with nothing but a misguided Game of the Immortals at her disposal. A scent of horror that can't be scented drifting on the wind . . .'.

Liu Chun gazed bleakly at the wooden Wheel of Samsara. 'You can still leave if you wish. San Lung is floating into a ghost world. Best to run. The Thzan-tzai scent can't spread all over China.' *Can* it?

'No,' responded the abbot firmly. 'That would be the ultimate surrender. None of the brethren would leave and betray the Buddha Spirit. The monastery is the home of our community – our Sangha. But you must depart, old friend. This isn't your affair.'

Rallying his spirits, the sage squared his broad shoulders. 'That *would* be the ultimate betrayal. And you're mistaken – this is my affair.' He drew a deep breath. 'Chia has saved my life twice. And she's a girl – or woman – I never know what to call her – whom I fell

212

utterly and completely in love with the first time I met her, the way men do in tales and songs. I know I'm not the only one. I also know it's hopeless; that she responds only to a female touch. But for all that, Chia is life to me. If Chia's long life ends in San Lung, then mine ends here too.' He took an even deeper breath, expelled it loudly. 'There,' he declared. 'Now I've said it. And probably never will again.'

A long, heavy silence followed the sage's outburst. Nagarjuna, in spite of the dangers that seemed to be closing in on every side, found the vivid image of Chia forcing into his thoughts. He had long been aware of Liu Chun's love for the sorceress, but the Indian had always seen Chia as a bewildering mixture of mother, sister, daughter. One thing was sure, it was impossible to be indifferent to her.

'There must be a chance of her surviving the Mound,' he thought out loud.

Liu Chun rubbed his hairy jowl. 'Perhaps,' he conceded. 'With Green-Eyes anything's possible. I was eighteen when our paths first crossed, a young officer riding with a detachment of cavalry near the mouth of the Yangtze. We were attacked by a rebel band that wanted to seize and dishonour the Imperial standard we bore. The rebel banner was a gold dragon on white, as I recall. A fierce battle ensued. Then Chia made her appearance.'

'And she saved the Imperial cavalry?'

'No. She attacked everybody and burned both banners. The sorceress never did like soldiers. But, by heaven, the way she fought ... Half the time you couldn't see her at all, she was so fast. And she jumped as high and landed as softly as a cat. We were the mice. And this mouse was the first to surrender. I've followed that cat ever since. You know, where other people might break up fights, Chia goes around breaking up battles. And all with a silver dagger.' Liu Chun nodded, his eyes

213

brimming with memories. 'Yes,' he breathed deeply. 'With Chia anything's possible.' Then the ex-warrior's eyes clouded. 'But one day death is sure to catch her out. Her flesh is mortal flesh. A dagger in her neck. A sword in her heart. Poison in her stomach. One day the true death will find her. The day will come. Perhaps it is now.'

The abbot could find no words to answer the look in Liu Chun's face.

Peng-t'ai sat with knees pressed to her chest, and arms hugging her knees in the dark, domed stupa. All about her, where she sat in the centre of the sacred circle, was the invisible but almost palpable spirit of the newborn Chinese Buddha.

The flame of the Buddha had cured her flesh of the red plague from the hand of the man in the silver mask. She prayed that the Buddha Spirit in the candle-crowded dome would be strong enough to repel the Chao-thing and the masked ones.

And also – she sensed it coming – she prayed that the Buddha was mighty enough to withstand an evil that was blowing from the north. Yes, it was coming. An evil was coming. And the evil was aiming for the centre.

And the stupa was the centre. The stupa was the Buddha-heart of the temple. An evil was howling from the Death Mound in the north to turn the stupa into another kind of death mound.

It was a kind of loving madness, this evil. It wanted her. It wanted everyone.

And Peng-t'ai began to fear that nothing could stop it.

'Do you believe that Chao is truly possessed by Nyak?' asked the abbot, breaking the long silence.

The sage pondered for a space, then nodded. 'I believe that Nyak has projected his spirit into Chao's body as a ray of moonlight strikes below the surface of a lake. I believe that he is both Nyak and a mirror self – indeed, he could well be Nyak's mirror self.'

'If that's true, then what is the power he wields?'

'The power of T'ai Ching,' the sage replied without hesitation. 'The power of illusion cast by word or by thought alone. It's a power the Silver Brethren share, in lesser degree. Nyak and the Brethren can make you see or not see what they wish.' His eyes suddenly widened with alarm. 'Will of Heaven!' he exclaimed.

'What is it?'

'They could be standing right beside us now,' he said in a whisper. 'And we wouldn't even know!'

Nagarjuna flexed uneasily, glancing involuntarily over his shoulder. 'Do you think we should speak in a whisper?' he inquired in a quiet voice.

'That won't do any good,' Liu Chun stated firmly and regretfully. 'Whispering is their speciality, if Green-Eyes is to be believed, and I'm sure she is. All we can do is – well, talk as if they're not here.'

The abbot shrugged acceptance.

'We've got to have some sort of plan,' the sage insisted. 'Any sort of plan. Agreed?'

The abbot spread his mouth in a wry grimace. 'All I can say is that I'm silently praying for Chia to return through the Black Serpent Gate and deliver us from the nightmare in the temple.'

A sombre expression filled Liu Chun's battle-scarred face. 'Chia, for all her powers, is in the greatest danger I've ever known her to be. She's facing the Spirit Mirror, and unless she remembers the use of her spiral magic in time the Mirror will overwhelm her. And she's accompanied on this hazardous mission by a dubious girl and – of all people – Vinaya.'

'Why the reservations about Vinaya? Wolf Mask, as I like to call him, has one of the keenest minds in the Order.'

'I'm not gainsaying the keenness of his intellect – I'm merely repeating Dharmapala's doubts. He expressed misgivings about Vinaya's strange behaviour in the first few days after the Feast of the Dead. Also, he was the only monk to bring a haunted mirror into the temple.'

The grey eyebrows arched in surprise. 'You're mistaken, Liu Chun. It was Dharmapala who brought Nua's mirror into the garan.'

'Did you see him do it?'

'No.'

'Then who told you it was Dharmapala?'

'Vinaya.'

The abbot lapsed into silence as he absorbed the news. Liu Chun was on the verge of consoling his brooding friend when Amaravita appeared and swung the ponderous beam to ring the chimes, announcing the change from the Hour of the Boar to the Hour of the Rat. The chimes of doom, thought the sage as the brazen tones reverberated into the night. Looking past the tiered chimes he saw that the Wheel of Samsara was moving, without pressure of wind or hand, from right to left. His scalp still tingled when the unnatural motion ceased.

When the last echo of the chung bells had bounced into the distance and Amaravita had retired with an apologetic air, Nagarjuna faced his companion with his old, brown profile as stern as hard, chiselled wood. A new firmness sounded in his tone.

'As you suggest, the omens are inauspicious for Chia. But there's nothing we can do for her. Our task is to oppose the evil in the temple. We can't judge whether it's Chao, a mirror self, or Nyak – not for sure. Let's call it the Black Serpent. We must plot the downfall of this Black Serpent.'

'Don't forget the red silk stranger with the white face,' the sage reminded. 'So far we haven't got a clue of his rôle, and I'll lay long odds it's a significant one.'

The abbot nodded agreement.

In silence, the warrior-recluse contemplated the game

of Wei-ch'i. With a pensive expression he studied the results. 'I played with my heart on the side of the black,' he mutttered finally, 'but white has stolen the breath of the four winds from the greater part of the black stones. All in all, white has surrounded black.'

The Mimic in Chao's body cast the thought of invisibility into the minds of the monastic fools and walked unseen around the stupa, the Buddha Hall, the Cloud Tower. Also unseen, four Silver Brethren followed the Mimic, the Hearing, Nyak the Master.

Nyak-Mimic was amused by the blindness, the deafness, the madness.

For a time he stood on the crown of the Cloud Tower, listening to the ridiculous plots of the sage and the abbot. The Mimic laughed, unheard, at their pathetic scheming.

The Mimic looked to the north, expectant. Soon the Two would be One.

'Then you will all become me,' said the Mimic.

Deep into the Hour of the Rat the two men debated rival tactics to deal with the Black Serpent and the Silken Stranger. The hundred or more townsfolk that had elected to stay were congealed in tight, quiet groups centred on the hallowed dome of the stupa. The saffron brethren paced fretfully in the courtyard facing the north Gate of the Black Serpent.

A brief space after the mid-point of the hour had struck, they reached a decision. Liu Chun straightened his stiff spine and stretched his muscled arms.

'Then we're agreed, Mahayana Master. When Chao comes out of the cell I'll kill him with flame-arrows from the elmwood bow. He's flesh and bone, after all.'

Nagarjuna ruefully shook his head. 'This contravenes the rule of ahimsa. Is it lawful to protect a way of non-violence by the use of violence? But, reluctantly, I bow to your wish.'

217

'Excellent. I'll fetch the weapon now if you —'

'What's that?' the abbot cried, starting to his feet and peering to the north.

'I don't know, but I hear it too,' responded Liu Chun, rising. 'A distant rumble like a low growl from the earth . . .' He paused. 'It's getting nearer, I think.' He stared intently at the rolling northern landscape. 'Look!' he bellowed. 'Due north. A small patch of horizon and stars is wavering as if in a heat haze.'

'My sight is weaker than my hearing,' Nagarjuna murmured, screwing up his small eyes. 'I cannot see the shivering vision.'

The sage's voice was grim. 'It's growing larger.'

'Ah — I see it now. And the roaring of the wind is stronger.'

The rising wind fled like hunted prey from the oncoming apparition, fanning the weathered faces of the watching men. The approaching tempest, invisible as thought, slow as a loping tiger, snarled up the hill to the Gate of the Black Serpent.

Liu Chun, shocked by a sudden premonition, wheeled round to behold the grey figure of Chao stalking into the north courtyard with the red shape of the Silken Stranger in his arms. Chao lowered his burden and lifted his hand in invitation to the north.

A rending crash shook the timbers of Black Serpent Gate. The monks scattered in panic. The gate shuddered under a second impact, then shattered into a hundred fragments that were borne aloft like straw in a gale. A seething mist bawled through the broken mouth of the temple, a mist that darkened the hues and twisted the outlines of all it touched. A score of the monastic brethren were sent reeling from its onslaught as it fell upon the waiting form of Chao.

As the head of the tempest dropped, a chariot, its contours distorted by the boiling mist, thundered beneath the northern arch.

The two Fergana horses that drew the vehicle reared to a halt as the charioteer pulled violently on the reins. The driver of the chariot was flanked by two Silver Brethren.

The charioteer raised a fist in triumph or defiance at the Black Serpent and the Silken Stranger.

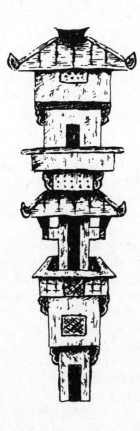

17

DEATH MOUND

'At least the horses haven't bolted,' said Vinaya. 'Do you
think we could outrace the Mirror Breath back to the
temple?'

Chia, still trembling from the shock of liberating the
dark gale, marshalled her thoughts. 'We could,' she
gasped. 'But I'm not leaving yet. I need to explore the
tomb. But you can go if you go alone.'

The monk waved the idea aside. 'I'll stay.'

'As you wish. First I have to return the spiral to its
frozen state to allow us to enter and depart at will. This
outward flow stops us from entering – the inward flow
will imprison us once inside.'

The act of restoring the Outward Spiral to the Unmoving Spiral was soon completed. She picked up the
Night-Shining Jewel and beckoned them to follow. 'Keep
your wits about you,' she whispered over her shoulder.
'We can't be sure of what's inside.'

With one stride Chia moved from moonlight to night.

Now the time is here, beloved Fu.

The skeletons shifted with a dry rattle as she brushed
them to one side with a bare foot.

*I'm here at last, gentle Fu. I've hardly dared to think of you
until now but now that I am free to think of you I'm filled with
dread of what I'll find in the burial mound. If you're not here
then the Spirit Mirror or Nyak and the Brethren have taken
you. And if you're here – if you're (dead) here – then you've
shared the tomb with the Spirit of the Mirror for more than a*

month and even if you had food and water you're (dead) bound to be suffering from the congealed Thzan-tzai, scent that saturated this place for so long and how could your (dead) spirit have withstood the congealed scent of the Thzan-tzai, the Masters of the Infinite Flesh who became the Unshaped Masters, and how is it possible that you're (dead) . . . You're (dead). You're dead.

Chia halted abruptly on the downward path. The tunnel was airless and heavy with cold, a cold that permeated the radiance of the blue stone, a cold blue radiance that illuminated no more than two paces of the dipping floor. The path was lined with mouldering skeletons shored against the dank walls.

No. Not dead. I will not let her be dead. That voice in my head that speaks of her death is the voice I resisted for three thousand li. Step by step of my long journey I denied that voice and I still deny that voice and I will not listen to the lie in the back of my skull. Fu is alive because I will not let her be dead. Never in my life have I set foot on Spirit Hill because it's the place I fear most in the world. Each time I passed by it I felt my shadow move within me but now I walk into its dead heart for love of you, gentle girl. And you're not dead because I'll not let you be dead. I refuse your death.

'Fundamental men,' rang out Vinaya's sardonic tones as he indicated the bones. 'We are the dressed skeletons.'

'Keep your fatuous comments to yourself, emaciated monk,' replied Chia. 'Flippancy is the garb of the mediocre.'

'And virulence the mark of the virago,' came the counterblast. 'But,' he added, 'it's good to see you've kept your fiery spirit even in the stomach of the Death Mound.'

Did you hear that, Fu? They see me yet they don't see me. My mouth says one thing and my face shows the same thing and that's all they hear and see. Nothing shows. I remain within myself. The Silver Brethren aren't the only ones who wear a mask.

They continued stealthily down the chill passage, each beat of Chia's heart pounding the same message, 'she's dead – she's dead – she's dead', but her mind ran away from the remorseless heart.

The patina-smeared doors at the end of the tunnel were open, and beyond them was a thin vertical band of golden light. Chia almost felt that she was reliving her dream on the Feast of the Dead. She almost imagined dream phantoms of Fu and her brutish captor stealing past her in the darkness.

Oh, Fu, be alive . . .

The sorceress turned to her companions. 'Wait here,' she ordered. 'Vinaya – keep watch on Nua.' She paused. 'And Nua – keep watch on Vinaya.'

Nua gave vent to a low chuckle of satisfaction as Chia crept warily to the far side of the chamber and the strip of golden light. The two at the door kept her indistinct figure under close scrutiny as her hands glided to the edge of the glowing gold. Suddenly the light expanded to a blazing rectangle of gold as Chia wrenched open the erstwhile secret door above the pool. A golden luminescence transfigured the stones of the vault and the ruinous triple coffin; the pool was liquid gold, the strewn bones and bone-dust were carven gold and gold-dust.

'What is fundamental in humans, Vinaya, depends on the light in which they're seen,' declared the sorceress, her voice voluminous in the Golden Chamber. 'Now, would you go and untie Ming's mirror from the chariot and bring it here, please? Take Nua with you – she may be of assistance, and keep both eyes wide for the Silver Brethren. Now, please, would you leave me?'

Vinaya laid bony hands on narrow hips and shook his head. 'No. That's a ridiculous request. I don't share your superhuman strength, Green-Eyes. It's physically impossible for me to lift that bronze mirror, even with the feeble help of the girl.' He waved a skeletal hand at the corpse lying beside the round pool in front of the secret door. 'That dead thing there would be as much use,' he sniffed.

Chia's head rose menacingly as her fingers bent into barbs. 'Don't tell me what's impossible, you bastard! *Just do as I say*! NOW!'

A tiger would have flinched at Chia in such a mood, but the target of her wrath simply gave an airy lift of his narrow shoulders and beckoned to Nua. 'Come, Mirror Girl, the mistress demands a mirror.'

They departed without another word.

Left alone, Chia closed her eyes. One look as she entered the chamber had been enough. Just one look was enough. That one look had almost stopped her heart. It wasn't that the rational part of her hadn't expected it. It had always expected it. It was just that Chia always had the courage to hope, and was never afraid of the grief-pain that struck her when hope was smashed into the ground.

The grief-pain was in her now, so much so that the pain in her breast was a physical ache.

Fu, gentle Fu. I loved you. I love you. There will always be love in my heart for you. Your pain is over. Leave this dark land called the world. Run through the shining forests of the Everlasting Lands. One day I will join you there, and we'll make love under trees that sing.

For a long while the sorceress stood with sealed eyes, adjusting her heart to the reality of Fu's death and strengthening her resolve to set right the horror she had unwittingly released into the world. And she let her hatred of Nyak grow with each inhalation of breath, for Nyak was behind Fu's death and the Mirror haunting. They had chosen to kill Fu because they had discovered that there was love between Chia and Fu. Nyak always killed and tortured the ones Chia loved. She still dreaded to think what might have happened to humorous, lively Yi of the generous heart and wide, cheeky smile – kidnapped by Silver Brethren two years ago. Now there was Fu.

'It's gone on long enough, necromancer,' hissed Chia between tight teeth.

She felt the hate and vengeance flowing through her limbs and tingling into her hooked fingers.

'It's time, Nyak. I'm going to make an end of our ancient battle. I won't just kill you. I'll exterminate you utterly. I'll make you nothing. You'll scream for hell but I won't let you run there.'

At last Chia opened her sad green eyes. She was ready. As ready as she would ever be.

She knelt beside the corpse of Fu where it lay spread-eagled face down by the round pool. The body stank like stale water. A mildewed paper lantern and rusty iron chain and collar lay beside it. Chia turned the body face upwards.

'Hell's fangs . . .' she whispered, wincing at the contorted features and vicious throat wound. Mastering a sudden upsurge of wild grief she studied the cruel rent in the girl's throat, a wound encircled by a slender chain and a black jade dragon pendant. It was the work of a crude knife, that rough gash.

Oh Fu . . . I do what must be done. I perform the task. But inside I'm screaming . . .

Impulsively, Chia clasped the body to her, momentarily seeing the vibrant girl that was once in the corpse that was now. From the pain and the hidden past Chia sensed the vitality that had once been Fu. Fu murmuring to her in the elm wood. Fu gripping the black dragon amulet at her breast. *Aid me, Little Dragon.* Fu riding her pony through sunlight and shadow in a pine wood. Fu – beaten and terrified in Spirit Hill Mound. Fu – despairing and dying . . .

Chia rested Fu's head on her breast and rocked it to and fro as if she were rocking a child to sleep.

'Safe now, safe. Not to worry. Not to worry,' she murmured.

But I mustn't think of this as Fu. Fu is running under the trees of the Everlasting Lands.

224

She let the girl slide from her embrace to the floor. The slight jolt as the head met the ground dislodged an eye from its socket. The silty orb dropped back into the skull from which it had once looked out at the world.

From the crack of the door, the gold ray struck the face like a sword. The Night-Shining Jewel which she had unconsciously placed beside the corpse bathed the corrupted lineaments with the softness of blue liquid. Chia wiped a tear from her cheek, unsheathed the silver dagger and gulped in loathing of the task that faced her.

This isn't Fu . . . Fu's in the Everlasting Lands . . . this isn't Fu . . . it's just meat . . .

'Forgive me.'

The blade tore through the damp red silk, exposing the decomposition of the body in golden light. It bit into the soft skin. It carved the stale flesh and gutted the innards.

Not Fu . . . not Fu . .

Finally, the grisly operation was finished and the rank viscera and web of veins revealed their secrets. Deterioration was far advanced, but Chia was skilled in anatomy.

A month dead though the girl was, the sorceress could tell she was drained of blood.

Drained of blood. But no sign of blood around the body, except . . .

Chia scanned the edge of the round pool. There were traces of old blood around the pool, but that was all. She peered into the pool. She could discern the faint green lines of the threshold spiral under its surface, the spiral that guarded the secret door to the inner chamber. But no hint of blood.

'Blood spiralling in water,' she mumbled, seeing blood memories behind her green eyes.

Forgive me for struggling to forget you, Fu. I must carry a stone heart for what I have to do when I enter the secret Golden Chamber. Emotion will destroy me in the Game of the Immortals.

In spite of her grief over the girl, it had been creeping into Chia's heart for some time. She couldn't name it. But it was there. Some form of dread was wafting towards her. She hadn't been conscious of it at first, but now she was. It was a fragile breath of fear that rose as much within her as it seemed to blow from without. It was nonsensical to feel thus after the shock of seeing Fu's body and the horror of opening her flesh like a fruit. But it was there, nevertheless.

And something in her knew its source. She slowly turned and looked at the remains of the threefold coffin in the middle of the chamber.

It was no more than a sodden, shattered old relic. Bits and pieces of rotting wood foundering in slime.

But it had a scent of fear about it.

Thzan-tzai? Was it Thzan-tzai? Was that the scent?

No. The scent of the Unshaped Masters was unde-tectable by the human sense of smell. The Thzan-tzai scent was manifested in memories, dreams, ghosts . . .

Bass thunder rumbled from the tunnel. She was startled for an instant, then remembered Ming's Mirror.

Goodbye, Fu. Time to wear the mask again. Time to play the sorceress role, inside and outside. If I don't, I'll die. And your killer lives.

The ponderous mirror in its red silk shroud crashed into the dark chamber with Vinaya running in its wake.

'Ah!' he observed. 'I see you weren't caught in its path.'

'And I see you've learned to live with dis-appointments.' *See how well I play the role, Fu?* She gestured at the mirror. 'Check that the drape isn't ripped or loose . . . Where's Nua?'

'Here.' The girl ambled into the room. 'You can't lose me, sister. We two are as one.'

Chia's eyes narrowed.

The Two that are One. The prophecy. The warning. The Two that are One – the Body and the Spirit of the Mirror. When the

226

spirals were frozen on the Feast of the Dead, the Body could be removed from the Mound. But the Spirit had still been imprisoned. Ah yes – ah yes – the Spirit was imprisoned until my Outward Spiral released it. Now the Spirit has gone to join the Body. The perfect madness has truly begun . . .

She turned to Vinaya, all grief for Fu suppressed in the face of the catastrophe she had initiated. 'I'm a fool, Vinaya. A complete fool. I've walked straight into a trap. Damn! I was panicked into action. Everything I've done has been foreseen by Nyak. If I had done nothing events would soon have returned to normal, for how long can the Two that are One be divided? A season, at most, before the Body perished from the deprivation of its Spirit. Nyak couldn't unleash the Mirror Breath so I was tricked into doing it for him – I, Chia the Fool. Chia the . . .'

She checked herself. Why was she unburdening her pack of woes onto a man in whom she placed slight trust? It was as if, in spite of her heightening distaste of the man, she regarded him as a comrade – even a brother. Chia disliked the new emotion, turned from it, pointed at the corpse. 'Who murdered her, Saffron Robe?'

The monk displayed indetermination with a show of palms. 'Who can say? Not I. And why presume murder? It could have been suicide.'

'Then show me the knife. And show me where she stored her blood. Her veins were squeezed dry at the moment of death but there are only thin traces of blood around this pool. The real question is where the blood has gone. What possible reason could there be for a narrow ring of old blood around a pool but none inside it? Any suggestions?'

He crossed his arms. 'None.'

A quirky smile twitched the corner of her mouth. 'If you don't know then I'll ask the pool. The circle of water has an unhealthy air about it. It's a kwai pool, if my guess is correct. It must have had some influence on the spiral it covers. Or perhaps the spiral influenced the pool that covered it. Either way, the influence was evil. It is haunted water, permeated by the presence of the Spirit Mirror. It may hold the memory of the murder and tell us how the spirals came to be frozen.'

She knelt by the pool and peered into its circle. Chia unravelled the days back to the Feast of the Dead and untied the hours of the festival eve to arrive at the Hour of the Rat, uniting her memory with the sleek surface of the water. The resurrected images she pictured in the pool were strengthened and reflected back by the pool. The Hour of the Rat. Fretful dreams.

Skies of wrath — grey shrouds, black shrouds, white shrouds savaged with knives . . . Two silhouettes scaling a jagged slope . . . Patina muting the bronze of the burial doors . . . A girl in a red silk gown and blue cloak rushes to the tunnel . . . Chao pursues her . . . The girl is hurled back by the Inward Spiral . . . Her grey-cloaked captor drags her back, dashes her head to the floor . . . Fu lies unconscious in the flickering lantern-light . . . Chao leans on the unopened secret door . . . Waiting in the dark with knife in hand . . . His swarthy face clouds . . . Whispered to death . . .

The swart face was swallowed in the black of the pool and the blank of Chia's memory. The vision vanished where her dream had ended. Compressing her lips in vexation she tilted her head to the narrow gold crack of the secret door.

'I must locate the Spirit Mirror. The Mirror Breath travels south, so it lies somewhere in that direction. It's time to play the Game of the Immortals before Mirror Body and Spirit are reunited.' Her voice was steadier than her heart.

Vinaya and Nua watched impassively as Chia lifted Ming's mirror and rolled it towards the Golden Chamber, bidding the monk to open the door wide. Squinting in the glare of the Golden Chamber she heaved the great disc to the centre of the glittering floor. The room had the light of a furnace and the cold of an ice lake. Silence saturated the blazing walls.

'Shall we follow?' the monk called out.

Chia leaned towards the entrance. 'Stay where you are. I'm going to move the door so that the slimmest of cracks remains, and it must stay in that position. Keep out of this room – preferably on the far side of the burial chamber – I can't predict what forces may be unleashed in the struggle of the Mirror Game.'

With a certain reluctance they withdrew, and Chia pulled the door inwards so that only the thinnest bar of darkness showed on the smooth golden walls.

'Vinaya,' she shouted through the crack, 'beware Nua. Nua – beware Vinaya. And both of you, keep a lookout for the Silver Brethren.

In the darkness of the burial chamber, the dim blue glow from the Night-Shining Jewel contoured Vinaya's angular face as he scowled at the even features of Nua, a scowl reflected in the girl's dusky almond eyes.

With a shrug of indifference the monk stepped back from the small girl. His sandalled foot caught a sodden plank on the outer square of the threefold coffin. He sprang away as if burned.

The girl laughed.

'Shut your mouth,' he snarled. 'I'm beginning to wonder whether I need another Chia, after all.'

'But what would you *do* without another Chia?' the girl mocked.

He didn't answer. The touch of the funeral wood had seared his nerves. The first moment he walked into the burial chamber he was riven with fear by the rotting relic. The very touch of it pained him.

And he had seen visions. Visions at the centre of the threefold coffin. Grey shrouds, black shrouds, white shrouds savaged with knives. And a tall man had risen from the coffin. A man with green eyes. And he mouthed a word that . . . that was terror to remember, and would not be remembered, never be recalled.

The green-eyed man in the coffin had haunted his dreams, but this was the first time he had witnessed the nightmare with waking eyes in a setting that he recognised as very similar to his dream. He dreaded the return of that waking vision. Come to that, he dreaded the whole Death Mound.

'I'm getting out of here for a while,' he snapped.

'Come back soon,' she said. 'My sister's starting to play the Game of the Immortals.'

'A game she's going to lose,' he stated as he strode out of the chamber. 'She doesn't remember the rules or the players.'

The monk's gaunt legs marched briskly up the tunnel and out into the open air before he halted and took a deep draught of night air.

Stretching his shoulders and flexing his wrists, the monk gazed down the bony slopes of Spirit Hill.

Then he scanned the southern horizon beyond the deep gorge of Shen Lung.

His mouth barely moved as a low whisper escaped the dry, parted lips.

'All flesh is pain. I am flesh. I am pain.'

Vinaya's wolfish face came to resemble the face of a wolf of stone, a petrified hunger, infinitely patient.

It was the hunger and patience of thousands of years.

Far below the southern fringe of the Forest of the Ancestors, the dark air in the vault vibrated with glee.

The emaciated hands of the long, lean, naked figure in the sarcophagus twitched spasmodically.

The exhaltation of life to the girl Yi who hung above became agitated and expectant.

The blinded, deafened Yi had almost paid the penalty for her crime, her terrible crime. The crime of being a friend of Chia the sorceress. Yi's time of punishment was drawing to a close.

Before sunrise she would be an object without utility, an item of rubbish. She would be disposed of neatly and efficiently.

The Hearing and the Sight had completed their tasks.

The perfect madness had been released.

The perfect madness would soon assume rich Spirit flesh.

And Chia would spin down into the whirlpool.

Down and down.

Without end.

Where am I, Chia? taunted the Sight.

Here, Chia – here – where you have not looked.

Here – in the rumpled jelly in the crown of the skull.

Here – in the flesh maze.

Hidden where the Sight could see Chia but Chia could not see the Sight.

The Sight resided in the warm, wet home of the maze in the head.

It was not a comfortable residence.

It was haunted, that labyrinth of flesh.

Haunted by the prior occupant.

Like an unfamiliar house crammed with tables and chairs and paintings that emanated the character of the deceased occupant, it was strange and haunted, this blood-nourished maze.

Memories haunted its living flesh, unfamiliar memories.

And the unfamiliar was pain to the Sight.

Pain is in me, thought the Sight, but I am not in pain.

I hide in the centre of the maze. I nestle deep within the folds of the rumpled jelly, supreme maze among mazes.

This maze has a million ways and corners, each an individual puzzle.

It has paths that run on forever.

It has paths that run to a sudden blind stop, blocked by a wall of impenetrable tissue.

The pulsating maze has plots, secret societies of rebellious notions, assassins lurking in the shadows, sharp twists and turns and steep drops and rises, and the omnipresent echo of the pad of running feet – unseen and multitudinous.

If you walked this labyrinth forever you could trace the history of the universe.

It was a maze among mazes, the maze in the head.

Chia's meandering steps and wandering mind were pitiful when pitted against the limitless maze in the summit of the skull.

Chia had reached the centre of her maze – the black circle in the square.

And the circle would become a spiral.

An Inward Spiral.

And into it she would go.

Down and down.

18

GAME OF THE IMMORTALS

The sorceress shut her vision from the pounding waves of light in the Golden Chamber but the light seeped through her eyelids. Her mind pitched and yawed like a wreck in the golden surges. A residue of evil from the Spirit Mirror lingered in the chamber.

Fighting a swelling nausea she stripped Ming's mirror of its scarlet cover and, eyes closed tight, awaited the outcome with trepidation.

Behind her lids, she perceived that the light was fading. Relieved, she opened her eyes and saw the brutal blaze subside to the placid glow of an aureate sunset. The luminous metal hinted at both gold and bronze properties but its radiant and icy surface implied an unknown element, doubtless mined and forged during the dynasties of Thzan. The chamber had been constructed by the same nameless hero who had spun the imprisoning spirals and it was obvious that the shining surfaces acted as a reflection trap for any mirror within their confines. The reflective room, devoid of shadow, was the first barrier to the Spirit Mirror; the spirals were the second. She hoped that the slender gap in the door-frame would not interfere with the chamber's capacity to restrict Ming's mirror – the entire room was meant to present a uniform face of gold luminescence.

The mirror had absorbed much of the light but its sheen had not intensified. Her brow contracted. The brazen circle was growing darker. Before a hundred breaths had steamed from her mouth the mirror had assumed a raven hue. It was a black pit in the middle of the gold floor. Chia shivered in the gelid air and extracted the Yin-Yang rods from her cowl, uncertain how to proceed now the cosmological signs were swamped in darkness. How could she play the Game of the Immortals on a blank circle?

A sudden burst of imagery from the broad black disc sent a jolt through her and she dropped the six rods. A fleeting glance showed that they had fallen into the Yang hexagram, the same arrangement that had puzzled her in the dawn cave. But the scene in the mirror commanded attention: a yellow lantern nimbus highlighted a prostrate girl and a squatting man. Fu and Chao the Braggart. And the scene began where the dream and the recent pool-glimpse ended. In fascination she leaned over the living mirror circle.

Whispered to death . . . Fear shivered the knife in Chao's hand . . . The swart features were clouded by a trance, responding to a prior command by the T'ai Ching whispering of the Silver Brethren.

Chia's eyes formed sharp slits. Chao's face. San Lung Town. 'I've seen that man,' she murmured. He had been among the stragglers in the exodus from the town, bearing a limp man in red silk on his massive back. The dream-memory had been too vague for her to identify him at the time.

In the vision inside the mirror, the man's gaze, seeing the unseeing, moved to the kwai pool near his booted feet. He bore all the marks of a man under a T'ai Ching trance. A bright image of the very chamber in which she now knelt bloomed from the haunted kwai pool. Chao lurched upright, knife held high.

The knife shimmered in the lantern-light as it descended to Fu's slender neck. The blade tore a clumsy rent in the delicate throat. The blood gushed like wine from a burst wineskin. Ponderously, Chao grasped his victim around the waist, hauled the slight body up and tilted it head downwards so that the red stream from the gaping throat poured into the haunted pool.

As the blood spattered the surface of the water it shrank into the tiny image of the Golden Chamber as if transformed into a crimson thread, or as if full red flowers suddenly dwindled into diminutive petals heaped in a distant cluster.

Chia saw that the murderer rotated the body slightly so that the red torrent struck the water in a gradually widening spiral. The transposed flow of blood spread in an outward spiral onto a miniature representation of a black circle in the phantasmal chamber. She was watching an image of the Spirit Mirror within the Mirror of Ming. The ghosted water of the kwai pool transmuted the wretched girl's blood flow into remote sorcery.

Chao squeezed the draining shape like a fruit from which the juice was being pressed. The crimson flow slowed to a trickle. A few drops. Then the drained vessel was flung to the ground, its purpose fulfilled. A red Outward Spiral smeared the black Spirit Mirror. The vision in the kwai pool dissolved as the secret door swung open behind Chao's brawny bulk. A boiling golden mist was revealed in the frame of the gaping entrance.

Chia gritted her teeth. So that was how the spirals were frozen. Primitive blood-sacrifice passing in the Outward Flow from the haunted pool to the incarcerated Mirror. An evil person could not perform the Outward Spiral rite, but the blood of an innocent victim transmitted its own Outward Spiral within the ritual. The pool was a kwai − haunted water which became, over centuries, a faint aspect of the Spirit Mirror. By the Blood Spiral rite the Outward Flow was mystically absorbed by the Spirit Mirror. The Outward Flow counteracted the Inward Flow, thus the threshold spirals were frozen in immobility. The subtle interplay between the threshold signs was disrupted by the out-curling blood. With this form of blood sacrifice it was the act itself rather than the blood which partially freed the Mirror. The act would haunt the spot a thousand years after the blood was wind-blown dust.

'May you suffer all the pangs of the Ten Deep Hells, Chao,' she cursed.

She bit her lip as she beheld the man raise his bare arms and cross them with palms turned inwards: it was the archaic sign of the Thzan-tzai cult. What resembled a Black Serpent tattoo decorated the back of his right hand. Rudimentary intelligence dawned in his gaze, and with that dawning she saw fear. Chao was watching something she could not see in the compass of Ming's mirror. The man was greeting a newcomer beyond the range of her sight.

A saffron shape strolled into vision and halted on the other side of the kwai pool. The newcomer was a tall, gaunt figure with shaven scalp and Mahayana robe.

Vinaya. It was Vinaya.

The monk crossed his arms in the identical Thzan-tzai sign made by Chao. For an uncounted procession of heart-beats the two held the unhallowed signs. Then they crumpled to the ground in unison. Chia glowered in mystification. What was afoot?

Vinaya was the first to rise, reeling drunkenly to unreliable feet. What lightning bolt had enfeebled his spirit? It was some time before the other man regained his legs. Chia nodded slowly, having expected the transformation. It was predictable that the Spirit Mirror would work a change in him. The stolid visage was subtly modified and the Black Serpent tattoo had changed to the left hand. Chao's body was reversed. Served the bastard right. But what was Vinaya's rôle in this change? As if in answer, the Chao-thing spoke. There was no sound, but Chia could read the words his heavy lips were forming . . . 'I am the Hearing. I am Nyak.'

Chia's lungs froze in mid-breath.

236

The burly killer in the vision strode into the bright, seething mist of the Golden Chamber. A fully recovered Vinaya watched and waited until his companion returned from the agitated haze bearing a large, unidentifiable object which she reasoned could only be the Body of the Mirror. The monk gestured and left and Chao followed. The images faded and the Mirror of Ming resumed its blackness.

The sorceress heaved a deep breath. So that – if Ming's mirror did not lie – was how the Body of the Mirror was freed.

She was still left with the problem of how to commence the Game of the Immortals. Failure to twist the mirror to her purpose would mean that the location of the Spirit Mirror would lie undisclosed. And what was she to do about Vinaya?

What happened in Egypt, Chia? What happened in Egypt? What made those ominous words of Nua intrude into her mind all of a sudden?

A disturbance in the black mirror startled her – a stark shock of yellow burst in the circle. A mild wash of blue seeped down from the uppermost arc, meeting the yellow in an unrelenting line. Pyramids upreared from the yellow expanse. The bronze shield of the sun burned in the blue enamel of the sky.

'The Kingdom of the Nile,' breathed Chia, golden Nefertiti swimming in her memory. 'The Land of the Pharaohs.'

It was her personal shrine. A sanctuary from any T'ai Ching Master's attack. Her Egyptian refuge from any Chinese enemy attempting to invade her mind.

Egypt stretched out a welcome. The brown serpent of the Nile wound round her bare feet. Her fingers gripped the silver ankh. She heard the somnolent rustle of palm leaves, luxuriated in the brash embrace of the sun.

She was walking on the sands, the sacred sands of her beloved Egypt, calling for Nefertiti, disbelieving that the

237

queen was dust and brittle bone and her spirit an exile among the stars. Chia keened at the locked doors of the imperious tomb. She raised her face to the rich disc of the sun. 'Aten,' she prayed. 'God of Akhenaten and Nefertiti. Let my love come forth by day.'

The Sun Disc softened to a gentle bronze. A bronze shield hung in the skies. No – a bronze mirror, for it had begun to reflect her face. Her own visage smiled down from the mirror of the sun. A green evil slanted the eyes of the image, and the smile was crooked. The Death Whisperers had invaded her private imagery, her secret symbols.

The horror of that perverse face leering down from the huge sun mirror almost overwhelmed her. She was almost fooled into seeing it as an image of final defeat, but all she had learned in the last hour showed her the way to vanquish this mirror self. She lifted her hand and traced the path of the Inward Spiral across her face in the face of the Sun Disc. The Inward Spiral imprisons, she laughed in her mind. Be imprisoned, Mockery of Aten, be drawn into yourself.

She did not see, but she sensed, that at her back an immense door of darkness opened in the Egyptian world. Hot sand tugged her left foot. Chia thought of the hands of the buried, warmed in the scorching earth. The sole of her foot was sinking into the moving sand – she couldn't wrench it loose.

They're pulling me down to the land of the dead. They're dragging me down into the halls of the dead where Osiris sits on his judgement throne. And when I'm judged I'll be found guilty and cast down into the pit of perdition. Osiris will turn his white face from me. There will be no redemption for the Death-bringer.

She looked up once more at the sun. It was still a bronze mirror and the face reflected in it was still a mockery of her own. It was her mirror self, her dark self, that image in the bronze sun. It was her Shadow.

'Aten!' she yelled at the treacherous Sun Disc. 'I believed in you because Nefertiti believed in you. I was a fool. In my heart I never believed in you. To hell with you, God of the Sun!'

Yes, she confessed to herself. I lied to my soul. The moon is my god and the night is my goddess, for silver and black are the colours of Chia.

She tugged frantically at her foot as the panic scrabbled like talons in her breast. She tugged with manic strength.

'Moon Goddess, save me. Moon-silver power, save me.'

And the foot began to work free by tiny degrees. Chia laughed aloud as it gradually came loose.

A huge voice fell from the sun. Chia's voice. The nightmare Chia's voice.

'Oh no, Chhhiiiaaa . . . Go down into the Dead Lands or ascend to the sun mirror. Enter the mirror or sink into darkness. One or the other, Chhhiiiaaa . . .'

Chia glared at the bronze mirror that wore her face. She took a deep breath and pointed a finger at the sun mirror Chia.

'No, Mirror Chia,' she hissed in defiance. 'Neither one nor the other.'

Chia let power stream through the finger pointing at the sun. Luminous power. Moon power. Night power. Chia power.

All of Chia poured through that sunward pointing finger. All her love, all her hate, all her memories, all her dreams. And all her blood. It streamed to the sun.

And the pointing finger traced her blood and soul across that mocking visage of herself. A crimson trail of Spirit blood splashed an Inward Spiral over the false Chia in the sun mirror. Chia poured herself in an inwardly spiralling path into the sun. The face in the sun grimaced as if in pain.

'There, you bitch. I've trapped you this time,' smiled Chia.

239

But what was this door of darkness behind Chia's back?

Chia's blood-streaming finger reached the centre of the Inward Spiral. 'There, now you're caught, you shadow of me,' she sneered.

What was this immense door of darkness in the walls of the Egyptian world?

The moment the ritual of the Inward Spiral was completed the sorceress glanced down. Her foot was trapped in the sand, more firmly than before. And it was sinking faster. She threw a look at the sun. Her face had faded into the heat of the sun.

And the sun, too, was vanishing.

Why was there a huge door of darkness in the walls of Egypt?

The booming laughter sprang from everywhere. It bounced off the walls of Egypt. It reverberated from the blue enamel of the Egyptian sky. Colours deliquesced. The pharaoh world, shaken by convulsive mirth, shattered into a million splinters.

Dull gold walls replaced the Land of the Nile. Nua's low chuckle displaced the booming laughter.

Chia realised that she was in the Golden Chamber. And that her finger was pointing straight at the grinning face of Nua. Behind her, Chia glimpsed with a quick look, the door to the Golden Chamber gaped wide.

The sorceress lowered her pointing finger from Nua's mocking features. Chia could only just form the words on her trembling lips. 'Who are you?'

Nua smiled in answer. 'Your sister.' The voice was the faintest of whispers.

Then Nua glided gracefully from the chamber.

Chia, finally collecting her wits, made to pursue her but was pulled short by the grip of the black mirror. Her left foot was caught in the metal as it had earlier seemed to be in the clutch of the shifting sands of Egypt. She couldn't tear free, and her alarm thrummed at a higher pitch when she realised that her foot was slowly sinking into the mirror. The metallic grasp was as cold as the imaginary sands were hot. The cold mirror was pulling her down. Down – into what? Dreams? Hell? The Mime Realm?

'Oh, Moon Goddess, be with me,' shivered Chia.

Vinaya left Spirit Hill to its rocks and spirits, entered the mouth of the mound and strode confidently down the gullet of the dark tunnel. But nearing the burial chamber with its baffling threefold coffin, he hesitated. Nua's shape was seated firmly in the middle of the coffin within a coffin within a coffin as though attempting to convey a cryptic, macabre message to him or Chia. In his weakened state he couldn't face the interior of the mound and the sight of the threefold coffin. They fed the darkness and fear inside him. No, he wouldn't go in there – not yet.

There was a task to fulfil. A duty to perform. But there was a disharmony in the flesh. A weakness. A loss of power. He needed rest. A short rest.

It didn't occur to Vinaya to question the logic of this decision, or its motivation.

Vinaya leaned against the wall, slid gradually down its slick surface – and fell asleep.

And the shadow that had grown in him from contact with Spirit Hill began to stir in his sleeping body. And the shadow reached out to the Golden Chamber . . .

Chia's foot had disappeared almost to the ankle. No amount of physical effort was adequate to wrench the foot from the black suction, but she persisted in straining her muscles in an attempt to pull free.

Pausing for a moment to wipe the sweat that trickled from her brow into her eyes, she suddenly became aware of something slipping into the chamber. It was nothing the five senses could detect. But it was there with her in the Golden Chamber.

Shaking off the sensation of a presence in the room she prepared to resume her struggle to rid her foot of the mirror suction. She was stopped by a cramping, folding feeling in her stomach. It felt as though the skin was crumpling. Drawing the side-slit in her gown up and across, she looked down at her bared stomach.

Around her navel there was a moving circle of puckered flesh like worms burrowing under the skin. Then Chia gasped with the swift pain of the stretching navel. The hole of her navel expanded to the size of a small mouth. Her stomach felt as if it were being pulled inside-out. The circular dance of skin worms became more animated.

Wincing, she dropped the hem of her gown in disgust.

The lively flesh rippled the black silk lying over it. The open mouth of the navel didn't show under the silk, but the tearing pain of it made its presence all too evident.

Then the navel spoke. It had the tone of a voice speaking through a flute.

'Disease is the flesh at play.'

Chia groaned inwardly. This infantile display and reedy words bore all the marks of Nyak's handiwork, but whether this was a conscious projection of the necromancer or flotsam from his fragmented nature she wasn't sure.

She bit back the pain and squashed the sense of physical violation. 'What are you?' she asked.

'Eloquent flesh,' piped the voice from her navel. 'The voice from within. Do you like me playing with your flesh? I like playing with it. I like being inside you, Green-Eyes. Do you like secrets?'

This wasn't the cold, self-righteous voice of Nyak's conscious self. It was an errant element of his being, and it would soon return to its source. These fugitive phantoms were invariably more revealing than the

242

necromancer himself. Painful and revolting as the phenomenon was, she hoped that the intruder wouldn't flee too quickly back to Nyak's hidden personality. It could tell her much, if its mercurial nature inclined to spout its secrets.

'Who are you?' she demanded.

'A bad mood aspiring to be a tumour,' the navel lips replied. 'Would you like to give birth to a tumour? A whimsical notion, is it not?'

'Where do you come from?'

'Oh, a very holy place.'

She grimaced as her navel distended with a sharp abruptness. She clenched her teeth even as she ground out the words: 'What holy place? The temple?'

'Oh no, no, no,' piped the hole in her stomach. 'I've nothing to do with him. He's the wrong way round. And I don't like travel.'

The sorceress, despite the bizarre manifestation and the pain it caused, tensed at the import of the taunting hints which the contorting flesh had let slip.

Chao is the wrong way round. Reversed. In the mirror vision Chao said he was the Hearing and Nyak. The voice isn't from Nyak-Hearing. So who?

'Do you like secrets?' fluted her stomach.

'Yes, I do,' she replied, feeling as if she were holding a conversation with a spiteful child. 'Will you tell me some?'

'No. I've changed my mind,' warbled the mouth in her stomach.

'I don't think you know any secrets,' sniffed Chia, hoping to goad the taunter into a fuller revelation.

And the flute voice was goaded into a fuller revelation. A violent revelation. A revelation of the flesh.

Chia's clamping teeth bit blood from her lower lip at the sudden agony that speared her midriff. She felt as though she was splitting from the centre. She felt as though her insides were coming out.

Yanking up her gown, Chia's eyes widened at the grotesque spectacle being played out on her exposed flesh.

The puckered skin in the middle of the stomach was smoothing out as it rose into a mound. And the mouth atop the jutting mound was opening like a fresh wound. It seemed incredible that the stretching lips on the bulging mound didn't rip her belly in half.

The voice pitch of the broadening mouth slid down the scale to the lowest note: 'Would you like to give birth to a tumour, Virgin Lady? A tumour is such playful flesh.'

The pain was so excruciating that Chia pressed her hands onto the swelling mound and tried to force the gaping mouth shut, but it continued to yawn wider.

Something was congealing inside the taut mound. A lump was growing. And as it grew the body rejected the inflating tumour, pushing it up the throat of the mound to the pink lips of the gaping mouth. The top of the tumour protruded like a swollen, livid tongue.

The navel-mouth racked her bulging stomach with a last distension, and ejected the purple sac of the tumour with a heave that flung it well beyond her trapped foot to a spot near the centre of the black mirror. It flopped onto the metal with a sound like impacting sludge. Her stomach mound subsided and the navel shrank to its earlier size of a child's mouth. Chia gasped with relief at the considerable reduction of the pain, and lowered her hands and her gown.

The tumour did not lie still on the darkened bronze. It squirmed, and it spread as it squirmed. It was like soaked clay being pressed and kneaded under a potter's hands. As the livid lump was flattened out on the black surface, rudimentary features were moulded from its flaccid substance. Bestial features. As the silty material spread ever more thinly, the animal features were enhanced. The tumour that had sprung from her stomach now resembled a mask of mud in the form of a wolf's face. A wolf mask.

A hole budded open in the snout of the wolf mask and it spoke with a low whine: 'I can see you but I can't hear you,' it complained.

Then the mirror seemed to gulp down the fleshy mask in a single swallow.

'Wolf Mask,' breathed Chia. *Vinaya. Wolf Mask. And it's sight, not hearing.*

'I know another secret,' fluted the navel hole. 'Look up at the ceiling.'

She lifted her eyes to the ceiling.

There were chains with cruel hooks hanging from the ceiling. The hooks were thrust into the eyes and ears of a naked girl who dangled in the air.

Chia started to tremble. The hanging girl resembled . . . that old scar on the left thigh . . . that small mole on the right shoulder . . . she was . . . the girl was . . .

'Yi!' screamed Chia in rage and anguish.

At her screaming the navel closed tight as something fled from the chamber.

The monk woke the moment that Chia screamed. He sprang to his feet and padded down the tunnel and across the damp floor of the burial chamber. His sandalled feet splashed in the kwai pool as he glanced over his shoulder at Nua's rounded body where it sat inside the threefold coffin remains. Then he was inside the Golden Chamber before he realised that the screaming had stopped.

Chia, one foot buried in the mirror, stood with bowed head.

She was aware of the tall monk's entrance but ignored it.

Ah, Moon Goddess, Chia sighed inwardly. When will it stop? It was a vision and the vision was brief but the vision was true. When will they stop killing the women I love? Do they think they can crush me by slaughtering my loves? Never! Never in eternity. I'll not even weep. Anyone can wear a silver mask. But wearing a flesh mask is the hard thing. And wear it I will. Nyak wants contrition. He wants my tears. He wants to see the face of pain and hear the voice of pain, but he'll never see or hear them. I'll continue to play the sorceress, nonchalant and impregnable. I remain within myself.

She turned to the figure in the doorway.

Yi had hooks in her eyes.

'I hope you're well, Nyak-Sight,' she greeted.

Taken by surprise, he nodded. 'Well enough. But the same can't be said of you.'

'Give my regards to the Hearing when you see him.'

Yi had hooks in her ears.

'Stop acting, Chia,' came the patient sigh. 'I know you too well, and –'

'Not as well as *I* know you,' smirked Nua's face as her small body brushed past Nyak. 'I know you better than you know yourself. I am you. Your Shadow.'

Chia gave a rueful nod. 'The summoning. It drew my shadow self into you.'

'Nua's hun souls were driven from her body a month ago,' explained Nua's mouth. 'The pho souls remained in the flesh to maintain the functions of the body. A T'ai Ching trance was placed on you and others to make me invisible to your eyes. I was an empty husk lying in the abbot's cell until your spirit was stretched to its limit during the summoning. I sucked in the shadow of that spirit, unknowing. You were delayed in the gorge so that my shadow spirit would have time to grow in me.'

'So,' Chia shrugged. 'You are me. No wonder I felt strange when I lay on you in the cave. I was trying to make love to myself.'

And no wonder I felt an absence in myself after the summoning. She who has no shadow is an incomplete thing, a less than human thing. No wonder my memory wandered in a maze. It wasn't the madness before the dying time. That Death-bringer madness is on me but I know its ways and tricks. It was the loss of shadow spirit that enfeebled me.

246

She glanced at the black pit that was slowly ingesting her body. The lower part of the calf was already engulfed and the flesh and bone below the dark metal were numb with cold. Pushing against the floor with the other leg and twisting away from the mirror she fought the icy suction, but to no avail.

Nyak's voice broke in on her struggle.

'Hopeless, sorceress. Hopeless.'

'That's right, Green-Eyes,' confirmed Chia's Shadow from the mouth of Nua. 'I know the inside of you. I know your Egyptian spirit refuge. I entered it. And you drew the Inward Spiral across my face, thinking to imprison me. But I am you, Chia. What you saw in me was your own face. It was your own image that you trapped in the sun mirror. And the mirror sucked you in. No one but you could have released the Spirit Breath of the Mirror. You did it. No one but you could have trapped your body in a mirror. You did that also.'

Chia transferred her attention to Nyak. 'I suppose that you'll be wanting to rush off and join the Hearing in the temple. Don't let me keep you.'

Nyak-Sight met her green eyes with a stare as steady as her own. 'It's not too late, Chia,' he declared. 'Your cheap wit isn't amusing, Mistress of Sarcasm. I would have thought the prospect of being gulped by the mirror would have curbed your sharp tongue.'

'The sooner the scent of the Infinite Flesh swallows you and your so-called children, the better,' retorted Chia. 'As for this Shadow here, she has my pity.'

'Pity?' he echoed angrily. 'What of you – a shadowless woman, a half-woman . . .'

Chia's fraught mind leapt back to Shen Lung cave. No shadow had stalked the deeps of her meditation at dawn. The six rods had fallen into the Yang hexagram, symbolising light, heaven, the absence of secretive darkness. There was no darkness in the hexagram because her darkness had risen in Nua. Chia was a world cleft asunder. And the moving line in the Yang hexagram: 'The dragon lies hidden in the deep' . . . it had warned her to abstain from action until certainty illuminated the right course. She had not abstained from action, and the augury of the Teh-kuo hexagram had shown the result — catastrophe.

'If your stolen Shadow hadn't left you deficient,' Nyak was saying, 'you would have recalled that all mirror beings are reversed, and it was central to my strategy that you should be in some doubt of the girl. Almost symmetrical though her appearance may be, you would normally have known how to put her to the test . . .'

'The heart,' acknowledged Chia. 'I remembered when I touched your chest in Nagarjuna's cell, but the summoning sucked out the knowledge.'

'The heart,' echoed her incarnate Shadow. 'When you lay upon me, Sister Above, didn't you feel my heart beating on the *wrong side*?' Chia heard a travesty of her own laugh issuing from the rounded lips. 'We're changing places, you and I. The reflection will live *here* and you will live *there*. I hate you, sister. And I love you. I love you and I whisper you to death. You shouldn't have shut your ears to the words of the ebony shaman, Kabo the Wise — the words would have shrunk my spirit. I would have ceased to grow in you.'

'You've spoken enough, Shadow Chia,' Nyak said sharply, as disturbed as Chia by the reference to Kabo the Wise. 'There's a question I must ask before Green-Eyes sinks into the mirror.'

He leaned forwards to his snared enemy, inquisitive eyes expanding like the orbs of an owl. 'Who are you, Chia? Who?'

'House of the Twilight Owl,' she muttered to herself.

'What?' stabbed Nyak's sharp voice.

'Nothing, Master of Corpses. Take your questions to hell with you.'

'You have to tell me!' The pitch was shrill. 'I must

248

know! The legends say you're the fruit of a union between a Celestial One and a woman of the Ko Dynasty,
but the legends are false. The Celestial Ones – curse their
light – were invisible and impalpable to mortals. It's
impossible that your father was such a being. Now tell
me the truth. Who are you? Who was your father?'

'Spin on in your journey to the inner hells, Lord of the
Dead, Duke of Disease,' she sneered. 'The learned are
acquainted with the name of *your* father – Glak-i-kakthz,
a Thzan-tzai, a demon, an abomination. Wasn't it said
that his human semblance between metamorphoses was
the colour of bile? Do you think that Glak-i-kakthz was
bile-fleshed when he raped the woman that spawned
you?'

A flicker of anger plucked the monk's cheek, then
Nyak shrugged the monk's shoulders. 'So be it. You
refuse to slake my curiosity. It's to be expected. But don't
adopt a defiant posture with me, Black Dragon, for you
go down into the black pit. Our millennial battle is over.
You sought to defeat the Mirror Kindred by Liu Po exorcism – the Game of the Immortals. But the real game
was elsewhere – its board was the Dragon Empire, its
major pieces you and I. I was bound to win. I've lived ten
thousand years, offspring of Glak-i-kakthz, last of the
Thzan-tzai to flee from the fury of the Celestial Ones . . .'

Chia yawned ostentatiously. 'Here we go again.
Another speech.'

'I grow in knowledge and power with the sift of each
century, forgetting nothing,' he went on. 'Compare me
with you – compare the mightiest being under the sun
with a guilt-humped, fear-ridden bitch who needs a reg-
ular steeping in the Sleep of Rebirth to sustain her three
thousand years. Your life's no more than a cycle of rebirths. Your immortality is bought at the price of your
true name. We're the Immortals, Chia, and we've played
the game of death through long dynasties. But with your
wheel of renewal you're always forgetting the true

nature of the Game, while I always remember. The struggle between us was the Game of the Immortals, and you, finally, have lost.'

Her leg was now buried up to the knee in the black metal, making the tilt of her body so acute that she brought the other leg onto the surface to compensate. The mirror caught the foot in a frigid grip.

She thought of the Mirror Breath in Ming's chamber. It had been illusion, probably conjured by Nyak-Sight and the Chia-Shadow. Probably the Tao magus had not been taken by the mirror at all, perhaps the whole event was a charade imposed upon her and the wizard. But there was the Third Way. If she imagined that her feet were free – if she imagined strongly enough . . . Then she realised her hopeless position. This illusion sprang from the Sun Disc, from the core of her spirit – and it was powerful enough to transform imagination into reality. In truth, she was being swallowed by the mirror . . .

Nyak's laughter boomed about the golden walls. 'That's right, Green-Eyes. The Third Way is no way out for you. There is no way out.'

Chia gnawed her lower lip in frustration. The necromancer had lost none of his skills. He could perceive any clear image she fashioned in her mind. But – that could be used against him . . .

'Come,' commanded the necromancer, beckoning his strange companion. 'Chia can't escape, and we've delayed too long. We'll take the chariot and race the wind. When the task is done there'll be ample time to observe her in the sacred mirrors, enduring torment in the reverse rim of the world. I will –' Abruptly, a deep frown disturbed his narrow forehead and he fixed Chia with a sharp stare.

The sorceress had not noticed his look. She was absorbed in the contemplation of the silver ankh. As a ruse, she had placed her palms fractionally above the haunted metal as if the hands were caught in the mirror

250

suction – her shoulders flexed in the pretence of struggling to pull them free. And throughout the deception she held a vivid image of the silver ankh before her, mentally repeating the words: 'Through the golden Sun Disc they ensnared me, but the ankh is the silver of the moon. By the sun mirror they entrapped me, but by the moon I shall be delivered. Let my enemies not discern the secret of the silver ankh.'

Nyak continued to stare. He was receiving the impression of the silver ankh and the drift of the words in her mind. Doubt made his frown more pronounced. Was the looped cross a specially powerful talisman? Was there a moon mystery in the silver ankh which could counteract the golden prison of the sun mirror and the trap of the black mirror?

Inclining his angular head to Nua he pointed at the sorceress. 'You're Chia's Shadow – tell me what power lies in her silver amulet.'

The girl mirrored the necromancer's frown. 'I can't say.' She pursed her lips in a manner reminiscent of the true Chia. 'It has *some* power – I can't tell what.'

He nodded slowly. 'Then you had better take it from her. She's unable to resist – her hands are locked in the metal. But be careful not to touch the mirror.'

The girl adopted a defiant stance. 'Why don't you do it if there's no danger?'

'It's wise not to disobey me,' he said sternly. 'Learn from the fate of your creator.'

She shrugged submission and moved to the rim of the mirror, her hand reaching for the silver chain.

Chia reacted instantly, seizing the girl's wrists and forcing the wriggling hand onto the mirror. First one finger adhered to the mirror, then another, and another, until half of the Shadow's hand was drawn into the icy metal. She screamed in fear, tearing to break loose. The sorceress smiled without humour.

'Why do you protest, Sister Below? You're returning to your own world, your own kin.'

The Shadow swerved crazed eyes on its true self. 'You don't know what it's like, Green-Eyes – it's a place where nothing was ever meant to be – there's no kindred among the Death Whisperers – you don't know what you're sinking into – they make you eat your eyes . . . My only comfort is that you're falling with me. It was you who condemned me to the Mime Realm three thousand years ago. You were my gaoler, Sister Above. It was only justice that the positions of prisoner and imprisoner be reversed.'

Chia glanced at Nyak-Vinaya. He had not moved. His rebarbative expression had not altered. It was plain that her trick had not come as a complete surprise to him. Nua's possessed body coiled to confront the impassive necromancer.

'Why can't you release me?' she shrieked. 'Free me from the mirror!'

He shook his head and laughed. 'I would if I could, Shadow, but the only way out of that mirror is down. It's unfortunate that Chia felt compelled to make this futile gesture. I was looking forward to keeping you as a – a memento of Green-Eyes, but perhaps this way is safer, after all. It was becoming clear that you have inherited Chia's hatred of me, in a diluted form. By the way, Black Dragon, compliments on your attempt to get your hands round my throat. Using my own thought-discernment against me was a clever bluff, but I'm too wary for such deceptions.'

Chia curled her lip in contempt. 'You mean you always have servants to take your risks for you. What a clever coward you are.'

Her insult fell like dusted snow from his robe. Hers was the defiance of the defeated, hollow at heart. With a dismissive wave he turned to leave.

'Now I must go and show the Temple Master who's the master, Chia Sorceress, Chia Shadow, before I return to my body and while away many pleasant hours observing the two of you rend one another in the realm of reflections. I have a number of ancient mirrors that show visions of the world of silent whispers. I'll be seeing you, although you won't be seeing me. Fare ill, old enemy. The Game of the Immortals is over.'

With a sardonic bow he left the Golden Chamber to the two victims of the black, swallowing mirror.

19

THE SIGHT

瞁

Vinaya-Nyak unhitched the skittish horses, bounded onto the chariot deck and shook the reins with a loud cry. The Fergana team, eager to flee the precincts of the Death Mound, sprang as one beast down the erratic trail.

Nyak, whose power did not extend over animals, fumed at the pace of the thudding hooves. Swift though the chariot plunged down Spirit Hill, impatience made it slow in his eyes.

'Faster, you red brutes, faster . . .' he hissed between bared teeth.

The whirring wheels scattered the fragments of the stick man and bumped over the bottom-most ridge of the hill. The intention had been to perplex the sorceress further by the sight of the draped wood with its silver mask, but she had been unimpressed. No matter. A skull-grin parted his leathery features. Green-Eyes was never easily impressed.

A worthy enemy.

The only enemy.

As the chariot rumbled up the mild incline of the moor to the undulating lip of Shen Lung Gorge a contrary emotion began to stifle the charioteer's exultation. The more he fought to suppress the unfamiliar emotion, the louder it clamoured.

Remorse? Remorse for Chia?

No. He was Nyak-Sight. He was the son of Glak-i-kakthz of the Thzan-tzai. In the ancient tongue, Nyak's name meant Game Master, Glak-i-kakthz meant Last of the Changers. He, Nyak, was the Game Master from the last of the Changers of the Unshaped Masters. How could such a one as he feel remorse for anyone? He was above sorrow. The emotion was a disorder caused by too long a stay in Vinaya's body that gave him the illusion of sorrow. Not only did he suffer the discomfort of tenanting foreign flesh, but he – the Sight – was separated from the Hearing in the temple. The awareness that what he thought of as himself was no more than an aspect of his true self was disconcerting to his sense of identity. The separation from his true body far to the south and the split between Sight and Hearing was painful and confusing. No wonder ignoble human emotions troubled him.

But then – perhaps he just regretted the end of the game, the conclusion of the battle. Perhaps he needed an adversary to test his metal and add a tang to the air he breathed, and who could replace Chia as his adversary? The future landscape was arid and bleak without the black figure of the sorceress. Friendship meant nothing to him – it was folly and weakness. But mutual hatred – was that something precious to him? Had he lost a necessary enemy in Chia?

Who was she? What were her origins? And what *had* happened in Egypt?

There had been that final backward look in the burial chamber at the golden rectangle and the shapes of Chia and her Shadow sinking into the black mirror – then the urgency of his mission had driven him into the tunnel and out into the night. The burial chamber – why had it lanced him with such a sharp dread? Chia had seemed unaware of the inimical aura of the vault. It was centred on the sodden remnants of the triple coffin and the foetid slime that ringed it like a slug trail. It sent shock-waves back to the blackness before his earliest memories. He had felt the presence on his first visit to the tomb on the

Feast of the Dead, but it abated after he cast the Hearing into Chao. But this time he had received the full brunt of the presence. It was as if an ancient spirit still breathed in the damp chamber.

It angered him that he could be intimidated.

The wheels bounced over the rim of the gorge and the chariot clattered down the gully it had previously ascended. Nyak-Sight got a tight grip on the reins as the lurching chariot threatened to topple over with the frenzied speed of the horses. The risk of crashing into the walls of the straggling gully exorcised the fear raised by the damp vault and the ruinous coffin. He grew alert and banished the memory of Spirit Hill Mound. It was foolish to jeopardise his plans so near to completion.

The Shen River was moon-silver and the fans of water in the wake of the black chariot shimmered with a lunar glow. Deft handling of the Fergana team brought the vehicle safely onto the southern shore. He allowed no respite to the stallions – the scourge of an unrelenting whip forced them up the slippery trails to the stark silhouette of the Wolf Tower.

Eight of the Silver Brethren were waiting outside the tower. Two raised bandaged hands in salute. Their master had returned victorious from Spirit Hill and they had played their part in alarming and distracting Chia so that she delayed crossing the river until such time as Nyak-Hearing had entered the monastery. Vinaya-Sight slowed the team as the chariot neared the tower, and the Sight within the monk's skull cast commands into the minds of the two brethren that had lifted their hands in salutation. Obediently, they mounted the wide deck and stood to each side of the Master. Nyak cracked the whip and the Fergana horses resumed a full gallop on the winding brown road to San Lung Town.

Suddenly Nyak gasped, handed the reins to a Silver Brother, and slumped to the jarring deck. The arduous casting of thoughts in the tricking of Chia had taken their

256

toll. The Sight was threatening to burst from the spindly body. Possession was always an unstable state. The natural affinity between body and spirit did not exist in possession and the lack of affinity between possessing spirit and possessed body caused the forms and functions of the body to rebel against the invader.

The narrow neck swelled to double its normal width, becoming a bloated bag of blood. Blood hammered in the head and pulsed the straining temples. For an anxious space, Nyak-Sight was afraid that he would explode from the dome of the skull and re-enter his true body far away.

The pressure shifted to the lean torso, which vibrated like a panting lung. The Sight battled to regain control. When an alien spirit left a soul-less body in haste, there was no returning. The internal force generated by such an expulsion was tremendous. The Sight would blow the body to bits if it was expelled involuntarily.

In the turmoil of his Spirit Vision, he sensed the spaces of the dark vault. The ruddy glow of torches smouldered the murkiness. The hook-hung girl dangled above his true body in the open stone sarcophagus. The life-breath descended with the blood-drops from the sacrifice and the blood-spirit sustained the Deep Self within his silver-masked shape. The Deep Self in the sarcophagus returned a trace of the blood-life to the suspended victim, protracting her unnatural existence. Inside her head, madness boiled.

Her hooked eyes, crying blood, gave strength to the Sight. Her hooked ears, trickling blood, gave power to the Hearing. From her blindness, the Sight. From her deafness, the Hearing. And from her madness, the integrity and tranquility of the Deep Self.

The vision of the torchlit vault flickered out. Nyak-Sight gradually regained control of Vinaya's body. The grotesque swelling subsided. The crisis was over. He sighed his relief.

Soon Sight would be reunited with Hearing.

And the Spirit Mirror would be whole.

And the Rites of Desecration would be performed throughout the Dragon Empire. Blindness and deafness and madness would be manifest.

And Nyak would make all mortals into reflections of himself.

And then . . .

What then?

Where could he then find an enemy? What of the deadly Game? Would his cleverness atrophy in the unrelieved boredom of a world without challenge?

He smiled.

When the boredom became insupportable, he would do battle with the Spirit Mirror – at a distance. The game would begin again.

He rose unsteadily and reassumed command of the Fergana team.

The blurring hooves devoured the distance to the south. The chariot hurtled down slopes, bumped over a bridge, laboured up inclines. But Nyak was never satisfied by the horses' efforts and showed his exasperation in the constant use of the whip.

On two occasions a smile ruffled his grim lineaments. Ten li south of Spirit Hill, the chariot approached the crushed body of a woman lumped in the middle of the road – he had told Chia that the corpse was a wolf after he had run the wretch over. Fourteen li south of the hill he encountered the man whose head he had succeeded in cracking under the iron-banded wheels.

It was the Hour of the Rat when the necromancer swung the team around the silent walls of the town. He grinned as he remembered the wizard's dumbfounded expression in Ming's chamber. The Sight and the Shadow had joined forces with Ming's mirror to impose the mirror wind illusion on him and Chia. Chia had been fooled into believing that the mirror had inhaled the magus. But in fact he had merely collided with the bronze surface and been stunned. The magician had revived in time to witness the sorceress conversing with Nyak at the door, but had been temporarily robbed of speech, paralysed of limb, and made invisible to Chia's eyes. By the time the T'ai Ching trance released his mind Nyak would have put considerable distance between the magus and Chia. The wizard would have had some strange reports to make of the Black Dragon Sorceress when he reached the temple.

Nyak-Sight chuckled as the chariot thundered past the Pavilion of the Red Phoenix and over the stone bridge where he and Chia's Shadow had pretended to push the sorceress over the parapet. The deception had contributed to Chia's confusion – it had made her suspect Nua all the more without being quite certain. It had continued to divert suspicion from himself and kept his adversary's attention from the crucial Outward and Inward Spirals.

As each li shrank to the north Nyak began to peer ahead anxiously. They should have caught up with the Mirror Breath by now. The Breath would follow the winding ways of the dragon paths of feng-shui. It would track the land and water forms that were shaped and directed by the ch'i flow. Such a circuitous path should have enabled the relatively straight course of the chariot to reach the Spirit Breath before it seeped into the monastery.

At last he glimpsed, within sight of Celestial Buddha Temple, the thing he raced. A writhing, distortive mist stormed across the shallow valley that skirted the northern slopes of Celestial Buddha Hill with its monastic crown. He yelled in exultation and lashing the foaming horses to the pitch of their endurance as the chariot made ground on the seething Mirror Breath. From the Cloud Tower the midnight chimes announced the midpoint of the Hour of the Rat.

The dense vapour of the Spirit Breath ascended the rolling rises to the Gate of the Black Serpent. With a final spurt from the winded horses the chariot merged with the turmoiling mist.

Wild whispers thronged the air around the Sight and the two Brethren. Nyak-Sight sensed an urgency in the Breath — a craving to achieve its goal. As if through clouded water Nyak saw the sturdy oak gates shiver and crumble under the might of the Spirit Breath, revealing two figures, one in a grey cloak and one in a red silk gown.

Nyak-Sight urged the terrified horses to surge with the streaming mist into the courtyard and raised his fist in a gesture of triumph to Nyak-Hearing.

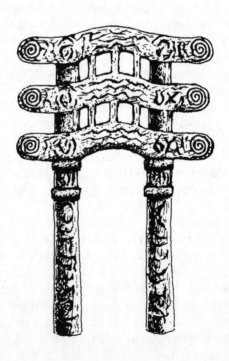

20

CHIA DEATH

Merging into the black mirror was like sinking into an icy well that robbed the limbs of sensation.

Chia had sunk to the waist in the black metal and her legs and hips were chilled into numbness, severed at the waist. Her Shadow, in the shape of Nua, was resigned to despair and slid sideways without a murmur into the tenacious mirror, her limp neck lolling, her jaw drooping.

The muffled din of the chariot had died into the distance. Nyak had departed the burial mound and she was alone with her Shadow. Chia had resisted the temptation to panic at the suction of the haunted mirror; her obdurate nature unwilling to concede defeat until the terminal stroke. The necromancer had spun as cunning and complex a plan as any she remembered, but she knew there was no such thing as a perfect plan – even the spider's web was not perfectly symmetrical. Somewhere – if she could find it – there was a strand awry in Nyak's web. What she needed was time . . .

Then the idea came. She carefully drew out the long silver dagger. She held the Shadow's glance.

'You'll have to die, Sister Below.'

The Shadow nodded and sighed in resignation. 'Yes, Sister Above, you must kill me. Separated, we drop into damnation – together, there's a faint hope . . .'

Chia nodded in return, unsettled by cross-currents of emotion, swung back the knife and plunged it into the girl's heart. Her arm was drenched by the gush of blood. But the Shadow continued to stare through Nua's face, seemingly unperturbed by what should have been a death blow.

'It's not so simple to drive out a Shadow,' Chia's mirror self said, a crimson dribble staining her mouth. 'Beheading is the quickest way to force me from the body before we're swallowed by the mirror.'

Chia took a deep breath, seized the girl by the hair, brandished the silver dagger.

'Now,' pleaded a plaintive voice. There was terror in her doe eyes as she gazed at the sorceress.

Chia gulped back her revulsion. She swung the dagger. The blade hacked and tore at the pliant throat.

It was a hideous operation that made Chia sick to the pit of her stomach. She felt guilty of the worst kind of murder – it was like dismembering a sleeping child. After ripping loose the muscles and ligaments she pulled back hard on the head and snapped the pinnacle of the spine. As she wrenched the head free, a long strip of skin came with it and dangled like a ribbon from the stump of the neck. With a shudder of self-loathing she threw the head with its adornment of long black tresses and red ribbon of flesh into a corner of the Golden Chamber. The headless trunk still pumped a livid flow across the black metal surface.

Chia returned the dagger to its sheath and locked her eyes to the butchery. She was clad in blood.

A sudden shock ran through her body and her eyelids sprang open to behold the corpse lying *on top* of the mirror as if it were any ordinary bronze surface. The spirit gone, there was nothing for the Death Whisperers to call – they only accepted living bodies. And her horror at the decapitation began to recede. She felt whole, something she had not experienced since the illusory summoning of Nua, for Chia's Shadow had returned to renew her ailing faculties. She had not committed murder, but rather set to rights a spiritual anomaly. The Shadow was one with her spirit. Chia was free of Nyak's T'ai Ching.

Memories returned with the return of the Shadow . . . Dragon Shadow . . . The speech she had delivered in the Buddha Hall . . . her strong suspicion that the Spirit Mirror had not been fully released . . . her conviction that the 'mirror hauntings' were partly illusions spread by Nyak and the Silver Brethren . . . Her firm intention to shape the Inward Spiral at the door of the Death Mound . . . Her instinctive suspicion of Vinaya – suspicion at first sight.

All this insight had deserted her when her Shadow sprang out and entered Nua. Small wonder that the summoning in the abbot's cell had left her feeling drained and confused.

She had sunk almost to her chest in the black mirror.

Hastily marshalling her thoughts, she sifted all the dross she had accreted on the journey to Spirit Hill and sought the gold of illumination. What had she learned of the truth? She knew that Nyak was responsible for the release of the Body of the Mirror, that the mirror 'invasion' of the past few weeks was partly a product of T'ai Ching from Nyak and the Silver Brethren. She knew that Nyak had infiltrated San Lung as the Sight in Vinaya and the Hearing in Chao. She realised that she herself had been required to unleash the Mirror Breath. She had learned that the Body of the Mirror had been freed by an Outward Spiral of blood striking a haunted pool – an Outward Spiral of innocent blood . . .

She drew a swift breath. The Outward Spiral of blood on the Mirror . . . If outward spiralling blood could release the Mirror Body, then why not her?

And the dark mirror was covered in the blood of Nua.

As quick as the inspiration, her hand stretched to the centre of the mirror to begin the outward movement traced in blood. The hand was caught fast, fingers trapped in the bronze.

Chia cursed her stupidity. Anything living that touched the black metal was caught instantly in the hungry suction of the mirror mire. Exhilarated by the sudden idea of escape, she had not stopped to think.

The black surface had risen to her chest. Her time was as short as the stump of a guttering candle. Chia felt as if, below the region of her chest, her body had vanished, was made insentient, transmuted to metal. Cold, tingling vibrations jingled up her spine and into her skull.

A terrible fear trembled in her brain – a fear of being altered, of being unmade and remade. Better to die. The Mime Realm did not take the dead.

She set her fingernails to the side of her neck and prepared to tear the skin. Chia would gouge the flesh and veins from her neck before she permitted the Mime Realm to take her soul.

'*No*,' whispered a vast, deep voice inside her head. A force took control of her hand and flung it from her neck to the bronze, which immediately trapped it.

'The Whisperers,' she sighed. 'The hungry ghosts won't be cheated of their food.'

'No,' repeated the huge, soft voice. 'You will not hear the Whisperers until your ears sink beneath the haunted mirror. I am not of the Mirror Kindred. I am the Spirit of the Tomb. I am the breath of the soul of the body that was interred in the burial chamber three thousand years ago. I am the ghost of the threefold coffin.'

Chia recoiled from the phantom voice. The words thrilled her with the kind of awe that is a distillation of the alien and the familiar. And its disclosure stirred a buried memory. She stared with wide eyes into the murkiness of the death chamber and the smudged contours of the wrecked threefold coffin. The perennial nightmare of grey shrouds, black shrouds, white shrouds flapped and waved in her skull.

'Who are you?' she shouted, dread driving her pulse.

'You know my name,' rolled the melancholy intonation. 'I am the one who raised Spirit Hill Mound and imprisoned the Spirit Mirror with the Inward Spirals of Thzan, evil restraining evil. Here I was entombed after my children slew me, the one in hatred of what I once was, the other in hatred of what I had become. Three thousand years this mound has stood, and for three thousand years it has housed the dust of my cadaver and my dwindling spirit.'

'Three thousand years?' she breathed. 'But the Death Mound is ten thousand years old . . .'

'So would Nyak have you believe, as he believes. Spirit Hill Mound is no older than you. Nyak is no older than you.'

The grey, black and white shrouds shook her memory. The high-pitched, nasal chant of Kabo the Wise echoed from the Egyptian past. Chia teetered on the brink of a revelation she refused to face. There was nothing, nothing she would not endure to avoid the unbearable truth. Worse than the fear of being altered was the terror of all you had thought hidden shown in a clear mirror. 'Who are you? Who?' she cried out, unsure whether she meant herself or the sighing spirit.

'You know my name. Remember that the true mystic is a bright mirror that reflects all worlds and the heart of eternity. If the mirror is clouded the vision is faulty. Disperse the dark mists in your mind, Chia. Confront your Shadow. Your spirit is trapped in a tight circle. Break free, Chia. Begin the outward journey to the Everlasting. Meditate on the night. The night will redeem you from the Shadow. Death will redeem you. Remember Egypt and Kabo the Wise.'

The mirror pinioned the outspread arms. The gelid metal had reached almost to her neck. She sealed her eyes in acceptance of imminent damnation. Better to exist as a witless shade among sad ghosts than to suffer the horror of self-knowledge. The terror of one's self was the mother of all fears in all possible worlds. Her fears

265

had been the grave-diggers of a thousand births in her past. And the live burials would not be still beneath the soil.

The voice of Kabo resonated from the yellow womb of old Egypt, intermingled with the sough of the Tomb Spirit. The words she had ignored by the brown banks of the Nile came to her again and this time she could not evade them.

The sigh of the Tomb Spirit and the chant of Kabo the Wise merged into an echoing incantation . . .

' . . And the Unshaped Ones that were old in the First Time of Men were dark with a darkness that frightened the River People and the Mountain People. Wearing the many forms of things that slide and swim and creep and jump and fly, they gobbled the entrails of the gods of the land. And the name of them was Thzan-tzai. In other forms they were clothed, unlike the shapes of the beasts of the land or the waters or the semblance of the gods and demons of the Upper and Lower Worlds. Their forms are not named in the Book of Unas. And the Thzan-tzai took dominion in all lands and beneath all waters. And the Sun Eye darkened at the iniquities of those who hid in a thousand shapes, and the Warriors of the Sun Eye cast down the Thzan-tzai, all but one. And the name of the one was Glak-i-kakthz who was upright in the Sun Eye, and not as the other Thzan-tzai. For taking human shape and teaching the Children of Men, Glak-i-kakthz was exiled from the host of those whose forms are not named in the Book of Unas. And in the shape of a man he took the vows of land and water and sky and swore allegiance to the Sun Eye and the Moon Breast, and his shape did not change. Thus Glak-i-kakthz was named Last of the Changers. And the servants of the Thzan-tzai could not oppose him, and their inheritance was a hundredth part of the rites of desecration. Glak-i-kakthz made his dwelling in the Land of the East where the servants of the Thzan-tzai had made their dynasties of the Unshaped, and Glak-i-kakthz bound them with a secret sign . . .'

Chia, the sweat from her face moistening the stains of Nua's blood, groaned in agony, pleaded for Kabo's voice to stop, begged that the last revelation be withheld. But the voice persisted.

'. . . And a thousand years were numbered to seven, and Glak-i-kakthz raised his arms to the Upper World and said: "Lo, for seven times a thousand years my kin have been chained in the Regions of the Spirits, and I have renounced their deeds in your sight every day, Eye of the Sun. I have walked as a man under the Sun Eye, and have not changed for seven times a thousand years. I will take to me a woman who will bear me children." And he took to him the woman Chi of the Huan Tribe and she bore him a son and daughter. And the son was named after the Owl and the daughter was named after the Twilight. And the names of the son and daughter were Nyak and Chia . . .'

'No!' Chia screamed. 'It's a web of lies!'

'. . . Now Nyak and Chia were twins, and each knew the other's ways . . .'

'No!' *These are the killing words . . . This is the killing time.*

'. . . And when they were twelve years beneath the sky the paths of Nyak and Chia parted. Nyak went into the darkness and Chia went into the twilight. And Glak-i-kakthz beseeched them to return to the Sun Eye, saying: "The colour of my eyes is in your own, and my life of many days I give to you, age to age. Before seven times a thousand years I was of the Thzan-tzai race and a scourge to the Children of Men. In the First Time of Men I was worshipped as a demon. But my own race I have renounced, and have become as the Children of men, though great in years."

'Now Chia hated the ways of the Thzan-tzai while her brother worshipped their memory. For the sister it was a grievous thing to be born of that which was born

Thzan-tzai, and for the brother it was a spear in the breast to be named as the son of a man. So Nyak came from the south to Chia in the north, saying: "You hate our father for his Thzan-tzai birth and we have been at enmity for it is his human rebirth which is hateful in my sight. But let us conspire to destroy him, marrying our hates until the time of his death." And Chia consented, being in the twilight.

'And Glak-i-kakthz had built a tomb for a demon mirror on a hill of spirits. And Nyak and Chia came to their father, saying: "We have returned to the Sun Eye, one from darkness, one from twilight, and you are whole in our sight. Show us the Mirror Tomb that we may guard it from the dark servants when your time under the sky is done." And the father was deceived, meeting Nyak and Chia on Spirit Hill, and the darkness and the twilight went with them. And the children slew the father and laid the clay of his spirit in a threefold coffin in a chamber of death . . .'

Chia groaned softly as her chin touched the black metal and her haunted eyes were afflicted by the ruinous coffin in the dimness beyond the Golden Chamber. 'No,' she sobbed at the tormenting voice. 'You're killing me. No . . .'

'. . . But the spirit pained Nyak and he was driven out of all the shrines of the demons and the skin on his feet could not touch their ground and the eyes in his head could not look upon them. And the spirit spoke to Chia in sleep and gave many warnings, but she feared to walk in the Sun Eye and clove to the twilight. And Chia forgot that her name was named after Twilight. And her thoughts became tangled thickets and she was strange in her own image, and her image said that the blood of her father was not upon her. And her father became strange in her sight and she named him one with the Warriors of the Sun Eye. In the trouble of her spirit she fought for the Children of Men and the sickness of the false image fell upon her and her sleep was like death.

'And Nyak moved further into darkness and took upon himself the power of the Thzan-tzai. His hatred of the

268

father did not die with the death of the father, for Nyak loathed his flesh that was not Thzan-tzai. And the mother whom Chia loved, Nyak slew . . .'

'Moon Goddess,' moaned Chia. *The silver dagger weeps tears of blood.*

'. . . And Nyak slew his mother in anger that she was as the Children of Men, and he sought also the life of Chia for he wished to stand alone upon the mountain. And he grew strange, saying: "My name is not named after the Owl, but is the name of the Game Master." And in his darkness he was made alone though Chia lived, and he stretched out his hand, saying: "I have no sister. And the father of Chia is not as my father. He who sired me was a demon and never a man." And Nyak knew that the Thzan-tzai had fled all the lands and all the waters for seven times a thousand years, and Nyak crossed his arms in the sign that is not named in the Book of Unas, saying: "I have breathed the winds of the Middle World for seven times a thousand years, sprung from the seed of Glak-i-kakthz who was cast down with his brethren by the Warriors of the Sun Eye." And Nyak took dominion over the Rites of Desecration and drew all things evil to him. And the dynasties of men beheld a change in his flesh and he hid his form in the labyrinth of the south. And Nyak hated Chia above all who walked beneath the sky. And Chia named him as the Enemy of Light, and her hatred was as great as his. And Nyak declared that his father was a demon of the Thzan-tzai. And Chia declared that her father was a Warrior of the Sun Eye, whom she named the Celestial One. Thus Nyak renounced the father from the south and Chia renounced the father from the north. And the battle between the brother, no brother, and the sister, no sister, has not had an end.'

The black metal of Ming's mirror covered Chia's mouth as her deep green eyes gazed into time and her soul.

On the golden walls of the Spirit Mirror chamber was all the past.

Aromatic smoke at dusk in Twilight Owl Village (re-named after Chia and Nyak) by the upper Yellow River and the simple hut where she looked from the green eyes of her brother to the green eyes of her smiling father and asked the question that banished the smile: 'Father — who were the Thzan-tzai?'

On reliving the memory a part of Chia died.

Orange sunrise over the Yellow River Valley and bitter parting. Nyak had left for the south in rage at their father's renunciation of the power of the demons, pro-testing that he had been cheated of his birthright as the son of a Thzan-tzai. After a meal whose savour was remorse she bade farewell to a mournful mother and a stricken father, unable to endure the proximity of a man who had once belonged to the dark masses of the Elder Race. Ashamed of her disgust, she avoided meeting his green gaze. The orange sun was huge and the villagers silent as she left, travelling north to Black Dragon Mountain.

Another part of Chia died with the memory.

Black Dragon Mountain. Solitude shrinking the past to a drop of water in the palm of her hand. Rejection of her Thzan-tzai genealogy forcing her deeper into the caverns. Dreams in which her father's shape was squamous and the colour of bile. Nyak's arrival and the murderous pact. Spirit Hill, and the sharp blades and their father's blood splashing over Nyak and Chia's black cloaks and spreading in a crimson spiral in a puddle on the tomb's floor. The savaged corpse, its ripped robes become shrouds, grey, black, white, sealed in a sumptuous threefold coffin. Grey shrouds, black shrouds, white shrouds savaged with knives.

Another death in Chia.

Egypt. Serpent-circled brow of the black shaman and the throat of the jungle and the mouth of the Nile. Kabo the Wise, cloak of snakeskin, talisman-decked staff sparkling in the sun. Nefertiti, who had made her sane

270

with the only love she would accept, trembling for Chia's sanity. The black words of truth, heard only by the Shadow, the Khaibit, growing in shadow.

The death of Chia.

The hard black line of the metal surface slid over her eyes and a dense silence poured into her ears and crammed her head. The tenuous spirit of her father receded into the tiny golden world above.

In a moment, or an age, she floated in infinite black space-watching a gold circle ebb into the distance until it was a spot of light, a golden star.

The void was suddenly populated with a universe of phantoms.

The starved ghosts of a million denied dreams congregated around Chia and she saw them and saw through them. Sad phantoms, exiled aspects of what men would not face in themselves. Banished traces of men's souls, blindly searching to rejoin the soul that had cast them out. Searching, yet forgetful of their spiritual homes, trapped in their false freedom, lost in their illusion of selfhood.

Dark selves, shadows, wispy traces of the scent of the Infinite Flesh.

Pitiful spectres.

And they whimpered and scattered at the sight of Chia.

Chia's being was not dispersed in the void. Her death hung around her like a talisman. And the mirror ghosts could not endure her gaze. They could whisper death to life, lie to truth – they could not whisper death to death, truth to truth.

Chia had died to Chia and there were no mirrors facing her eyes to reflect the Shadow. She was one with the T'ao, was of Nirvana, was Brahman-Atman. Chia was a mirror reflecting all things. And the kindred of the Mirror saw, in Chia's eyes, the secret terror of their frail existence. They saw the truth of their nature – unreality.

The one thing in all the cosmos which the Mirror Kindred could not look upon was a mirror.

The phantom hosts fled.

Slowly, magic stars and paradise worlds appeared in the void, linked by silver threads of silent hymns.

Suspended from the invisible thread between life and life, the sorceress was irradiated with the knowledge that nothing ever dies except that which was always nothing. Time was an illusion, dying from moment to moment, but the past river and the past girl and the past mountain did not die. The past was an eternal land, and in time its eternity was revealed.

No barriers remained. She could soar to everlasting freedom. The skies beyond day and night invited her spirit to blissful abandon. The surging seas beyond the rim of all worlds swelled her heart with a longing deeper than any ship-skimmed ocean, fiercer than any storm.

Time might have passed.

The stars and worlds faded, the ideal they enshrined now no more than a Higher Illusion. She was gliding out of the universe of Higher Dreams. She was awakening.

For an instant that was the instant of a moment and the instant of a hundred kalpas she was free to go forwards or return to the dying illusion of time. All pasts and all futures called her with a weaker voice than the tones of eternity, but the very frailty of the voice inspired a vast compassion. It was the voice of birth and death and suffering and hate: creation groaning under the creaking Wheel of Samsara. It was blind, deaf children stumbling over blind, deaf children, tortured and torturing. And she saw the Spirit Mirror for what it was – a thing of terror for the blind and deaf children. It was the combined reflection of the Thzan-tzai, a reflection congealed into a shape and power of madness. The Spirit Mirror would bring madness to the lost children who called themselves humans.

Her choice made itself. It was the way of the Bodhisattva, the one who turns from the Great Awakening to redeem the suffering of the worlds. This was the Great Death, to forego eternity, to plunge into the unceasing death of time in response to the calls of anguish. Chia chose to descend from the last summit to Heaven as a redeemer, a Bodhisattva.

Her soul leaned down to the turbulent trail of the Mirror Breath and flowed in the wake of the seething mass as it stormed out of the Death Mound and hurled the body of her former self and its companions aside. She tracked the maelstrom as it roared down Spirit Hill and across the moor to Shen Lung Gorge, her bliss diminishing as she pursued. Joy spilled from her like sparks from a comet's tail. The surges of eternity ebbed as valley and river and hill fell back. Enlightenment streamed and was lost from her condensing body.

The Wheel of Samsara. Dying into birth and born to death again.

Once more she was the Sorceress of Black Dragon Mountain, fugitive in time. Soon she would have to enter the world and inhale its dusty air, her form fixed, her flesh, once more, mortal. Her mind, once more, trapped in the fleeing time.

The Mirror Breath rampaged up the slope of Celestial Buddha Hill and smote the temple gates. Chia perceived that a chariot with three figures had merged with the boiling mist. Ah – Nyak and the Silver Brethren. It was to be expected.

The gates burst asunder and the mist and the chariot roared into the courtyard. And Chia saw the Body of the Mirror. And her spirit, condensing into human form, winged towards it in grim determination. She would claw her way through the Body of the Mirror.

She would break through the Body and into the haunted temple to battle with the haunters.

Mortal again, the last droplets from the sea of enlightenment falling from her body, Chia thrust her flesh and bone hand through the Body of the Mirror.

The Spirit of the Mirror was waiting on the other side.

21

BODY OF THE MIRROR

訟

'Spirit of Heaven!' Liu Chun cried, striding from the parapet of the Cloud Tower to the lantern-crested door of the stairway. 'The mist from Chao's mouth was indeed a mere breath to this sorcerous gale!'

The abbot shuffled in the steps of the warrior sage, praying silently to the Bodhisattva Avalokitesvara, Lord of Compassion; divine intervention seemed their sole hope.

The courtyard was a commotion of discordant sounds and fuming fog. The townsfolk had fled to the southern precincts. The monastic brethren huddled by the outer walls. Chao's uplifted arms were frozen in welcome. The Silken Stranger sprawled at his feet, dormant. In the vague chariot, a mere wraith within the turmoil of mist, wavered the outlines of three passengers – a blur of saffron flanked by grey shadows crowned with silver. The noble horses, made insubstantial by the vapour, lay dying with splayed legs between broken shafts.

The smoky head of the storm arched like a cobra above the red silk bundle of Chao's companion. It darted at the Silken Stranger, withdrew, darted again, retracted, hesitated. Then it started to weave above the prone figure. To the onlookers it seemed to breathe into the Silken Stranger, but the breath flew back into the seething mist.

The spectres in the chariot descended and walked out of the streaming fog, changing from apparitions to solid shapes as they approached Chao. 'Vinaya — and two Silver Brethren,' whispered the abbot.

Sparing Nagarjuna and Liu Chun a meagre glance, the angular monk swept to confront the motionless, expressionless Chao. The monk wore a sneer.

Fear has made them as the stone of the temple, thought Nyak, as he cast his disdainful glance at the abbot and the sage. Advancing to the Hearing in its reversed image of Chao, the necromancer lifted his arms in the primordial sign of the Thzan-tzai, arms crossed with palms turned inwards, and summoned the Hearing to join the Sight within Vinaya's body. Woodenly, Chao's arms rose and crossed in response.

The leaning head of the Mirror Breath continued to circle above the Silken Stranger.

Chao's mighty chest stretched as it took a deep inhalation. The deep breath was held. And it was not released.

The veins in the muscular neck began to throb. The neck swelled and contracted, swelled and contracted.

The Hearing was straining free of the head.

The spirit was struggling loose of the body.

Spasms started to twist and shake Chao's massive bulk. The heavy face contorted into an agitated maze of ripples and twitches. Violent tremors racked the muscles of the torso. And the heart pounded like a drum. The wild beating speeded rapidly and mounted in volume. The thudding heart banged against the ribs. The ribs began to crack.

The throbbing of the neck rose to the head. The temples vibrated with the rushing blood-flow. A narrow split angled up the brow of the skull.

The ribs snapped and the skin tautened over the bulging, thundering heart. A large lump expanded the chest.

The bone of the forehead split and the blood-inflated brain squeezed through the gap.

The heart exploded the chest and spun far across the garan before squelching into a red mess on the hard clay. The bloated brain smashed the bony dome to splinters as it erupted from the skull and the eyes were blown from their sockets.

Crimson fountains gushed from the grotesque, swaying shape as the Hearing swept from Chao to the Sight in Vinaya.

The gruesome corpse wavered for a moment, then toppled backwards and crashed to the ground as the Hearing rushed into Vinaya, rejoining its overlord, the Sight.

Nyak uncrossed his arms, his teeth bared in a wolfish grin. Stronger now.

Stronger.

His long preparations for body invasion had involved an arduous and prolonged hierarchy of trances, subtly cadenced to the body-spirits of Chao and Vinaya. Little control had been required to guide the Hearing in Chao's shape, so Nyak had only been fully aware of existing in the form of Vinaya. But now the Sight and the Hearing were one. His grin widened. The last strand of the web was about to be woven.

The smile became fixed as his eyes focused on the white-faced man in red silk. The smile faded as his gaze moved upwards to the weaving head of the mist. Why did the Mirror Breath hesitate?

His stare switched back to the milky visage with its effeminate features and incarnadine eyes – the androgynous travesty of the girl slain by Chao in Spirit Hill Mound. The figure gave no sign of response to the mist coiling above.

Out of the corner of his vision, Nyak spied Liu Chun draw a knife and pounce in his direction. The necromancer signalled the Silver Brethren to deal with the assailant. With a few swift strides they blocked Liu Chun's path and started to ease the gauntlets from their diseased hands. Liu Chun halted in consternation, his nose wrinkling at the foetor of the Brethren, his mind lost in puzzlement over the rush of events. He was preparing to rush his masked adversaries when his attention was caught by the alarm that suddenly shook Vinaya's profile. He heard the abbot shout in surprise, and his own breath was expelled in a gasp when he followed the angle of Vinaya's stupefied stare.

A slender hand, smeared with blood, sprouted from the stomach of the prone Silken Stranger.

The hand rose higher, clutching at air, and an arm draped in a blood-stained black sleeve emerged from the red silk of the inert figure.

Nyak gaped in astonishment and rage at the ascending arm and the hooked hand. A black shoulder heaved from the slim red form. A head crowned with long, disordered hair arose from the frail torso. Another shoulder came into view – another arm. The Silken Stranger's body was undisturbed as if the rising figure was surfacing from water.

The head of the mist recoiled from the black newcomer and the body of the mist shrank back to create a crescent of unsettled haze.

The necromancer sensed a frenzied wrath and a shrill fear in the Mirror Breath . . . the one who was rising out of the feeble frame of the womanish man inspired terror in the Spirit of the Mirror. Stark fear shook the bones of Vinaya and the bones of Nyak's body in the dark vault beneath the Forest of the Ancestors. It was Chia, Sorceress of Black Dragon Mountain.

It was Chia, clad in black and blood.

Chia . . .

The tall figure of the sorceress stepped out of the limp, inert body, her silver ankh glinting in the moonlight, blood on her black woollen cloak and black silk gown and on her face and hands. She set her green gaze on the necromancer and in her ocean eyes he saw a

277

reflection . . . a green-eyed boy playing on the mud banks of the Yellow River with a green-eyed girl . . . a vision of a green-eyed man rising from a coffin. An old nightmare blazed the interior of his skull with the sheet lightning of revelation.

He staggered back with arm upraised, shielding himself from the mirror in Chia's eyes, and yelled for the Silver Brethren to follow as he reeled into the gusts and eddies of the Mirror Breath. The Silver Brethren, bewildered by their master's distraction, trailed him into the mist with tottering steps.

Liu Chun and Nagarjuna hurried to the sorceress. 'Chia!' greeted the sage in a tone compounded of delight and surprise. 'You were never so welcome, Green-Eyes.'

Chia averted her face and pulled up the cowl to cover her features. 'Don't look at my eyes, Liu Chun. You also, Nagarjuna – don't peer into my eyes.'

The deep, thrilling quality of her voice stole their breath. It was a dread of joy and a joy of dread voice. The sage scratched his beard and mumbled something incomprehensible. Nagarjuna folded his arms and lowered his gaze.

The sorceress bent and lifted the Silken Stranger. The pallid, delicate face was serene. The fixed pink eyes were baleful. 'A weighty burden in so small a pack,' she said. 'It would need Chao's brawn to carry it from Spirit Hill.'

'Who is he?' The sage scowled at the whey-faced man.

The black cowl shivered with the shaking of Chia's head. 'Not he – it,' vibrated her mellow voice. 'It's the Body of the Mirror masked in the male guise of its female sacrifice. Death had made her face white when the mirror mocked her form – the paleness of this parody's skin reflects her death face. It's dressed in scarlet silk, as was she. The Mirror Body is a male travesty of a girl who lies dead in Spirit Hill Mound. In this disguise the Mirror Body left the tomb, in this disguise it entered the temple. Freed from the mound, the Spirit of the Mirror rode the wind to the south to be reunited with the Body. The Two that are One.'

Neither man was able to absorb the full import of the compressed speech. Their attention was torn between the chalk visage of the Silken Stranger and the frenzied crescent of luminous mist. Liu Chun faced an unruly mob of questions: how was it that the Mirror could metamorphose into a scrawny man hanging loosely from Chia's arms? What in the name of Mo Ti had blown Chao's body apart? How had Chia passed through the disguised Mirror, and from where? What was Vinaya's purpose, and why did the Silver Brethren obey him? And why was Chia covered in blood that was obviously not her own? The questions jostled with a hundred others, clamouring for answers.

'What —?' he began, but the sorceress merely shook her head and strode towards the Buddha Hall.

Nagarjuna and Liu Chun started to follow. It was then that the crescent of streaming fog roared like the Hound of Heaven and raged under the walls of the garan, assuming a bright density. Swathing the brown walls with a mist that was now white, it raced to the southern side of the monastery. The few monks who had not been stunned by its initial onslaught fled for the refuge of the Buddha Hall. The wing-roofed edifice blocked the view of the southern courtyard, but it was to be presumed that the townsfolk had either escaped through the Red Phoenix Gate or hidden under the dome of the stupa.

Chia stopped, stared at the surging fog and the brethren flocking to the Buddha Hall, then turned and headed for the open door of the Cloud Tower. It was best that the Mirror Body be kept well clear of the members of the temple, for it drew the Mirror Spirit, and wherever the Body was, the Spirit would hover near, breathing death. Nagarjuna and Liu Chun traded looks, exchanged nods, and tracked the black profile of Chia. She waved them back but they continued to dog her steps. A backward glance showed Liu Chun that an arm of the billowing mist was reaching after them as they hurried under the lintel of the Cloud Tower portal. Again Chia signalled them to run for the Buddha Hall, but Liu Chun set his shoulders square, Nagarjuna breathed deeply, and both men mounted the stairs with quiet resolution.

The Wei-ch'i board, sheltered by the low parapet, was undisturbed by the tide of wind from the north – the white stones still circumscribed unbroken walls around a substantial number of the black. But the Wheel of Samsara creaked and rotated, west to east.

None too gently, Chia deposited the Silken Stranger near the Wei-ch'i game. She lifted her cowled head to the melon moon and drifted into silent prayer.

A plume of mist brushed the parapet, stroked the stone, and sank back. Liu Chun peered over the edge and saw the white fog wrapping round the foot of the tower, nuzzling its walls – the freshly painted wood was smeared with mist fingers. The Mirror Spirit was a milky pool frothing three men high, lapping at the root of their spindling refuge. Hidden in the billowing shroud – Vinaya and the Silver Brethren. What was their aim? The sage stiffened as he saw a young monk approach from the Buddha Hall, his robe yellow in the eye of the moon.

'Dharmapala!' shouted the abbot, 'Go back! Keep your distance from the cloud. 'See to the safety of the townsfolk.'

'They're gathered in the stupa,' the monk called back. 'About thirty of them. One of them is a T'ao magus who claims he saw Chia in the town.'

'Then go to the stupa and exhort the people to pray to the sacred images. Remain at their side.'

Dharmapala bowed and left.

'I wish they had all left with the coming of the Black Serpent Breath,' grumbled the sage, scratching his full beard. Flicking a look at Chia, who kept her back to him, he swept up the wineskin and gulped a noisy draught. 'I might as well get drunker,' he muttered 'I couldn't understand this affair with a sober head so I might as well look at it from a head brimming with wine. I knew this mirror haunting would be a nightmare, but it's proved a nightmare more complex than the Labyrinths of Kang. I find a pattern, but it leads me to a larger pattern which contains the first, which leads to –'

'Silence,' broke in Chia's low, penetrating voice. 'Stop your babbling.'

Liu Chun's mouth gaped, but the tongue stilled its torrent of complaint.

Nagarjuna studied the floor at his feet, bewildered beyond the simplest comprehension of the rush of bizarre events. The confusion in his mind was a merciful confusion; it subdued the fear of the white mist surrounding them like an ethereal sea. He dimly recalled the previous dusk when he had stood on the western parapet with Vinaya and mused on the sunset mist that made golden cloudscapes of the hills and deeps of the land. That moment seemed an age ago.

The sorceress continued to face away from the two men. Her hood-framed face of legend was uplifted to the melon moon, its refined features stained with Nua's blood.

She had just returned from the borders of Paradise. She had been radiant with the blaze of enlightenment. She had burst with bliss, bliss of the spirit in the body and the body in the spirit The true Immortal, beyond the flesh. Or beyond and within and above the flesh. Words failed . . .

Memory also failed. Chia vaguely recalled that she had been on the edge of the Great Awakening. But now the Great Awakening was itself relegated to a dream – a dream dreamed by someone else, somewhere else, long ago. The soiled and stained world of empires and time in the flesh had her in thrall again.

And the Death-bringer madness was rushing down on

281

her with the flap of gigantic wings. And in the wind of its wake was the dying time. The Sleep of Rebirth.

Her spirit was losing the last fleecy clouds of Enlightenment – they dispersed with each breath of her lungs.

But that was the way of things . . .

'Sorceress,' quavered Nagarjuna's voice. 'This Spirit mist rises. It's rising to the roof of the Cloud Tower.'

That was the way of things, she brooded, ignoring the abbot. Enlightenment is no rare prize. We have all been enlightened, time and again. And we have all forgotten. Small children walk every day in the Enlightenment. Then they grow old and forget. You wake in the morning from a dream that leaves a divine ache in your soul for the mystery that was in the dream. But the mystery is lost in the opening of an eye, and the dream is lost in the din of the morning. We have all been enlightened, and we have all forgotten. The trick is remembering. Memory is life.

And memory, also, can kill.

Yes, dark brother, she whispered in her mind. Memories can kill.

The scent of the Infinite Flesh was memory. Memory scent. Killing scent.

The Shadow was also Memory, and it housed killing words in its quiet dark.

'Sorceress!' the abbot repeated with alarm rattling his bony throat. 'The white fog . . . The Mirror mist . . .'

Chia spared a glance at the column of white cloud crawling up the wood of the tower. At the base of the Cloud Tower it spread in a foaming pool over twenty steps wide. Three shapes could be hazily discerned in the mist. Out of the corner of her black hood she cast a quick glance at the stair door. Fleecy fog floated out of the black square with a lazy sigh.

Then she turned her face once more to the yellow moon.

'Why are you just standing there, Chia?' burst out the

sage. 'Why don't you do something? At least tell us what surrounds us. I know all you've told me about the Thzan-tzai scent and the Spirit Mirror and Nyak and the Brethren, but what is the – the essence, the heart of the threat?'

For a brief spell her shadowed green eyes continued to gaze at the moon.

'Ourselves,' she replied.

The haunted mist hid the thoughts of Nyak and the two Brethren in its muffling folds. The enfolding fog wrapped them in a cocoon of vapour from the probing mind of the black enemy on the high tower.

Four Silver Brethren slipped into the billowing white shrouds and joined their two fellow-servants and the Master. Each Silver Brother turned his silver mask towards the saffron-robed body that housed their master.

Master, hear us, the six thought as one.

I always hear my children, Nyak thought back in answer.

Why has our enemy returned from the dark?

Nyak bent Vinaya's thin lips into a sardonic smile. *Why, my children? Because the enemy is cunning and strong. But do not be afraid of her, my children. Her cunning is the cunning of a hunted animal and her strength is the strength of hate alone. She is nothing. The Spirit Breath that surrounds us is stronger than her. And I am stronger than the Spirit Breath. I am stronger than the perfect madness. And what is this perfect madness of which I am the Master?*

The perfect madness is a mind without thought which is a world without thought, they answered as one.

And what is the nature of flesh? asked Nyak.

The nature of flesh is the residing spirit of flesh, be it skin, bone, blood, stone, wood, earth, water or wind flesh. Flesh is spirit. Spirit is flesh.

Yes, my children. And I am the Master of the perfect madness. While I exist it reflects me only. And I exist forever. And mastery of the flesh has always been mine. The seed of the

Infinite Flesh is in me, now and always. Do not fear the Green-Eyes, my children. She is less than nothing. She has escaped one trap to step into another, such is the confusion of her evil mind. From the circle in the square she is running to another circle in the square. The enemy runs always down a tangled maze, and the path she takes leads always to destruction. For I, my children, am the master of the maze. I am the maze in which she runs. And her trail leads to the centre of the maze. And I am the centre of the maze, reflected in the Spirit Mirror. And the Spirit Mirror will soon don the stone flesh of a god. That god will wear my face. And I will swallow the enemy. Down and down.

'Ourselves?' echoed Liu Chun in a bull voice charged with rage. 'You go too far, sorceress. I've had enough of your mystification and superior airs. The world is falling around our ears and you stand, hood-hidden, like an inviolate goddess. You've infuriated me often enough in the past, but this time you gall me beyond endurance. Do something, Green-Eyes, do something. That's the Spirit Mirror out there. The damned Spirit Mirror – the worst thing in the world. DO SOMETHING!'

White arms and hands of mist wove around the black figure of the sorceress. Snakes of white fog slipped across the wooden floor to the bare toes peeping under the bloodstained cloak.

'What is out there,' she said, 'is not the worst thing in the world. The worst thing in the world is everywhere. The horror of the Spirit Mirror and the horror of the emperor's torture chambers are, at heart, the same. They both break the spirit. The Spirit Mirror is no worse than those lords who stand on a hill made of corpses to make themselves seem tall and powerful. The Mirror steals thoughts. Men steal everything.'

Liu Chun, his anger expended by his outburst, contracted his eyebrows. Chia's voice had lost the magical quality it had when she emerged so spectacularly from the Silken Stranger. Not only had her tone lost its recent enchantment but it had sunk below its usual clarity. The speech was slurred and subdued.

She swung round without warning and the two men saw the blazing green power of the eyes beneath the hood. That green power charged them with such a shock that their hearts banged on their ribs.

'Ah,' she gave a wan smile. 'It seems my eyes remember what my heart forgets.'

Chia suddenly became alert, lifting her head as if catching a sound of menace or hope. She listened intently. Both men strained to hear the sound she hearkened to, but there was only silence.

She sat, knees pressed to her chest, arms hugging her knees, in the centre of the stupa. The hood of her dark green cape was thrown back, exposing the broad burn on her cheek. Her supple fingers stroked the charred, pointed stump of what had been a genially beaming Buddha statue.

Peng-t'ai wasn't alone any more in the sacred dome. Over thirty townsfolk and the pleasant young monk Dharmapala shared the stupa with her. Apart from Dharmapala, they all disdained to recognise her presence.

Peng-t'ai didn't mind. A short while ago she had seen her Bodhisattva in a resplendent vision. The vision hadn't hung in the air in front of her eyes. It had no bright lights or gaudy colours. It was in her mind, and all the more real for that. She had seen an Enlightened One at the threshold of Heaven, and Peng-t'ai had called out in that silent cry of the mute to the Englightened One. And the Enlightened One had answered her cry for help and turned from bliss to descend from Heaven to Earth as a redeemer, a Bodhisattva.

And Peng-t'ai knew that Bodhisattva. She was the Green-Eyes. Chia the Black Dragon.

And Peng-t'ai sensed the nearness of Chia in the temple. She also sensed an evil coming.

Chia . . . we need you . . . come to us . . . forgive me for denying you Heaven . . . please come to me, Green-Eyes . . . please come . . .

The silent plea poured out of Peng-t'ai's soul.

'What is it, Chia? What do you hear?' asked the abbot.

Chia shook her head. 'No questions.' She knelt beside the cream-faced image of the Mirror Body and studied the puerile gaze of the pink eyes. A finger of mist stroked its cheek. The sorceress breathed deeply to maintain an inner balance, but her spiritual resources began to trickle into the white fog, drop by drop. Sweat glistened on her intent face as the fear of failure – pummelling her confidence – increased the likelihood of defeat. She dared not lose the last shred of enlightenment left to her – it was all that might save them.

I heard your voice, voiceless one. It called me to the stupa, the centre.

But the dying time was heavy upon her and she swayed with swimming vision. Despite the craving to sleep and die she forced her attention to the whey face of the Silken Stranger. A sleek smile curved its bloodless lips. The lip-curve split and a satin whisper slid between the small, even teeth.

'Whispered to death.'

Ignoring the inane whisper, Chia hoisted the frail but heavy body onto her shoulder and stalked to the southern parapet, carefully skirting the dense fog gusts from the stair door.

'Whispered to death,' came the inane repetition from the bleached-bone face.

The abbot and sage dogged her steps but she motioned them back with a toss of the head.

Liu Chun was baffled. 'Chia! What are you doing?'

Taking the Body to the centre, you old drunkard. Housing the Body in the heart of the temple – the stupa.

286

She jumped onto the parapet, the Silken Stranger dangling from her arms. White Spirit mist tendrilled up to her and her burden. At the foot of the tower the frothy pool of white fog had spilled out into an even wider pool of swirling intangibility.

She straightened her spine, sank her mind into the long moment, swung back her arms and hurled the Silken Stranger far outside the rim of the mist. To her ch'i-raced vision the Body seemed to float like a leaf in a long arc.

As she watched the descent of the Mirror Body she flexed her thews and sinews and leaped in its wake. At the instant of leaping she unleashed her spirit in an upward surge that vaulted to the heavens and the power of Yang, and diminished the Yin power of the earth. The Yang force slowed her fall to an extent that was visible even to the incredulous gaze of Nagarjuna. Liu Chun smiled grimly as the Silken Stranger thumped to the ground shortly before the sorceress landed lightly at his side, her black cloak streaming like a banner.

Chia scooped up the Body and glanced over her shoulder. The cloud bulged towards her at a speed she could never have matched outside the long moment. She raced for the southern courtyard. The Spirit of the Mirror raged at her heels. Rounding the ornate Buddha Hall she sprinted under the torana and sped into the great dome of the stupa. Flinging the Mirror Body into the centre of the vault she bestrode the prone shape and withdrew from the long moment. The silver dagger flashed as she drew it and faced the entrance with a wild flame lighting each green iris.

Dharmapala gasped at Chia's abrupt appearance. She had been moving so quickly that his untrained vision failed to note her arrival until she stood in the middle of the floor: it was as if she had materialised from air. The stupefied townsfolk were under the same impression and stared round-eyed and wide-mouthed. Only Peng-t'ai smiled in delight at Chia's appearance.

I came, Peng-t'ai. And I was glad to heed your call. You're great-souled.

'Gather round me,' she ordered. 'Stay at the centre of the dome.'

They did not stir into life until Dharmapala sprang to duty and hustled the recalcitrant people into an untidy huddle centred on Chia.

'Shutter your eyes and lock your ears,' she said quietly without diverting her attention from the dark portal. 'An evil is coming.'

The evil came. The cloud, white as a funeral garment, seeped into the dome. It rippled along the walls, hugging the stony contours. In two stretching arms it spread around the small knot of humanity until the hands of fog met on the southern wall. Then the circle of luminous mist glided up the sandstone surface, thinning as it spread to a gleaming, opaque haze. At length, the whole interior of the stupa was radiant with a sheen of shimmering vapour.

Mahayana altars adorned with bronze shrines of Buddha Maitreya, Lord of the Future, and Buddha Amitabha, Lord of the Mantras; camphor wood figurines of apsaras; stelae of nimbused arhats; stone eidolons of Bodhisattvas – all were muted to soft outlines and sullen shades of brown by the gleaming mist. Yet a brooding sanctity inhered in the devotional images flanking the walls – a numinous presence, sprung from the marriage of India and China, haunted the perfumed air of the stupa and the ardent glow of a thousand candles. The Spirit of the Mirror faltered in the fragrant dome of worship.

Chia, momentarily distracted by the flimsy fog and the Mahayana effigies, returned her gaze to the mist-curtained door.

The angular saffron figure of Vinaya emerged from the mist followed by six grey-cloaked Silver Brethren, the long grey hair that flowed from the crowns of their silver

288

masks swaying as they walked. Forgetting Chia's admonition, Dharmapala and the San Lung people uncovered their ears and opened their eyes. A few paces from the circle of amazed faces, Nyak halted and twisted Vinaya's mouth into a parody of a smile.

'So you've bolted into your last hole, vixen. And I see that your eyes have lost their sorcery of a short time ago. Compliments on your mysterious escape from the Golden Chamber, but – alas – you've run from one trap to another. The Body and the Spirit of the Mirror are lodged in the temple's heart, and the Hearing and the Sight are united in me. You cannot oppose both the Spirit Mirror and myself.'

The smile came to resemble a death-grin. 'Now it begins, Chia. Now it begins. Desecration. Damnation. The Game . . .'

22

RITES
OF DESECRATION

囷

The necromancer's speech was interrupted by the sudden
arrival of Nagarjuna and Liu Chun. The sage took the scene
in at a glance and bunched his sturdy hands into fists,
prepared to launch his full weight on the gaunt frame of
Vinaya.

'Keep back!' warned Chia. 'Nyak is inside him. He'll
destroy you.'

Liu Chun halted.

'Indeed,' confirmed the necromancer. 'For many hours
four Silver Brethren have walked in the temple unseen with
killing love in their hands. For many weeks a part of me
walked through San Lung in the body of Chao, sustaining
the illusions that I and my servants fostered. At any time you
could all have been destroyed by the power of illusion.'

'Then why weren't we?' demanded the belligerent sage.

'He prefers slaves to corpses,' Chia cut in. 'And he seeks to
block the Path of the Buddha.' Liu Chun scowled, uncertain
of himself. 'Cavern of the Five Breaths,' she added.

Liu Chun nodded at the reference. Five years ago, in that
nightmare cavern, they faced enemies which only Chia
could oppose – enemies he had to flee if he wished to go on
breathing. The sage caught Nagarjuna's arm and pulled him
to the centre of the stupa. The bemused abbot offered no
resistance.

Nyak, who had looked askance at the cryptic message,
now realised its implication. He gave a crooked smile.

'Liu Chun was wise to run to your protection, woman. But you're foolish to think you can oppose me, Green-Eyes.'

Leaving the Silken Stranger in the middle of the huddled group, she stepped forwards to confront Nyak and the Silver Brethren. Nyak's servants fanned out, three on each side of Vinaya's possessed body. At a signal from the Master, the Silver Brethren speedily drew the silver gauntlets from their hands.

Six pairs of hands were raised in the dim light of the stupa. Twelve hands – four white as snow, four red as blood, two green as mould, two black as spiders – weaved in a sinister invitation. Long, metallic nails sprouted from twisted fingers. The outspread hands throbbed like hearts and stank like rancid pork.

A hapless cry of panic rang out behind Chia and a man of willowy build rushed past her for the door.

'Let me go,' he implored Nyak. 'I'm not your enemy. Please . . .'

He was making for a space between Nyak and a red-handed Silver Brother when, with an almost careless gesture a red hand ripped the light brown neck of the escaper. The victim recoiled with a choked cry. Scratching furiously at the infected skin, the man reeled to one side in an effort to reach the portal. Chia knew he was doomed. She had witnessed too many victims of the unnaturally virulent poisons of the Silver Brethren to be in any doubt of that. The man fell heavily, staggered to his feet, fell again, begged the abbot for aid.

'Help him, Chia, for Buddha's sake,' the abbot cried out, aghast.

'Stay where you are, Nagarjuna,' she shouted over her shoulder. 'Nothing can save him.'

The victim tried to crawl to the portal. 'I'm burning,' he wheezed. 'Burning.' His face was bathed in perspiration from the swift heat of the fever. His swarthy complexion darkened to the ruddiness of plague. He was seized with savage spasms as purple sores sprouted from his twisted features. A scream was stifled by the swollen tongue.

The head expanded to a ball of livid boils. Blood-washed eyes rolled upwards in their sockets. Distended lips formed two syllables: Burning. Then the red plague swept him to merciful death.

Chia had already steeped herself in the long moment although the pounding ch'i force it required nearly toppled her already exhausted frame. The world around her slowed down almost to a standstill from the view of her accelerated state. The six Silver Brethren looked like statues.

It is here, she thought. The killing time. The Owl and the Twilight meet. Nyak and Chia meet in their final conflict. It's the time of reckoning between us, we who are of the flesh of Glak-i-kakthz and Chi. Fu, Yi and the few other women I've loved in my overlong life — you've tortured and killed them all. But now it ends, Brother Owl. I, the Twilight, will end it. The time is here. The time of your death. Or mine. Or the death of us both.

She raised her hand to Nyak in the shaven-scalped, saffron-robed body of Vinaya, 'Greetings, Brother Owl,' she called out. 'Is the Hearing in you ready for the killing words of the Twilight?'

Nyak faltered momentarily, the sludge of buried memory stirring slightly at hearing the names of the Owl and the Twilight. Then he regained command and smiled indulgently at the sorceress.

'My name is Game Master,' he said softly.

Until his reply, Chia wasn't certain just how adept Nyak was in the art of the long moment. But it was clear that his command was superior to her own. To anyone outside the long moment her speech would be high above the upper limits of hearing. Nyak's chi-speeded mind was at least as fast as her own although

Vinaya's body displayed no sign of strain. Her body, she knew, was trembling in every muscle.

And the dying time was seeping through her labyrinth of veins. The Sleep of Rebirth was calling her exhausted spirit. There was little time before the dying sleep claimed her.

And if I sleep, I die. This time, surrounded by enemies, my Sleep of Rebirth will be changed into death eternal.

Less than a second of the world's time had passed.

'I know the killing words for Nyak the Owl,' she announced. 'They are the words of Kabo the Wise, the dark-skinned shaman, who recited them to me in distant Egypt long ago.'

The features of Vinaya's wolfish face twitched with the perturbation of Nyak's spirit. He felt ancient dreads rise within. Rejecting the spirit battle he had planned to wage with Chia, and wary of the mysterious power that still lingered faintly in her gaze, he reached into the minds of the Brethren.

My children, she stands before you. The Black Dragon. The enemy. She who has killed so many of your brothers. Now she is weak, and encircled by the mighty strength of the Spirit Breath. Let your hands drive her out of the world. Do you hear me, my children?

We hear you, Master, the six thought as one.

But don't attack yet, my children. The enemy claims to have learned new killing words. I think she lies. But if she uses words that pain my flesh, I will give you the words to attack and destroy the enemy. You – Brother of the Green Hands – you must lead such an attack. You have the power of the long moment. You will fight her until her power of the long moment fades. Then the rest of you can make short work of her. Do you hear me, my children?

We hear.

The perfect madness had thought the Green-Eyed One to be a goddess from the High Realms.

Now it knew better.

It was Chia. Chia the long-lived. But Chia the mortal.

And the perfect madness did not fear Chia. It had known her since she was a tiny child.

It had known everyone since they were tiny children.

It knew and loved Nyak the Master and his masked children.

The perfect madness was the scent of Thzan-tzai spirit flesh.

But Nyak the Master was the Thzan-tzai spirit flesh itself, and the perfect madness was his worshipful mirror.

I love you, Master. I wear your hidden face. And I will become a god for you.

The breath of the perfect madness nuzzled into the recesses of the stupa walls, shyly licking the Buddha flesh.

I mean you no harm, thought the perfect madness.

Here – in the China flesh of earth and water and wood and bone and stone and skin and fire – this god was new and unfamiliar in the flesh. Its unfamiliarity was a slight hurt to the white mist that caressed the stone flesh.

The perfect madness came, not from the unfamiliar, but from the familiar.

It was unsettled by the raw essence and scent of the Celestial Buddha. It was wary of godhood and the unknown.

But here – right here in the Buddha Dome, a point had been reached, a point of transformation from raw godhood to delicious god-flesh.

The god was merging with China-flesh, and China-flesh was familiar.

It was descending into the world of images.

And the world of images fed the world of reflections.

And the world of reflections fed the perfect madness.

And the perfect madness, mirroring the hunger of the Master, craved god-flesh.

It sniffed the Buddha stone of the stupa with love and longing.

If the Buddha-flesh was familiar enough, then the Spirit could reunite with the Body of the Mirror, and then the Spirit Body would become very familiar with the familiar Buddha-flesh.

The perfect madness tentatively tasted the enfleshed Buddha.

Ah – the taste was just about right . . .

Perceiving no immediate threat from Nyak and the Brethren, Chia withdrew her mind from the long moment. It would be folly to waste the power of the long moment needlessly, the exertion of maintaining it taxed her to the limits of her wearied condition. She had to struggle against the swoon that threatened to plunge her into the dying time, and, with Nyak's help, into unending oblivion. If she gave way now the Sleep of Rebirth would be the Sleep of Everlasting Death.

When Nyak's voice echoed in the great dome it also echoed in her head. She lifted her swimming vision to the gaunt figure of Vinaya-Nyak.

He stretched out his gaunt arms. 'People of San Lung,' he declaimed. 'You have been sadly misled. This devil-eyed sorceress here and the Buddha monks in this temple have brought you falsehood. The true Buddha Spirit is not as you have been taught. The true Buddha is a being of great splendour, but the true Buddha is not the Buddha in which these Indian monks believe. The true Buddha is the Buddha of the flesh at play. People of San Lung, let me show you the true Buddha . . .'

The arms stretched wider.

'The Buddha of the Infinite Flesh will be revealed to you in a vision,' he proclaimed. 'Listen to me, people of San Lung. Listen. Listen to me. Listen to my voice. My voice is all you can hear. Nothing intrudes on my voice.

295

My voice is all you have ever heard. It fills all the Nine Realms . . .'

Turning, Chia saw that the abbot's narrow shoulders and the sage's burly shoulders drooped in unison, their eyes clouded. The throng at the centre of the temple settled into a T'ai Ching trance.

Except, Chia noticed, for Peng-t'ai. The deaf girl was immune to the words of command. The hooded woman scowled at the necromancer.

Good for you, brave woman, thought Chia.

'. . . Behold the Temple of the Buddha Flesh,' intoned Nyak. 'Behold the God of the Infinite Flesh — see how the flesh slithers and squirms with a thousand visions . . .'

Chia allowed herself to drift with Nyak's words to see the picture he was forming for the others, and to gauge his strategy in performing this seemingly pointless act of T'ai Ching. Floating on the surface of the T'ai Ching words, she began to see a number of inane visions . . .

A bronze statue of the Buddha Maitreya swayed in a serpentine motion, its burnished hand bending from the mudra of blessing to perform an array of signs from Nyak's Thzan-tzai cult. The wooden head of an apsara lolled idiotically to and fro. The ascetic lineaments of an arhat underwent bizarre contortions like the face of a tortured monkey. The Buddha Amitabha executed a display of obscene and puerile gestures and his writhing lips mouthed profanities. The demonic spectacle clogged the mind and churned the stomach.

Withdrawing from the T'ai Ching trance, Chia observed the reactions of those caught within it. Liu Chun's craggy features were trembling. Nagarjuna's expression was one of horrified bewilderment. And, except for the deaf Peng-t'ai, the drawn faces of the rest were full of loathing and terror. This was the symbol of Nyak's private drama — the desecration of the temple. It wasn't enough to destroy the monastery or murder the members of the Sangha. The slaughter of missionaries meant martyrdom and martyrdom meant more converts. The way to extinguish the sacred flame of the Buddha in China was to implant a sick root at the heart of a shrine that nurtured the flame. Religions died when they rotted from within. A rite of desecration would unloose more evil than the despoiling of a thousand shrines. The darkest shadow always lurks by the brightest altar. And Nyak must be revelling in the thought of combining her destruction with the spread of a power that would poison the Buddha Spirit.

And she recalled the words of Kabo the Wise: 'Nyak took dominion over the rites of desecration and drew all things evil to him.' Here was her brother's chief delight — not games, but the perversion of all those things esteemed to be of the highest value. For all his erudition and remarkable powers he had the soul of a lewd brat.

'. . . Witness the glorious contortions of the Buddha of the Infinite Flesh as it –'

'*Silence!*' roared Chia.

Nyak's voice and the T'ai Ching trance halted abruptly. The knot of people at the centre of the stupa stirred and blinked.

Chia leant her head to one side, summoned the ch'i force, and then swept her glaring eyes at the monks and townsfolk, intense thought streaming from her.

Leave. Flee the stupa. Run from here if you want to survive. Run from here. Run.

The power of her thought blasted into their minds and they scattered and bolted for the door. Chia gave a sigh of relief as they streamed past the Silver Brethren without being harmed.

But Peng-t'ai remained, sitting at the centre of the stupa with a sharp stump of wood in her hand. She smiled fondly at Chia.

The sorceress frowned. *Why can't I control you, Peng-t'ai?*

The woman's smile deepened.

Chia was touched by a feeling of admiration for Peng-t'ai. Let her stay, if that was her decision. She would give Chia one more thing to fight for.

She turned to Nyak and the Brethren.

She had little time. The Death-bringer madness was raging through her head and the Sleep of Rebirth was close to dragging her down.

It was time, time to make an end of the brother who killed everything she loved. It was time to fling him into hell.

To hell, with the killing words.

She felt the ch'i power growling up from her breast to her head. The power of slaughter-love.

The Death-bringer madness roared in her skull.

The madness was strength.

The hate was strength.

The brawling ch'i power bellowed in her flesh and spirit, hurling her deep into the long moment. The hate rose like an angry tidal wave.

For Fu – squeezed like a wineskin. For Yi – hung by her ears and eyes. And for Peng-t'ai who relies on my protection . . . let the hate fill me, burst me.

Chia let the hate in her loose.

She leapt with a roar at Nyak, her right foot drawn back to crush the narrow skull he inhabited – crush it into shards, grind it into splinters, squash the brain it housed into a smear of blood-jelly.

Nyak dodged to one side and she landed on empty ground. Whirling round instantly, she jumped clean over the head of a Silver Brother to place herself between Nyak and the defiant Peng-t'ai beside the red-silked Mirror Body. But Nyak was drawing back. Although he was obviously using the long moment he was not so adept as to risk fighting Chia. Even the arrogant necromancer recognised her superiority in physical combat.

298

But one of the Silver Brethren was moving, and moving at the speed of her own ch'i-raced brain – ten times the rate of normal motion. She faced a Silver Brother who was also adept in the art of the long moment. She prayed that he was the only one.

His green, fungus-clumped fingers reached for her face.

Chia hurled herself backwards onto the floor and twisted sideways before regaining her feet. She swayed in her combat stance with feline grace and glared with tigerish eyes.

The green hands swung round, seeking her flesh – just one touch, just one brush on her exposed skin, and she would be dead in less than a minute. The green death in those hands would raise mounds of mould in her body. Fungus would sprout in her lungs, bulge her womb, riddle her dying brain.

She wove her hands and started to circle her enemy. The other Silver Brethren, unable to sink into the long moment, had barely moved in the mere second of normal time that had elapsed. She could win if . . . She glimpsed Nyak making for the Mirror Body in the centre of the stupa. He was moving much too fast for Peng-t'ai to see, let alone block him.

Chia hurled herself at the necromancer and punched the gaunt frame away from the woman's time-frozen face. She smiled at the sound of breaking ribs. The possessed body skidded across the floor, striking its head at the base of a benign Bodhisattva.

An inner alarm made her spin round to the groping green fingers.

She rolled and ducked under the stretching arms of mould so swiftly that her momentum carried her to the feet of a white-handed Brother. Recoiling instinctively, she spun round to challenge the green-handed Brother.

Green hands were reaching for the unknowing face of Peng-t'ai where she stroked her burned cheek – were

299

stopping a finger's length from her skin. The silver mask swivelled round to confront the sorceress with the plight of his hostage. The barbaric, beaten metal seemed to wear an expression of victory. The message was plain.

And Nyak, apparently unconcerned about the broken ribs of the body he controlled, was strolling casually to the centre of the stupa and the Body of the Mirror. He lifted his lean hand. And the tenuous mist quickly congealed near the summit of the dome and began to spiral downwards to the Silken Stranger. The Spirit was sinking down into the Body.

Chia bowed her head, opened her arms in abject defeat to Nyak and the Silver Brother who hovered above Peng-t'ai, and trudged like a chastised infant to the centre of the stupa.

The green-handed creature did not react to the sharp glance of warning from Nyak.

Like lightning, Chia grabbed the long grey mask-hair and wrenched the Silver Brother from the threatened woman. The green hands made a desperate effort to scratch her skin but missed by a nail's length. Screaming blood-fury, the sorceress swung her enemy across the floor.

Twisting the grey hair in her iron grip, she slammed her adversary back onto the floor by the mask hair, then readied herself for a massive exertion. Her mouth bent in a vicious smile.

Oh, how I love the hate . . . how I love the Death-bringer madness . . .

She thrust her foot in the small of her opponent's back and gave a muscle-wrenching heave of the grey hair buried deep in the silver mask helmet. The helmet tore loose of the chin, but so tightly-fitted were the Brethren's helmets that she heard a snapping of neck-bone and splintering of cheekbones before the silver mask helmet ripped free of the skinned head. What scraps of flesh remained were beaded with mould. The twist of the stretched, ruptured neck showed that Chia had almost yanked the head from its shoulders.

Out of the corner of her eye Chia spied Nyak heading for the Silken Stranger. It was evident that he was emerging from the long moment; he seemed to move as if pushing through deep water.

With a savage scream Chia whirled the mask helmet by its hair and launched it clean through the air at Nyak. But the combined ch'i force and speed was so enormous that it impacted with Nyak as if it were a boulder. It smashed into Vinaya-Nyak's ribs and slammed him backwards to the floor, arms flailing.

Chia hurled herself at the battered mask helmet and snatched it up before readopting her battle stance and quickly noting the Spirit mist. The diaphanous cloud still nuzzled into the carven recesses of the stupa's stone walls. Turning her gaze on Nyak she was filled with dismay.

He was climbing back to his feet, his rib-cage collapsed, his spine bent at an impossible angle, but he grinned and forced his shattered frame in her direction. Nyak's spirit could make Vinaya's body function even with a split spine.

And, Chia realised, her ch'i force was receding rapidly. The surrounding world was speeding up. A white-handed Silver Brother had advanced to within two paces of her. Before the ch'i power finally deserted, she poised herself to attack the advancing white hands.

But a noise from her back made her spin round. The broken-necked, unmasked green-handed Brother was reaching out a green hand to stroke her. She swung the Brother's own mask helmet at his head with all the hate in her. The silver helmet beat the head into a pulp like a squashed fruit.

Whipping round, she swung the helmet at the silver-masked skull of the white-handed creature.

The helmet mask bashed into the masked head with a

301

loud clang of metal and a cracking of neck-bones. The Silver Brother tottered, his head dangling back between his shoulder-blades, pale blood gushing from his torn, white throat. His arms flailed wildly.

Chia drew the silver dagger from her crimson sash. Usually the dagger was of little use against the Silver Brethren – daggers were for in-fighting – but there was one use a sharp blade had which wasn't shared by heavy, blunt instruments – a sharp blade cut deep. A sharp blade severed. With a fierce swing she sliced the white hand from the Silver Brother's wrist. It flopped limply to the floor.

But the Brother was dead even as she severed the hand. His stinking hulk juddered on the floor, then lay as still as butcher's meat.

Chia started to pant like a hunted fox. The ch'i force had gone. She was so weak she could hardly stand. Her ears boomed to the crazed beating of her heart. Her hand trembled as she replaced the silver dagger in her red sash. Her other hand trembled so much that it lost its grip on the mane of grey hair, and the mask helmet clanged to the floor.

She hadn't sufficient physical energy left to do anything but fend off the Brethren. And how much longer would the Spirit Breath linger on the stupa walls? How much longer before it seeped down into its Body?

A weary upward glance told her the answer. The mist had started to congeal at the centre of the dome's roof. It had started to coil down in a spiralling column of frothy fog to the spot where the Silken Stranger – the Body of the Mirror – sprawled like a doughy lump of flesh bound in red wrapping. The Spirit Mist was swirling down to the Body. And while Nyak lived, she couldn't stop it.

'Moon-silver Goddess, help me,' she whispered.

Peng-t'ai had perceived Chia's battle with the Green Hands as subliminal hints – a hint of blurring motion here — a whisk of movement there. But her tight stomach muscles and pattering pulse told her that the sorceress was battling for her life, and the life of everyone else.

The Green Hands' reappearance had startled her, and now she stared at his dead, sprawling shape with its unmasked, mould-patched head. Something had pulled the skin off that head as if removing a glove.

Chia, smiled the hooded woman. It was Chia. But how could she have done all that within the space of a few seconds? Ten seconds, at most?

A white hand flopped close to her feet, followed by the thump of a handless Silver Brother. Peng-t'ai glared at the rancid white hand of plague. The body of its erstwhile owner had fallen across the fingers and the dripping stump of the hand shifted slightly in her direction.

She felt the savage burn on her right cheek, glanced down at the pointed stump of the burned Buddha in her firm grip, and simmered with anger at what had been done to the blind and the deaf-mute by the hands of plague in the early days of the San Lung haunting.

She stabbed the hand stump with the sharp end of the charred Buddha figure and pulled it out from under the corpse of the Silver Mask creature. The white hand, stuck securely on the point of the blackened Buddha image, looked as if it had sprouted a tiny wooden arm.

The woman in the dark green hood held the hand aloft on its stick arm of wood and charcoal. She smiled grimly at her trophy. She had stabbed the hand of death.

The perfect madness was spiralling down to reunite with the Body.

It had tasted the stone Buddha flesh of the stupa.

It was satisfied with the taste of that god stone.

It was young and weak in the flesh of China, that god.

303

But not too young that it wasn't caught in the web of sacred images.

When it rejoined the Body, the Spirit Mirror would no longer be one and one, but the Two that are One.

It would be the raw, undiluted, strong scent.

It would be concentrated power of the Spirit Mirror, hungry to feed and free, after thousands of years, to feed.

Its hunger would soon be filled.

It would consume the flesh of a god.

And what the Spirit Mirror consumed, it became.

Spine-split, rib-cracked, Vinaya's body continued to crawl to the Body of the Mirror. The spirit of Nyak in the shattered frame forced it on, avid to feel the stupendous energy of the Spirit Mirror when Spirit and Body were made one.

The skin of the possessed flesh drank in the sights and sounds of the stupa as Nyak dragged his body close to the Body of the Mirror.

He saw the Spirit mist whirling down to the recumbent Body. He saw Chia emerge from the long moment and stand, head bowed, shaking — for all the world like a chastised infant.

Ah, you evil woman. You have slaughtered two of my children. My children sought to send you into oblivion, where there is no pain. You kill in hate. You kill in the belief that those you murder will plunge, not into the perfection of oblivion, but the pains of hell. Ah, deluded woman, you are the Death-bringer. You almost make me hate, so contagious is your evil. Before you die, I must bring you enlightenment. Ah yes, I will bring you enlightenment. The enlightenment of Nyak. Here, sorceress. In my mind. In this limitless maze of folded flesh under this shaven scalp. Here. Come here. Into the enlightening maze of my mind. Come, sorceress. Come. Into my mind. COME . . .

Chia's gasp was choked in her throat as she felt herself

coming asunder. In the fleeting instant in which her mind was wrenched from her body she knew, with terror, what was happening. It was the Calling of the Flesh Maze, and only Nyak had the power to make such a calling.

Normally she could resist the Calling, but she was teetering on the brink of the dying time, and her mind was sucked into the labyrinth of flesh in the possessed head of Vinaya.

There were corridors here, here in the maze of folded flesh, here where Chia found herself wandering. There were paths that went on forever. There were blind-alleys and sudden twists in passages that dipped and fell. There were hidden chambers and vast caverns where scudding thoughts and dreams and memories had never visited. Here, in the limitless maze, thoughts were tangible and ghosts were solid. And everywhere – unseen, always in another room or corridor – the pad of running feet, soft and multitudinous.

And, wherever she ran in the flesh maze, the omnipresent booming of Nyak's huge whisper.

Here, sorceress, is the enfleshed symbol of the Infinite Flesh. Here is the sole reality. Outside this maze there is nothing. Outside does not exist. There is no world. No nation in it called China. No Buddha. No gods. No humans. No Chia.

A final wisp of the Deathless Lands must have lingered in her trapped, lost spirit, because Chia recalled that shred of wisdom, that flake of truth.

She pressed the flesh of her palm on the flesh of a towering wall that led down into a forever tunnel in the labyrinth. And she thought one vivid thought that the walls of the maze would transmit to the Master of the Maze . . .

I am sister Twilight. You are brother Owl. We are one in the flesh from Glak-i-kakthz and . . .

The immense whisper seemed to howl down all the

305

corridors of the maze. The living flesh of the maze writhed and squirmed and . . .

. . . and rejected her.

She was hurled into the black oblivion of the Outside.

She opened her eyes when she found she had eyes to open and discovered that she was standing in the stupa with four Silver Brethren surrounding her. Chia had returned to her own body. Nyak's contorted mind had rejected her.

The mind of Nyak could endure anything but the truth.

She looked at Nyak as he crawled towards the Silken Stranger beneath the descending pillar of fuming fog. So, thought Chia, trembling from shock and weariness, his mind is shut tight. Nothing enters which might disturb the snug familiarity of the locked house.

Then Chia reeled and crumpled to the floor. And the Brethren moved to her with their killing hands.

Peng-t'ai witnessed Chia's collapse with dismay. The Men of Plague were within a few feet of her. What could she do against the Men of Plague?

Her gaze slid sideways to the possessed shape of Vinaya where it heaved itself closer to the Silken Stranger. Wasn't this man the Master of the Plague Hands? And if he was their master . . .

Peng-t'ai sprang towards the crawling figure. Its wolfish face looked up at the young woman in indignation. 'Out of my way!' he shouted. 'How dare you block me! How *dare* you?' He opened his mouth wide to bellow at her more loudly.

And Peng-t'ai rammed the white hand of plague on its wooden prong deep into the gaping mouth. With a strength she didn't know she owned, she crushed the plague hand into a compressed mass of skin and crunching bone as her grip on the burned Buddha stump pressed and twisted. With one last push and twist she crammed the dead hand of living plague fully inside the gaping cavern of the mouth.

Then, as though the protruding Buddha figure was keen to show a dash of magic, the entire mass of crushed white flesh was gulped down the bulging throat as the burnt wooden stump slipped out of the mouth and clattered onto the floor.

The eyes in the gaunt head bulged with outrage and the scrawny arms started to thresh on the polished floor of the sacred stupa.

Peng-t'ai whirled round to see what had befallen Chia.

The Silver Masks had stopped in their tracks. But for how long?

CHIA! screamed the deaf-mute's mind.

Chia's eyes flickered open. She gritted her teeth and forced herself upright. Her stance steadied as she caught the drift of Peng-t'ai's thoughts . . .

I've pushed the white hand down his throat. The Master's got the plague.

The sorceress nodded her gratitude as she staggered to a space near, but not too near, the diseased Vinaya-Nyak. She motioned Peng-t'ai to move well back, and the young woman obeyed without hesitation, warily eyeing the Silver Brethren as she did so.

The Brethren, confused by the withdrawal of their master's will, shuffled uncertainly, innocuous in their confusion.

'Green-Eyes!'

Chia spun round to witness the sage and the abbot entering the stupa. It had been Liu Chun who had called out.

'Stay where you are, you stupid bastards!' Chia yelled back. 'Stay at the door!'

The two men froze on the spot, just a pace inside the dome.

Chia returned her attention to Nyak. The leprosy spreading from the white hand in Nyak's stomach was of a nature and speed of growth not found in actual leprosy.

The White Death crammed a month into a moment. Nyak's face was already swelling into pale folds of dead tissue. Already his ears, lips and nose were beginning to rot.

But the eyes, fast disappearing under a flap of leprous skin, glared a vivid hatred at Chia. 'I'm not killed, bitch,' he croaked. 'The Sight and the Hearing return to my true body, that's all. I've not been killed.'

The tips of his fingers were starting to shred.

'The Body and the Spirit are becoming one,' he wheezed. 'The Mirror will assume Buddha-flesh. You've lost. I've won the game.'

She sat on the floor and folded her legs, then smiled mercilessly at her brother. Wrenching herself from exhaustion she cast diamond-clear thoughts into Nyak's decaying head.

Your ears are locked to my words of enlightenment, Nyak. But before you die in this body I must bring you the enlightenment of the killing words. I will bring you the enlightenment of Chia. I will bring it there, necromancer. Inside your mind. Inside the benighted maze of your mind. I'm coming, necromancer. I'M COMING . . .

Hurling her spirit in the Inward Spiral she spun into the Flesh Maze.

The maze was waiting for her when she plunged into its zigzag paths. Raging thoughts like massive boulders hurtled down corridors to crush her. Armies of vicious ideas swarmed from vast halls to annihilate her. On every side, Nyak's wrathful mind attacked the presumptuous invader.

Peng-t'ai witnessed the decomposition of the Master with grim satisfaction, recalling the plague-deaths of her deaf-mute and blind friends in San Lung Town. She felt it to be justice as she observed the ruin of the corrupting flesh. Fingers rotted off his hands. White flesh sank into the nasal cavity. The entire mass of flesh crawled with the White Death. She was reminded of a slug she had once discovered in a jar of salt.

The running of Chia's feet was as swift as thought itself as she bobbed and weaved and dodged her way through the murderous maze. The twisted path she took was down, always down. Embodied fury rushed at her heels. Thought incarnate hounded her down every corridor, huge and vengeful. But she kept to the tortuous downward track, indomitable in her resolve to destroy Nyak forever. All of Nyak's mind rushed at her back.

And she took that mind into the deep, dark regions where secrets were stored and memories buried. She knew which buried memories she wanted to unearth. An inner compulsion made her dive down a tunnel which suddenly widened out into a burial chamber. In the centre of the chamber was a freshly constructed threefold coffin. Inside the threefold coffin lay a tall man clad in savaged robes of grey, black and white. Two black-robed figures stood beside the coffined corpse, their long silver daggers dripping blood on the floor of the chamber in Spirit Hill Mound. The kin-slaying Nyak and Chia of three thousand years past stared at each other over their father's body.

And the Nyak of the present — the Game Master — charged into the deep chamber in his mind to obliterate his ancient enemy. The Master of the Maze found himself trapped in the black heart of his own maze. He found a dead father — and a sister.

Soaring from the maze in an Outward Spiral, Chia left Nyak confronting himself.

Chia opened her eyes to behold Peng-t'ai engrossed in the decay of Vinaya-Nyak's body. She sensed acute danger in the dome. *Peng-t'ai. Go outside. Quickly.*

The woman hesitated, then, with a nod, strode briskly to the door and the open air.

Chia studied Nyak's crumpling face. It knew. It peered at her through lumps of dead, wrinkled skin.

'Black Dragon, you're killing me,' he managed to splutter. 'Killing *me*.'

Her eyes narrowed to cruel rents. 'Does the memory live again, dark brother? Sunrise over the Yellow River and the green eyes of our father . . . the conspiracy on Black Dragon Mountain . . . grey shrouds, black shrouds, white shrouds savaged with knives. Is the past resurrected?'

Fitful life still flickered in the mass of putrefaction. Nyak was living his lifelong nightmare – a man with green eyes rising from a coffin, and now he could hear that word that was silent in sleep: son. He peered fuzzily at the stern visage of Chia – his arch-enemy and sister. His heart crumpled like a rotten apple squeezed in her hand. 'No, no, no . . .' he wheezed.

'Yes, brother, yes. I'm your mirror. You are what you see.'

The monstrous shape resembled slug skin in a crude human form.

'Die, Chia,' it hissed softly.

'Die? Not me. Not –' Chia tensed. The white disease in Vinaya's body carried enough contagion to eat into her flesh. If it touched her . . .

The pale, stinking heap swelled; split through the saffron robe. The possessing spirit was bursting free. Bursting . . . contagious flesh . . .

Chia hurled herself away as the bulging hulk suddenly blew apart with the expulsion of the screaming spirit.

Deadly white flesh flew in chunks from a red explosion of brain, heart and entrails. Leprous lumps spattered the walls of the sacred dome.

The long, narrow body in the open stone sarcophagus shook as the Sight and the Hearing howled south to be united with the Deep Self in its flesh.

In the dark vault far beneath the roots of the southern limb of the Forest of the Ancestors, terror struck the Deep Self in the body of Nyak. The torches on the dank walls flared wildly, catching the spirit of fear.

The unholy blood-spirit exchange between Nyak and the blinded, deafened Yi was disrupted. Natural decay released the tortured spirit of the girl.

Her soul fled rejoicing to the Deathless Lands.

Her body crumbled slowly.

Nyak's naked, masked shape threshed in its sarcophagus. The Sight and the Hearing were bringing a knowledge from the north, a knowledge that was dread.

Screeching far above the pitch of human hearing, the spirit-selves plummeted into the vault. The Sight and the Hearing, torn by truth, gushed into the emaciated body of Nyak. The Hearing, the Sight and the Deep Self became one. The spirit of Nyak was fully present in the body. Present, and twisted with truth.

The girl's skull decayed and the brow-ridges and temple-bones snapped free of the cruel hooks. Her withering corpse dropped onto Nyak's body as the agonised shape bulged with a truth it could not contain. The girl's rotting corpse was blown aside as the necromancer burst asunder, howling to hell.

A silver mask spun in the murky air and clattered to the damp flagstones.

The torches erupted in a lurid blaze, then quickly guttered.

Total darkness and utter silence filled the vault.

23

SPIRIT MIRROR

Chia flung herself into the massed flames of the candles on Buddha Maitreya's altar.

She bathed her face and hands in the sacred fire as gobbets of corrupt white flesh dropped and sizzled around her. When the scorching became unbearable she pulled away and turned her blistering face on the Silver Brethren. She threw off her cloak and the morsels of flesh that clung to it. A burning sensation afflicted the skin of her face and hands – but she was untouched by the abnormally powerful contagion of the white disease.

The four Brethren were lumbering forwards. The Master had given his last order: Die, Chia. She had survived the explosion of the White Death, but the Master had said she must die. They would obey.

'You're going to burn like a torch, woman,' one of the red-handed Brethren whispered hoarsely through the ornamental mouth of his silver mask.

She shook her head firmly. The Silver Brethren had weaker wills now that their master's will was withdrawn. She was sure that the truth had flown back with the fleeing spirit to Nyak's true body, wherever it lay. And the truth would destroy him. Her lips bent into a lethal curve.

'No, you walking diseases, it's *your* time to burn.' She held up her hand in a gesture of command. 'You will burn, Silver Brethren,' she said in a loud whisper. 'You are struggling to ignore my command but it is a hopeless struggle. The more you battle against my will, the stronger my will becomes. Try not to think of burning.' Her depictive speech cast the vision of their burning bodies into their dull minds. 'Try hard not to think of burning. Try hard. Burning . . . You're trying, but you're failing. You will set your cloaks to the flames of the candles. You have a craving to purge your rotting bodies in fire. You can't ignore the craving. Burn your ulcerated flesh. Burn it . . .'

Nagarjuna and Liu Chun hovered by the door. The abbot began to frown. 'Sorceress,' he called out. 'Don't seek revenge. Leave the Silver Brethren. Escape the dome. The Mirror – flee the Mirror!'

'Be quiet, old man,' she shouted back. 'It's my turn to be a Death Whisperer.' Ignoring the pain of her scorched face and hands, she directed the Silver Brethren like wooden puppets to a tier of yellow candles.

'Chia! Come on! Get out!' Liu Chun pleaded.

'You will set your cloaks to the flame of the candles,' she continued remorselessly. 'Set light to your cloaks. Burn, Brethren.'

Out of the corner of her eye she glanced at the column of mist writhing down from the roof. It had almost touched the Mirror Body.

Soiled grey mantles draped over the fire. Flame licked tongues of light along the tattered grey wool and the Silver Brethren roared in terror. They were powerless to move as the fires ran greedily up the cloaks and set alight the long drapes of dead hair that flowed from the mask crowns. The cloaks blazed and bellows of agony rang from the burning. They ignited like torches dipped in oil as if the flames were keen to scour the world of their corruption. The livid, prancing ribbons cast a crimson glow on the walls of wispy mist.

Satisfaction creased the corners of her mouth. 'Burn, burn, you bastards.'

'Chia!' implored the abbot. 'Run!'

The fog-pillar was a hand's breadth from the Silken Stranger.

Chia watched, smiling, as the Brethren dropped to the floor, engulfed in flame. For a brief space the fires raged, smouldered, then dwindled to dull embers. At last there was nothing but four piles of sizzling bone and ash. And four silver masks.

She started to leave the stupa, but was frozen in her tracks by an abrupt agitation in the walls of mist. Cloaks of mist, sleeves of fog, scarves of vapour were thrown out in churning currents by the gyring motions of the Mirror Spirit.

The central pillar of Spirit mist had coiled down to a finger's breadth from the Body of the Mirror.

'The stupa has been polluted by Nyak and his slaves,' exclaimed the abbot.

As Chia walked unsteadily to the portal the turbulent mists evanesced into rainbows of dazzling colour. A fluctuating mass of indistinct torsos and arms and heads flashed and cavorted in cloudy formations. Silent whispers wove.

Then the cloud exploded. It exploded into living walls of wild flesh, limitless and whimsical. The stupa became the fleshy walls of a translucent maze of abandoned thoughts. The stupa became like the dome of a skull. And in this skull there were playful thoughts, the thoughts of the Buddha at play, the whims of the flesh at play.

The Spirit and the Body had united. And the Spirit Body, the Spirit Mirror, had donned the flesh of the sacred dome. It had usurped the sanctity of the stupa. It had assumed the flesh of a god. It was the Buddha of the Infinite Flesh. And the labyrinth in the skull of the Flesh Buddha was the infinite maze of the mind of a mad god.

Trapped in this God Maze in the Flesh Dome, Chia would have lost her mind in an instant, and for ever.

But the true Buddha descended.

Not dramatically. Not with resounding music and resplendent rainbows, but with a fire.

It wasn't even a fire that could be seen with the eyes. It was Vision Fire, an ardent pillar of power. It was fire from heaven. And it scoured the stones of the stupa of the scent of the Infinite Flesh. The dome became dark and still.

Recovering her wits, Chia raced for the door, but her companions' stupefied gazes halted her. She wheeled round, and saw it. She saw a tall, slim woman in a black gown with a crimson sash. A silver ankh gleamed on her chest. Her green eyes probed Chia's eyes.

For the sage the Mirror was the sage. For the abbot it was the abbot. For Chia, Chia.

The whole world slid down to that reversed vision of her face.

The whispers came to the three watchers, each in their own voice. Puerile susurrations trickled into their heads. Obscene whispers, snide whispers from the inner stranger with the borrowed face. Chia knew that the whispers came from the Mirror, but they seemed to come from herself. The Mirror wore Chia's semblance so that what was Chia and what was the Mirror was difficult to distinguish.

Whispered to death.

The image of Chia slunk across the floor of the dome, a sick smile curving its lips. Cold, silent whispers swarmed in the skull of the sorceress. The Spirit Mirror, in her mimic's voice, was debilitating her soul. A witless world was draining her energy.

'Shrug off the burden of reality,' the voice sighed. 'Become a spark in sun-water, a moan in the breeze, an echo of an antique apparition.'

'Diminish.'

'No!' she shrieked, tearing her gaze from the approaching mirror self. With a violent shove she pushed her companions out of the portal and into the clean night and the faces of Dharmapala and the townsfolk. The two men visibly shook off the cloying dreams.

'What happened to us, Green-Eyes?' Liu Chun mumbled.

'We looked into the Spirit Mirror. If it weren't limited by the remaining power of the stupa that glimpse would have been the end of us.'

The shadow of the Spirit Mirror fell across the threshold, different in outline to each onlooker. The shadow spilled across the courtyard, swamping the moon faces of the small crowd. It stretched up the north wall of the monastery. It climbed into the heavens, swallowing stars. A shadow stretched from the stupa door to the high sky.

A giant shadow looked down on the earth.

Liu Chun saw the broad black contour of Liu Chun. Nagarjuna saw the spindly silhouette of Nagarjuna. Chia saw Chia.

Chia stared at her black profile overlording the world. *The universe is I*, came the single mad notion.

'It's illusion,' the sage roared, more in fear than anger.

His outburst restored some of her senses. She whisked out the silver dagger. 'Only one thing left to do,' she said, placing the blade on her forearm. She had scant hope that the ritual would work – there was no innocence in her . . .

'What are you doing?' demanded Nagarjuna, a strange look enlightening his features.

She disdained to answer. There was no time to explain about blood spirals and the faint chance of imprisoning the Mirror. In several heart-beats the Spirit Mirror would emerge from the dome. And when it was free of the sacred dome they would all become shadows.

In the moment Chia took to think about the blood spirals a host of memories stormed through Nagarjuna's mind . . . boyhood temples in Mathura . . . the sacred

316

Ganges ... the trek to the Dragon Empire ... the construction of the stupa ... the toil of building the monastery ... the weary climb to an unseen summit ... the torana ... the torana – and the vision, the blood spiral between the pillars of the torana ...

With a deft snatch he plucked the dagger from Chia's fingers. '*My* life, Black Dragon,' he smiled. 'My life for the Buddha and China.'

'What –?' she began.

'The Inward Spiral of blood,' he said.

Then he sliced a deep rent in his throat.

Chia was the only one not dumbfounded by the abbot's actions. 'Don't interfere, the rest of you!' she yelled as she caught the Indian in her arms and assisted him to the stupa's threshold. 'Don't waste the gift of his life.'

Lifting the abbot so that the blood spilled like wine on the door's threshold. Chia slowly moved it in an Inward Spiral. The crimson spiral spattered the trampled clay.

As the blood circled inwards the Shadow in the sky began to shrink and descend to earth.

As the last loop of blood completed the spiral, Chia cupped her hand over the ragged gash and hauled the old man to the torana gateway. A storm of protests erupted from the crowd but Liu Chun shouted them into silence.

Standing under the crossbeams of the torana she released her hand and the hot blood spurted again. Once more Chia guided the blood-fall into the pattern of the Inward Spiral. She concentrated on the inward movement to the last drop of her vitality.

The Shadow continued to shrink.

'Murderer!' accused the T'ao magus, glaring at Chia. The crowd took up the chant. 'Murderer – murderer – murderer ...'

'Keep the path between the torana and the stupa clear,' she managed to gasp.

Liu Chun bellowed her order and the townsfolk

reluctantly moved back. With quivering shoulders Chia swerved the abbot's draining body to trace the last bend of blood in the spiral.

The Shadow slid back down the north wall, back across the courtyard, and dwindled into a dwarf before it was swallowed by the mouth of the stupa.

A huge whisper, silent as space, deafening as a thunderclap, keened its misery from the dark dome and faded into itself like an echo flying down endless corridors.

Silence.

Natural silence.

The sorceress carefully placed the dying abbot on the ground. He blinked, smiled feebly, then quietly let his soul slip away. She fell with a groan at his side.

Liu Chun rushed to her and dropped on one knee.

Her eyelids flickered. Her fire-blistered features trembled. 'The Sleep of Rebirth is taking me,' she murmured. 'And the sleep of death has taken Nagarjuna. I don't want to wake here. Carry me to Luminous Cloud Mountain. And I need the Night-Shining Jewel – it's in the Death Mound, no longer a dangerous place.'

She tried to rise but failed. 'The stupa is the new tomb of the Spirit Mirror,' she said breathlessly. 'Centuries ago, before they were made into shrines of the Buddha, stupas were death mounds. From the Death Mound of Spirit Hill to the Death Mound of Celestial Buddha Temple. At the door to Spirit Hill Mound and on the threshold to the inner chamber there were once Inward Spirals that trapped the Mirror. Now there are Inward Spirals of blood under the symbolic gateway of the torana and on the threshold of the stupa. The Spirit Mirror is imprisoned. No one must enter this temple again. The monks must see to that.'

'It will be done, old friend.' Tears coursed down the sage's cheeks – tears for Chia, more tears for Nagarjuna.

She smiled wanly. 'Nyak – my brother . . . the unthinkable is the truth. The truth was something he couldn't bear. I think it will destroy his spirit. Yes, I think so.'

With a painful effort she turned her head to the abbot. Dharmapala was bowed grief-stricken over the body. 'Tell the people that Nagarjuna saved them,' she whispered to Liu Chun. 'They mustn't believe it was me, for in the end it wasn't. Promise me.'

'I promise.'

Rousing herself to a final exertion she reached out a hand to touch the abbot's dead fingers.

'They will say that the Light of the Buddha defeated the Spirit Mirror,' she smiled sadly. 'There will be many converts to the Noble Eightfold Path. Are you happy now, old man?'

Liu Chun knew it for a sympathetic illusion, but he fancied that a wisp of a smile softened Nagarjuna's features.

Chia's voice meandered to a low pitch and her eyelids closed. The Sleep of Rebirth had almost claimed her. 'Nagarjuna,' she muttered, 'if Gautama did manage to become the Celestial Buddha of All Worlds – when you meet him, tell him I could do with a little help . . .' A final flicker disturbed her eyelids. 'Liu Chun . . .' The voice was barely audible. 'How did he know about the Inward Blood Spiral? How did he –?'

Her head flopped to one side and she was deep in a sleep that neighboured death, her long fingers touching the dead hand of Nagarjuna.

Liu Chun rose and confronted a crowd of curious stares. 'The abbot came from distant India and gave his life for you,' he proclaimed. 'He brought with him the sacred flame of the Buddha, and that flame has vanquished the mirror hauntings. You are free. Now return in peace to your homes.'

They departed silently, all but one man who was dressed in the red Kang-i garment of a T'ao magus. He stood over the sleeping sorceress and gazed on her face of legend. While Peng-t'ai hung back in the shadows the monks gathered quietly round the prone forms in the fitful moonlight. The magus crooked his lips and spat on the black silk gown.

'Chia the Death-bringer,' he hissed, then swept away with an imperious swirl of his rich garment.

No! wailed Peng-t'ai in her distraught mind, witnessing this final insult to her beloved redeemer. She raced out of the shadows and knelt at Chia's side, lifting up the lolling head and cradling it in her shaking arms.

Peng-t'ai had stayed in the background since leaving the stupa. Staying in the background was a habit that deaf-mutes learned young. You didn't interfere in the affairs of others. You kept to the edge of the crowd.

Ever since Chia emerged from the stupa, Peng-t'ai had longed to run to her side. And when Peng-t'ai had seen her own shadow rearing into the night she had ached in every bone to rush into Chia's protective arms. But habit made her keep her distance.

Not now. She couldn't stand by and watch Chia being spat on like a straw dog. She held the sorceress in a tight embrace, feeling the diminishing warmth in the body. As she held Chia, she felt words drift into her mind, faint and remote.

I'm lonely.

And Peng-t'ai couldn't tell whether the words came from her or Chia.

24

SPRING IN AUTUMN

Dharmapala rested from the day's labour, reclined on a smooth shelf of rock, and gazed up the slopes of Spirit Hill.

Where there was barren soil there would be rich loam; where there were wild, dry stalks there would be lush grass; where there were stunted trees there would be tall oaks, stately elms and stalwart birches.

Celestial Buddha Temple was lost to the Sangha. The monastery that had surrounded two years of the young monk's work and meditation had, in a single night, been invaded and desecrated. It's heart had stopped beating – the heart of the stupa, the heart of Nagarjuna.

A mild autumn breeze strayed down Spirit Hill. The land was warm and dusk.

Work on the new temple had started immediately after Nagarjuna's funeral and Liu Chun's departure with the sleeping sorceress. Already a passage had been constructed to cover the path from the torana to the door of the stupa. Now the foundations were being laid for the structure that was to enclose both stupa and passage. They were faced with an arduous task, but the burden was lightened by the assistance of the San Lung people, all eager to gain favour with the Buddha. Dharmapala had recently heard that the townsfolk wished to make Nagarjuna a local god in gratitude for his sacrifice; the request had been politely refused. The cause of Mahayana had been greatly advanced, but at what a cost . . .

More than two hundred murdered bodies had come to light after the spell of the T'ai Ching Masters and the Spirit Mirror had been broken. Some who thought their friends and relatives still alive suddenly discovered that they were dead. It was a dark time, the time that followed the end of the T'ai Ching illusions. The first he had witnessed was a broken-necked little girl called Red Blossom lying near the west wall of the garan. Then the eyeless body of Sung the vagabond nearby. Then – there were many others. But some thought dead were found to be living. The illusion had worked both ways. Mostly, it was a time of confusion. And the townsfolk, on the whole, blamed the ill-reputed Chia.

Celestial Buddha Hill was soon to be renamed Shadow Hill. And Celestial Buddha Temple was to bear the new name of Tomb of the Spirit Mirror.

It was almost evening. The sunset was a drop of honey on the brink of the world. It was the autumn Equinox, and day and night were in balance, poised for the gradual descent into darkness.

With a pensive air he studied the mound on the summit. The imposing exterior of the dome was being scraped and prepared for the long years of patient conversion. One distant day it would be a stupa whose dimensions would far outstrip those of any yet built. Fu's and Nua's bodies and the bones and coffin relics had been removed from the inner chambers and buried in the hillside. Ming's mirror had been hidden in a secret place. Before the snows came Mahayana statues would smile in the sacred candlelight of the transformed chambers of the mound.

Around the erstwhile tomb, makeshift quarters were clustered, prefiguring the walls and cells and galleries and hall and tower that were to come. Before the snows of the Black Serpent fell from the north, Amaravita, the new abbot, would dub the Death Mound and Spirit Hill with fresh titles – Temple of the Buddha Spirit and Hill of the Buddha Spirit.

All beginnings were endings, all endings beginnings – it

was a founding precept of the Way of the Buddha, but never had Dharmapala been so acutely aware of the truth it contained. To the south a sacred temple had been desecrated, and now in the north a profane tomb had been sanctified. There was a transformation-wind surging through all times and all worlds; nothing was constant. It might be that an age would come when Mahayana would die in India, but a transformed Mahayana would enlighten China. And if the flame was extinguished in China – well, there were ten thousand worlds in which to be reborn.

The wistful monk sighed, clambered down from the rock, and slowly climbed to the domed summit. He was a sadder man than he had been in the spring, but his faith was firmer.

He glanced to the west, then to the east, and a smile surfaced in his thoughtful face. Yes, his faith was firmer.

Four months. Framed and articulated on the tongue, four months was a moment. Considered in the mind, the elapsed time was a kalpa.

It had been late spring then, on the night of the Mirror Shadow, but a cold spring night. Now it was autumn, and a languid warmth was recumbent with the delicate mists on Luminous Cloud Mountain.

Liu Chun was not the man he had been four months ago.

When he had renounced the capital and settled in his small cave on the mountain three years past it had been in the manner of a grand gesture of contempt for the Imperial court. A rejection, in time-honoured T'aoist style, of public affairs and private intrigue. He had played the part of a recluse like a mummer on a lonely stage.

His stolid features were as impassive as granite as he surveyed the Valley of the Five Ways from the crest of a rugged crag. Since the night of Nagarjuna's death, the

Sung An Mummers had stopped performing the silent Mirror Dance. So it was said.

His gaze wheeled to the western mountains. From the west, said the myths, sprang the White Tiger, herald of autumn, bringer of cold. But with the setting sun the warmth was from the west and the mists on the upper western slopes were ablaze.

There was no warmth in the Green Dragon of the East, King of Spring: dark clouds walled the eastern horizon like a tall forest.

How long had the wagon journey from San Lung taken? Twenty days, perhaps. He smiled wryly. Chia asleep was an innocent child in the back of the shaking wagon. Her breath was inaudible and her face untroubled. Chia as an innocent child – quite a spectacle.

After a week on Luminous Cloud Mountain she had woken with the memory of San Lung virtually expunged. Her scorched face and hands were healed, with not a hint of their burning. She looked even younger than before. He had never seen her so carefree, lost in wonder at the swaying of a flower, the flicker of a butterfly. Often she would laugh with unbridled delight. And he would laugh with her infectious mirth.

But in a handful of days the laughter faded. She reassumed the brooding quality that was the epitome of the Chia of legend. Old hauntings returned to her green gaze, which was most frequently fixed on the east. Often she was silent, and he knew that she was trying to remember, trying to forget. Her mood worsened. Fragments of memory spilled into her mind, each warped beyond recognition.

'I remember, Liu Chun. I cut the abbot's throat above a water mirror and released the Death Whisperers with his outward-spiralling blood. What demon was in me?'

'No! You didn't, Chia. He gave his own life to imprison the Mirror.'

She looked dubious. 'As you say.'

He had attempted to describe the major events in San Lung and touch on the brambly subject of her birth, but at such times she became as a deaf-mute, or as one under a deep trance. She did not hear a word.

On the tenth day she donned her borrowed cloak and prepared to leave. 'I must go,' she muttered. 'Wei is alone, waiting for me in Black Dragon Caverns. And I need her.'

Liu Chun knew then that all hope for Chia was gone. Wei had died over thirty years past. A young man, he had been with her at the time, in Owl Village near the Great Wall. Chia had spilled a trickle of her blood in an Outward Spiral in a water mirror bowl. It was a powerful form of meditation in which she lost herself. Wei had been walking by the river less than a li away. She was raped by a couple of Imperial soldiers. Then they ripped her heart out and threw it into the wet mud of the bank. Wei's young blood streamed into the river. The sorceress soon tracked down the men who killed her lover. She tore them apart with her bare hands, then scattered their remains in the village lanes.

Chia, as was her nature, had blamed herself for the girl's death. Then, to alleviate her guilt, had convinced herself that Wei was still alive. That conviction turned into a terrible madness. She shared Black Dragon Valley with an imaginary Wei, spoke to an imaginary Wei, made love to an imaginary Wei.

He had hoped that the dying time might have cured her of that. The dying time – the thought made him frown. He liked to remember only the later stages of the Sleep of Rebirth, when Chia was like an innocent child, but he was unable to shake off the memory of the early and middle stages of the process. The sight of Chia's body regenerating wasn't a sight for the squeamish. It lowered her in his estimation, somehow. He liked to think of her as the beautiful, inviolate goddess and not – not what he saw on the road from San Lung in those first harrowing days.

He shuddered. Best forget it. If he could.

One thing was certain. He was incapable of adoring the Black Dragon Sorceress anymore. He had been pursuing a dream all these years. Now the physical reality behind her death and rebirth had shattered that dream.

What was he to do now that adoration for Chia had fled?

Ordinary love seemed inappropriate for Chia.

Friendship, of course, was out of the question.

Liu Chun sighed. Yes – at last he had summed up Chia. She was a creature of dreams and memories. She was incapable of love or friendship. At least that was so as far as he was concerned. Chia was just a glamorous ideal. An illusion of divinity. He wanted no more of her. He could even begin to understand why so many men hated the sorceress. She was the tormenting lure of the un-attainable. The mountain that made all men shrink into foothills. In short, she was Trouble.

'To hell with you, Chia,' he muttered, scratching his beard.

Chia watched the hooded woman laboriously ascending the steep and tortuous trail up Black Dragon Mountain from where she stood on the ragged crest of a crag over-looking Celestial Tiger Forest.

When at length the woman reached the crag's edge Chia stepped forwards and gave the visitor a long, warm embrace.

Finally, Peng-t'ai stepped back from Chia's hug and threw back her hood, revealing the angry, livid scar on her right cheek.

Chia took Peng-t'ai by the hand. *I can live without a lover*, she thought to her deaf-mute companion. *But I think I need a friend.*

Yes, thought Chia to herself. I need a friend.

326

GLOSSARY

ahimsa The Buddhist principle of refraining from any action harmful to a living creature.

Akhenaten Pharaoh of the XVIII dynasty, and founder of a form of monotheism; an heretical religion centred on the Aten – the Sun Disc.

Amitabha One of the Buddha-Aspects, he was known as the Buddha of Boundless Splendour and Lord of the Western Paradise. The paradise he ruled was a world of bliss perched between earth and heaven.

apsara Originally a Hindu fertility goddess, Buddhism transformed her into a number of angelic nymphs attendant on the Buddha. Buddhist apsaras were often pictured as heavenly dancers.

arhat Roughly equivalent to a Christian saint. A buddhist 'perfected being'.

Aten The Sun Disc of Ancient Egypt, or rather the divinity immanent in the image of the sun. Its worship began and ended with the rise and fall of Akhenaten.

Avalokitesvara The Bodhisattva Avalokitesvara was the Buddhist Lord of Compassion, and one of the most loved of Buddhist divinities. The Chinese later feminised this being into their most revered figure – Kuan-yin, Goddess of Mercy.

Bodhisattva An Enlightened One (i.e. a Buddha) who has renounced Nirvana to return to earth as a redeemer for the sake of unenlightened humanity.

Brahman-Atman The identification of Brahman – Ultimate Reality – with the soul dwelling within creation. Usually expressed as the recognition of the unity of the human soul with the reality of Brahman, couched in the phrase 'tat tvam asi' – 'thou art that'.

Buddha The name means 'the Enlightened One'. First applied to Gautama, a sixth century B.C. Nepalese noble, who founded the precepts of Buddhism, according to legend, after sitting under the Tree of Enlightenment. After his death, Gautama was virtually deified, and gradually a whole host of Buddhas were conceived in order to portray the various aspects of the apotheosised Gautama.

ch'i Ch'i is a T'aoist term which signifies the Vital Spirit which infuses all of creation. It is literally the breath of life which circulates earth and heaven and the lines of force within the human body. Breathing exercises were believed to be a means of summoning and concentrating the ch'i within the body, enabling the individual to perform remarkable physical and spiritual feats.

Chuang Tzu Philosopher-poet (*c.*350–275 B.C.) of the Warring States era. A major exponent of the T'aoist school of philosophy.

dragon paths (*lung mei*) These were lines of force in the earth, connecting sacred locations. They were formed by the operations of feng-shui – wind and water – and were usually understood as the strands which kept the fabric of the earth intact. Crooked, meandering lines were benign; straight lines were malign.

feng-shui Literally translated, 'wind and water'. Feng-shui was the moulding of the earth by the ch'i force of wind and water. The term was also applied to the art of geomancy where it represented the search for 'auspicious' locations and the avoidance of 'inauspicious' areas. It was, for example, highly inauspicious to site a graveyard on a dragon path; the dead might be inclined to rise with the energy of the ch'i currents beneath them.

garan The physical enclosure of a Buddhist monastery, typically containing a Buddha, or Golden, Hall, a Lecture Hall, a Cloud Tower (which later was developed into the pagoda form), and a dormitory and refectory within the four walls of the temple.

Han This dynasty (202 B.C.–220 A.D.), more than any other, was the one responsible for forming the Chinese character. After this period, the Chinese frequently referred to themselves as 'the people of Han'. The Han dynasty was divided into two periods: the Western Han in which the more westerly city of Chang'an was the capital (202 B.C.–25 A.D.) and the Eastern Han in which the easterly city of Loyang served as the capital (25–220 A.D.).

Hours (animal) Each Chinese hour was equal to two Western hours. The first hour of the Chinese clock started at 11 p.m. and ended at 1 a.m. Each hour, like each year, was named after an animal. The first hour was the hour of the Rat, then came Buffalo (or Ox), Tiger, Rabbit (or Hare), Dragon, Snake, Horse, Goat, Monkey, Cockerel, Hound (or Dog), and Boar (or Pig).

I Ching System of divination, using Yin and Yang symbols, to construct and interpret hexagrams formed by the symbols. The I Ching (Book of Changes) contains sixty- four hexagrams.

Jagannath This means 'Lord of the World' in Sanskrit. Jagannath was one of the ten avatars of Vishnu, the Hindu god of compassion. At the feast of Rath Yatra, a towering, sixteen-wheeled vehicle is pulled by hundreds of devotees from the Jagannath Temple to the Garden Temple a mile away. As the massive chariot gathers speed, it becomes a death car for anyone who is caught in its path. Jagannath is the source of the word 'Juggernaut'.

Kang-i The ceremonial robe of a Wu magus, or T'aoist magician. This red garment, bordered with emblems of lightning and clouds, was worn during the practice of ritual magic.

Kali A Hindu goddess, she was the consort of Shiva. She represented the savage side of nature, and her image is adorned with a necklace of human heads.

kalpa The period, in Hindu cosmology, between the creation and destruction of the world. It was calculated to be 4,320 million years.

Karma The principle of the cumulative consequences of actions, good or bad, which in turn affect predispositions in future actions. An individual who has accumulated bad Karma is predisposed towards bad actions and, in a loose sense, is 'fated' to perform evil acts, while someone who has gathered a 'store' of good actions is predisposed to good actions in the future.

Kung Fu Tzu The original name of which 'Confucius' is the latinised form.

kwai Chinese word for a ghost or evil spirit.

Lao Tzu A sage – sixth century B.C. He is traditionally regarded as the founder of T'aoism.

li Standard Chinese unit of measurement. About a third of a mile.

Liu-po A game popular in the Han dynasty. It involved gaining control of the centre of the board by forcing the opponent into the margins.

Mahayana This was a form of Buddhism which developed in Gandhara in the second century A.D. The name means 'Greater Vehicle', a term which was intended to raise it above the earlier school of Buddhism (Theravada), a school now dismissed as 'Hinayana' (the Lesser Vehicle) by Mahayana Buddhists. It was Mahayana that introduced a vast wealth of supernatural imagery and ritual into Buddhism, and lifted the Buddha to the status of a god. And it was in the shape of Mahayana that Buddhism spread through China and Japan in later centuries.

Maitreya One of the major Buddha-Aspects. He is Buddha as the Lord of the Future.

mandala A circular symbol, usually divided into quarters, which is believed to possess magical properties.

mantra A repetitious chant, originally derived from Vedic hymns of praise, directed towards focusing the thoughts of the worshipper.

Mathura An ancient city by the river Jumna in India. It rose to prominence under the Kushana empire during the first century A.D., and was renowned for its red sandstone statues of the Buddha.

Mo Ti A warrior-sage of the Warring States era. He established chivalrous rules and the notion of obedience to the 'Will of Heaven', as well as adding significant contributions to scientific thought.

Moving Sands The deserts to the northwest of China.

mudra A Buddhist hand gesture that conveys a religious message, such as the abhaya mudra which reassures the onlooker that there is nothing to fear.

Nefertiti Wife of the Pharaoh Akhenaten, and reputedly the most beautiful woman who has ever lived. Her name means 'the Beautiful One is here'.

Night-Shining Jewel The name given by the Chinese to a luminous stone.

Nirvana The Buddhist domain of bliss, where the enlightened being is freed from the process of change.

Peng-l'ai A mythical island to the east of China which the legends described as a mountain which perpetually recedes as you sail towards it.

prana The living energy of the cosmos. It has close similarities with the Chinese conception of 'ch'i'.

pranayama   A system of breath control which enables the yoga adept to achieve harmony with the energy of the universe.

rakshasas   Demons, who, in Hindu mythology, used the island of Sri Lanka as their abode.

Samsara   The cycle of rebirths which is the fate of anyone who has failed to find enlightenment. Reincarnation, in this context, is viewed as a curse – an entrapment in an eternally revolving wheel.

Sanchi   Located in Madhya Pradesh in central India, this is the site of three stupas, one of which – the Great Stupa – is the best preserved Buddhist monument in India.

Sangha   The community of Buddhists in a monastery.

Set   In Egyptian mythology, an evil god who dwells in the desert and flies on the desert wind. He is the slayer of Osiris, who is resurrected by his sister-wife, Isis.

Shang Ti   The ruler of the Chinese heaven.

Shatavahana   An empire which replaced that of the Shungas and Kanvas in central India and endured from *c.*50 B.C.–250 A.D.

shen   Chinese word for 'spirit'. Shen are essentially benign spirits, unlike kwai which manifest themselves in hauntings.

Ssu Ling   The four sacred animals of the Green Dragon of the East, the Red Phoenix of the South, the White Tiger of the West and the Black Serpent (or combined Tortoise and Snake) of the North.

stupa   In their origins, stupas were simple burial mounds. During the Shunga and Shatavahana periods, stupas evolved into large, imposing domes, often surmounted by stories of 'umbrella roofs'. The stupa was widely regarded as the architectural body of the Buddha, substituting for his vanished earthly frame.

Sutra A Buddhist canonical text. There were a great many sutras, together forming a corpus of Buddhist doctrine.

T'ao The harmony of Yin and Yang. The balance of opposing forces. The true, or proper, way of things in nature.

t'ao-tieh The most sinister and mysterious of all mythical Chinese creatures. It seems that the t'ao-tieh masks (fashioned during the Shang dynasty: 1550–1030 B.C.) were a confusing mixture of a number of animal faces, including those of a bull and a tiger. The image was highly stylised, containing many symbols whose meaning was unknown even to Chinese of the Han dynasty. The monster itself was said to consist of only a head or, more drastically, no more than a face.

T'ai Shan The most sacred mountain in China, situated on the border of what is now the province of Shantung.

torana A symbolic gateway to a stupa. Carved in stone, the torana comprises two pillars surmounted by three architraves, or lintels. The entire structure is covered in flamboyant reliefs. One feature common to the ends of the architraves on all toranas is the volute, or spiral, representing a rolled-up scroll.

Unas Last Egyptian ruler of the fifth dynasty (*c.*2300 B.C.), King Unas was the supposed compiler of the Pyramid Texts, referred to in the novel as the Book of Unas. The first of the Pyramid Texts contains a passage known as the 'Cannibal Hymn' due to its almost unparalleled gruesomeness in the history of religion.

Yang The active principle in nature, symbolised by the sun, the south, fire, and all phenomena associated with the positive aspect of the universe.

Yin The passive principle in nature, embodied in such phenomena as the moon, the north, water, and all features considered negative. This negativity did not imply any inferiority or evil, but simply a counterbalance to the bustling activity of Yang.

yun-t'ai A Cloud Tower, so named after the winged 'cloud roofs' on each level of the multi-storied building. It was the precursor of the pagoda.